ANGEL
EYES

ANGEL EYES

TENSHI NO ME

STEVEN W. CROSS

ISBN: 978-1-3999-5245-3

The story, all names, characters, and incidents portrayed in this production are fictitious. No identification with actual persons (living or deceased), places, buildings, and products is intended or should be inferred.

Book Cover & Design by Clipped104
First print edition 2023

Angel Eyes takes its influence heavily from Japanese anime and manga, an art form has provided me with so much entertainment and has had a lasting, emotional impact on my life. Fans of the medium may notice some familiar tropes in Sasaki's journey. I hope that the characters and the journey in this book can stick with you like so many other writers' work has stuck with me.

Angel Eyes was occasionally a difficult story to write and may at times cover sensitive topics that may be tough to read for some. Sasaki's journey is a troubled one, and her experiences include some of the very worst things that the human existence can push on us, including self-harm, depression, loss and grief. If you're suffering in this life, please reach out to whoever you can. There's always someone available to help you.

Speaking of support, without my wife Emily, one of my closest friends Anita and my mother Marilyn, I'd never have been able to tell you Sasaki's story. They've all helped me so much throughout the nearly 15 years it's taken me to bring this book to you. Thank you all for the feedback, opinions and emotional support that you've provided me throughout my life.

I'd also like to thank Clipped104 for their amazing work in bringing Sasaki to life on the cover. Without her dedication and hard work Sasaki would forever only be a girl living in my head. Clipped104 can be found on https://clipped104.carrd.co/

Chapter 1

fwip...*thud*, *fwip*...*thud*

The briefest of smiles passes over my lips as my arrows crash directly into the middle of the targets. Well, maybe not a smile but one side of my mouth turns up slightly. That feeling of euphoria at the sound of a bullseye is long gone, but it's still satisfying in a small way. I begin to fire arrows into the targets I've set up in a mechanical, unfeeling way.

The school gymnasium has become almost a second home to me, each day allowing me a sanctuary from my thoughts as the hours pass. There's a small range in the garden at home but it's just not really big enough, so this is the only place I get to practice. The echoes of the arrows flying through the air forms the background music to my lonely, quiet life.

"Umm, Kyu."

The timid voice from the doorway startles me out of my spiralling thoughts and I turn, bow still cocked and ready to fire, to see Yamamoto Miyu. She flinches at the sight of the arrow pointing directly at her for a brief second before I remember to lower my bow. She's a diminutive figure, a few inches shorter than me and her slender frame contrasts with my blocky stoutness. I look into her big eyes under the beautiful, flowing black hair and feel jealousy rise in me. I push a lock of shaggy, almost white-blonde hair out of my eyes and look away from her instinctively.

"Sorry Yamamoto, you surprised me. But I've said before I don't like the informality of you using my first name anymore," I say in a timid but steady voice.

"Sorry, Sasaki then. I'm just about to go shopping with a few friends and we wondered if you wanted to come along."

Her friends don't really want me there, no one does. Miyu is friends with everybody in the class, in fact practically everyone in every class. She doesn't need me after what happened before. The way I broke down and took out my sadness and frustration on Miyu in public after my sister died four years ago made me a total outcast. My sister taught me everything I know about archery; in fact, she gave me my very first bow as soon as I was old enough to hold it. Other than Sis, Miyu was the only one who seems to understand me, but the guilt I felt then still burns my soul all these years later. I ran out of school that day knowing I'd lost the only friend I had, just like I've lost everyone who I ever got close to. Miyu always seemed to have such an innate understanding of how hard it is for me to form those bonds with other people, how I can't read people's intentions and that helped at the time.

She still tries to reach out to me like this every now and then, but I just know that it is out of pity rather than anything else. I can just imagine the reaction of her friends if I turned up with her. The mocking voices run through my head. I'm not wanted, and I don't want Miyu's friends to hate her because of me.

"No thank you Yamamoto. I still have lots of practice to do."

My short answer seems to knock the impetus out of her as she bows solemnly and apologetically at me.

"Ok, if you're sure... But before I go would you show me one of your tricks please?" she says.

She often asks to see a trick shot, even though I'm sure she just does it out of politeness, but there's a fleeting feeling of happiness within me.

"Ok," I say looking at anything except directly at her.
"Great, thank you!"

I stride to the other side of the gym and start pulling on ropes that rise into the rafters. Since I am the only one that does any kind of archery and there's no official archery range anymore, the school are happy to let me make some creative adjustments to the targets they have left over. Such was my sister's influence and prestige at the archery club that they disbanded it straight after her accident. I shake my head to disperse the momentary distraction as Miyu steps into the gym and leans on the wall behind me. I pull on another rope, causing five targets to descend from the heavens in a rattle of chains and cogs.

When they're are all in place, I take three deep breaths, push my hair out of my face and swing the quiver from my back over my shoulder. It moves around my torso in one fluid motion, returning to my back where it settles, but there are seven arrows in my hand now. I finger the link of the chain from my sister's bike that keeps my quiver clasped to me. They saved her bike after the hit and run but I snuck the chain off before my parents threw it out.

I readjust the stupid pink bow around my neck to be as unobtrusive as possible. I hate the ribbon so much because it's gaudy and is in the worst place for an archer. With my white shirt untucked and the accompanying jacket discarded to the darkest corner I know I look unkempt, but why does it matter what I look like? I only wear what I have to while not falling foul of the uniform rules. It's not like any boys are interested in me anyway, they'd much rather chase after the popular and beautiful girls like Miyu.

Putting the anger and jealousy aside for a moment I check my arrows, place one against the string, rest it and pull it back to my face. As I steady myself, I return my glance to the end of the bow in front of me and see the fire burning in the reflection of my blue eyes in the metal plate on my bow's shaft. When my sister handed over her bow to me she said she called it "Tenshi", the Angel. I was besotted with him from the moment I laid eyes on him, hefting him as hard as I could until my arms ached. He really is a thing of beauty. He's a classic looking recurve bow with polished, decorated wood and a steel plate running down the middle, engraved with angelic wings and a diamond embedded in it. I spend far more time caring for him than I do myself. I clean and oil him every day and polish the metal frequently. He's never left my side since I was given him. He sleeps next to me, goes to school with me, and I spend my spare time with him.

Flicking my eye over the targets in front of me I set my sights and calculate my shots in an instant. It's a gift that I've always had, the pure understanding of maths, angles and mechanics that allows me to calculate the flight of every arrow perfectly and see the path they will take traced out. This is the real reason I'm so good at archery, but my sister is the only one that knew about it. People always wanted to know my secret but I always reply with something non-committal for fear of embarrassment if people knew the truth. They think of me as a weird loner now so I dread what they might do if they found out about this.

After all this has gone through my mind, in just a brief moment, I begin to unleash a barrage of arrows onto the targets. One shot to the target on the ceiling pierces a sandbag behind it, making one to my right drop suddenly from the rafters. My second shot is already in flight and catches it halfway down before it hits the ground with a loud crack. Before the impact happens, I've already nocked two arrows at once and fired them at the two targets either side of the one directly in front of me.

For the target above me but facing away I fire one arrow into the boards of the ceiling before taking a split second to adjust and fire another which cannons off the end of it and into the bullseye. With one last movement I nock my final arrow and, panting slightly at the effort, I pull the string, swing my body in a full circle and unleash the shot halfway through.

My body spins to a stop, my hair dancing around my face, as the final shot thuds into the wall about six inches from

Miyu's face. I open my eyes to see her grimacing in fear as the arrow wobbles to a standstill next to her head.

"Sorry Yamamoto, I only added that one recently," I say as I wipe the sweat from my brow and run my hands through my messy hair.

Miyu begins to giggle slightly as she finally breathes out. She should know that I would never put her in danger but that was probably a bit too close.

"That was wonderful Sasaki, you really are amazing."

"Thank you, Yamamoto."

She applauds my efforts gently as I go about retrieving the arrows from their targets and resetting the course. The lingering feeling of closeness and the glow of happiness inside me dies out like the last ember on a campfire as she leaves the gym. Miyu is the one person I desperately wish I was more like, and one who I wish I could be with. She made me a happier person. Every night when I'm staring at the ceiling in the darkness instead of sleeping, she's in my head.

I spend some time practising on the normal targets, trying shots from different angles but I'm back to the robotic, unfeeling actions. Every arrow hits home better than if I could walk up to the target and place them in by hand. That brief happiness I had has completely vanished now with jealousy, self-hatred and loneliness taking over again.

When I look up the sky has turned a deep orange and I realise how late it must have gotten. It darkens even further as the setting sun gets blocked out by deep purple clouds, like the sky itself is battered and bruised. I sigh as I head to the door, realising I don't have an umbrella. Heaving the quiver and Tenshi over my shoulder, I set off home. The weight is heavy but reassuring. I'll always have them with me.

Soon after I leave the school, the clouds close over, and the rain begins to pour. My shirt sticks to me and the pink bow droops on my chest as I trudge along. As the darkness closes in quickly the pools of light from the intermittent and poorly maintained street lamps get further apart the closer I get to home. We only moved here a few months ago, and I hate living on the wrong side of the tracks. It's grim and full of people who just get on with their horrible lives while never enjoying themselves. Even my parents fit that description perfectly now. Once Sis was gone, they just collapsed. I barely know who they are anymore, and they don't seem to care about me at all. They just mourn and live with a heavy cloud of depression hanging over them.

I stumble and stutter through the dark streets letting my feet lead my body as my brain becomes overwhelmed by the negative thoughts. Before my sister's death my parents were both happy and healthy in good jobs. We lived in a large house on the more affluent side of the city and had a normal life. But after the accident my mother had a breakdown and had to leave her job. Although my father did his best to not show his sadness at the loss of his eldest daughter, he still had to take a reduced role at his company. Now he's doing everything he can just to keep us housed, even if it is in a small, dingy house away from the light airiness of our old place.

The rain makes me think back to the day that Sis was taken from us. That day great rivers flowed from the sky as we were taken to identify the body. My mother spent the entire journey crying her eyes out, and although I wanted to join her in the outflow of emotion, I just found myself numb to the idea that the sister I had only seen a few hours ago at school was gone. We were taken to the cordoned off area where all we could see was her mangled bike a few feet away from her lifeless body in the middle of the road, her battered legs poking out from under a modesty blanket. There was blood everywhere, like she had been hit by a thresher. I can remember the horrible, bloody mess as her face was revealed to us, her golden blonde hair was stained a deep red by the damage.

I remember thinking at the time that a normal person would have cried, or shouted, or fallen to their knees but I just couldn't do anything. I couldn't even speak. I barely spoke for the next six months as we begun the readjustment process, but I knew things would never, ever feel even remotely right again.

A loud impact and a feminine scream erupt over the thunder, snapping me out of my flashback. I don't even recognise where I am, I must have been walking in the rain for ages. It's pitch black now and the rain is pouring down from the sky like it's angry with the world. I let instinct take over me, pushing the fear back down, and desperately try to work out where the scream came from. If I can help someone in trouble, then at least another family won't have to go through what I have felt for the last four years. Maybe if someone had been there to help my sister she wouldn't have died and we could have been happy. My anger at the murder of my closest friend makes me seethe. I frantically start to run as another scream accompanies the roll of thunder splitting the sky.

After a few turns I find a small kids park behind some large bushes. I dash into them trying to get to the noise but the rain seems to have gotten harder and I can barely see through the water streaming down my face. Something inside me is screaming to me to hold back, but the desperation to help this girl has overtaken all my other senses.

I crash through the undergrowth into the park before the sheer horror of the scene in front of me. A large grey mass of muscle and sinew has the screaming girl trapped under one of its six giant claws. The thing must be at least ten feet tall, with glowing black eyes and long fangs coming out of both upper and lower jaw. It's emitting a low growl as the girl struggles against its vice grip, her blood flowing over its skin. She must be at least ten years older than me, her white-blonde hair covering a look of agony on her face.

The blood, the dirt, the rain, the screaming...it all calls out to the anger inside of me. It burns like molten lava in my veins. My brain superimposes images of my sister on top of this helpless girl. When the monster removes its claw to swing a final death blow, framed in a flash of lightning, something deep within my soul calls to me. A voice on the edge of my hearing whispers something, making my body act on its own. Without taking my eyes off the poor girl, without my expression changing or making any noise, I nock an arrow, pull the string back in an instant and shoot the monster directly through the eye. The arrow made of steel and wood pierces it's brain, an explosion of grey matter following it as the shot leaves its body. The thing collapses, leaving just the noise of the rain overlapping the scene. I jump through the black smoke coming from its corpse as I push my way to the woman's side.

I throw Tenshi to the ground which clangs as it collides with another bow, half buried in the mud. Her arm and chest have been demolished by the claws and her breathing is getting shorter as the injuries take hold. Blood is oozing out of her from the gaping holes in her torso. Without saying anything I start to press on the worst wound in her chest, going through the motions of rudimentary first aid while her groans and rasps of pain pierce my ears. She tries to say something but her injuries are so bad she can't even finish a sentence. Her eyes open and look straight at me as I lean in to hear her. There's something in her eyes as a flash of lightning illuminates us, but I can't tell what.

"Your wounds are bad, don't speak," I say, but she continues, only to be cut off by another round of thunder.

The storm is practically overhead now, pounding the world into submission. After another crash of thunder and flash of lightning her eyes begin to glow, and her voice regains enough power for me to be able to hear it.

"Darkness reigns in blackest night."

She pauses and coughs blood into my face. I retch at the feeling of the warm fluid all over me, trying to wipe it off desperately, but she goes on.

"Give me thine weapon."

Another cough of blood interrupts her.

"Take up the fight."

I gasp in agony. Looking down I see an arrow going right through my stomach. The glow in her eyes fades as she passes out, and after a second unbearable pain overtakes me, making me keel over on top of her. My sight fills with the white of her dress as my fingers clutch my heaving stomach. I vomit blood before eventually feeling consciousness slip away from me.

Chapter 2

A sudden, searing light pierces through my closed eyelids. The whiteness is so bright I don't dare open my eyes in fear of having them melt from my skull. I roll over gently to try and avoid the pain but all I can feel is the overpowering sensation of light. A clink of metal makes me reach round to my back and the feeling of my quiver under my fingers brings some solidity into my world. I reach out, eyes still shut, and feel a bow in front of me. My fingers trace the engraved design on the plate, and I know that it's my Tenshi. I decide to play dead for a bit longer and await my fate, a multitude of thoughts, slow and logical, running through my head. Am I really dead? Is this the afterlife? Purgatory? Hell? Despite the brightness, it doesn't feel hot. If I am dead, why would I still have Tenshi? Why would he feel so solid and real?

After what seems like an eternity the light begins to disperse, allowing me to see the darkness of the inside of my eyelids. Taking a calculated risk I open my eyes to a slightly anticlimactic scene, one with red sand stretching in front of me all the way to the horizon, dotted with large irregular rocks and little outcrops. It looks like a normal desert, but a brief look upwards brings with it a sky that is a light, summery blue with fractures running through it that reflect the light in strange ways. There's no sun, but where a sun should be there sits a gigantic red moon dominating the world. The seconds pass and it continues to just sit there, imposing itself over the landscape but lighting the place bright enough to make my eyes hurt. I gently rise to my knees and look for the arrow in my stomach, but there's not even a wound or scar.

"Ah so you've managed to make it this far have you?" A sweet female voice addresses me from somewhere behind my kneeling form. "I didn't think you would have had it in you, but I guess I should have known. Get to your feet."

The voice suddenly takes on an authoritative tone with an edge to it that makes the hairs on my neck stand up. It's probably not in my best interests to antagonise her just yet so I begin to make my way to a standing position. I do it slowly though, giving myself as much time as I can to get my brain together. I grimace slightly as my leg twinges on my way up. If I am dead, then why am I feeling pain? What would I even be feeling pain with? The clink of arrows over my shoulder is the only sound as I manage to stand to my full height, the noises behind me meaning I've probably got a full quiver, minus perhaps one or two arrows.

"Turn around, now," demands the woman in the same flat authoritative tone.

Questions flood through my mind as I turn around to face her. My breathing doesn't change but I can't help but raise an eyebrow at the sight of the figure in front of me. It's the woman in white, the one who I just saw kill me with her last breath. She's standing tall, a striking figure against the bare backdrop. Her whole being including her skin, hair, dress, and gigantic pair of wings seem to emanate light. She's also holding a bow, just like me.

"So, I am dead then? And you are too?" I ask in a matter-of-fact tone, nodding at the angelic wings she sports.

"No Sasaki Kyushiro you're not dead, but you will be soon."

I let the threat wash over me as I go through the actions of the last few minutes, although it could be hours or days.

"What about the wings then? You're dead. You killed me after I tried to save you from that thing, and then you bled out. Now we're here in whatever this place is. Why did you kill me?"

The winged woman doesn't seem to take kindly to my insistence, furrowing her brow in anger.

"How dare you talk to me like that you little shit. You stand here before me without fear or terror? You should be bowing before me, not demanding explanations."

I don't really know why she's so annoyed...what have I said that's wrong?

"How do you know my name?"

"It doesn't matter you impudent little girl. Soon you'll be dead, and no one will remember your pathetic little existence."

Her words cut me deep into me, made worse by the fact that she's seeming to echo my own negative thoughts.

"If we're not dead then why are you, an angel, here, in the afterlife?"

"You think this is the afterlife? You don't even have a clue!" she scoffs.

She raises her hand to the sky, ripples appearing as if she were dropping a stone in a lake, making the image of another place form above us. I remain passive as the rain flows upwards onto what clearly is a scene of myself, leaking bodily fluids on top of the body of this woman. We're entwined in a horrible mix of blood, bile, earth, mud, and rain. Unmistakably, protruding from the mud at the side of the scene is a pair of wings. Her wings. Presumably white when they're not completely buried in the grime.

"Ok, so you had wings all along," I state, "what are you then?"

shhnk

She's suddenly in front of in a flash, leaving a metallic noise ringing in the air. I didn't even see her move but now she's face to face with me. Her hand closes around my collar, lifting me up violently.

"I am an Angel! I am a voice of God himself! I am sent on his mission to bring his word to everyone!" Her voice bellows with a force that would make a normal person cower. For once, I'm glad that I'm not normal. "And I've come for you Sasaki Kyushiro. Your body and soul will be ours. Yield your power to us so we can continue the fight against those that rule the darkness and go against our message. We can and we will take that power from you if you don't give it up willingly."

I continue to stare at her, unflinching, her face mere inches from mine. My restraint appears to spur her to even more anger.

"How can you stand there in silence? Do you realise that you're going to die? You are a useless little worm who has never done anything to help anyone, not even your sister. With the power inside you and the right attitude you could be a lethal weapon in the fight against evil. How can you stand by and do nothing? I won't let you slip through our hands. You will fight with us."

I feel like I want to react but just don't know how, so I continue to stare at her obstinately.

"Say something!"

The cracking blow to my cheek sends me flying backwards, the sound echoing around the empty world. I wince as I crash against a rock, knocking the air from my lungs, causing my head to fall to my chest as the pain rebounds through my body. Through a rapidly swelling face I look up at her, engulfed in a mixture of rage and pain.

"What did you say about my sister?"

"I said that you couldn't help her! Ah yes, you could have been there and saved her but you didn't. If you embraced the power within you would have saved her. You're a useless piece of crap Sasaki and everybody knows it, especially you."

"If I'm so useless then why do you want me?"

"You're useless because you refuse to use your power. All that strength you have and it's going to waste because you won't use it. Your sadness and guilt rule you, trapping you in a prison in your mind. They make your mind and soul into this barren desert with nothing as far as the eye can see. But I am strong, we are strong. We can use your power better than you ever could, and we will take it!"

"What do you mean pow..."

fwip

My reactions kick in and before I've had time to think I've thrown myself face down into the sand as an arrow thuds into the rock behind me, splitting it in two. The creak of the string betrays her intentions and I roll behind a small outcrop as another arrow buries where I'd been.

I yelp in pain as the arrow hit my foot, but when I instinctively reach down to pull it out my hand grasps at nothing. I'm perfectly unharmed, the arrow is just sitting there, half covered in sand. I swear that hit me, I felt it. Shaking my head, I dispel the thoughts and try to come up with a plan before she catches me.

"Come out you little fucker. You're just going to hide as normal? Aren't you even going to fight me?!"

The thought of attacking her had never even crossed my mind. I don't have any reason to harm her. Violence has never been my thing. I usually find that people will leave me alone if I sit there and don't put up a fight.

"Why would I attack you?"

"You're not even going to attack someone who's threatening you?"

"No. You won't kill me. You said you need me. Look, I just want to know what's going on. Who are you? What power could I possibly have that you need so badly?"

"Anyone who won't attack when faced with an enemy is a fool."

She's trying to goad me, but if I go for her and miss I'll be wide open. My eye catches the disintegrated rock as I hear her string creak again. Rolling to one side I narrowly avoid another shot which destroys my cover.

"If you want information off me Sasaki then you'll have to prove to me that you deserve it!"

I think there's a mocking, almost childish tone to her voice. Scrambling to a crouching position I can see the girl standing at least fifteen feet away. She seems to be at ease, holding the long silver bow I saw by her side in the park.

shhnk

That strange noise penetrates my ears again, but before I've even finished processing the signal she's in front of me, her free hand holding my chin gently and raising my face to hers. Her eyes are beautiful, stunning emerald green masterpieces that fill my world and captivate me.

"Are you a fool Sasaki Kyushiro?"

Her voice is low and thick like syrup, and the feeling of her skin touching mine sends shivers through my core, raising my temperature.

"H...how did you do that?" I ask in an almost breathless whisper.

I'm lost in the green, burning fire of her eyes that seem to be swallowing me whole. Our lips are almost touching and I can feel her breath mingling with mine. My thoughts feel like they're melting. Another tingle passes through me as I feel something brush the back of my neck. I instinctively collapse to the floor before seeing her wings slam together. I clutch my chest with my lungs desperate for oxygen.

"Sasaki, you're so adorable, but the time has come for us to claim our prize."

She extends her wings and she's gone again, with that noise hanging in the air once more.

"Back here Sasaki."

I almost wrench my neck in an attempt to follow the strange movements. The wings flap again and again she's gone.

"How did you do that?" I repeat as I turn to come face to face with the glint of a silver arrow inches away. It's deadly still, without even a hint of swaying. "Just tell me who or what you are. Please?"

The arrowhead seems to drop a little. My chance!

"No."

The arrow lets fly but I'm already halfway through a spin, pulling the quiver up to take the force of the blow. The thump of the arrow burying into the thick wood has such incredible force that it knocks me down. I scramble to my knees quickly, pulling Tenshi into my hand and inserting an arrow into the string so it's mirroring the silver one she's pointing at me. My breath is still short and my arrow sways in my hand compared to her rock steady grip.

"Oh Sasaki, you have a bit more spunk than I gave you credit for. You've seen me teleport before, do you really think you'd win that race if we both fired? Hahaha!!"

Her laugh grates on me making my emotions seethe inside, starting to get the better of me for once. I lose control for a split second and foolishly call her bluff by releasing the string. Just as she promised, she disappears from sight with that strange sound, the arrow sailing into the distance until it vibrates to a stop in mid-air, point disappearing in the sky.

I think part of me is glad she avoided the attack. I don't know if I could really bring myself to kill someone. Even though I predict the counterattack, I've spent too long contemplating things to be able to avoid it. The silver arrow punctures my right arm, dropping me to the ground. I scream at the pain, but I think I did enough to avoid a lethal attack. The blood flows out of me, painting the sand an even deeper red.

"Very impressive Sasaki, you even predicted where I would attack from, but it looks like you weren't quick enough. We will enjoy having you on our side."

"And who is your side, really? Who are you?" I pant.

"I told you; we are the Angels. I am Lailah, the Angel of the Dark Mind. We come from God with a message. 'We are the protectorate of the human race, and we are the only beings that can save this world from the Fallen, the enemies of humanity.'"

She seems chattier now, I think fuzzily through the throbbing in my shoulder. My attack must have done something to prove my worth.

"Where are we?"

fwip

The sound of an arrow whistling away from a taut string sparks my reflexes again, but my injury is slowing me down. I try to move out of the way but this time her shot slams into my left palm, leaving it buried in the red sand. As I pull it out and the mix of sand and blood streams off me there's a strange tingling sensation in my fingers. The fog of pain and blood loss in my brain makes thinking for more than a few seconds impossible.

"And once again you lie here on the floor, alone and dying Sasaki. If you look up there you'll see your physical body doing the same, while in here your soul dies before me."

I follow her finger back to the vision of what appears to be the 'real world', focussing on the park scene. Through the haze of pain, it looks like there's another figure there, kneeling over me.

"That is your body and this is your mind. A world entirely created within your psyche. A desolate, sandy wasteland with a moon that imprisons your true self."

"My mind?" I whisper.

"I used the arrow to put my blood inside you, now I can overcome your inner being and steal your body and soul. You can put up a fight but when I win, and I always win, all that dwells within you is mine to control. I'll absorb your strength, take over your body and use it to fight for us. Now your time has come, your final defeat."

I fuzzily look up and see her aim an arrow for a lethal shot, directly between my eyes. Time seems to slow down as she releases the arrow which curves and spins towards me. All I can think of is my sister. Sis, I wanted to make you happy, even after your death, but it looks like I've failed. I wish I could have done more. I'm sorry.

Chapter 3

A loud crack of thunder suddenly bursts through my fading consciousness, bringing my vision back to me, but all I can see is darkness. As I tilt my head the darkness morphs into a silhouetted figure blocking my view. I wince as rain falls on my face from a quickly receding circle above. As it closes it brings back the distorted, blue sky of my mind.

"Wh...who are you?" I squeak.

The figure turns her head and my eyes bulge as the gentle, long features of Yamamoto Miyu stare back at me. Shock courses through me at the sight of her in a long, loose, purple robe covered in twinkling stars.

"Don't worry Sasaki, I'm here for you."

"Look out Yamamoto!"

I flinch backwards as another arrow flies towards us but Miyu makes a strange hand movement like she's pulling a bed cover over us. The arrow smashes into some kind of barrier, bouncing off and leaving strange ripples of blue around us. Even with the pain flowing up my arms I'm overcome with amazement and disbelief. She turns and faces me with a calming smile on her face, a look of warmth and loving kindness that even I can decipher.

Lailah fires another few shots, each bouncing to safety. Miyu doesn't even flinch as she leans down and places her hands where the arrows are piercing my body. She mutters some words and small glyphs appear around their shafts before they explode into tiny fragments. The holes they left close up before my wide eyes, not even leaving a scar. She bows her head so our foreheads touch, a feeling of calm flowing through my veins. I stare deeply into Miyu's eyes before finally letting out a sigh and feeling a real smile draw across my face. Sudden quietness envelops us as the arrows stop raining down, bringing with it a fragment of peace to my mind.

"Are you feeling better Sasaki? And please, call me by my first name like you used to."

Something pricks the doubt in my mind, replacing the insincerity in her voice with genuine concern.

"I don't know what I'm feeling, but I'm happy to see you Miyu."

Calling Miyu by her first name isn't something I thought I'd ever get to do again. I tremble as a tinge of embarrassment fills me. My head drops only for her to pull it up with a gentle hand.

"I'm glad, Sasaki. Can we talk like we used to? I've missed your friendship." I nod carefully, impeded slightly by Miyu's hand. "Thank you Kyu. Now listen carefully to me because we don't have time for questions. We're inside your soul, please take that as face value. Your body is in the real world and it's in a bad way, so we have to get back quickly before your injuries take hold. I tried to stop the bleeding before I came but I had to get here before it was too late. I can't hold my shield forever and we have to stop her. Will you be able to help me do that?"

"I don't think I can kill her Miyu. What if she has a family that will miss her like I... That monster was the first thing I've ever killed and I...I didn't even know what I was thinking when I did it. I don't even know if I was thinking!" I wail.

"Ok Kyu, but if we're both going to survive this then you might have to. I don't want to hurt her either but I'm here to help out ok? I know your senses work orders of magnitude faster than anyone's, so you're going to have to use those. You can do this, even if you don't want to, but we're going to have to do it together. Ok?"

I nod in agreement but the fright at the idea of killing someone still grips my heart. She clasps my arm and I feel soothed again.

"I know you can do it Kyu. Ready?"

"Can I have one second to prepare Miyu?"

She nods as I close my eyes. Without looking I swing the quiver around, pull an arrow out and rest it loosely against Tenshi's string. With my other hand, but still with my eyes shut, I draw diagrams in the sand playing out the possibilities of the fight in front me. Archery is nothing but energy, angles and momentum, and a fight is nothing but predicting the enemies moves.

"Drop the shield when I say Miyu."

"Whenever you need it, Kyu."

Surprise, that's the key.

"Now!"

Miyu drops the shield and both of us duck to the right to avoid the inevitable shot.

"Block!"

Another arrow flies towards us but Miyu holds up her hand and shouts an incantation, producing a circular shield of blue energy which dissolves the arrow in mid-flight. Lailah teleports around the battlefield firing at us again and again. I stand with my back to Miyu as she continues to dissolve the arrows that come at as. I spin us around, the shaft of my arrow brushing against Miyu's thigh as I try to find the opening. Every time I think I've found it I can't bring myself to take the shot. Miyu is panting with the effort of protecting us, but every time I try to shoot I come up against a wall in my consciousness. I simply can't kill this woman, despite her attacks.

"Kyu, you have to do something here. Her attacks are getting stronger."

I can hear the desperation in Miyu's voice but I just can't shoot her. Miyu's knee buckles under the intense job she is having to do just to protect me, making me bite my lip to push back the guilt and the tears. Behind her I see Lailah's wings flinch as she disappears. The right, she's going to come from the right. I turn and unleash an arrow that collides with the silver arrow from Lailah's bow on my right side, smashing both into pieces. Yes, I can guess her movements. I can feel where she's going to be! Lailah disappears again, and I go to block it but I'm too late, all I get to see is the silver shaft bury itself in Miyu's side.

"Miyu!" I screech.

I catch her in my arms as she flops down, anger seething inside me. My friend is hurt because of me, because of her! I turn my tear sodden face to Lailah.

"I thought it was me you wanted, why are you attacking her?"

I ask the question instinctively, but I know it's because she's trying to goad me. Miyu is clearly in agony, but when she speaks it's in a clear, calm voice.

"Kyu, you have power inside yourself. I've always known that. I'm sorry I couldn't protect you."

Her apology sets something off inside me. It's something cold, dark, and hard, deep in my soul. How could she possibly apologise for not protecting me? I should be apologising for making her come here and getting her hurt. I can't let her die. I'll do anything I need to do to protect her. Something pricks my mind as I think about killing Lailah, not fear but...something. I push it down inside me and gently put Miyu down on the sand, rising to face the Angel.

"How dare you hurt her you coward!"

"Hah! You stand there and call me a coward! You have been running from yourself for years Sasaki Kyushiro!"

"I saved you from that monster and this is the thanks I get? You come into my world, you nearly kill me and my friend. Where's your gratitude Lailah?"

She stares for a brief moment, so I use the opportunity to whisper to Miyu, "I need your help once more Miyu, please? Can you do that?"

She stifles a scream of pain to nod gently out of the corner of my eye. I look back up to Lailah who seems to be thinking carefully.

"Gratitude does not save the human race does it? No, only strength can do that. Are you going to give us your power willingly to save that girl and everyone else?"

It sounds lovely, but how can I possibly trust this woman? Instead, I trust my instincts and steel myself. Slowly I take a deep breath and shut my eyes, feeling the fire of emotions burning within me.

"No."

The sound of her first arrow beginning its trajectory towards me hits my ear, the shot heading directly for my right pupil, my weaker eye of course. Rather than dodge it completely I move my head slightly to avoid it by the narrowest of margins, the point grazing my cheek as it rushes past. With my eyes still shut I pull the string tight and aim it to my right.

"My left Miyu."

Following my instructions Miyu plants a shield to where I told her to. Her moan of pain at the effort bites into me, but I think this is the only way we can win. Having had her first shot destroyed by Miyu's spell Lailah teleports to my right. I fire the pre-aimed arrow before spinning on the spot and swinging my bow up in a complicated fashion. I pull two arrows from the quiver and nock them against the string. I take a millisecond to adjust before letting both of them go in a V-shape formation in front of me. Immediately after they leave my bow I pull Tenshi up and fire another shot, before twisting him around to deflect one of Lailah's arrows off his metal plate. To my right and left my arrows clatter against Lailah's attacks, knocking them both out of the air, leaving four arrows fallen in the sand.

As I open my eyes Lailah is exactly where I felt she would be, with my arrow sticking in her chest, pointing towards us. She looks down at the tip in disbelief and gasps for breath. I point behind her to the arrow stuck in the sky as it vibrates gently to a stop. Just like back at school, the arrow provided the perfect obstacle to bounce a shot off, allowing me to attack from Lailah's blind spot. The silence is over now, as she begins to pant and gurgle. Ignoring her for a moment I drop down to my knees, trembling next to the prone form of Miyu. She's breathing but it's short and weak. Everywhere around us stained in her blood.

"I knew you could do it," Miyu says breathlessly.

Her trembling voice makes the tears well up and run down my face as I hold her head to my chest and feel her arms touch mine.

"Don't cry, it's not that serious," she says.

Even if this is all just my mind the feeling of Miyu's soft robe on my skin and her breath on my chest is as real as I've ever felt. It's been so long since I could enjoy the closeness of another human being. I desperately want the moment to go on forever, but Lailah's retching forces me to finally lay my friend down and stand back up. I walk over to her unsteadily, her white dress turning crimson before my eyes as her chest wound pours with blood.

"You didn't even look. How could you know where I would be? How could you fire that accurately with your eyes shut?"

Her voice is almost a mumble, just like it was in the park when I first found her.

"You told me this was my soul didn't you. That means this sand, the rocks, the air around me is all part of who I am. Earlier I felt like I'd been shot in the foot when your arrow hit the sand beside me. I can tell you the location of every grain of sand here. Every time you touched the ground I knew exactly where you were. Every arrow you shot I could tell the flight of by the way it disturbed the air."

"What?" she splutters, blood dripping off her chin, "no normal person could do that, that's impossible."

"Well, I guess I'm just...not normal then? Look, I'm sorry I can't help you; I can't give you what I have. I just wanted to say...thank you. Being here and seeing this has really helped me understand. I didn't know this was all here."

As she collapses back to the floor under the weight of her injury, I step over her body and pull Tenshi out. I carefully reach over my back and pick an arrow, pushing it against the string. Aiming directly upwards I unleash the arrow before looking down at Lailah.

"Thank you."

The arrow whistles upwards before ploughing into the gigantic red satellite above us all. A crack runs through it like a pane of glass before the entire thing shatters into millions of fragments. There's a feeling of pressure being released suddenly, like a massive shock wave through my whole being. Where the fragments hit the sand green shoots begin to sprout. Within seconds the entire vista is covered in plants, trees, flowers of all shades from beautiful delicate white to ultraviolet purple. Thick vines erupt from the greenery that's growing around Miyu's feet, coiling around her legs and arms, lifting her up to a standing position. The arrow wound in her side disappears into the undergrowth before the greenery gives way, showing nothing but flawless skin where her wound had been.

This feeling is incredible. There's power, calmness and beauty all here within me. I am not useless. I am not worthless. A sense of purpose erupts from every pore of my being and tears of joy seep from my eyes. In front of me a tree bursts up, growing hundreds of years' in a few seconds before blooming with beautiful pink blossoms.

Vines pull Lailah up, encompassing her until her back is pressed against the bark. Her arms are outstretched and trussed up like she's being crucified. I don't really understand what's going on so I pull an arrow just in case. Holding my normal, flat, emotionless expression I draw the string back in a threatening motion.

"Do you want to die here Lailah?"

"You can't kill me and you know it."

Shit. It's like she can read my mind.

"Let me go...so we...the Angels...can save you and your friend from the Fallen," she gurgles breathlessly.

"I don't need you to protect me, or to protect Miyu. Why should I do anything to help you and your group against these so-called Fallen?"

"Because they killed your sister," she gasps out before her head drops to her chest.

I run up to her and grab her hair, yanking her face upwards.

"What did you say? They killed my sister? What do you mean?!" My voice suddenly screeching with anger.

Her mouth is opening and shutting but the wound in her chest is obviously causing her too much pain.

"S...save me."

"Tell me what you meant!" I shout, but nothing comes back.

"Kyu!" Miyu says from behind me, putting her hand on my shoulder. "I patched up your body before I came here but we have to get back to the physical world and get you medical attention. We can't hang around waiting for this. We have to go now!"

"No, I have to know what she meant!"

"I said we have to go! Please!"

Turning to Lailah, strung up helplessly and bleeding profusely, I shut my eyes and concentrate before letting out a small sigh.

"Lailah, I won't let you die here. I will find a way to come back and talk to you again."

I concentrate, pushing the power inside me towards a specific cause. Suddenly the vines undulate towards the wound in Lailah's chest. As they cover it she begins to heal just like Miyu did.

"Thank you, Sasaki," she gasps with relief as breath re-enters her chest, "Dr Michihara, at the General Hospital, go to her, she can help once you release me."

I turn to Miyu when suddenly a loud gasp from Lailah makes me spin back round. The vines around her snap tight around her limbs and cinch around her neck. She starts to gasp loudly as she struggles for air, her face quickly turning red. The sound of her babbling and gasping is horrifying. I swear I can feel her pain flowing through her binds and vibrating through the tree trunk, down through the ground and up through my feet.

"What are you doing?!" The panic in Lailah's voice is evident even with her breath being cut off.

"I don't know! I just wanted to heal you and keep you here! The vines are moving of their own accord! I don't have control over them!"

"Helllllllpppp!"

Her screams get cut off as she passes out.

"Do something Kyu!"

"I'm trying Miyu! I can't stop them!" I shout as I grasp at my head.

I desperately wrack my brain looking for an answer. The tears are back again but this time they're tears of panic and terror. I run up to the tree and start pulling at the vines around Lailah's neck, but they just seem to get tighter and tighter the more I struggle. I scratch and pull at them, drawing blood from my skin as I scour myself on them. I throw Tenshi to the floor, pull the arrow I had aimed at Lailah and start hacking away with the point.

"Help me Miyu!" I shriek as she joins me, pulling at the noose around Lailah's neck.

This is all part of me isn't it? Why can't I control them?! Why are they attacking her?! I didn't tell them to do that! Despite both Miyu and I trying our best we can't prevent them tightening further. I wail and cry as I collapse from the effort of the battle knowing that there's nothing we can do. Lailah has stopped breathing entirely and her face has gone purple as her eyes roll back in her head. The vines crawl down her face and nose, moving down her chest before driving outwards and then returning to stab her directly in the heart. I let out a long, ear piercing howl as Lailah's body becomes mummified by her restraints. I can't kill. I can't. How could this have happened? I wanted to save her! The feelings of remorse are quickly replaced with burning anger, and those replaced just as quickly with corrosive self-hatred.

I scrabble vainly again at the roots of the tree but within a few seconds wracking sobs take me over. My tears are still dropping into the grass, rolling down the blades like morning dew as Miyu grabs me. She pulls me to my feet and her hand brushes my cheek.

"Kyu, look at me."

Miyu's voice is tender and soft but I don't want to look at anyone right now. I just want to kill myself and to die in a pool of my own blood at the feet of the horrible, Angel shaped cocoon.

"This wasn't your fault Kyu; you didn't control those things and you didn't choose to kill her. You couldn't do that. I know you couldn't."

I throw my arms around Miyu's neck and bury my head into the soft hem of her robe until the tears refuse to come anymore. Looking up at Miyu, I search for some kind of solace in her eyes but all I can see is her mouth open in amazement.

"What?" I sob.

"Kyu, your eyes! They're not right!"

I flip Tenshi around and through the tears in the reflection I can see that she's right. My irises have become a bright, glowing, emerald green rather than my natural faded blue. I move the bow slightly and gasp as a pair of gigantic white wings unfold from my shoulders.

"What's going on Miyu?"

"I don't know Kyu, but we have to go! We have to get back to the real world. Now! Hold my hands and I'll take you back to your body. We can try and work it out later."

I grab Tenshi and swing him over my shoulder before reaching for her hands. Lailah said this group called the Fallen killed my sister. I need to find out what really happened. As I take her hands, I look down at them and seize up slightly at the contact.

"Here we go, get ready Kyu."

She starts reciting something under her breath. A rush of wind, cold and rain hits my face as I look up into an opening portal above us. Miyu suddenly pulls me up through it as I take one last look at the light, shining, verdant surroundings. The wind burns my skin as it blasts past me through our short trip through the darkness. Then with a thunderclap everything goes black and still.

Chapter 4

I open my eyes and the only thing I can see is the recessed fluorescent lighting in the ceiling. My mind is fuzzy as I try to recall everything that's happened. I gently turn my head and try to get my bearings in the plain and pale room, flinching and groaning at the pain in my stomach as I shift my body. The tubes coming out of my arm and the beep of a monitor next to me makes the word 'hospital' present itself. That means I must be alive. The constant stabbing pain in my stomach continues to befuddle my thoughts, derailing them and making me only capable of thinking in tiny bite sized chunks. Alive. Hospital. Pain. Accident? Images of Lailah pass across my eyes. The wings, the voice, the arrows piercing my skin. Miyu rescuing me. It all runs through me, threatening to overwhelm me.

I close my eyes, breathe slowly and concentrate on pushing the calmness through me. Within me I have that beautiful place, filled with greenery, somewhere that shows that I have worth as a person. I clench my fists and try to feel the sensation of being there. Positive feelings spread through me in a way that they have never done before.

I'm interrupted by the door to my room sliding open where a female doctor, correction, a very female doctor enters my room, followed by Miyu. Thank goodness! She's ok! I try to speak but barely anything comes out of my mouth and another stab in my gut reminds me that I shouldn't be trying too much. I manage, just about, to say Miyu's name with relief. She sits next to me and grips my arm in a caring way.

"Kyu this is Dr Michihara, the one Lailah told you about," she whispers into my ear.

The beautiful feeling of her breath in my ear and her soft skin on mine makes me close my eyes and smile ever so slightly. It doesn't last long though as Dr Michihara yanks one of my eyes open and shines a pen torch in it. The brightness makes me flinch, eliciting another howl of pain. Miyu grabs my arm tighter as the physician continues to check out my wounds.

When she finally sets me back down on the bed there are blue dots jumping in front of my vision. I avert my eyes from the ceiling only to be confronted by Michihara's chest filling my vision. A blush flows over my face and something that sounds like a stifled giggle escapes from my right.

When Michihara stands up I get to see all of her for the first time. Her low-cut top complimented by a loose medical coat. She has glasses on but is wearing them quite low on her nose, almost as if they're just for affectation. She looks over them at me and sighs with what might be annoyance. What could I have done wrong when I'm cooped up in a hospital bed?

"Your wounds seem to be healing well Sasaki and it's good to see you beginning to deal with the pain. The stab wound in your stomach was bad, and frankly you're lucky to be alive. From what your friend here told me you ran into my compatriot. Can you tell me what happened?"

I try and speak but it hurts too much and I'm forced to give up.

"Hang on, let me help you out," Michihara says.

She lays her hand on my stomach and an aura envelops her entire body. I shut my eyes as I feel an energy run through my stomach, my chest and out to the rest of me. It fills my veins, replacing my blood and flowing through me. When I next open my mouth, my breath comes easier and the pain has fallen from a demonic stabbing to a dull, aching throb.

I start to recount the situation that led me to running into Lailah, how badly she was injured and how after saving her she attacked me. Describing the events finally make me really think about the monster that I killed, causing my voice to trail off. I knew that when it had come to the time where I needed to kill Lailah I couldn't do it, but that monster; I killed that thing without even thinking. I didn't even have to look at it as my arrow pierced its brain. It felt like something overcame me in that moment, controlling my actions.

"Sasaki?" Dr Michihara's voice cuts through my confusion and brings me back to her.

"Sorry Doctor."

She sighs again, sounding exasperated.

"Look, I know full well about Lailah and her powers. She's highly regarded among the other Angels. Tell me what happened after she transferred herself into you."

"So, it is real then? You are an Angel? This is all real?"

"Yes, it is and yes, I am. What did she tell you about us? What happened to her?"

"She told me that some kind of monsters called the Fallen killed my sister. It was four years ago and I have to find out if it's true." My words suddenly come out short and sharp, interrupting Michihara's question which I don't really feel like answering right now anyway. I can't face the thought of being the one who murdered Lailah. "Is it true? How did she die? Did they kill her?"

"Your sister? Hmm, if I remember there was another girl called Sasaki among the people I investigated."

"What do you mean investigated?" Miyu asks, drawing a glare from the doctor.

"I'm charged with examining all of the bodies that come here for evidence of Fallen activity. As far as I remember there was nothing special about her death. She was just a girl hit by a car. The only thing even remotely out of the ordinary was that her life force was entirely extinguished by the time she reached my table. Usually, bodies contain some trace of it for many days after death so to have a subject with none was slightly unusual. I guess there is a possibility that the Fallen killed her, but I don't think even they have the capability of destroying someone's life force like that."

"How can you talk about her like that? She isn't...she wasn't a piece of data for your group to dissect! She wasn't a nobody! She meant everything to me!"

"Whether she was or wasn't isn't important right now, and the fate of the human race is what's at stake. We need Lailah back. We've recovered Lailah's body but her soul isn't inhabiting it. Release her to us Sasaki."

"Tell me what is going on here," I say obstinately, causing Michihara to sigh loudly.

"Honestly I'm so busy at the hospital that I don't get told the whys and wherefores of everything that goes on with the whole group. I am a physician and I don't have any more information for you."

"Then take me to someone who does," I demand. She sighs again.

"Very well. Perhaps the others will know what to do with you. Follow me and I will take you to the lab."

"Let me help you Kyu. Can you walk?"

"She can," Michihara says over her shoulder as she storms out the room.

I struggle out of bed, dressed just in the skimpy hospital gown and try and take a step before stumbling. Miyu is under my arm immediately, taking my weight and guiding me towards the door. When we get there Michihara is already most of the way down a corridor heading towards a pair of big double doors. She hasn't even looked back for us as we start off, slowly, towards where she's going.

"Thank you Miyu. I couldn't have done any of this without you, but I have so much to ask."

"I know Kyu, but you want to know about the Angels and your sister more than you want to know about me."

"How do you know that?"

For a few seconds, the only sound between us is the padding of our feet slowly down the tiled hospital hallway.

"I didn't know how you would react if I told you. I'm not even sure you'd have believed me. I've hidden it from you all this time, but when I found you in trouble I had to do something about it."

"Hidden what from me? What are you? Are you one of them?"

We stop in the middle of the corridor with Miyu looking straight ahead. She doesn't give an answer for what feels like forever.

"No, I'm not an Angel, I'm a mage. My mother and father are both mages, and I have been raised as one in secret. We practice and specialise in empathy and telepathy magic. I can tell what people are thinking, I can influence their thoughts a little, as well as some other stuff. I'm so sorry I couldn't tell you before."

I look up to her with an air of minor surprise, which is about as much emotion as I ever show when someone isn't trying to kill me.

"But...that's...ridiculous."

I guess if she is a mind reader of some kind then she must know my reaction to all this already. I feel stupid for even uttering the feeble attempt at disproving her. But then, Angels are ridiculous as well and Lailah was one. I think back to those wings I saw on my back in Tenshi's reflection and wonder.

"I know it's hard to believe but you have to trust me. Magic is real and mages have been on this planet for thousands of years. There are various sects that have waged secret magical wars for centuries, to the point where the craft is almost dying out. My parents and me are the last mages of the entire Eastern sect. They trained me in private and they forbade me from telling anyone, or ever showing my power outside of a life and death situation."

My face drops again and we start off again down the empty hallway.

"Ah I see you believe me now!"

She looks at me with another smile but I still find it hard to look directly at her. She really can tell what I'm feeling.

"Is that how you knew I was in the park?"

"Yes Kyu. Your pain was so strong it seared into my mind! Sharing in your agony was one of the worst things I've ever felt. I know you've gone through so much over the past few years and I've always known you've been suffering but this was on another level. I'm so sorry I couldn't get there in time. When I did eventually arrive, I could sense that something was happening inside you."

Silence envelops us again as we struggle towards the double doors that Michihara has left swinging. It feels like there's something welling up inside of me but I don't know what it is.

"Don't you say sorry to me."

"What?"

"I said don't you dare apologise for helping me. How can you be sorry when I'm the one that's sorry Miyu? I didn't want to cause you any of that pain. I didn't want you to get hurt. I can't bear the idea that you got hurt because of me."

At the top of a cold, grey staircase she suddenly pulls me round and puts both her arms round me, bringing our faces close.

"Kyu," she says sharply, "you did not cause me any of that pain. I could have shut you off at any time over the past god knows how many years if I really wanted to. I kept your emotions close to me because I knew you deserved it, and I came to get you because I knew you needed me. I will go through anything to protect you because you've always been my friend. Even when you couldn't accept it, I've always been here for you."

"Ladies we're here," Michihara shouts from the bottom of the long staircase, "please come down to the Sanctum and meet the rest of the Angels."

"Catchy name," Miyu whispers in my ear as we make our way down the stairs and enter the Sanctum.

Chapter 5

The sheer size of the place makes the view overwhelming. it must cover a good chunk of the lower floor beneath the hospital. Rows of machines and tables fill my vision on every side. Everywhere I look there are warning labels, trefoils, lasers, and loose wiring. Through a small window in the door there's a person handling a diamond into a piece of apparatus using a long pair of safety tongs. He or she seems to be being extremely careful.

"Hello there pretties! Who are you now? Are you our next victims?"

A woman steps in front of my view, blocking off the window to the lab and smiles a big, gleaming, pointy toothed grin at me. My normally dulled social senses are now screaming at me about how dangerous this woman is.

"Keiko, don't intimidate our guests."

"Aww I was only having a little fun Professor!"

The woman flashes me another powerful grin which makes the hairs on my neck stand on end. Trying to ignore the adrenaline spiking in my body I turn towards the voice that scolded her, which came from a middle-aged man flanked by a woman with a tablet. The man is immaculately dressed but his face is wrinkled and tired around his square framed glasses. The woman beside him is giving me a one-eyed stare from behind an eye patch and has the same gaunt look. Both of them tower over me in a way that would intimidate if I didn't have a combination of pain and exhaustion running through my body to help keep that at bay. The reassuring clasp of Miyu's arm around mine reminds me that I'm not alone.

"Thank you for bringing them to us Michihara. You can leave them to us, I'm sure you're needed back upstairs."

The man speaks with a strong tone, but other than a short sigh from behind me followed by a "Yes Sir" from the doctor there's no noise of dissent. I turn to watch her go, desperate to thank her for helping me.

"She'll know how you feel."

"Stop doing that Miyu! You've got to give me some privacy."

She stifles a giggle, which causes me to drop my head in embarrassment. Despite her having a special place in my mind it's still hard to know that I can't keep any secrets from her. I don't like feeling so naked, as if my skin has been shredded from me to reveal my inner workings to the world.

"Young ladies I would like to pass on my thanks to you. Your actions have rid us of one more of the scourge that is the Fallen and thus there is one less threat to humanity. You have done the Lord's work."

The words come out of his mouth in a calm and quiet manner but when I run them back through my mind something doesn't sit well.

"Allow me to introduce myself, I am Professor Hashimoto Shinsei, the leader of the Angels. I want to reward you in any way I can for helping our cause, but first I need to know what happened to our sister Lailah. Tell me where she is, or what happened to her Miss Sasaki."

"Not unt..."

I start to speak but then I look into his eyes and the fear hits me like a cannonball. There's a halo of burning fire around his brown irises and a pressure that pushes me to the floor. In my mind's eye the rest of the lab falls away until there's just the two of us remaining. Miyu's skin melts from around my arm where she'd been holding me, sloughing off into a pit in front of us. Flames start to rise from the floor making Hashimoto's shadow grow and take on a form of its own, towering over me. Terror fills me up like a reservoir in a rainstorm, and as the banks begin to overflow I drop to my knees to see demons of black fire cackling, trying to pull me in. The shadowy hands reach over the lip, wrapping around and crawling up my legs, all lit in an eery, fiery glow. I try to scream but a hand grips my throat and stifles me. I struggle my head upwards until I lock eyes with Hashimoto who is staring directly into my soul. As quickly as it came, the whole scene vanishes and reality flows back in.

My tear flecked eyes dart around the room, but I can't see anything out of the ordinary. Miyu gently pulls at my arm, but I yank myself away forcefully and sink back to the ground. I despise this feeling, like someone has dug claws inside my mind and shredded it. I hate it, I hate it! Between Hashimoto, Lailah and Miyu I've encountered three people who have made me feel like I can't hide anything and I can't stand it. An urge to scream and run away rises in my throat like bile, burning me and shocking me, but I swallow it down. The pull of being able to find out what these people know about my sister helps overwhelm the fear trying to drown me, keeping my head above the surface.

"If I share what I know with you, will you be able to tell me what you know about my sister?" I pant.

"I will tell you everything I can to help try to settle your poor, restless soul Miss Sasaki."

I stand back up and steel myself, finding the last remnants of calm inside and calling them forward.

"I found Lailah in a park where a monster was attacking her. It had her pinned to the ground. She was screaming in pain and bleeding badly." My lip starts to quiver a little as I remember the scene. So much has changed since then, but it must have only been a day or two ago. The thing I remember most is the way the monster looked at me, with its pitch-black eyes right before my arrow pierced straight through it. "I killed it without thinking. What was it? Was I wrong to do it?"

"No Miss Sasaki, what you did was absolutely right. That thing was a monster we call the Fallen. They are horrors that are intent on destroying the human race and taking this planet for their own. If you had not done so then both you and Lailah would be dead now."

"Lailah is already dead."

It slips out before I can stop it. I gasp and clap my hand over my mouth as I realise what I've done. My face drops and the tears flow down my cheek. I sob loudly at the attempt to keep the memory from overwhelming me, but the effort is to no avail. Seeing that beautiful person, with hopes and dreams and emotions and family being speared, choked, and crushed in my own mind makes me despise myself.

"What did you say?"

There's no sound anymore, just seven pairs of eyes staring at me, boring into me. They're all looking at me with a mixture of horror and worry, except for a young boy who has a soft smile on his face and a welcome lightness to his being. The man he is standing next to could hardly be less welcoming, staring a deathly, dark look at me from under long, black, greasy hair. The woman he called Keiko has been joined by a heavily built man who looms over me intimidatingly. She walks towards me with a look of rage painted on her face until the man places a hand on her shoulder. I feel surrounded. I'm trapped. I take a step back in panic where I collide with Miyu, her yelp in my ear causing me to wince.

"Sorry."

"It's ok Kyu," Miyu says as she leans in, reducing her voice to a whisper, "maybe it's time to confess. I don't think we're going to be able to get out of this without telling them."

I wipe my eyes with my gown. Of course, she's right. I recount my story to Hashimoto about what happened including all of the details of how Lailah met her end.

"I tried to stop it I really did! I tried everything I could to protect her and it was never my intention to...I mean I never...please don't kill me."

After a few seconds of silence, Hashimoto beckons to the lady with him and they both stride over to me. The older lady leans close to my face and looks me over with her one good eye, her breath rasping on my skin. She gently grips my chin and moves my head to the side before Hashimoto does the same. After an awkward few seconds, they stand up straight and begin whispering to each other. I can't make out what they're saying but the way they stand over me makes me feel insignificant, like an experiment to be measured. Hashimoto cuts the woman off and turns to me with a sigh as he rubs the bridge of his nose.

"I think we have a problem here. I don't think Lailah's dead. The bad news is that she's clearly not here, and you may have somehow managed to absorb her into your soul. She's never been defeated before so we don't know if that's what actually happened but...however unusual it seems, it's the most likely outcome right now. This could give us some serious problems because we need her power. We cannot be down a member, and especially not her."

"What does that mean?"

"In short, we need what's inside you. Until then, I think you may have actually, in some small way, become an Angel."

"But what exactly is an Angel? What are you?"

"Ah, I thought you would ask that question, Miss Yamamoto. Allow me to introduce you to us."

He gestures to the eye-patch lady beside him and she bows stiffly towards me.

"This is Tachibana Kameko, she's my second in command here. Furakawa Naoko and Furakawa Keiko are the pair over there and behind us are Kagawa Hiroshi and his son Kagawa Satoshi."

"Good morning Sasaki," Satoshi pipes up in a welcoming, upbeat tone of voice.

"Yes, quite. And of course, you know Michihara and Lailah as you've already encountered them."

Satoshi is the only one to say a word to me through the introductions. Hashimoto turns to him and I can't see his face, but it's enough to make Satoshi quickly avoid his gaze. Keiko has begun to growl at me like a dog until she also gets stared into silence.

"We're a group of scientists working in this lab and have done for decades. Four years ago, there was an accident here which turned us into what we are today."

"But what are you?" I just about manage to ask the question through the sense of nausea rising in my stomach at the talk of an accident.

"We are Angels Miss Sasaki. Before then we were a neuro-medical research team working on anti-depression drugs in a hope to help the growing numbers of people out there who are suffering. Everyone has something that holds them back from enjoying life, something that imprisons them within their own souls. There are things that people can't or won't face up to. We need to help these people because they won't seek the help they need themselves. Have a look at this."

Hashimoto picks up a small piece of the crystalline material lying around and hands it to me. It feels light, almost weightless. As I turn it over in my hands a beautiful shimmering rainbow appears within it. I start to feel the nausea dissipate in my stomach as I stare in rapture at the weird reflections.

"We discovered this, a new type of mineral which has some tremendous properties. The results we have been getting are exhilarating. It's called udomite, and when light is shone through it the reflections induce a sense of calm and happiness in those that are exposed."

"How could that possibly work?"

"We don't know precisely. The accident allowed us to delve deeper into our minds until we could connect with another level in this Universe, bringing forth something we never thought possible. We're all logical people, but we cannot deny the reality of our new situation where God speaks through us. We believe the other benefits are merely symptoms of the crystals helping us access this new world. Unfortunately, the accident also allowed those Fallen monsters to be created.

"Lailah said the Fallen killed my sister. Is that true?

Hashimoto sighs at me, causing my head to drop again and my cheeks to flush. Everyone must think I'm stupid and selfish. To them I must look like I'm just concentrating on myself and my own problems when so much else is going on.

"The best information we have to go on is that yes, they killed her. And do you know why? Because the Fallen are monsters Miss Sasaki. They murder humans in cold blood because they are out to destroy us, and not just us. They are out to destroy everyone and everything we hold dear and we will not rest until we stop them. They even took my wife from me."

"I'm...I'm so sorry."

The silence between us is painful to sit in as his face crinkles up.

"Why did they take her, Professor?"

"They want revenge on us. They blame us for the accident that created them and kill indiscriminately out of rage stemming from that. But the details of that are not for this time. The thing you need to keep at the forefront of your mind is that they are monsters, and they will try to kill you, your friends, and your family. If you actually are an Angel after what happened then that is even more true. Let me show you what we really are and maybe you will understand a bit better. Satoshi, can you come here and show our guests what I mean please?"

"Certainly, Professor!"

The unrelenting cheerfulness makes me smile a little as Satoshi skips towards us. He comes to a halt between us, with his black hair framing his warm, welcoming smile. He puts his arms by his side and looks to the ceiling, lowering his head slightly to give us another big grin and a wink which makes something stir inside me. Closing his arms over his chest he clasps his hands together. Suddenly there's a soundless explosion of light so bright that it overwhelms all my senses. I shut my eyes but it burns so much I can still see it. I spin round and bury my head into Miyu's shoulder to try and escape the pain.

"You can turn around Sasaki. I won't hurt you," says a melodic voice behind me.

As I slowly turn around the sight in front of me makes my mouth gape and my heart race. The feeling of my breath shortening and blood rushing to my face scares me and exhilarates me in equal measure. He stands tall, his uniform replaced with a billowing blue shirt and a pair of huge white wings shaded with purple. His skin is practically glowing, making him to look like a ceramic doll. My feet want to walk forward and my hands want to clasp around his body, so much so that I have to work hard to prevent myself from doing it reflexively. The memory of Lailah holding my chin, our faces so close, causing my whole body to paralyse comes into my head. Not for the first time in my life my mind feels both overwhelmed with conflicting emotions but also empty because I can't hold on to any of them. I can't help but want to be next to him, like being near him might take all my troubles away. His wings sway gently, making the purple in them shimmer like oil in a puddle.

"Satoshi..." I say in a strained voice.

"Ah, ah, ah Sasaki," he says waggling his finger at me in a voice that rings in my ears with odd harmonies. "I am Hesediel, the Angel of Mercy. You can just call me Hesediel, and when I'm not here you can call him Satoshi. It's a pleasure to make your acquaintance."

As he smiles and holds out his hand to shake mine my skin warm significantly. I absent-mindedly wipe my hand on my hospital gown and hold it out, not taking my eyes off the beautiful, loving smile that is spread across his face. Our hands touch and I physically jump from the jolt of electricity that flows through my veins. He grips me harder and holds me for what feels like many minutes.

"P...pleased to meet you too," I stutter.

"I know I'm very different but I assure you, part of Satoshi is still here, safe and sound. I am Hesediel and I live inside his soul. But I can come out when I'm called or when our life is in danger. I'm here as an Angel of the Lord to protect humans from harm."

"Thank you Hesediel that'll be enough." interrupts Hashimoto.

Light blinds me again as Hesediel disappears, leaving Satoshi back in his place. As the room fades back in, I realise my head is still full of a sensation of warmth and comfort. It's like the feeling of a relaxing day at home during summer vacation, practicing my archery. The vision of the summer's day in my head is punctured by the image of my sister approaching and talking to me. The pain of missing her slams into my soul like a freight train.

"Once someone has communed with the Angel that's connected with their soul we can channel them through us and allow them to take our bodies, gaining access to their powers."

"But why did my sister have to die Hashimoto? What the hell did she have to do with anything? She can't have been involved in all this."

Even with my usual steel there's a tremble in my voice.

"She was just in the wrong place at the wrong time, and the Fallen didn't care. That's the explanation. In the same way Lailah can absorb people's strength to add to our group, we know they have the ability to turn humans into Fallen to boost their own forces. They must have tried and failed, disposing of her when they'd used her up."

Something about the explanation makes me uneasy, but before I can say anything Hashimoto kneels close to me.

"Miss Sasaki, we have to protect humanity against the Fallen. If you do have Lailah inside your soul then they will want your power and they will come for you before long. If you come with us and commune with Lailah then we will help you find what you are after. Somewhere in their deceptive and evil group will be the person who hurt your family. If you do what we say you'll have the power to go after them, defeat them, and make them tell you why they did it. We can take you where you need to be. Wouldn't getting your revenge on them be what you want?"

The lust for revenge in my head tingles, thinking of what they might have done to her. What if they had gotten her and turned her into a monster? I retch as that image fills my head until it overflows. I have to find out why those things hurt me and my family like this.

"I want to find out why they did it. If you can really help me get that then I will do my best to help you," I say open-endedly.

After what feels like many minutes Hashimoto nods at me and turns back to his group. He dismisses me with a hand wave, telling me to come back as soon as I was recovered. As I limp through the double doors with Miyu supporting me under an arm the adrenalin that was flowing through my body begins to drop away. I fall to the ground, gasping for breath as Dr. Michihara magically turns up at my side and punctures my arm with a needle, causing the pain to drop away and unconsciousness to take me.

Chapter 6

My eyes open to a cold, shivering darkness. Pulling my head back and focussing it turns out that I'm nearly submerged in long, wet grass, not quite the bland, sterile hospital room that I was expecting. As I struggle to stand up a scream rips through the air above me. It's a brutal, visceral noise that forces my legs to work on their own, scanning the horizon for the source. There's nothing but a foggy savannah in all directions with trees, rocks, lagoons, and long, long grass everywhere.

I take off in a random direction in a panic, the thick turf clinging to me and slowing me down when the scream erupts again, shredding my ears from behind. I spin and try to keep moving but the grass begins to entangle itself around my waist and legs. My breath is short as fear grips my heart, but for lack of any kind of implement on me all I can do is start ripping at my shackles with my bare hands. The harder I tear the more it seems to cling to me like it doesn't want me to escape.

The cry comes again, this time it feels like it's right behind me and the shock forces me to my knees. I scratch manically at the grass around my legs, a wail escaping my lips as I tear my skin apart. Ripping at the last of the undergrowth I struggle forward on my knees, the dirt and soil mixing with the fresh blood to cake me in scum as a blinding flash of white fills the world.

I spread the grass apart and see an Angel in front of me with wisps of fog obscuring it and licking at its body. The thing is wholly shades of grey and dirty white, wings protruding from its back. It hunches down over something before screaming yet again, its voice filling the world until it dies down only to be replaced with the horrifying sounds of bones cracking and teeth chomping. I inch forward with terror filling my soul until the remains of a body being eaten come into view. The Angel thing delves into it and rips out a handful of ribs, tendons, and organs before shoving it in its face. I try to scream at it to stop but the sounds it's making are so visceral that it causes me to vomit instead. Gasping for breath I rush forward and try to pull it off the body but to no avail. In an instant the creature turns, screaming like a hawk from a face with no features. The blank face is millimetres in front of me before opening to show row after row of triangular teeth that pierce my skin as the being engulfs me.

***

I wake up screaming and thrashing in my bed. I struggle, shouting and kicking violently as the doctors and nurses struggle to hold me down while the horrors that attacked me in the night refuse to leave my vision. The pinch of the sedative being injected into my arm barely registers past every neurone in my body firing all at once, but it seems to do the trick, forcing me to settle back down. My voice is hoarse and my mind is filled with cold fog that reminds me of the thing in my nightmares.

After the commotion of my awakening, the silence of the room is overpowering. I tilt my head slightly and notice through the haze that I've been moved to a new room, one with the luxury of a window letting the evening light in. I roll over, grimacing at the pain in my stomach and jump out of my skin when I see Miyu sitting under the window, watching me with the golden evening light flowing across her. I try to smile sheepishly at her.

"What was...that?"

"Don't speak Kyu, you were having a night terror."

I squint as something flashes across my vision.

"Did you see something just now Miyu?" I whisper.

She looks around the room with a quizzical look on her face.

"No Kyu, I didn't see anything. What was it?"

"I...I don't know, something looked odd," I say as she looks around again at the sunset filtering through the leaves, "I guess it was nothing. What do we do now Miyu?"

Quick as a flash she puts her hand on my head and soothes the slight twinge of panic that is rising in me.

"You need to get better that's the important thing."

Yes, I need to get better, physically and mentally. I'll find the thing that killed my sister and make them tell me why. But I have to do it while protecting Miyu. I owe her a life debt, so I have to do everything in my power to make sure she never comes to harm again. The thought of losing her again makes my heart hurt.

"Hashimoto said we should go back when you were healed, maybe we can work out what's going on inside you and try and fix it? Remember what happened when we were both in your soul?"

The image of the faceless, winged Angel eating the corpse in my dream immediately fills my vision and bile rises in my stomach. But then I remember before that, there had been that feeling of elation as those wings grew out of me. In the reflection of the heart monitor beeping away next to me my eyes are still the same old dusty blue that they usually are. The reflection in Tenshi back then had definitely shown a pair of bright, green irises looking back at me.

"Hashimoto said you had absorbed Lailah's soul and that you might be an Angel. I think he might be right. There's something different about your mind but I can't work out what it is. Maybe the Angels can tell us what's happening in your head. I fear that it could be something that might hurt you, and I don't want you to hurt that much again."

"Don't worry Miyu, I'm going to try and be stronger now," I say in an attempt to soothe her. I can feel it too, something is different. I feel like I have a purpose now after four long, rudderless years. "If Lailah is inside me then I doubt she will try and hurt me."

"I hope so," she says with a faint hint of trepidation in her voice, "we should go if you're feeling well enough?"

Even in this state I can tell Miyu is worried about what's happening, but I won't achieve anything just lying around in bed. I push past the pain and stand up before falling to the ground.

"What's going on here? My legs feel like they haven't been used in a week!"

Miyu looks up at the ceiling suspiciously.

"I've been asleep for a week?!"

"No Kyu, it's been five days."

"Five days?! Why have I been out so long?"

"They couldn't wake you up. You've been alternating between deep sleep and screaming from nightmares. Every day and night you'd scream and thrash as if fighting off something. I was so scared for you. When no one was around I tried my hardest to find out what was going on inside your head but every time I tried I was prevented from getting in there."

"You mean you can't read my mind anymore?"

"There's something in there stopping me from seeing as clearly as I used to be able to."

"What is it?"

"I don't know. Sorry, describing how empathy magic works is really difficult with words. I mentally prod and poke at the wall to try to find a weak spot but can never open up even a crack. I can follow it in all directions but it never changes."

The nightmare spills back into my head just as I'd managed to banish it for a bit, that toothed monster ripping at flesh and bones. The noise and feeling of despair all come back to me in a flood of unexpected emotion.

"Is it Lailah?" I choke, almost hopefully.

"I don't think so. After she was killed I fel...oh I'm sorry Kyu, I didn't mean to..."

Remembering the feeling of killing Lailah makes all the grief and horror resurface, combining with the fear of that faceless thing. Miyu told me I didn't do it consciously but it was my fault. I was the responsible party and I will bear that burden. Every time I think of her the weight gets heavier.

"Hashimoto said she isn't dead, maybe, so try not to let it upset you."

"Let's just go see the Angels," I say tersely.

Maybe if I get up and get moving I can try to ignore the bad thoughts. If I avoid them a little bit more maybe they might go away and not come back. Miyu takes the hint of strength in my voice and I think she realises that complaining right now isn't the right thing to do. In silence she wraps her arms around me and slowly helps me out of my bed. Needing more cover than just that which is provided by the hospital gown I change into the clean uniform Miyu had brought over. After the damage from the fight, she went and got my father to bring one in for me. Apparently my father had sat at my bedside for two days before the pressure at work got too much and forced him to go back. The fact that my mother never came to visit, and that neither was here when I woke up leaves a bitter taste in my mouth. I want to go back to them, but if they don't care enough to be here then I'm going to carry on. I know I can never live up to Sis in their eyes, but maybe if I avenge her they'll take more notice of me. She was their golden princess and I'm just a pitiful, broken version of her.

When I pick up my bow and quiver there's a sudden pang of regret in me. Not firing him for almost a week is an alien concept to someone who has nothing better to do but practice every day. I spin the quiver around, looking for the wound it should sport from deflecting Lailah's arrow but there's nothing but the well-polished wood design and gold leaf swirls. The pain I felt there was so real but it doesn't seem to have had any lasting physical effects, unlike the arrow that Lailah drove deep into my gut which still leaves me wincing as I move.

Hoisting Tenshi over my shoulder a flood of relief flows through me at having the weight on my back again. My fingers immediately fall to the clasp made of the bike chain and caress the rough metal. I turn and look at my reflection in the mirror to see a girl who looks the worse for wear staring back. My skin is pallid, there are bags under my eyes and I look thin and gaunt after being drip fed for so long. It'll have to do though; I've got to find out what happened. I have to be strong and fight through the pain. In these four years I've learned to live with hurt and loss in my heart, but I've always had to be strong enough to get through it. Miyu looks at me in the reflection, her long face filled with worry.

"Let's go," I say with as much energy as possible.

With that we set off through the corridors of the hospital, winding our way through bright hallway after bright hallway. The bustle of patients being wheeled about and nurses going about their caring is the only noise between us. I don't feel like talking much anymore anyway. I feel like doing. I want answers.

After a few minutes we come to the stairwell which leads down to the Sanctum. I don't even hesitate before limping down the stairs as I'm consumed with the need to get things moving. Miyu calls out to me but I ignore her, reaching the double doors at the bottom and bursting through them with my shoulder. I go to shout out but freeze as the eyes of the entire group of Angels fall on me following my boisterous entrance. Miyu pulls up behind me, calling my name as the anger and courage I had leaves me stranded, facing their accusing looks. For what feels like eternity I stand there staring, wanting the words to come. I want to order the Angels to start out on my quest for the truth but that's just what it is, my quest, not theirs. What will happen when they find out I can't kill any of these Fallen? Will they desert me and leave me to die in the mud like they did to Lailah?

"Good morning Sasaki!"

The joy in Kagawa Satoshi's voice startles me out of my funk. Looking up into his charming, welcoming face makes me blush furiously. Hashimoto stands up and turns to me while the rest of the group go back to whatever they were doing before my interruption.

"Thank you for coming to us again Miss Sasaki. We are worried the Fallen will attack while we are without Lailah so I don't want to waste any time here. You definitely have some power within you, all of us have sensed it and I know your friend has sensed it too. However, I must insist that you take your leave of us now Miss Yamamoto."

Miyu wraps an arm around me protectively as Hashimoto makes his proclamation.

"Yes Professor."

I have a feeling that she knew she would be asked to leave, but how easily she accepts it still takes me by surprise. Now that I have had Miyu by my side I don't think I could bear to let her go. As her arm drops from around mine it seems like a tiny piece of my resolve is taken with her.

"You're going to be ok Kyu," she says as she turns to me, "I spoke to Dr Michihara a lot while you were asleep and I think I can trust them. If you come to harm, they've lost their only link to Lailah's powers. They need you, remember that."

"Ok Miyu," I mutter.

Even with her assurances I feel hurt and abandoned. She should be putting up more of a fight, unless maybe she doesn't really care about me at all. I instinctively reach back to Tenshi, the one thing that will never leave me. I watch Miyu as she leaves the lab, wishing for her to come back and protect me. When I turn back I jump as Hashimoto had silently bridged the gap between us and crouched down so his face is level with mine. His burning eyes feel like they're boring into me, searching. Despite wanting to be brave, I retreat slightly.

"I'll be frank with you Miss Sasaki, this is going to be a painful, dangerous and difficult process but by the end of this I hope we will both be in a better place. You will know what happened to your sister and we will have defeated those that seek to destroy everyone and everything we hold so dear. I can't describe how bad it will be if we fail in this endeavour because it would be unimaginable. I need you to be aware of this before we begin, because we need to be able to rely on you once you've gone through this process."

All these terrible words float into my ears, overwhelming my brain.

"What if I don't want to join you?"

I try to keep my voice level as his words sink in. He looks back at me, silently staring into my soul. With a long slow breath, he stands up again.

"We know that what you want is worth the price we are asking you to pay. Hopefully, you will become closer to us as you find out what we are, and about yourself."

I can't help but stand there in silence, thinking this over. He knows he's right. He knows I'll go along with them. Damn it! The fact that he seems so certain about it, like he knows how my mind works, fills me with revulsion. But finding out what happened to my sister is something I would pay almost any price for.

"Ok," is all I can muster.

"Then we must begin immediately. Angels, we now have a new mission. Sasaki Kyushiro has agreed to join our cause and getting her into shape is our top priority. All our energy must be put into unlocking her power. Even if she survives the communion you know that we are not out of the woods. The Fallen are strong. They're getting stronger by the day and will stop at nothing, so we must get a result here and fight them back."

The words 'even if she survives' run over and over again in my head as the rest of Hashimoto's speech washes around me. As my knees start shaking and I fight to hold back tears I realise that what's going through my head is fear, fear for my own life. This is the first time I've felt it. In the last few days, I've felt so much horror, revulsion, disgust, and fear but always for others. The thought of dying and being left in a pool of mud, rain and blood like Lailah overtakes me and makes me want to do nothing more than turn and flee. I pull Tenshi over my shoulder and grip his shaft until my knuckles are white.

"Naoko, Keiko, Satoshi, I'm going to need you to come and assist us," says Hashimoto.

"Aww come on!" Keiko shouts. "Why do we have to deal with this little brat, isn't our work more important profeeeeessssor?"

The whine in her voice accompanied by that toothy grin of hers leaves me with no illusions about how much I dislike her.

"This is our work Keiko, and I will have no more of this insolence! Do you question my judgement? Without a trusted leader all armies will fall, now follow my orders."

The outburst was as powerful as it was unexpected. Keiko huffs before pulling on a long red coat and stalking over to the corner where Hashimoto is. Naoko follows in silence while pulling on his own coat. Skipping slightly behind them is Satoshi who gives me another of his bright smiles.

"You need to come with us too Miss Sasaki. We're going to get you to commune with Lailah so we know what we're dealing with. We need to know if Lailah is still inside you. Step into the elevator with us."

The wall in the corner of the lab slides back silently to reveal a tiny, coffin like elevator. I struggle against the feelings inside me but manage to make my legs move, shakily approaching the box. As the five of us cram into it we're joined, soundlessly by Tachibana Kameko. She wasn't asked to come down, but I get the feeling that as second in command she knows what Hashimoto wants. The box begins to descend and I feel Keiko's breath in my ear.

"Oh we are gonna have some fun with you Kyu."

I glare at her in the reflection of the doors. How dare she call me by my name like that in such a casual way. She just stares back with her teeth gleaming in a sneer filled with malice and her sky-blue eyes piercing into me, leaving my skin tingling and my heart still racing. She makes me feel something awful inside and I want to get away from her as quickly as possible. I swear the Angels can sense my claustrophobia and are closing in on me to make it worse. My breathing is shallow and quick as nausea begins to overpower me. As the elevator shudders to a stop and the doors open I burst out and drop to my knees, vomiting yellow bile on the ground. The sound of me retching echoes through the silence as my stomach wracks with pain.

Gulping oxygen, I wipe the sweat from my face and take in the colossal room in front of me. Rough stone floor extends in all directions with pile upon pile of glittering crystal everywhere. They shimmer and glow as far as I can see, reflecting the pale light in such ways as to make the room look like it goes on forever. In the middle of one side of the room sits a single, huge crystal in a kind of support bracket. It looks like an egg sitting and waiting to be hatched, except for the light coursing and pulsing in the middle of it. Everything around me seems slightly translucent, but the stone on the table has a core of solid white light laced with green and turquoise flecks. The energy fills the stone until it's almost leaking from the edges, thrumming, and vibrating. As I rise to my feet the turquoise explodes into a panoply of colours before my eyes. It's beautiful.

"This is the biggest concentration of udomite in the world," says the stoic Furukawa Naoko, "you'd be amazed at the potential that this much has."

His spiky blonde hair and long, sharp face are framing the words with the same forcefulness as his wife, but it comes out like granite slabs rather than sharp barbs. I stare up at him as he flexes the muscles under his shirt. Keiko shoots me a dark look before throwing her arms round him and kissing him salaciously.

"So much power that my husband and I could wield. No one will stand in the way of our mission, not the Fallen, and certainly not you little girl."

"May I remind you that we are not here for power Keiko, Naoko, not for its own sake. We are here to protect the human race."

The shock of hearing the aged and so far silent Tachibana Kameko startles me. She's staring down the fiery Keiko with her one good, grey eye. Keiko looks like she's going to complain but seems to think better of it and backs down instead.

"And we are here now to do that we need to awaken Miss Sasaki's power," says Hashimoto batting the concerns of his associates away with a simple flick, "Naoko, Keiko you are here to get the job done and if either of you complains again there will be serious ramifications."

Under his fierce gaze they nod in agreement. Kameko backs into a corner, bringing her tablet up and placing a small camera on the ground. Keiko drops down from embracing her husband and pads over to me, bending down to look at my bow.

"It's good that you have that with you. What a gorgeous jewel that is in there," she says as she reaches out to touch it. I instinctively pull it away from her which elicits a snort. "I'd get that ready now if I were you," she says as she smashes me in the face with a punch that knocks me to the floor.

Chapter 7

I spit blood on the cold, rugged floor as flashing lights swirl in front of my eyes and the shimmering room spins around me. The blow has left me feeling groggy and in so much pain that I can barely move. Just as the threat of unconsciousness is all but gone, the light in the room gets blocked out by Furukawa Keiko leaning over me with an evil grin on her face. Something in her stare makes me want to throw all my force into slapping that stupid grin off her face.

"I told you this was gonna be fun Sasaki!" she laughs.

Her mocking tone makes it all the harder not to lash out at her. Instead, I settle for rubbing the blood off my face so she has one less thing to be so fucking proud about. I don't think I've ever felt such anger and hatred before for a single person. It's draining just to stop myself from confronting her every second that goes by.

"What are you doing?" I ask.

Instead of an answer something heavy thuds between my shoulder blades. I let out a muffled cry at the pain while Keiko just stands there smiling at me and laughing. Craning my neck, I see Naoko floating behind me, being kept aloft on silver wings. Every now and then they flap gently, causing him to bob up and down. His clothes have been replaced by a shining pair of white, ragged trousers and not much else. Emblazoned on his bare, muscular chest is a yellow lightning bolt. He seems bigger than before. Broader. His bulging arms grip a long silver staff that he occasionally twirls between his hands.

"Who are you?" I ask, trying to hide the amazement and fear in my voice at being faced down by such a huge specimen.

"I am Barachiel, the Holy Lightning."

After stating his name, he just hovers there holding me down with the long spear. A flash of light makes me avert my eyes from in front of me. With how bad Keiko is now I can only begin to imagine how frustrating her Angel is going to be. It makes the hairs on my arms stand on end in anticipation, but when the light fades the being standing in front of me is not what I expected. Unlike Barachiel her wings are smaller and more rounded, looking soft and yielding rather than jagged. She's wearing a brass armour chest plate instead of any clothing on her top half with a swirl roughly carved into it. She beckons her husband to her, who releases the pressure on my back and joins her in front of me. I push myself up to my haunches and face them down with a grimace.

"And I am Ariel, the Holy Roar. It really does pain me to have to put you through so much trauma Kyu. Well, actually, I guess it doesn't, I don't actually give a shit about you. You won't stand in the way of the two of us. Together we will take the fight to those disgusting Fallen and we will win. We will win and we will take back our rightful place. Since we were told to go through you to do that, then that's exactly what we will do."

Ariel's voice is deeper, and less mocking than Keiko's but I can still hear how little this new being thinks of me. She's just another person who seems to hate me, despite having never encountered me before. I never knew I could inspire such rage in people, I've always felt like a speck of nothingness on the tapestry of humanity. I got beaten and bullied by the other girls because I'm different but that wasn't because I angered them, they just do it because I'm an easy target. But now I'm stuck between two beings that seem to want me to suffer, one who takes pleasure in trying and one who just seems to follow unthinkingly. Does Hashimoto just want them to beat me while the rest of his entourage watches? If Keiko...or Ariel wants me gone, then there's no way I'll give her that pleasure.

I make a move to stand up, purposefully dropping to the side as I do. The clatter of arrows on the side of my quiver filters through to my ears and I use the opportunity to mentally count how many I have. I reach my feet before Ariel flaps her wings and disappears above me, leaving the metallic noise echoing after her. I was hoping that that was something special that only Lailah could do. With her out of my field of view, I get to my feet and turn to Barachiel.

"What is your rightful place?" I ask.

shhnk

She teleports back in front of me, inches from my face.

"For years now we have protected you. We may have been hiding in the shadows but we have prevented your pathetic race of low lives, cheaters, liars, and scum from being devoured. We get no thanks. We deserve to be worshipped as gods in our own right! Once the Fallen are destroyed we can take our place again at the top of this world, living not in darkness but in the light."

I look over at Hashimoto and Tachibana, expecting them to leap in but they've remained still throughout this outburst.

"Is that really why you're here Barachiel?" I ask, but there's no answer from the stoic lump. "Why have you set your loyal attack dogs on me?" I ask Hashimoto.

Before he can answer, a gust of wind flies into my face. Keiko sweeps away from me before circling round like a hawk hunting its prey. I strain against the gale, shielding my eyes before the teleporting noise hits my ears and my vision becomes filled with the Holy Roar firing towards me like a missile. In the fraction of a second before she knocks me down I swear I could see that gurning face of hers, happier than ever at being able to cause me more pain. I keel over backwards and smash into the rocky ground. Shaking my head to brush the cobwebs away, I wish with all my heart that Miyu hadn't left me here.

"We are here to drive you to reveal your true self to us Miss Sasaki. We need you to commune with your Angel so you can unlock that power within you. You are part of a much bigger plan. To win the game the king must put his pieces in danger," Hashimoto says as I clamber to my feet.

The pain is so bad that I have to use Tenshi as a crutch to stop me from falling over. Another evil giggle comes out from behind me and the wind picks up again, blowing my hair over my face. As I try and turn their strikes land upon me. Ariel hits me from the back while Barachiel spins his staff before ploughing the blunt end it into my chest.

"You want me to kill your dogs, is that right?" I whisper at Hashimoto through the pain.

"Yes! Come on Kyu, come and kill me!" That voice of Ariel reverberates around the cavern, the piles of gemstone giving the command strange harmonies.

"Fine."

I nock and fire my first shot in a fraction of a second, but it whistles off into empty space.

"That wasn't very good Kyu, I barely even had to move. Surely you can do better than that?

It did miss but I meant it to be a warning shot. She'll find out how much I can do that's for sure. Two superior foes intent on driving me to the edge and here I am, alone, again. The flames of anger and loneliness burning deep within me spark and crackle. I know after years of suppression there's an erupting volcano worth of wrath within me somewhere. It's like an itch that I can't scratch. The last time that fire burned out of control I killed that Fallen creature without a thought and got Lailah into this mess. I always suspected that if I gave in and let it blow out of control I could do something stupid, and when I killed the monster all of my fears were realised. I can't let myself be like that again, however much Ariel antagonises me or however strong Barachiel and the others are. I cannot lose control again.

"You're right, I can do better."

It's all I can manage as I nock another arrow and shoot directly at Ariel's face, knowing that she'll avoid it anyway. There's no way someone like that could be taken down by me, and a flap of the wings greets her disappearance and reappearance a few feet away.

"Ah, better. Better Kyu. I could feel your rage in that. Next time maybe you might even land a scratch on me."

I try again, another arrow for the face and a second at the position where Ariel stood before. As she reappears just inches away from where the second arrow strikes the wall I turn and fire twice at Barachiel. The attack seems to take him by surprise, but he avoids coming to harm by teleporting next to Ariel. Even I can tell that the frown on her face was because she nearly fell into my trap. The thought of her being vexed by my skills pleases me immensely. I won't be able to kill her but I'll bloody hurt her if it is the only way to save myself. I fire another two shots towards the pair, but Ariel puts out her hands and blows a gust of wind that knocks them to the ground. Another shot, another empty threat as she deflects it again. I'm outclassed.

"Barachiel."

"Yes Ariel?"

"You know what to do."

"Yes."

They sound like an old married couple, Ariel giving out the orders like a controlling shrew and Barachiel following them without ceremony. With both of them hovering in front of me they start to move their hands in a swirling motion. The wind picks up again, coming from all directions, making shards of loose crystal and feathers fly around.

"Where is this wind coming from underground?" I shout to the onlookers, covering my eyes.

"Ariel is the Holy Roar; she has control over the wind! She can manipulate air pressure in individual pockets to create vortexes as she pleases. Please be careful!" Satoshi shouts over the increasingly loud howling. Occasionally one of the loose shards of udomite flies past me, scratching my skin and tearing at my clothes.

I start to take a few steps backwards and nock an arrow, changing my aim from one to the other. I fire at Ariel but before my shot can reach her she snaps her eyes open and flings her hand up. The arrow follows the trajectory in a sharp deflection and buries itself in the ceiling up to the flight. Delight fills her face as her hands come together in an almighty clap which sends a dense tunnel of circling wind crashing into me, blowing me backwards until I smash into the wall. I drop to my knees and cough blood on to the floor while the dust in the air filling my beaten lungs makes it a struggle to breathe. I raise Tenshi in front of my face to try and protect my eyes from the storm but I can barely see through the tears streaming out of me.

Then a crackling noise filters down to me and I force my eyes open just in time to see blue electricity arcing towards me. It barrels through the twister that pins me back, swirling around the eye of the storm before careening into me, causing me agony as the electricity courses through my body. I scream louder than I've ever screamed before. It feels like it's burning away my skin, stripping my muscles to the bone and tugging on every single nerve ending in my body. I'm thrown into the air from the force, continuously screaming until the pain makes my voice to give out. My body goes limp at the top of my arc as gravity pulls me back down to earth.

shhnk

Ariel and Barachiel appear directly above me with that sickening noise of their wings flapping. Barachiel hits me with an arm across my stomach and Ariel grips my throat as they push me forcefully towards the ground. My wide-eyed stare can only see her gleeful, gloating face as she chokes what little air there is left in my lungs. We hit the ground with a terrible force, causing rock and gemstone to flow past me as the crater swallows me up. I gasp in silent agony as the feeling of broken bones floods through me. Blood soaks my clothes until they cling to my skin.

I can just about make out the Angels through the haze, hovering above me, weaving their hand signals for another attack. I try to raise my hand and yield but without any air in my lungs and with the pain wracking my body nothing but a small croak comes from my throat. I manage to raise my arm a few inches off the ground before it's pinned back by Ariel. My body feels like it's beginning to completely collapse as Barachiel's lightning sparks through the air towards me.

"Ssk...Sask...Sasaki."

The voice saying my name pounds into my head over the noise and the sound of my impending electrical doom. It sounds like Lailah, but with a tinny and hollow edge to it echoing through my consciousness.

"Let me save you, Sasaki."

***

I shut my eyes, and when I open them again I'm not in the cavern anymore. Instead, I'm looking up at a sky full of grey cloud with tinges of purple. In the small gaps between them there's dazzling blue light trying to force its way though, lighting the overgrown meadow. The voice pleads with me again through the air on the stiff breeze. My body floats up and spins silently until I'm upright again, standing shin deep in the grass as a cherry blossom falls from the gigantic tree that fills my world. It's stunning visage entrances me as I float over to it, running my hand along the rough, flaking bark. All my senses say that this is a real tree, everything about it is beautiful; the smell, the touch, the colours, they're all so physical. I flinch suddenly as a human face becomes visible in the bark. It speaks to me from inside the trunk with Lailah's voice.

"Let me out and I will save you Sasaki, I promise."

I touch the area around the face and I can feel the voice vibrating up my arm and into my brain. She's alive? I didn't kill her! A sense of relief floods through me as the wind picks up to a sudden squall around me.

"There isn't much time. Release me and I will save you from them. Break me open now. You need me."

Something is there on the edge of my hearing, trying to get me to listen, but I can't make out what. I shake my head and push through it. Stepping back, I place my hands on to the massive trunk underneath her face. The bark underneath my fingertips suddenly goes from rough and solid to soft and yielding. I pull a handful of it away like it was clay. I tear and rip at it with vigour until I'm removing huge portions with each handful, but it still stands there, tall and strong.

"Hurry Sasaki!"

The voice is definitely clearer now. A white glow is emanating from the centre of the hollow trunk and as I rip the last pieces away a figure pulls itself out. I smile with tears of joy in my eyes as it starts to come back to me.

"Lailah!" I cry.

As soon as her glowing form pulls itself out from inside the tree she lunges at me, screeching. I don't have time to react before my entire world goes white.

***

Suddenly back in the real world my eyes focus on the Angels above me. I can feel my ribs starting to knit together again and I realise the attacks they've launched are dropping towards me much slower than before. My arms instinctively come across my face to protect myself and I shut my eyes.

shhnk

But the pain I expected doesn't come. Instead, my body is light and floaty in an unsteady fashion. I lower my arms and open one eye to see the ground behind Ariel and Barachiel below me. Without even thinking about it I've pulled Tenshi round and have an arrow held tight against the string. Everything seems to be happening at a slower pace now. Staring down the backs of the Angels I can see the reflection of my fiery green eyes in Tenshi's metallic plate as I draw him up and pull the string back.

Time returns to normal as the Angels turn towards me with shock in their eyes. I concentrate on Ariel's face, holding her gaze in mine for a fraction of a second before I unleash the arrow at Barachiel. Unlike my previous shots, it moves so fast that he doesn't have time to react. It's a perfect shot straight through his palm, forcing him to drop the spear and scream. Ariel spins back to see blood explode from the wound with a look of horror besetting her face. I shift my arm gracefully, whipping Tenshi round into a horizontal grip and smashing it over the side of her face with all the strength I can muster. The force of the blow travels up my arm and through my body as blood flows out of her face, arcing through the air in a glorious symbol of my power as she collapses to the floor.

The sight and the feelings stir something inside me, making bloodlust rise up in my soul. This bitch deserves to die for what she's done to me. She deserves it! The rush of adrenaline floods into my brain as I flap my wings, teleporting directly in front of her. I hover above her prone body and nock another arrow, watching her eyes follow the tip as it comes within an inch of her face. The look of pain and terror filling her despicable face is electrifying.

"Excellent, excellent!" Hashimoto says as he takes a few steps towards me, clapping slowly with a small smile on his wrinkled face. "Thank you for showing yourself Lailah."

That comment fans the anger within me and before I know it I'm doing things without even considering my actions. I grab his coat by the collar and thrust him backwards until we hit a wall. The sound of everyone else in the room gasping and setting themselves to attack stances filters through to my ears as Hashimoto holds his hand up. I'm hovering slightly above the ground so I can be face to face with him. His smile hasn't quite moved as much as I expected to as he stands inches away from me. He doesn't fear me at all.

"I am NOT Lailah," I shout, "I am Sasaki Kyushiro. I will never, ever be one of you as long as you can cause this much pain to a young girl! You set these violent thugs on me! I could never be a part of that!"

He still hasn't moved an inch despite my anger directed at him. I feel bolder and stronger now. Lailah, or whatever that thing was tried to take over me but I think I'm in control, like I've fought it back. The lust to kill seems to have dissipated in the face of this broad, handsome old man who can face me down without fear.

"Oh, but you are a part of us now Sasaki. You don't mind if I call you Sasaki do you, now that we've joined together?"

Before I can answer, he puts his hands on my shoulder and throws me into the ground hard enough to send shards of rock upwards. I try to flap my wings and teleport away from his grasp but I can't move even a single inch against his iron grip. He leans closer to me before speaking in a low voice.

"You agreed to help us Sasaki, and if you don't I will be forced to prevent you from becoming problem. I am the leader of this group and I will do anything to save this world. If I have to hurt a little girl to save millions of lives then I will thrash you to within an inch of your life and leave you paralysed and helpless."

There's that tone again. The words seem to come across almost as if they were honourable and worthy but only if you don't scratch at them and look below the surface. I let out a scream as black fire erupts from every pore in my body, drifting upwards and leaving behind a feeling or crushing loneliness and emptiness.

"What the hell did you do?" I gasp. He leans in so he can whisper into my ear.

"I didn't want you losing control now did I. I did what I had to do."

Hashimoto releases his grip on me, dropping me to the ground. He stands up, straightens his clothing, and turns to the others. As he walks away from me I lift my arm up and see scratches and blood all along it. Pain floods back into my body as the adrenaline dissipates. I check my reflection in the polished metal of my bow but all I see is my normal blue eyes staring back again. The Angel has gone.

"I hope this process was helpful to you Sasaki, and I hope you've all learned something too. Send the message to Michihara to come down here immediately and tend to their wounds."

I can barely see through the haze of pain as Satoshi's face comes into my view. The blinding smile that's always been there is completely gone now. He looks angry I think, and maybe sorrowful as he puts a hand on my shoulder. Despite the pain the touch of his hand still sends more electricity through me.

"Help me," I whisper to him.

"Don't worry, Michihara will be here any second," he says.

The increasingly familiar sound of an Angel teleporting accompanies the flash of black and white that welcomes Michihara to my side. She places her hands on me and a flow of energy connects through us. The warmth eases my pain, begins to heal the rest of my broken bones together and sutures the deep wounds I have.

"I'm sorry Sasaki," Satoshi says, "I wanted to help you but if I had done anything they would have..." he trails off.

I look behind him at Hashimoto and Tachibana whispering together while studying the camera. He held me down with ease without even transforming. His sheer strength of will kept me pinned down practically on its own.

"He's right though. I did agree to help the Angels, and I'm not sure what you could have done about them," I say pointing to the happy couple now groaning and limping towards us, "did you have to go through this too?"

"Sort of," Satoshi says after a pause. "Sometimes communing with an Angel is easier than others, but often it requires being pushed to the edge like that. It all depends on the Angel and the person. I had to fight for mine but after watching those two I'm glad that it was only against my father."

"Hashimoto set your own father on you?"

From what I've seen today it's quite easy to believe that Hashimoto would do something like that even if it is barbaric. He must be telling the truth when he said he'd do anything, and now I have to go along with him. What have I got myself into?

"Yes, the experience was very painful for me, well for both of us. I think," his voice has suddenly lost the timbre that makes my soul feel like it's on fire.

"I'm done Sasaki, you should be ok to leave on your own now. You should take these," Michihara says abruptly, dropping something at my side and departing in another flash of black and white. I pull myself up to a sitting position and grasp what she left for me which turns out to be a large bottle of pills. The label has characters that I've never seen before, it looks almost alien. Satoshi holds out his hand and helps me to my feet.

"What are these?" I ask him. He takes the bottle, turning it round making the small white pills inside glitter and shine in the light.

"It's a bottle of pills that have udomite in them. It's a medicine that we've been developing that helps heal injuries. It'll help you get better Sasaki," he says as I stare at him. "It's perfectly safe," he says, looking away from me.

Michihara may have helped me, but I'm still a bit wary of taking unknown pills with this seemingly magic ingredient in. I mentally shrug my shoulders and take a pill from the bottle, holding it up to the light. It looks strange, glistening in an odd way, but I take it anyway.

"I'm sorry about your father," I say as I look up to him. The smile has returned to his face.

"That's alright Sasaki! It made me what I am."

I start limping towards the elevator and take a quick glance back at everyone in the room. Interestingly, Michihara didn't heal either Ariel or Barachiel, choosing to leave them there with their wounds instead. I guess I didn't do that much damage to them after all, but damn it felt good. My vision blurs and I feel dizzy and nauseated again as I stumble, using Tenshi to prop myself up.

"It looks like your exertions have put you at a disadvantage Sasaki. Be patient and time will heal you."

"Yes Professor Hashimoto."

A sudden pang of loneliness fills my drained soul. I want to see Miyu. I want to see my sister. I want my parents to love me and hug me. I stumble again, Tenshi clanging onto the ground. Satoshi helps me up for the second time, cradling my arms and shoulders in his as I find my feet. The weakness that I'm showing makes me feel awkward so I brush him off once he has completed his good deed for the day. I reach for the lift button that will take me away from all this.

"Sasaki," my finger pauses over the button back to freedom as Hashimoto calls out again, "this was just the beginning. You've communed with Lailah and we know she's in there, but you'll need to use her. We will come for you again. It will be soon, and if you don't fulfil your duty then you will lose your chance to find out what happened to your sister. Do you understand?"

"Yes Hashimoto."

It's all I can muster before closing the doors behind me. The gentle whirring and feeling of pressure on my feet lets me know that I'm heading back up towards reality. I let my head fall against the cold wall and let out a long sigh. The lift glides quietly upwards and I step out into the now almost empty lab. I can already walk slightly easier, as if the medicine was kicking in already.

The only person left in the Sanctum is Kagawa Hiroshi, sitting at a desk, his face bowed under his greasy black hair and his head in his hands. He looks over to me through his fingers with deep set and darkened eyes whose bags imply that he hasn't slept well for a long, long time. I try to imagine how he must have looked battling his own son, hurting him to the point of death to awaken his powers. I avert my eyes from him but I can feel him silently staring at me as I exit the lab. After I'm through the double doors I lean against the wall, another heavy sigh escaping my lips. He's scary, in fact they're all scary in one way or another, except Satoshi.

A chilly wind hits my face when I finally pass through the exit and into the darkness of the night. I try to take stock of everything that's happened recently. The memory of smashing that smug bitch Ariel in the face with my bow makes me smirk. It's a genuine smile, using muscles I haven't used for a long time. The look on their faces when I was behind them! Ha! I remember how those wings felt, wonderfully light but combined with a miraculous strength. I felt I could easily throw my whole body around in an instant on those things.

I get my phone out of my pocket and flip it open. Scrolling until I highlight Miyu's name, my finger hovers over the 'call' button. I want to hear her calming voice and get her to soothe my worries. The feeling of the Angel was amazing but I barely felt in control, and then Hashimoto just ripped it away from me. I desperately want to press the button but I just can't make myself do it. I can't stop the tears from escaping my eyes and falling down my cheeks at how pathetic I am. The tiredness, pain, and loneliness are just too much as I collapse to my knees on the deserted pavement. I need someone to hold me and take me away from everything. No, I don't need it, but I want it. What I need to do is keep going, on my own. Miyu might be around but I have to be able to rely on my own power. I must. I take a deep breath and push myself up and onwards into the night.

When I make it home the house is quiet and dark. Mum is on the couch sleeping with nothing but the TV illuminating her. There doesn't seem to be any sign of Dad. It's later than I thought, he must be working overnight again. I stand in the hall, looking at the dozing form of my mother. I want a hug, I want consoling, I want to be protected like any young woman does, but after a few seconds I decide to leave her be rather than waking her.

I sneak past and pad upstairs to my cramped bedroom. I stand in front of the large mirror next to my desk, stripping off my clothes slowly to observe my wounds. The cuts and scrapes on my arms are healing already, but the scabs and scars are still visible. Thousands of small abrasions cover every part of me, only broken by the large pock mark scar on my stomach from Lailah's arrow. It's rough when I run my fingers over it. The memories of murdering the Fallen monster and of causing Lailah's potential death come back to me for what must be the hundredth time.

Where are the good feelings from when I smashed that moon inside me and got my true self back? Why do I feel like I hate myself so much when I felt so good back then? The tears flow again, cutting rivulets through the dried blood on my cheeks as my emotions overtake me. I throw the medicine bottle against the wall in a fit of anger before collapsing on my knees. Crying uncontrollable, I pull the bed clothes over my body to hide my wails. My thoughts are barely comprehensible as I let the sadness and anger take me over until I fall asleep.

Chapter 8

By the time the morning comes the tears have receded again as they always do, replaced with an empty, hollow feeling inside as I get up and put a clean uniform on. The long socks hide some of the worst of the scarring but most of the evidence of last night's training has already disappeared. I lift up my shirt slightly and see that the arrow scar on my stomach hasn't gone though. I run my fingers over it and fill my head with thoughts of that night, but instead of letting the sorrow and anger overtake me I push them down. As I turn to go, I trip over something and land heavily. Picking up the bottle of mystery pills that I slipped on, I unscrew it and cram another pill into my mouth before dropping it into my pocket.

I bound down the stairs, stopping abruptly at the bottom when I notice my mother is still asleep on the couch, surrounded by mess. She hasn't moved since last night. In fact, she's barely moved from that spot for an awfully long time. She just lies there with the news on all day and all night. I slide my flat shoes on, slipping out into the cold, sunny autumn morning and make my way to school. I pull the bottle of pills out of my pocket and try to read the scrawled text on the side but it might as well be in another language.

"Kyu! Good morning!"

The voice from behind me cheers me up immensely as it rings into my ears. I turn around, quickly shoving the bottle back into the recesses of my pocket. The sight of Miyu jogging towards me makes my heart flutter a tiny bit. After everything that's happened, I desperately want to run up and hug her but my body just won't co-operate, so instead I stand with my eyes lowered to the floor as she catches up to me. It feels like an eternity since I last saw her. I wonder if she knows how much pain I went through, or whether she knew what would happen to me.

"Are you alright Kyu?"

I struggle to look her in the eye. Despite her saving me, and us becoming friends again, I still feel that I should guard myself and not get too close to her, however much I want to.

"It was a difficult ordeal, but I am ok."

"What happened?"

I don't know how she would react if she knew what happened. Knowing she can read my emotions I force my brain to flatten out the bad feelings, locking them away.

"I had to go through a test. Something to do with working out what happened with Lailah."

"Are you alright? Did they hurt you? I couldn't feel even the tiniest part of you when you were down there."

"I'm ok now Miyu. I managed to find Lailah. She's definitely alive inside me! But it felt like she took over me somehow. I had all that power, the wings, the speed. I'm...helping them now. I had to promise that before they agreed to help me find the one who...the person who...my sister."

She doesn't say anything as she leans in a little closer, which makes me instinctively lean back. Before I know what's happening Miyu has thrown herself around me. I can't help but let a little gasp of happiness escape my lips. I shut my eyes and just drink in the tiny drip of joy being fed through my subconscious. Knowing that what I went through didn't cause her all that pain again brings some relief.

"I'm so glad you're safe Kyu."

"I'm sorry I worried you Miyu," I stammer.

She holds my head and makes me look into her deep brown eyes.

"It's ok Kyu. You're alright and that's what matters."

Miyu's phone beeps, interrupting our little moment. As she reads the message I try and go after the memories and feelings that I've experienced in the last few days. Everything has seemed so alien to me and every time I try and pin down a thought it runs off, scuttling back into the recesses of my mind like a spider hiding under a rock.

"Kyu, we're already late for school," she says, showing her phone to me.

We set off at a run towards the school, but having Tenshi, my bag, and my quiver makes it difficult to keep up with her. I long for the feeling of wings propelling me through the air again.

"Come on Kyu!" Miyu yells from ahead. "Let me take some of the load for you."

"Thank you, Miyu," I say, handing her my school bag but keeping Tenshi wrapped round my body. We arrive just as the morning bell finishes chiming and race to the homeroom. Miyu gets to the door ahead of me and abruptly stops when she pulls it open. With the extra weight behind me I can't help but go careening into her, knocking us both down onto the floor and spilling my arrows everywhere. I can feel myself blushing at the stupidity and awkwardness of the situation as my classmate's giggles filter through the air. A shadow passes over me and a face that is full of smile and happiness emerges into view.

"Good morning Sasaki! Can I give you a helping hand?"

"Satoshi?!"

The embarrassment fades in an instant as he takes my hand and the rushing of blood in my ears and face distract me from reality. The sight of his beautiful face filling my view makes me feel like I'm almost floating as he helps me pick up my arrows.

"What are you doing here?" Miyu asks.

"I..."

"This is Kagawa Satoshi," interrupts our teacher, "he just transferred to us today. Since you already seem to know him Sasaki, he can sit next to you."

Satoshi just gives Miyu a big smile by way of explanation and takes his seat next to me. I untangle myself from Tenshi and sit down at my desk at the back of the class now surrounded by Miyu on one side and Satoshi on the other. I sheepishly look sideways towards Miyu.

"Sorry Miyu," I whisper.

Either she doesn't hear me or doesn't think there's anything to say as she just ignores my apology. I lower my head to my hands on the desk and try and block out the waves of embarrassment and self-hatred passing through me. I've brought shame on Miyu with my clumsiness and now she doesn't want to speak to me. I knew I'd ruin this again. I can hardly concentrate as the morning passes me by. By the time the lunch buzzer goes I feel like the loneliest and most isolated person in the world.

"Well, that was certainly dull wasn't it huh?"

Satoshi's voice knocks me out of my trance and brings me back to the real world.

"Yes, it was, wasn't it," I stammer.

"Can I join you for lunch? Maybe you could show me where everything is?"

Another disarming smile makes me start to nervously fiddle with Tenshi's string.

"Certainly, Satoshi. Shall we go Miyu?"

"I'm afraid I've got to go do something Sasaki. I'll see you later."

The pain of uncertainty burns inside me as she turns and leaves the room.

"Hmm, looks like I have some work to do, don't I? Shall we have lunch together then Sasaki?"

"I always have lunch in the gymnasium."

"Excellent! I'll join you."

We walk towards the gym with Satoshi doing the small talk for both of us. He babbles and yammers in a light-hearted way, but I can't find the words to respond as the thoughts of Miyu fill my head to breaking point. When we get to the gym I sit down in the corner next to all my practice targets piled up.

The silence is broken by Satoshi's ringing voice echoing through the empty hall.

"So, it would appear you're a pretty good archer then Sasaki?"

"I'm ok yes."

"You're modest. Back in the Sanctum I saw how good your aim was. If you weren't against two people who are so far above you in ability I'm sure it would have been very different."

"But I beat them anyway," I protest loudly. Don't try and take away my victory. I won that fight despite being against two Angels.

"Well, Lailah won that fight really didn't she?"

I stand over him, pouting angrily.

"That was not Lailah! That was me! It was all me! Whatever you think, I swear that was me. I don't let others fight for me. I will be the one to find out what happened to my sister. Not Lailah, not you, not the Angels. Me!"

The stress and anger and fear of reprisal running through me are so powerful that I feel like crying again. I'm weak and incompetent. I'm useless just like Lailah said. She had me all worked out, but now she's locked away inside me.

"Sasaki," he says wistfully.

He entwines his arms around me so quickly that I drop my lunch on the floor, the noise of the plastic box bouncing is the only thing I can hear. After the paralysing shock begins to fade I start to think about things a bit deeper. This isn't a nice thing to do, it's awful. He's trying to take the easy way out of the situation. How dare he try and sweep my problems under the carpet with a hug! As if a simple thing like this would change the fact that I'm so useless. I push him away forcibly.

"Go away! Why are you even here?!" I cry.

"I'm here to protect you Sasaki."

"I don't need protecting from any more of your monsters. I've shown I can handle myself," I struggle to say from my burning throat.

"Sasaki...I haven't been sent here to protect you from the Fallen. I've been sent here to protect you from yourself."

"I...I don't know what you mean!" I yell in bemusement, putting my head in my hands as the tears flow out onto the floor. "I can't understand you!"

I start running to the door but Satoshi catches my arm, leaving me struggling against his rock solid grip.

"You've begun to understand yourself a bit haven't you? Lailah always knew how to open people up. But I can help you understand yourself more Sasaki, you have to give me a chance."

"Stop it, you're hurting me!" I shout, struggling even harder.

"Bolt!"

Even through the cries I hear the voice and the fizz of something pass close to my face. The beam zips past me before smashing into Satoshi's chest and knocking him against the wall, his head cracking hard against the painted bricks. As blood starts to leak out I panic, fearing that he might be dead. After a few seconds with my heart in my mouth he groans loudly and grabs at his head. Miyu walks across the hall towards us.

"Don't you dare hurt her," she says, "whatever you are, you will not hurt her while I am still breathing."

Satoshi slowly gets to his feet, looking dazed and confused.

"What was...look, I don't want to hurt her, that isn't my intention Yamamoto. She's with us now, and all the Angels look out for each other. Look, let me show you tonight. Both of you come to the park and I can show you my true intentions."

With the meeting proposed he gently gets to his feet and shuffles out of the gym, rubbing his head. Through my tears and anger and fear I can see the spatter of blood that was left on the wall following the impact.

"Thank you Miyu" I say in a small, timid voice. "What did you do?"

"It's a simple energy bolt used for combat. I can do a few simple aggressive spells like that for when they're absolutely necessary."

"I'm sorry about earlier."

"I don't care about earlier, but I don't trust him Kyu. Something about him doesn't sit right with me and I don't trust the rest of them either. He's here to keep tabs on you and I don't know why."

"But you said that you thought it'd be fine to leave me with them?"

"That was before they did what they did. You didn't tell me the full story but it was painful wasn't it? I might not have been able to experience it when I was with you but I can see your socks are higher than normal, your shirt is done up more and you're hiding bits of yourself away. They made you suffer didn't they? I know that they almost certainly won't kill you because they need you, but I don't think I can trust them if they can do that to you."

The school buzzer sounds again, spelling the return to class. We quickly clean up Satoshi's blood that's dripping down the wall just before the afternoon volleyball class filters in and speed back to the classroom. I struggle to keep up with Miyu as we walk back to class. My head hurts. It feels like there's the sound of grinding teeth or scraping nails on metal running through it.

As I shove my hands in my pockets one rattles the bottle of pills. Michihara said they'd help with pain right? I quickly and stealthily pop another one into my mouth. The grinding sound dampens slightly but continues to pound at my head hour after hour as I struggle my way through the afternoon classes. Finally, as the end of day chimes ring out I rush to get myself back to my safe place.

My breathing is pained as I reach the gym, clutching at my head until I can get through the door and slam it shut. When I'm alone I finally start to feel some respite from the pain. I drag the targets from their corner and set them up before slipping into my usual practice routine, taking big deep breaths as I try to overcome the grinding. The calm and repetitive method of shooting doesn't make it go away, but it helps. I walk around the room taking shots from different angles and at different targets, filling the gym with the rhythmic sound of arrow hitting cork.

After a few seconds of collecting arrows from targets to refill my supply the abhorrent rasping returns with a vengeance. Every time I stop and take my pauses it hurts so much that it feels like I'm going to lose my mind.

Then, gradually, the grating begins to filter through my brain even when I'm in my zone. I keep up the volleys of arrows, trying to put more and more into each shot to try and block the noise out. After an hour of the pain steadily increasing, I am putting so much effort into it that Tenshi is emitting a whining sound as the string pulls at his joints. The sawing is unbearable now and my breathing is shallow and loud as I put everything I have into firing in the hope that the pain will stop.

As I unleash my last arrow, I collapse to my knees wheezing, the target crashing to the ground as my shot splits it in two.

"Kyu!"

Through my pain I recognise Miyu's shout, but I can barely see her through the buzzing behind my eyes. She puts her hand on my head and the noise drops from a high pitch whine to a persistent but low frequency throbbing.

"What happened to you Kyu?"

"Couldn't you hear the noise?" I ask.

I suspect there might be petulance in my voice. The fact that I've barely been able to keep up with all the nonsense that's been happening recently has been getting to me.

"I couldn't hear anything Kyu."

"I guess it was just a migraine or something. Thanks for helping."

"How long have you had it?"

"Since lunch."

"Kyu I'm worried about you. The confrontation with Lailah, whatever the Angels put you through and now this. Something is wrong."

I can't say I hadn't come to the same conclusion.

"When I defeated Lailah I felt so different, more like a real person. I'm sure it's just taking time to get used to it. Maybe Satoshi can help us understand it if we go see him like he said?"

That's it, I need to understand everything, but here I am with more and more things happening that I can't explain. I feel lost.

"Ok Kyu, let's go and meet him."

Chapter 9

We take the short walk to the children's park entirely in silence. Just being here again makes my heart beat faster until it feels like it's going to leap straight out of my chest. I don't know if it's fear or anticipation but there is something seeping into my veins. As we walk through the park I can't help but let the raw fire of emotion and memories of what ran through me bubble up to the surface again. The sight of Lailah's body trapped under the massive claw about to be snapped in two, the look in the eyes of the monster as it turned to notice me. I didn't even think about whether I should kill it and save her, I just did it. The inferno of anger at the sight of a beautiful young woman dying in the mud completely took away my conscious mind, leaving me to do what I did. Lailah looked so much like my sister that night it was terrifying, but whatever went through my head at that time, I can't let it control me again.

"Thank you for coming Sasaki," says Satoshi from the top of a slide, "I'm glad that you're both here."

"Tell me what you meant when you said you were here to protect me from myself," I say pointedly.

"Look, I'm here to help you and I really wish you would trust me. Being an Angel is a difficult business and I want to help you learn about your powers. As I said, we look out for each other in this group."

He seems less happy than usual. That beaming smile that usually fills his being and makes my heart race is conspicuous in its absence.

"What do you mean difficult? You said that you could help Kyu. You said you could show us your true intentions. Do as you said you would."

Miyu is usually such a soft-spoken girl but she's showing so much forcefulness. Even when I would sit in class and watch her I could never see this in her. She always radiated trust and helpfulness with everyone in the crowd. I always wanted to talk to her, to try and rekindle our friendship but I would inevitably chicken out. All I had was practicing archery and going home to cry myself to sleep.

"Whoa there, please try to remain calm Yamamoto. I'm still hurting from before," he says, rubbing his head to make his point, "I really don't need any trouble with you, and I genuinely am here to help."

"Why should we trust you Satoshi?"

Miyu is now just saying what I'm thinking. He said he would show me his true intentions and explain what he meant.

"Look, I'll show you how I can help, you'll just have to wait a little bit longer."

"What do yo..." before I can finish he interrupts.

"Quickly, over here!"

He bolts towards us, dragging the two of us into the bushes at the side of the playground.

"Wh!"

"Shut up!" He hisses, clamping his hands over our mouths. "Please just sit tight and stay quiet."

I sneak a look at him and see that his brow is furrowed. Having Satoshi's hand over my mouth feels...odd. His skin is so soft and warm yet makes me feel restricted and claustrophobic. My breathing is short and the heat of my own breath feels almost suffocating. I snatch his hand away and pull an arrow from my quiver, pushing the tip against his neck.

"Just tell us what is going on, now," I whisper to him forcefully through gritted teeth.

"Sasaki, I know more about you than you can possibly imagine. We all do. We've all been briefed on you. I know you would never push that arrow into my neck."

My arm is shaking at the amount of anger that his words send through me. I can't stand people putting me down and making me into some harmless, worthless nothing. Is he any better or worse than Keiko or Naoko? I've lost myself and I've killed before. How can he be so certain it won't happen again? I push the arrowhead that tiny bit harder to try and force that message onto him.

"Just be quiet and look over there," he says as he pushes the arrow down to the floor.

He points to two men walking around in front of us. They're both tall, dapper gentleman wearing pressed suits, one clad in maroon and one in dark blue. They don't look older than their mid-twenties and look so similar they could be identical twins, with highlighted dark hair parted around their faces. Between them they're carrying what look like tools, one carrying a shovel and the other carrying two large sledgehammers, one over each shoulder. The hammers appear to be linked by a long chain which is draping down and dragging along the floor. They talk to each other in low voices as they look around the park, like they're searching for something. After a while they seem to agree on a spot and the man with the shovel starts digging.

A vision of Lailah's body being pinned to the ground flashes before my eyes. Her white dress covered in blood and mud under the massive claw of that Fallen monster. It's the exact spot where she was attacked, the same spot where she stabbed me with the arrow that led to all of this. I lean forward slowly to try and overhear what they're saying in between the sound of digging, but their thick British accents make it hard to decipher.

"Why do I 'ave to do the digging bruv'?"

"Because I'm carrying the 'ammers. Fair's fair after all. Just get on wiv it. Let's try and find it and then get back before it gets too late."

"What are they looking for?" Miyu asks Satoshi.

"They really are disgusting creatures. They won't find anything of worth left in that soil."

I'm surprised to hear such annoyance from Satoshi who has only ever appeared to be a beacon of happiness.

"Wait, are you saying these guys are Fallen?"

"Yes, they…"

His words trail off as the anger bristles inside of me. These are the bastards!

"Kyu don't!" Miyu shouts as she reaches out to me, but it's too late.

I burst out from the undergrowth, bow in hand and arrow at the ready, aiming directly at the man doing the digging. He stops shovelling and has the decency to look surprised as the tip of the arrow glints in the moonlight.

"What the fuck are you and what the fuck did you do to my sister?!" I shout.

It feels like I'm losing control as the anger erupts from my body, pushing me to do things I would never normally countenance. Darkness fills my head and my soul.

"I'm sorry girl but you 'ave us at a disadvantage," one of them says in that earthy cockney accent, "should we know oo you are?"

"Maybe she's somebody famous?" The other one chimes in.

"Nah she's not bootiful enough for that is she."

Their cacophonous laughter scythes through my consciousness. The fires flare within me, overcoming my mind.

"You ran over my sister didn't you? Didn't you? ANSWER ME!"

"Sasaki, please calm down!" Satoshi says appearing at my side, pulling my shoulder.

Miyu quickly joins me on the other side, trying to physically hold me back. The Fallen brothers are both looking at me now. Despite my friends attempts to stop me they can't sway my aim which switches between their foreheads.

"Ran over? Oh yeh, there was that girl a few years back weren't there? 'It by a car? Over in the industrial area?"

"You might be right bruv', it rings a bell don't it? I remember the boss mentioning something about it. But she was much prettier than this girl. They couldn't be sisters."

"You're right bruv!"

There's the laugh again, that loud, ringing sound that pierces my brain like a hot knife in butter. Miyu yells something that I don't hear as my arrow takes flight. The split second after I've unleashed the shot I'm suddenly filled with dread at the possibility that someone else might die at my hand as it rips towards the blue suited man. Time seems to slow down as my vision clears and I feel like I can see everything that's going to happen. I stare deep into his vile face and the smile makes me realise it's not going to work. He's not moving, just standing there with that arch grin on his face, eyes fixed firmly on mine as the lethal arrow speeds towards him. A loud clang echoes through the air as it slams into the face of the spade that the red brother has wrenched in front of his sibling.

"Well, well that were a surprise weren't it bruvverr? I didn't fink she'd do it."

"It was. Now are you going to tell us oo you are little girl?"

"Not until you tell me what you are, who you're working for, what you're doing, and what you did to my sister four years ago."

"She wants to know oo we work for bruvverr," the blue one taunts.

"We work for the boss little girl," the other one retorts.

"She wants to know what we're doing bruv'," he says with glee in his voice.

"We're carrying out our orders after you murdered our friend little girl."

"Shall we show 'er what we are?" The blue clothed man is practically jumping with excitement now.

"Let's show 'er bruv!"

The red brother throws his shovel onto the ground and tosses a sledgehammer to his twin. They swing in a long circle like Olympians until they smash their hammers together, causing an explosion of light to erupt from the contact point. We shield ourselves as the force of the blast sweeps us up and dumps us on the ground. I hop to my knees quickly and go to Miyu to see if she's alright.

"I'm ok," she says answering the question I had yet to ask.

"You don't 'ave enough time to sit around little girl!"

Miyu pushes me abruptly to the ground as something crashes into the spot I stood in. The blow completely obliterates the earth around us, showering us all with mud and shards of concrete as the noise of the colossal strike rings loud in my ears. Thank God Miyu got to me first, I'm not sure any Angel medicine could have healed me from that. The point of impact begins to crackle loudly as the smashed, melted stone begins to cool down. The alien feeling of fear is welling up in me as my eyes dart side to side. They must be insanely powerful! Part of me feels like I've lost already, and that bit wants to just lay down and cry, to take the hammer blow and end it all.

"Kyu!" Miyu shouts, reaching towards me as I turn to see her beautiful face.

The suicidal part of my mind gets smashed down by a wave of purpose. How could I forget that I have a duty here. She saved me once and I must protect her. Her shout makes my body move on its own in a controlled panic as I frog jump away. The ground below me glows with the same heat as before where the hammer impacts it.

"Miyu, stay back these guys are really dangerous. Please protect Satoshi and I'll deal with these two."

"She finally gets us bruvverr!" The clear and ringing tone has become a rasping, echoing, almost electronic sound that's loud enough to reverberate in my ears.

"Too right bruv'." The other voice intones with the same horrible timbre.

I stand up, turning my back to Miyu and Satoshi and feel the moonlight illuminate my face brightly.

"I will protect you Miyu, Satoshi, I'll do whatever it takes."

I will not let my friends die at the hands of these gruesome things. Transformed they stand at least seven feet tall, with the veins pushed up against their gleaming skin by their bulging muscles in the dim light of the night. Their chests are huge, with two arms protruding from each side. One pair of arms looks normal; well, they could probably rip a person in half, but they're still human arms. The others taper into large metal hammer heads at each end. Between them there is a long, thick chain embedded into them, connecting them together. Their mouths are wide and grinning, showing massive white teeth under arched noses and thick brows. One of them feints at me and I flinch to my side, keeping my eyes on both of them.

"What are you?" I say steadily.

"Sasaki, they are Fallen, Munkir and Nakir, the Deniers," Satoshi says from behind me with a croaky voice, struggling to his feet, "it is said their hammers can shatter worlds."

"'ow dare you put me second," shouts Nakir, "it should clearly be Nakir and Munkir you bastard."

"What are you talking about bruvverr? 'e got it perfectly right."

Munkir laughs loudly as Nakir hisses.

"I'm clearly the better one. I'll enjoy crushing your little girl 'ead and melting what's in it."

"Both of you are useless, hypocritical, stupid savages. Neither of you can claim to be the best of anything. You will never achieve your goal to defeat us," Satoshi quips.

They react badly to his insults, hissing loudly before leaping towards us. I nock two arrows at once and fire a shot at each. I can't get enough power when firing multiple arrows to do any serious damage but it might slow them down a bit. With a speed that belies their size, both brothers swing a hammer arm and with a sizzle my arrows drop out of the air glowing white hot.

"We can propel our 'ammers so fast that it splits the air like a nuclear reaction little girl, a pathetic arra' like that won't be enough," says Munkir.

Something is happening to my body. It feels like there's a heavy mass flowing through my veins that paradoxically makes my limbs feel light and snappy. My mind feels...clear, but translucent. Something is driving me forward to attack. Something dark and deep inside me flowing into my soul.

"How about this then?" I say as I place another arrow into my bow.

I've done this thousands upon thousands of times until I can do it as quickly as the eye can see. Within an instant I draw the string back far further than normal, until it's way past my ear. The arrow flies out so fast that they can't react, burying itself deeply into the mass of one of Munkir's shoulders. The reverberations of his scream erupt across the park like a wave across a beach. I look back and see Miyu and Satoshi cowering on their knees, being eroded like a stone in the sea's salty wake. It looks like it should sound louder, but something in my brain is dampening the sound, making it manageable. I smirk slightly at how successful the attack was.

tssng

When the scream of pain is over Munkir launches himself forward at me, a red glow in his murderous eyes. The noise he leaves behind is quickly overtaken by the smashing of earth below him as he hurtles towards me at a speed that something his size just shouldn't be able to muster. But something inside of me is projecting calmness and certainty into my mind. With the fear and the panic blocked off from me, I can concentrate on the metallic ringing that follows him. So similar to the sound an Angel makes, but with a subtly different undertone.

Munkir swings a hammer towards me, but before it can land there's a snap of metal as Nakir swings round, pulling the chain that links them and forcing him to a complete stop just a few feet from me. Munkir struggles against his brother, grasping at me with his tongue lolling out of his mouth and a low snarl permeating from him. Just out of his reach, I hop back calmly and smack him on the arms with Tenshi like a teacher punishing a child. The school like gesture annoys him no end, causing him to emit another roar.

"Bruvverr calm daahn! You know that it's my turn to kill this one. You can have the idiot and the coward over there but this girl is mine."

Munkir settles down, his roar replaced with loud snorts.

"Fine bruv, I will!"

He reaches up to the arrow in his shoulder and wrenches it out with a horrifically painful crunching noise. He looks directly at me with his demonic eyes and crushes the arrow between his fist until it's nothing but dust. I stare back at him blankly.

"Don't talk about my friends that way," I say, surprising myself.

Even with everything that happened today with Satoshi I do feel something there. He might be an Angel but he's so open and pleasant. I have two friends! That's two more than I had a week ago. The happiness presses up against whatever is happening inside me, causing me to smile briefly. I feel like I can stand here and do what I'm meant to do. I will protect them. Sorry Sis, I will find out what they did to you but right now I need to do my job.

"You 'av no idea what you're gettin' into little girl. The Deniers will show you what your pafetic friends really mean."

Throwing his head back, Munkir roars with such force as to even make me cover my eyes. It's followed by Nakir dropping the chain, putting his head back and roaring in unison with him. The sound is visceral, almost physical. I shield my face and turn to see Miyu on the floor with tears on her cheeks behind Satoshi. His cuts are oozing blood from his head but his eyes are wide open, taking the full force of the brutal sound. I mouth a 'thank you' at him.

I hold Tenshi up in one hand and push my head against the force of the screams. The things in front of me are monstrous. Their hair flows away from their heads and their skin is glowing red hot. They're like the personifications of some brutal, unstoppable force. I reach over my shoulder to pull an arrow out when the roars stop abruptly and the Deniers fix me with a blazing stare. The red glow of Munkir's demonic eyes focus over my shoulder while Nakir's clamp directly onto me. The silence echoes around us after the cacophony of noise.

Munkir turns his back to me and grasps the chain between them. His muscles tighten, boiling under his skin as with a massive heave he launches Nakir into the air, who lands just inches away from me. I try to shoot an arrow but in a split-second Nakir snatches the slack in the chain from his brother and pulls it in. Like a top he swings around in a circle, hurling Munkir around me and towards Miyu and Satoshi. The speed of movement is bewildering. I turn my head towards Miyu just in time to see Munkir coming down from above with his hammer arms swinging. I grab an arrow and pull the string back but Nakir's voice penetrates my consciousness deeply.

"You don't 'av time to worry about them little girl."

He grasps my shoulders so hard that I drop the arrow. I'm completely immobilised as I look up to see his hammers raised, ready to crush my skull. I desperately call out inside myself, asking Lailah to grant me her power, but nothing but silence greets me. That voice inside me has abandoned me just when I need it most! Inside my head I shout a stream of expletives at that Angel for deserting me. I thought you were my power now! I did everything I could to save you! The words echo around my head silently with no answer forthcoming.

znng

A fizzing sound fills my ear as a green bolt of energy skims past me before smashing into Nakir's eye, spraying dark blood over my face. He drops me and screams in pain, but it's Miyu's scream that fills me with dread. I look back at her just in time to see Munkir's hammer as it connects with her side. She has one hand up to fire that bolt left her only one hand to summon a magical shield which shatters in an instant, the force of the blow sending her flying into the air. Blood explodes from her, turning the grass red beneath her. Miyu arcs through the air, her large, scared looking eyes catch mine before she loses consciousness. The sight triggers something primal in me, channelling all the fear and adrenaline and horror towards my core. I feel darkness rising inside me, filling me up as I push my head back and scream like the Deniers did.

Chapter 10

I awaken in the increasingly familiar garden, where the cool breeze and bright sun have disappeared beneath grey clouds. The gigantic cherry tree in full bloom looms over me in the centre of my world. Unlike the last time I was here the tree is just sitting there. I don't hear Lailah, there's no face in the trunk, there's no glowing energy, just bark and branches covered in pink flowers.

Without thinking I calmly reach my hand forward and put it through the trunk. It doesn't break, my hand just passes straight through it as if it's made of mist. I close my hand and grasp something within.

"I know you're in there. You're my Angel and I need you now but I don't have time to wait for you to come out. You're mine, you'll do what I say."

I pull back my hand with no resistance at all, bringing with it a ball of thick, white liquid. It's viscous and glows white as it runs heavily between my fingers. I let it drip down, covering my face in the thick, treacle like material. It blocks my eyes but in the blackness behind my eyelids all I can see is the look of agony on Miyu's face.

***

Back again in the real world it appears that Miyu has only moved a few inches since I left. I must have been gone for only a fraction of a second. I push out from my shoulders and feel my wings extend from the light inside me.

"Oh no you don't," laughs Nakir.

His breath is disgusting on my neck, rasping in short, sharp bursts next to my ears.

"You think you can stop me?"

I swing Tenshi under my arm and feel it bounce off the mass of muscle. It doesn't do much damage but it's enough to knock him away and allow me to flap my wings to escape. The rushing air and the odd sound that Angels make when they teleport fill my ears as I land behind Miyu, catching her in my arms. I could probably carry her without the help of the wings but now she feels almost weightless, although the inertia sends me skidding when my feet hit the ground. I place her down and gaze at her face. She's unconscious and blood is oozing from underneath the right arm of her cloak. My hand immediately clamps on the wound to try and staunch the bleeding but that only succeeds in getting my hand covered in the warm blood of my friend. Looking at her makes anger rise up inside me. Someone is hurting because of me, again. The light of the Angel is mixing with something painful, deep inside me. I try to filter it out but the weight of it swirls in my soul.

I call for Satoshi to come and help but Munkir's roar interrupts us as his hammer arms coming crashing down at me. I instantly fire an arrow and see Miyu's blood flowing through the air behind it. Both get evaporated by the hammer as it breaks apart the atoms in the air before a bright flash overwhelms my eyes.

clang!

The blows crash off of something, leaving the two of us unharmed and sending Munkir flying backwards. Above me is Hesediel, standing over us in Satoshi's place. He's breathing hard but a bright blue shield encircles us. Munkir growls, both hammers crashing down on Hesediel's barrier, but the Angel stands solid with both hands up to reinforce his protection.

Munkir's roar of frustration mingles with the constant clatter of hammers hitting the shield as he rains down blows on us.

I look past the two godlike beings fighting above me and see Nakir's blue eyes piercing through the darkness as he raises himself to his feet again. His face is burned where Miyu selflessly pushed that bolt into his face. I look back down on her, still unconscious but breathing lightly, and I can feel my resolve strengthen.

"Now Sasaki! Do something now!"

Hesediel's ringing voice shouts down at me over the roars and the clashing of hammers. I roll to the right, end up on one knee while pulling an arrow and firing it in one movement. Nakir slashes it out of the air and follows through until his hammer smashes into the ground, using his momentum to catapult himself towards me.

tsnng

In an instant he's over me, the other arm swinging down with murderous force, but with a flap of my wings I'm gone too. Two can play at this game. I pull another arrow but he's on me before I can fire, forcing me to retreat. Again and again, he comes at me, using his arms to generate momentum, but my wings allow me to escape every time with a twitch and a rush of air. The feeling of speed is exhilarating as I dodge and weave around his attacks that leave the earth carbonised beneath us. The mixture of my teleportation sounds and his attacks plays a ballad around our dance, merging together in harmony as a battle of strength becomes one of will and stamina.

"We know your weakness little girl," he says to me in between swings.

"And how could you know that?"

But before he answers he's gone again. Both his hammers smash into the ground sending him past me rather than at me this time. I turn around to fire but again he disappears.

"She's there for all to see 'in she," he says as he leaps towards Miyu. I react by adjusting my bow and shooting multiples shots through the chain connecting him to his brother, anchoring him to the ground. As the slack runs out he gets tripped up, allowing me to teleport in front of him, lifting my bow and forcing him back.

"Don't you dare lay a finger on her!" I shout viciously, preparing for his next move.

He grabs the chain and whips it, releasing the arrows from the ground, making metal fly around me. With a pull the links bind around my wings and my arms, preventing me from firing the shot and stopping me from being able to escape.

"You're easily distracted ain't ya? You care about 'er more than winning the fight. Well, now you've lost."

He leaps to go past me and straight towards Miyu. My eyes see a protective play and my body reacts by going for it without considering the harm I might come to. I throw out a leg and kick the chain up in the air just in time for Nakir to trip over it, sending us both flying to the ground painfully. He snorts loudly as he scrambles up, raising one of his weapons to the air before teleporting towards Miyu.

The impact of being thrown to the ground hurt like hell, but it did at least loosen the chain around me slightly. Munkir sees it happen and breaks off from attacking Hesediel to pull it tight and lock me in again, but it only tightens over empty space now that I've put myself between Nakir and Miyu as his arm descends. I take the only option available to me, putting myself between them and absorbing the hammer blow square in the chest. I reach forward and grasp his arms with as much force as I can muster through the agony as my skin starts to burn from the heat. My tiny hands can barely fit around his huge arm but I hold on for dear life, knowing that if I slip up now Miyu will die. The sight of his other hammer coming in for a swing sends my brain into automatic mode. A calculation passes through my head, in fact a flood of tens of thousands of them flows before my eyes as time seems to stand still.

When the flow of time is restored I pull one of my wings up and fan it to its full breadth, deflecting the blow with just enough force to push it into the ground instead of its intended target. Using the momentum of Nakir's flailing arm I spin, throwing him away like a wrestler. He crashes into the earth, throwing up mud and dust until he slides to a stop in a long trench. The chain pulls on Munkir causing him to stumble in his personal battle with Hesediel. Hesediel lands a blow but he's clearly built for defence rather than aggression.

Before I have time to think, Munkir yanks the chain again, sending his brother towards me. I flash an arrow into Tenshi's string, pull back with all my might and fire it at the oncoming monster. The noise of it puncturing Nakir's knee is brutally loud. I fire another into his upper thigh, and another in his other leg making him crash to the floor like a felled tree. Hearing the impact tweaks something inside my soul. I can't help but put a few more arrows into his legs, stopping his movement completely.

Whatever was in him before is getting stronger. His Fallen form is raging with pain as, to my amazement, he uses his arms to raise himself up off the floor and continue coming at me. I fire another arrow as quick as a flash into each of his limbs, causing him to go back down again, face planting in the ground. A voice quietly mutters inside me.

"He won't be getting up again."

shhnk

I flap my wings again and now I'm standing over him, pointing a shot directly at the back of his head. I pull the string tighter, making sure to give it all I've got so he won't be able to hurt my friends again.

"Do it Sasaki!" Hesediel shouts over the din, but he's drowned out by that voice coming back into my brain.

"Yes, kill this beast. He doesn't deserve to live."

It rings clear and true in my head, leaving me wondering where it came from.

"You killed his friend, now you know you can do it again. You have to," says the internal voice.

Yes, I did kill the monster that was going to kill Lailah, but I promised myself I wouldn't do it again. But no, I must do it. I need to defeat the Fallen so I can find out what happened to Sis. But I can't. It feels like the internal struggle is going to overcome me completely.

"Come on you coward. Prove your worth."

The voice is terrifying, sending waves of dread through my spine and down my legs. I refocus on Nakir who's staring up at me from his gleaming, cobalt eyes which practically glow in the moonlight. I can't do it. The string wavers on my bow as I sink to my knees. I look across to Hesediel, still protecting Miyu from the horrid blows of Munkir.

"I can't," I shout to him, "even if he's my enemy, I can't kill him."

"You made a promise to help us defeat them! How dare you not keep that promise! Hashimoto will come after you if you don't kill them. Do not face his wrath Sasaki. Please, please don't cross him!"

I look back down at Nakir's face and the blood leaking from his arms and legs and an idea forms in my brain.

"I don't have to kill them to defeat them. All I promised was to help you."

My usual, calmer self returns as the purity fights back within me, the onrush of emotion stifled for now. I drop my stance, return the arrow to my hand and kneel on Nakir, his heavy, rasping breaths punctuated with groans of pain.

"Just because I'm not going to kill you doesn't mean things are going to be easy. Your group messed up my life and you've attacked my friends. You will pay for that."

He looks up into my eyes as I push my wings back and throw myself into the air before returning with an almighty crack of Tenshi hitting his skull. His head collapses to the floor with a thud as I settle back onto the dirt. With my job done I turn to the remaining Fallen, ready to jump into the fight, until I realise I can't move.

"That's not enough. Don't leave it there," the voice inside me says suddenly, sending another paralysing surge through me. The blackness suddenly rages in my soul as the voice continues, *"you are a boiling mass of frustration, anger, dread, malice, and bloodlust. Stop him from hurting anyone ever again."*

I struggle as my body begins to move on its own. Slowly my arms come around, pulling an arrow out of my quiver. I pick up the slack of the chain and start methodically wrapping it around each of his arms and legs.

"Yes that's right! Do it!"

Inserting an arrow into the chain I begin twisting it, tightening the tourniquet around each joint. I try to cry out, but even my mouth is paralysed. Suddenly I realise what's going on, and my stomach drops out from under me. No! No! You can't make me do this!

"Deep down you really want to! I couldn't make you do something you didn't really want to!"

I cry silently as the voice inside takes over my body. It reaches round and pulls a handful of arrows out of my quiver. It nocks one and draw the bow back. I put every ounce of my remaining strength into stopping it, whatever it is. I shout obscenities within my own head, holding on for a few seconds until my meagre resistance fails. The arrow flows out and into the unconscious Fallen. Nocking them one at a time, I fire shot after shot at him, methodically ploughing them into his arms from close range. I scream in agony as the force of the metal tips shreds his muscles. The blood flows from his wounds, staunched to a non-lethal amount by the chains around him. The sound and sight of the arrows ripping the ligaments from his skeleton is horrific. I can't be doing this! This can't be me! But one by one the arrows fired from my bow do more damage, until his arm is hanging by a thread.

I manage to force my body to pause briefly before the arrow takes his arm completely off, before moving on to his other limbs. When the job is complete, I lean down and grab his hair, holding him up for the world to see.

"Munkir! Look what happened while you raged like the monster you are."

When he looks across to me he stops with the shock of seeing his brother, a limbless, broken mess.

"This is a message to the Fallen. I am here and I will find out the truth of what happened. Do you hear me?! Take that back to your leader and let him know that Sasaki Kyushiro is after you."

With a look of horror on his face he starts pulling at the chain that used to connect them, dragging his brother's dismembered arm until it reaches his fingertips. He sinks to his knees, breathlessly whispering his brother's name over and over again. He jumps towards me, but a simple twitch of my wings pushes me into the air. Behind me he collapses on the mutilated body of his brother. I teleport back down to Hesediel and Miyu, her body still lying limp.

"Sasaki, what did you do to him?" Hesediel says.

I look up from Miyu's unconscious form, my hand resting on her blood-soaked cheek.

"I made sure he couldn't hurt me, or any of my friends again. Ever. They did worse to my sister, to my whole family, to Miyu."

"What's going on with you? Why are you acting so differently?"

I grab my head to try and push the pain away.

"I don't know," I say.

"This isn't you Sasaki, who are you?"

I can't take it anymore. Rage fills me, making me leap into the air above Hesediel.

"I AM SASAKI KYUSHIRO!" I bellow into the night.

That darkness within me clutches at my soul again, pushing anger and hatred out of my body like a physical force. The wind begins to whip around me loudly, pushing me around in the air. I struggle to stay airborne on my new wings.

"How fucking dare you question me! You, the group who have pushed me to the brink of death on multiple occasions."

I zip down until my face is almost touching Hesediel's. I can feel his breath, fast and sharp on my mouth. From so close I can see nothing but the fear and confusion in his angelic eyes.

"Don't you ever question who I am again, or I will find the truth on my own, even if it's against you. Even if it is against every, single, one, of you."

My voice comes out loudly but it feels distant, like it isn't mine, exacerbating the problem of feeling like I'm not in control. A squall of uncertainty rises within me, dragging me down into the space it occupied. I want to strike him, to put my hand straight through his face.

Just as my voice fades away, I'm blasted by a bloodcurdling scream of agony and a fresh gust of wind from behind me, sending me sprawling down on top of Hesediel. The closeness to him leaves me flushed with embarrassment and boiling with shock.

I quickly push off and flip around on my wings to see Munkir, head back and mouth wide, raging at the sky. The roar passing the rows of sharp teeth in his wide mouth is guttural and painful to my ears, making me cringe. He's surrounded by an aura of red light and his skin is glowing white hot. He finally stops screaming and pulls his head down, his eyes glowing with the same crimson fire. The aura flickers around him as he speaks, barely pushing out the syllables past his gritted teeth.

"How...dare...you...hurt...him," he says.

He holds his arms apart and vanishes with a warble. The heat hasn't even dissipated from the air where he stood as he reappears underneath me and strikes a blow with two fists right into my stomach. I gasp in agony as the force thrusts me up into the air before he launches himself towards me. He lands blow after blow on me with a rapid pace, causing unimaginable pain to run through my body. I try to escape but he's just too fast. He clasps his hands together to aim for one gigantic strike at me, moving inexorably towards me surrounded by blazing heat and fire. Just as his arms brush the bottom of my skirt a sideways force knocks me away. I look up into Hesediel's serious face as he carries me to safety, his expression so contrasting to

Satoshi's. My wings are curled up, my arms folded and my knees are against my chest while I lay in his arms as he teleports us away from danger. Welts are coming up on my skin and blood is soaking into my clothes, but for a brief second I feel a pang of safety and security pierce through the pain. I haven't felt like this since my sister was taken. With my head being pushed into his chest I can feel the heat of his body mixing with the slight musty smell of sweat and dirt.

The brief moment of tranquillity doesn't last though. Munkir teleports behind Hesediel and smashes him hard in the back. The pain knocks the pleasant feeling out of me when we land hard on the floor. He grimaces loudly as his arms give way, sending us rolling along the ground. I finally come to a stop face down in the grass, whimpering at the burns and lacerations all over me. Hesediel is on the floor a few yards away, his face covered in an agonised look. One of his legs appears to be broken from the force of the blow he took.

Munkir walks over him, but he doesn't even look down as he steps towards me. His eyes are fixed only on me, those glowing red sockets burning with hatred and loss bobbing up and down in the dark night. Hesediel tries to grab a hold of his ankle and stop him but he is easily kicked off. As the flaming monster strides towards me he cracks his knuckles. I try to steel myself and think of something I can do.

I look from the unconscious Miyu to the damaged Hesediel and time flows to a standstill as life-preserving panic begins to set in, causing the colour to drain from the world. Inside myself I hear a voice whisper something and feel myself fill with energy. I have to move. I have to move! I'm the only one who can stop this thing. The energy envelops my wounds, giving me just enough power to try and keep going.

Managing to put the pain to one side for now I jump up and teleport backwards while firing an arrow. Munkir snatches it out of the sky, disintegrating it with the heat from his body. Another two shots get through but they barely scratch his tough outer form, bouncing off and dropping to the ground. He disappears again with a crash of thunder before appearing in front of me, but I manage to dodge him with a flap of my wings. He comes at me again, and again, but every time I evade, and every time he comes I can see the subtle movements in his muscles clearer and clearer. His panting becomes grunting as he starts to get frustrated.

"Push him to the edge."

The voice is so overwhelming that I can't help but obey it. The next time he attacks I wait an extra split second to catch his eye and give him a wink as I escape. True enough his fury overtakes him, and he starts comes straight at me.

"You...hurt...Nakir!"

"He hurt me first," I say sticking out my tongue.

He screams at me as I telegraph his rather obvious moves, dodging side to side as his punches come thick and fast. He's lost all semblance of control, each swing leaving him more and more open. I dodge another attack, this time working enough space to fire two arrows deep into his shoulders. Despite the force I put into the shots, the arrows ending up an inch deep in him, it doesn't stop his wild, flailing swings.

He comes again but this time I've worked up enough time to undertake a shot that should do it. I flit behind him, taking a second to brace myself with as much power as possible before slamming two arrows into the back of his knees. He falls to the floor, his legs shattered, roaring his agony into the world. I float back down to earth, straddling him. The flow of adrenaline rushing through me makes me feel alive with power. I grab a handful of Munkir's hair and force his head up from the ground.

"Do you see your brother over there?" I say coldly, "you let your boss know that this is what will happen to the rest of his people until I find out the truth. If you think the Angels are weak then you're wrong because I am here. Learn the name: Sasaki Kyushiro."

Munkir lets out another growl and his fists beat the floor. One massive wrist grabs me round the ankle, searing my skin before I can teleport away. Standing in front of him now, a safe distance away I nock an arrow and point it at his forehead.

"I think you need to calm down, or do you want to end up like your brother?"

"We win," says the voice inside my head.

He erupts in one, final, ear-piercing roar, the fire in his skin glowing white hot with anger. The light builds inside his body, causing his chest and arms to expand. The bright glow burns my eyes and the energy radiating off him sears the skin on my face. The heat becomes so powerful I can hear the air whining as it fuses around him. I try and flap my wings in the instant I have to escape but it's too late. The force of the explosion feels like it hits me from all angles as the world turns white and hot around me.

The blast still rings in my ears well after it's dim enough to see again. Somehow, I'm here, alive, feeling the grass on my face. I reach out and touch hard, compacted ground, seeing black, scorched earth around me. I panic at the thought of Miyu being caught in the blast but a soft hand from my other side shocks me as it grabs my arm. I look deep into Miyu's eyes as she holds on to me. She looks groggy after the battle and falls back into unconsciousness without letting go.

"Hesediel! We need to get Miyu to hospital, now!"

The reply comes from behind me but all it really amounts to is a strangled scream of pain. I pull myself up to my haunches to see the sorry sight of Hesediel with his face buried in the ground, lying motionless. Some way behind me he lies in a cone of healthy, flowing grass surrounded by destruction. Either side of us the blast completely destroyed everything, melting the ground with the intense heat, but here we were protected.

I try and flap my wings to get near him but nothing happens. I reach my hand over my back but nothing is there other than my quiver. The cold steel of my own thoughts and feelings come crashing in, flooding as if from a broken dam, extinguishing the boiling hatred. I feel broken and empty inside again. Without the Angel driving me I can't help but think how out of control I am. As I reach out it's clear that Hesediel is in a horrible state. His legs are covered in blood and both look to be broken in awful ways. There's sweat and tears running down his face as he lays there gasping in pain.

"Just hold on," I say to him, looking from him to Miyu, "I'll get you both to hospital."

I get my phone out and flip it open to call an ambulance but I'm greeted with nothing but a black screen. I randomly stab at the buttons but nothing happens. It must have been fried in the explosion.

"If you had just shot his brother instead of torturing him this would never have happened. You pushed him over the edge and he went nuclear. You could have killed him before then but you taunted him, didn't you? We knew that you wouldn't be able to kill them yourself. That's why I was here, to protect you from the consequences of your own actions. Hashimoto sent me here for that reason."

"Why you? Why am I worth protecting like this? Why am I worth putting yourself through such suffering?"

Hesediel is struggling to talk now as the pain overwhelms even the Angel's regeneration. I want to put my hand in his, to comfort and reassure him but as I inch my hand towards him I end up pulling it away at the last minute.

"Because...you..." he whispers.

shhnk

Michihara and the greasy figure of Kagawa Hiroshi punctuate the silent darkness. Hiroshi puts his hands on his sons' shoulders before staring a deep, dark look at me from under his tired eyes. As quickly as he turned up, he's gone, taking his son with him.

"We need to heal them. We're taking them to the Sanctum where they can receive their care. Take the udomite pills and they'll heal your wounds," Michihara says to me.

She also disappears, taking Miyu with her and leaving me alone at the scene. I sink to my knees and look up to the dark sky, wanting the tears to flow from me, but they don't come. I lift Tenshi to look into the reflection of my deep blue, bone dry eyes.

Through the yearning to just lay here forever I hear the sirens in the distance which force me to my feet.

As I exit the scene, I realise that without thinking I've reached for the bottle of pills and pushed two of the shiny capsules into my mouth. Crunching them mournfully, I start to trudge back home. My brain is completely blank, my movements cold and robotic right up to the point where I'm through the door and my mother comes into view. I hover behind her, wanting to say something, wanting to ask for some sort of advice, wanting to break down and cry to someone, but I can't. She's still just lying there staring at the TV with no reaction or noise. The thoughts run through my head again and again as I stand silently behind her, staring at the people on the screen. Suddenly they disappear, replaced by a young, trite, female newsreader.

"We're disturbed to bring you reports of a terrorist attack at a local park. No group has claimed responsibility and officials are unsure as to whether any casualties have occurred."

Pictures flash up of the park I was just in and my eyes widen slightly. I realise that with the explosion there isn't even a trace of any of us from there. The small circle of grass with a long conical strip behind it shows where Hesediel protected us from the blast, while everywhere around it is destroyed. All my discarded arrows were completely incinerated. Nakir and Munkir both went up in flames. Something nags at me as pictures of the site of my hollow victory flash on the screen.

"If you know anything about the incident, please contact the police immediately."

The report cuts out and I realise what's bugging me. My mother still hasn't moved. Even a supposed terrorist attack in her own city, where her only remaining daughter might be in danger won't get her to react. I obviously don't mean much to her if she can't even muster a surprised glance. I pad upstairs, disgusted, and curl up in the corner of my bed. I cry myself into a state, coiled up in the corner against the wall.

Chapter 11

I awaken to nothing but thick fog. It's cold, so cold I'm shivering, and I can barely see a few feet in front of me. Something doesn't feel right. This doesn't feel like the last time I was here. I try to take a step forward but the fog feels almost tangible to the point that it resists me, like walking through syrup. I try another step but it's even harder than before.

"Kyu!"

Miyu's voice rings out in a scream from somewhere nearby. My body temperature drops sharply as if the cold fog has entered my veins through my skin.

"Miyu?"

I call back in a voice that scratches my throat as it comes out. Suddenly, out from the fog the faceless Angel that I've seen in my dreams comes crashing through, pushing me to the ground and mounting me. It opens its mouth to reveal the disgusting rows of sharp teeth with saliva dripping off them onto my face.

"Kyu!"

The Angel warbles in a metallic, grinding voice that sounds like Miyu being fed through a synthesiser. It makes me feel sick to my stomach, but now it's on top of me I can't move. This revolting creature has pinned me down, its featureless face just inches from me. No eyes, no nose, just a mouth full of shark teeth. Inside I'm screaming in terror as I push against it. The mouth opens again and its breath hits my face. The creature lowers its maw towards me and closes it, the teeth digging into my flesh. I try to scream as my shoulder muscles separates from the bones.

***

I panic as I awaken, turning and slamming the alarm clock to stop its incessant screeching. My breathing is shallow and fast after the nightmare. When I put my hand to my head it comes away soaked in sweat. I pull the clock around to see the sight of 6:02am glaring back at me in the darkness of my room.

I throw my legs out of bed and wince as I try and stand on them. My ankle still burns from last night where Munkir grabbed at it. It's starting to heal up a little at least but the flesh is still charred and painful despite the effects of the pills. I can clearly see the outline of a hand in the scarring. I struggle up on to it and swallow two more tablets from the rapidly emptying bottle.

I don my school uniform, grateful for the knee-high socks that will cover the injury during the day. Very briefly I check my eyes in the mirror but I'm disappointed at just seeing my normal self. With Tenshi and my arrows in place over my head I limp off to the school gym again to practice.

Because it takes longer than usual to set up the targets with my injuries I have to accelerate my training regime, giving myself even less time than normal to fire each shot.

thud, thud, thud

The arrows bury deeply into the targets around the room, each one hitting the central spot I painted on them. I take some time while collecting them up to reflect on the last few days. Between the Fallen, the Angels, and whatever is inside me I've had a lot of adversaries to fight against. The Deniers are gone, dead, but I'm no closer to finding anything out. They said their boss knew about her, so I guess I have to keep pushing forward. The only way I'm going to be able to find out the truth about my sister, to protect Miyu, and to defeat the Fallen is to keep going.

I challenge my injured leg to hold my weight, to push further through the pain barrier as I force the arrows into place faster and faster. I have to get better, and I need to do it quickly.

thudthudthud

I demand more of myself, jumping around the room, hitting shot after shot as fast as I can. More, more!

thdthdthdthdthd

Five arrows hit home with an almost musical tone. I reach back and realise that all of my arrows are gone. I frown at the realisation because normally I can keep track of exactly how many I have left by intuition alone. I must not have replaced the ones I used in the fight last night from my store of them. A memory passes through my head, bubbling like sea foam before solidifying into something that touches all of my senses.

***

It's summer, the sun is bright and sweltering despite being halfway under the horizon. The cicadas are chirping in the quiet dusk. I'm sweating profusely, holding a bow that is a little bit too big for me with the string pulled back as tight as I can. The neat grass in the back garden feels prickly between my bare toes. I release the string which slaps into my side due to my poor technique, causing me to wince at the pain. The arrow flies through the thick summer air with a slight wobble until it hits the centre of our homemade target. It pierces the small yellow bullseye in between the others that might be called 'decent shots' by a normal archer. I turn to my sister slouching on the steps next to me and a huge smile passes across my face.

"I did it Sis!" I cry in a slightly squeaky voice.

"Well done Kyu! Only a few months ago you could barely pick up the bow, and only a few weeks ago you couldn't reach the target but here you are hitting a bullseye like a pro."

She gets up and disappears into the kitchen, her long, golden blonde hair flowing behind her. Before I can question her, she reappears with a cloth.

"Archery is in your veins," she says wiping the sweat and grease from my face, "it lives within you and flows through your soul. Eventually, if you work hard enough you might even be able to beat me!"

She smirks before taking my bow away from me, as well as two arrows from my quiver on the floor. Her eyes are glowing a fiery golden colour in the light of the dusk as she looks down the range. She nocks the arrows and fires them both into the target, hitting so close to my one that they take the flight off and just leave the shaft. My eyes are wide as she fires another shot so quickly I can't even see or feel her take the arrow from me. It whines through the air at a frightening speed before piercing the shaft of my arrow, shattering it completely. I turn and pout as she giggles.

"Ah you are adorable Kyu," she exclaims as she drops my bow to her side and gives me a big, enveloping hug.

Being in my sister's grasp makes me smile and I bury my head in her chest while squeezing her as hard as I can. It's such a beautiful evening and I feel full to the brim with happiness. I can probably get a few more minutes training in before the sun sets completely so I reach back for another shot but falter when I can't find any arrows.

"Kyu! I told you to always keep track of how many arrows you have! It's important to know all the information about the situation you're in. You can't let yourself get caught out like that."

A painful silence falls between us. Even the cicadas have paused, making it all the more embarrassing.

"I'm sorry Sis. I just lost c...cou," I stutter.

"Don't do it again. You have to be better Kyu; I don't like being disappointed in you."

She turns from me and disappears inside the house, leaving me alone with tears flecking the corners of my eyes. Her outburst hurts so much. I'm sorry Sis. I promise I won't disappoint you again.

***

The memory fades from my eyes, the feeling of horridness bashing up against my emotional walls. I want to make things right for her more than ever. I need to go back to the Sanctum after school and talk to the Angels. I'll make sure Miyu and Satoshi are ok after last night while I try and find out as much as I can.

As I make my way back to the classroom I put a couple more udomite pills into my mouth. When I take my seat there's a group of my classmates discussing the front page of the paper about the 'terrorist bomb' in the park. I can't help but listen in on their conversation, my eyes shut.

"Why would they bomb a park?"

"Well, it doesn't even say who it was so we don't know do we."

"I know, it's just a really strange thing to do."

"Do you think that anyone was hurt? Kagawa and Yamamoto aren't here, do you think they were caught in the blast?"

"I doubt it. They seemed to be getting on well the other day, maybe they're off somewhere together if you know what I mean."

My eyes snap open at the implication. Anger flows through my mind as their giggling pours into my ears. My teeth grind together and my mouth contorts into a snarl. I close my eyes, put my head down and try to quell the rage and jealousy that hit me so suddenly. Why do I feel so strongly about this? The idea of Satoshi and Miyu together repulses me but I don't know why. The sound of the crunch as my teeth slam together, crushing the udomite pills, rings through my head. Repeated images of Miyu in Satoshi's arms flash through my brain as I put my head in my hands. The echo of my grinding teeth becomes the sound of a chainsaw cutting through my anger. As I clamp my teeth together the sound morphs into the painful, inescapable whine that I heard the other day. I run my hands through my hair and grab huge handfuls of it, pulling to try and distract my body from the pain. The laughs from my classmates seem to go on forever, getting louder and bouncing around the inside of my skull around the sawing in my head. It hurts so much; I can't take it anymore.

I rush to the bathroom, slam the door behind me and grab the side of the sink as I retch. Tears stream down my face while my hands grip the counter so hard that they hurt. I stare at the falling teardrops mixing with the running tap as I try desperately to keep my emotions inside and the noise down, so as not to draw attention.

When I look up into the mirror again the Angel monster is there, staring back at me. I scream in horror and scramble away from it until my back hits the cubicles as panic melts my bone marrow. I sink down while flailing to protect myself, covering my tear-stained face with my hands. After a few seconds of nothing but the sound of running water, I pull my hands away and look around in horror. I swear that it had been there! I definitely saw the toothed, white winged, faceless beast from my nightmares. It had been there staring at me with its grinning mouth open, rows of teeth ready to bite down on me, just like last night.

I look at myself in the mirror and see nothing but bloodshot blue eyes staring back. The scare has jolted all my emotions out of my body. I don't have any fear or horror left in me anymore, I'm empty again. I clean up quickly, splashing my eyes with water before rushing back to class. I pause at the door and look back again expecting it to be there, waiting to devour me, but seeing and hearing nothing I slip through the door and back to class. No one even notices as I slink in and sit down in my seat.

After school is done I go to the gym to practice again, but my heart isn't in it. Images of Miyu and Satoshi keep flicking in front of my eyes, only to be interrupted with the sight of that disgusting white creature chasing them all away. Through it all I can hear that background grinding which tugs at my nerve endings.

After ten minutes straight practice suddenly the unthinkable happens...an arrow I fired misses the target entirely. I'm completely taken aback as the sound of it clattering onto the floor fills the room. I wrack my brain but I honestly can't remember the last time I didn't hit a bullseye. I shoot an arrow; it goes where I want. It just...happens! It's my thing! I stand there for a moment in the silent gym, looking at the arrow on the floor. A deep-seated unease surrounds the blip of panic.

It feels like I'm not in control of my own body as I sit down on the floor with my legs crossed. I place Tenshi on the floor next to me and draw a single arrow from the quiver, weighing it in my hand. I stare at the missed shot while twirling it around my fingertips. The sawing in my head is even louder now, the sound of wood on linoleum interrupting it only briefly. My ears are buzzing to the point of deafness and my eyes are drying out from staring at the fallen arrow, just sitting there on the floor next to the target, mocking me with its very existence. My breaths start to come rapidly as panic fills me up. Without taking my eyes off it, my fingers curl around the shaft of the arrow I'm holding without me wanting them to. The ear-splitting noise in my head drowns out everything as I turn the arrow towards me. I can't stop myself! The point begins to move towards my neck. The panic rises to a crescendo as the cold metal tip touches my skin despite me fighting it with everything I have.

When it punctures the surface, pain starts unwinding through my body. As it floods through me the pain suddenly overtakes the sawing noise, causing it to disappear sharply from my ears. I cry out and fling the arrow down on the floor where it rattles to a stop next to its fallen brother, a small trail of my blood following it. When I put my hand to my neck it comes away stained in crimson. Something's wrong! I don't know what's happening and I'm scared! I've been in control for so long, why is this happening to me? I have to go! I tell myself I need to see Miyu and Satoshi to see if they're alright, but fundamentally I know that deep down I'm scared to be alone right now. I'm afraid of what might happen next. The Fallen, the Angels, the noises, someone had better have answers for me. I collect my arrows up, use a handkerchief to wipe up the blood stains on the floor and rush for the door.

As I make it outside, I start to jog in the direction of the hospital where the Sanctum is located. The noise of Tenshi banging against my quiver and the arrows rattling around with each alternate step is interlaced with my breath clouding the cold air. I struggle after a few hundred meters and have to stop, putting my hands on my knees and screwing my eyes shut as I gasp for breath. I raise my head to the sky, my chest still wracking, and concentrate. I need the Angel within me. I need to be able to get there quickly, and this is the only way I know how to do it. I reach down inside myself to find the Angel, that part of me that has taken to coming in my time of need, but there's no response, again. Nothing. I open my eyes and let out a short scream of frustration. I want to stamp my feet and punch the ground like a child.

"You always let me down," I say through gritted teeth to the being within me, "I will not let you dictate my own life to me. At some point I'll find out how to control you."

Every second of running feels like hell, and after a distressingly long time I arrive at the hospital. Everything hurts and I can barely breathe. I can't let people see me like this, I can't draw attention to myself. Walking slowly around the side of the hospital grounds I find a side entrance into the area where I think the Sanctum might be based on my guess of the architecture. I slip into the corridor and start padding down the dingy hall. People give me strange looks as I pass them. The eyes of those doctors and nurses are boring into me and I hate it. God, I can't take this anymore. They're judging me, always judging my actions, how I look, my very soul.

I turn down another corridor but it's just another generic hallway. Shit! I scamper to the end and turn left but I'm faced with another corridor. I walk around under the judgemental eyes of the hospital veterans for what feels like ages trying to find the stairs down. Every time I make a turn my hopes are dashed by more plain walls and doors going into infinity. The panic returns as what feels like miles pass under my feet. Another turn and this time it's a dead end. A blank wall. I spin 180 degrees and I'm faced with another dead end. I'm trapped. There's nowhere to go. I'm trapped in a closed corridor with four walls and no doors. I spin round again and see a darkened corner so quickly dart into it for cover. My breath is so loud that I can't hear anything else. Stay hidden, stay down. I just can't take any more! I need to get to Miyu!

The image that pops into my mind is the one thing I wanted the least as I imagine her with Satoshi again, entwined in his arms. The jealousy and anger hit me like a brick, forcing me to cower down in the corner with my head in my hands, trying to silently stop the tears. I hate myself. I'm useless. Of course she'll leave. Of course he'll leave too. I'll be alone again like I've been for years. Why aren't you here to help me Sis? I need you so badly.

tsn

The tiny half noise snaps me out of my stupor, the tears instantly drying up on my now wide eyes. I definitely heard something in this prison. It sounded a little like the noise Munkir and Nakir made when they teleported, which is subtly different to the noise the Angels make. My body is filled with ice cold terror at the thought of facing another one of the Fallen in my current state. I try and push it down, but it keeps rising like an inexorable tide. What if I can't protect myself? What if Satoshi was right? I'd be a failure again.

I try to think of that garden within my soul to calm myself. The luscious grass, the trees and plants all pass through my inner being. I know I can do this. I have to do this. I pull

Tenshi round and concentrate, rubbing my hands over the decorated wood and metal. I take a deep breath and try to push my fear down. To my surprise, this time it moves. I push harder as it seeps deeply into the soil beneath my metaphorical feet. I continue and my mind absorbs the fear like the morning dew soaking into the ground. When the last trace of it has disappeared, I open my eyes to see an exit in front of me. The corridor is suddenly back to normal, a sign pointing me to the research centre.

"I'm coming for you Miyu, Satoshi, Sis," I whisper to myself.

I turn the corner and there's the door to the Sanctum. I found it, finally. I rush down the steps to the lower level of the hospital. Each time I've been to the Sanctum it's been bustling with the noise of machinery, computers whirring away and the babble of the Angels discussing their work. But now there is nothing but the echoing of my shoes on the stairs.

The silence makes me hesitate at the big double doored entrance to the lab. Where is everyone? Michihara said she would bring Miyu here for treatment, her burns and the wound in her side were pretty severe. The memory of holding Miyu in my arms, my wings spread as her blood leaked through my hands, homes into my mind. My head drops again at the pain I know I've caused her. She'll leave me again for sure. Then her voice rings out through the silence. I know it's Miyu's voice. It resonates within me.

"Thank god you're better Satoshi."

I push the door open gently and see her sitting on a medical trolley in the middle of the room. She's bandaged heavily, her wounds peeking out from underneath the white school shirt she's wearing. I move the door a fraction of an inch but an invisible hand grips my shoulder with just enough ethereal force to make me stay here.

"I'm glad to see you're doing better too Miyu. When I saw you get attacked I could barely control myself. I was desperate to do anything to save you."

"Please don't blame yourself, you did all you could but you were fighting a force of nature. I understand that you had to protect Sasaki."

My brow furrows slightly at the formality.

"Yeh I know, if it had just been the two of us I don't think it would have been a problem. Hesediel isn't the strongest Angel but he's fiercely protective of me and those that I love. Sasaki's recklessness put us all in danger."

The sentiment shocks me, leaving my mouth agape. They really think I was the problem? That I caused them to get hurt? The cold metal of the door comes into contact with my head as I slump against it. The sound of their conversation becomes slight echoed but I can still hear every word of their damnations.

"I don't want you to think badly of her, but I think you're probably right. She shouldn't have confronted them like that. But all that matters is that you're safe Satoshi."

"We know you're the last mage in your family, the last of all the big orders. It's more important that you're safe Miyu."

She nods at him gently, moving slightly closer. My heart begins to beat faster in terrible anticipation as mere inches separate them. The air feels electric. All the hairs on my arms and neck are standing on their ends.

"You're very knowledgeable Satoshi, but you're not the only one who does their research. Our order has known about your existence since you were created. We've been looking into you as best we can. It feels like you are here to take over our duty."

"There will be no more mages?"

"No, there can never be another mage. I have no one with the sort of immense power needed to bear one."

She pauses and stares at him, her eyes practically sparkling across the dimly lit room. My hand finds my chest as hurt blossoms in me.

"Miyu, did your research ever find what would happen to a child born of Angel and mage?" She nods at him and moves closer. He puts his hands around her back. "We can't be certain but imagine a being made of magic and God's power. A person with the strength to protect everyone. Someone who could rule the world with kindness," he says in a deep, thick voice.

My lungs have stopped working as I gag for breath. I collapse on my knees as they embrace, the coming together of the two people I care for the most. The choking noise fills the silence but they don't seem to notice. My vision clouds as Satoshi's lips find Miyu's. The energy and passion from them stabs at my heart. My thoughts slow down as my head scrapes against the door on the way down. They're going to be together, the perfect pair with the power to protect the world. Why am I here if they have everything they need? Why do they need me? What fucking use am I? I... My thoughts trail off into nothing as asphyxiation sets in.

I collapse to my knees as someone opens the door I'm leaning on. The impact hits me like a punch to the stomach, collapsing my diaphragm and forcing my lungs to gasp for breath. Through loud rasps I look up to see a black clad figure looking away from me, blocking the view of my closest friends. Dark, greasy hair spills down his neck and over his hunched shoulders. As Kagawa Hiroshi turns towards me I realise he's quite short for a grown man, but the way he hunches over makes him look tiny. His dark eyes bore into me as he raises his arm.

"The next Fallen is here. Satoshi and the others are in danger. Go to the school. Now."

"But they're just in th..." I say pointing past him.

"Go, now!"

He shuts the door and then disappears from view. As I push it open again there's no sign of Satoshi, Miyu or even Hiroshi, just me, alone with my breath rasping against my throat in the darkness. Where did he go? There's nothing else here, I'm completely alone. They've all deserted me. I can feel the self-hatred pouring through me, filling me up until it should be leaking out of my pores. My world is plunged into darkness as my head finds my hands, the depression creeping through my psychic barriers and pounding on the door of my being. I hate myself. Why can't I just be normal, someone who makes people want to be around her? Why do I make everyone leave me? The salty tears are a symbol of my weakness and a testament to what a pathetic person I am. The negativity encompasses my entire being, leaving me feeling both empty and completely full at the same time.

"Sasaki."

The voice corrupts the silence. It sounds familiar now, its vibrato tones swirling through me. I collapse onto my side, my eyes staring at the shadowy grey walls until they hurt. They just used me to get to Miyu to replace me with something better.

"You must go after them. The Fallen must be stopped."

That voice, the same one that promised me power when I was facing Naoko and Keiko. It helped me out then, but then when I needed it again it wouldn't come. I had to go and take it.

"Just who are you?"

"I am you Sasaki. I am the power of which Lailah spoke. You need me to achieve your goals. I am your Angel."

"What? I don't have an Angel!"

The silence that follows clangs in my ears. Nothing. My breathing is shallow again, emphasising the roaring quietness around me.

"I am here Sasaki; you can deny that all you want but I do exist. I am part of you."

I don't even know what that means. I have no power. No real power. I just have the empty facade of something that promises to protect but can't. Anytime I use it people just end up getting hurt. Any time I need it, it disappears.

"Get up," the voice says.

The order is said with a quiet forcefulness that prods at my brain, before coming up against the cyclone of depression and pain and hatred in my soul. Not a single muscle in my body moves from the cold, hard floor.

"If you won't obey me then I shall show you what you can do."

After a brief pause the floor begins to drop away. My body curls as my arms, legs and head get dragged down by gravity, the floor a few feet away beneath me. I manage to turn my head around and there they are, those wings that carry such unfulfilled promises of speed and strength. They brush against the wall as they unfurl to their full span. There's a newfound strength inside of me, like a calm blanket of light enveloping the deep purple and black tornado of pain that rages in my soul after seeing Miyu and Satoshi together. It surrounds it completely before compressing downwards on itself like a collapsing star, pushing the bad feelings into a core until it disappears completely.

The vacuum within me is a breath of fresh air after the torrent of negativity. I feel light and airy in such stark contrast to before. My arms and legs raise as if I've had weights removed from them. I rise up, arching my back and shutting my eyes while the white tube lights bathe my face. Yes, this feeling is good, this makes me happy. The wings keep me up with the simplest of flaps, moving me back and forward ever so slightly as I get used to them again. I can go anywhere and do anything on these.

"They need you Sasaki."

Something doesn't sound right, like there's a noise underneath the Angel's voice trying to get my attention.

"Who are you?"

"If you try hard enough and live long enough, you will find out. Now go to your school, show them what you can do."

I flip over and hover in the air, pushing down my doubts.

"Yes. I'll show them what I can do," I say to no one in particular.

I close my eyes and flap, teleporting upwards to get out of the building before crashing my head on the ceiling and falling to the floor. I hear a humming from the voice in my head, although it might be a snigger.

"That sounded painful Sasaki."

"Yes, I am aware of that thank you," I say sarcastically as I rub the quickly swelling lump on my head. There's another snigger inside me. "Why didn't that work?"

"Your wings don't teleport you through things, that's not how they function. What they do is allow you to move very quickly. When you flap them they can transport you from one

space to another in a straight line and at an appreciable fraction of the speed of light. You'll need to get outside first."

There it is again, something mumbling in the background as the voice talks. I do as it says, heading towards the outside.

"Will you be with me?" I ask tentatively, but the voice doesn't answer, instead just a single noise like the ghost of a fingernail down a chalk board rings in my ear.

I want to wait for a confirmation to anchor myself but I can't wait any longer. I might be on my own again but the power flitters calmly within me, not a raging storm but a smooth pool of potential. I start to walk slowly, trying to find my way back. As the memory of my journey here comes back to me, the fear of getting lost and delayed rises again.

I pick up the pace and soon I'm running through the hallways, passing bemused people but leaving them far behind as I reach a top speed. The clattering of the arrows in my quiver as I skid round corners fills the air before I burst through the door into a small courtyard. I don't even slow down as I jump on to the decorative fountain in front of me. My foot just taps the surface of the water as an almighty flap of my wings carries me upwards, leaving behind a splash of water and the angelic ringing noise in the air.

The wind feels tremendous on my face, blasting into me like ice every time I teleport forward. The houses and office blocks zip below me as I speed through the air with great arcs and twirls. I'm so free and so alone up here, but in the best possible way. There's no one here to judge me or to question me. Here I am the real Sasaki Kyushiro. I pause to catch my breath in the shallow air above the city. Extending my wings fully I can see the late evening sun moving below the horizon. The world is pure here. I spin slowly around to feel the beautiful rays fall on my face, a great smile spreading across me for the first time in years.

"Sasaki!"

The voice from within me reverberates through my bones before being cut off abruptly. It returns but seems to be strangled and in distress.

"The school. Go. You are needed. Now!"

I push my head down and flap with as much force as possible, propelling myself through some 40 metres of air in a brief flash. I continue to put all my effort into my wings, covering the distance between me and my school as quickly as possible. I push myself through another surge forward, then another, and another, filling the world with the echoing tones of my magic. The tall skyscrapers start fading into small office blocks and eventually become the archipelago of small buildings that make up my school district.

The low-rise main building of my school appears only a few hundred metres away. I stop and hover in the air to try and compose myself a little. In the dusky light the school is a beautiful place, surrounded by trees beginning to shed their browning leaves. I wish I could just sit on my own underneath them and feel the bark against my back. But before I have time to consider the potentially blissful scenario the voice returns. It sounds edgy, as if laced with metal, disturbing the harmony within me. Prickles of anticipation pass over my skin.

"They're in your classroom. You must save them. Now!"

The voice sounds almost in pain. As it's cut off I eye up the second-floor window that leads to the room I've spent so many unhappy hours in. It's a place where I'm surrounded by people who hate me, who laugh at me and judge me. I can see my desk at the back of the class as I head for another battle.

shhnk

I flit towards the window before the noise is cut off with a brutal, silent explosion from within me. The feeling of lightness is gone, and a weight comes back to my body as I start to tumble downwards. I suppress a scream as black fire erupts around me, seeping out of my skin, out of my eyes, nose, and mouth, dissipating into the air along with all the feeling of power. The burst from the magic leaving my body leaves me hurtling towards the window at tremendous speed. I reflexively put my arms in front of my face as I go smashing through the glass. The shattering pane buries piece after piece into my skin as I go careering into the room at full speed.

Chapter 12

I groan and grimace when I come to a stop against the door. Large fragments of glass are embedded in my skin with rivulets of blood oozing from them, mostly in my arms but I can feel blood on my face too. My clothes are full of rips and tears. I gently use the nearest desk to pull myself up to a stoop. The only sound around me is my blood dripping down onto the wooden surface, punctuating the encompassing silence.

After a few seconds my eyes focus and it becomes clear that the desk underneath my arms is already covered in blood, with mine falling on top of it. My stomach knots tight with dread as I look up and see every desk is covered in dark, sticky, tar-like blood. It's everywhere. On the desks, the floor, the chairs, even the ceiling. My eyes reach the front of the room where someone has pushed some desks together which are dark to the point of almost being black. There are two bodies on them, propped up and bound together.

"No..."

Satoshi...

"No..."

Miyu...

"No! No! No! No!"

A scream erupts violently and primally from my throat as I collapse to my knees. On the desks lay the blood-soaked and decimated bodies of my two best, and only friends. They're tied together with enormous amounts of thick rope which is also black from the blood. I scrabble towards the front of the room, dragging myself up with Miyu's bindings. I try to pull them off but they're stuck tight to her, digging into her arms. All my efforts do is cause her head to loll forward. I push my battered face in to the side of her head, feeling her matted hair scrape against my skin. Another scream escapes from my lips and I slam the desk with my fist, punching the desk again and again, each of my fists leaving horrible blood stains in the wood. My eyesight is fuzzy through the tears but I can clearly see the gigantic hole in Miyu's chest. Seeing her heart and vital organs spilling out of her disgusts me until the vomit rises from my throat and pours onto the floor. A tiny sound filters through my ears, but the sheer anger coursing through me is destroying all my conscious thoughts as I continue to bawl my eyes out.

"Where the fuck are you now?!" I shout at the Angel inside myself. "I could have fucking saved them! We could have destroyed those Fallen bastards before they did this but you had to go and fucking desert me didn't you?! You left me like everyone else did didn't you? Answer me!"

I start clawing at my back, desperate to feel the wings coming out from where they disappeared just moments ago. The feeling of nothing but torn clothes pushes the hurt and anger at my desertion further into my heart. I slam my head on the desk in some vain attempt to get the Angel to respond, causing blood to pour down my face and pain to crack through my soul like a lightning bolt.

"I'm useless, I don't deserve to fucking live. You don't deserve my body to live in either, you bitch!"

My eyes fall on the largest piece of shrapnel in my arm.

"You wanted my body for the power it had but what use is it now huh?! You left me and let my friends die!"

My thoughts begin to slip away as emotion overtakes me. The glint of reflected sun from the glass blinds me a little before being blocked out by a shadow over my shoulder.

"You can't fucking have it! You betrayed me, all of you!"

I clench my fist around the shard and rip it out from my arm, an eruption of blood following it. I raise the makeshift blade towards my throat, staring as one drop of blood falls to the floor. My hand starts shaking as it closes in on my flesh. They can't have me! She left me and now I'll leave her. I scream with pain as the sharp edge begins to slit my throat. The beautiful, deleterious pain will take me away from all this.

zing

A loud noise bursts from behind me, quickly followed by the sound of something slamming into the wall to my left. All that is left behind is a gentle fizzing noise as I collapse to the floor, the clanging of the glass vibrating to a stop in front of my eyes. The twinge of pain from my throat beats through me in time with my heart.

"Kyu!"

The magical intonation of Miyu's voice filters through my static body, filling my mind.

"What happened here?! Oh my god you're bleeding! Let me get that."

The purple, star flecked robes fill my vision as whoever is claiming to be Miyu crouches down in front of me. When she puts her hand on my neck the familiar healing and calming sensations that she's bestowed upon me before seep into my veins. It must be her. The world revolves around me as Miyu struggles to lift me up by the shoulders.

"Miyu," I whisper.

"It's ok Kyu, I'm here."

"But you're...dead, the body," I stammer quietly.

Miyu backs off, her large eyes staring at me wider than normal, filling her beautiful face with disquiet.

"What are you talking about?"

A groan from behind me disturbs us. I look over my shoulder to see a young woman crouched in the corner with smoke coming off her. Her cropped, black hair frames her small, charred face. It might have been heavily made up before Miyu's attack burnt her skin, but there's still a distinct look of kohl around the eyes and dark lipstick. Her clothing follows a gothic pattern with an ultraviolet corset accentuating her hourglass figure with a ragged, lacy, black and green skirt underneath. Pressed against the wall behind her are a pair of black wings that look small enough and damaged enough to not be able to carry even her slim frame.

"Kyu, please stay here. I'll deal with her."

"But, last time..."

Miyu turns and looks me in the eyes, speaking carefully and forcefully.

"You have protected me before, now it's my turn. You're seriously injured and I'm afraid what will happen if you try and join in. Stop trying to do everything for everyone and let me help you instead."

I look disbelievingly at my bloody arms and clothes before staring back up at her, then past her to where the desks were that held up her body, but there's nothing there now. As she turns and walks away towards the intruder I surreptitiously take another handful of udomite pills to help stem the worst of the bleeding.

"Who are you?" She asks.

Her calmness strikes me and I realise that it's what has always impressed me about her. Whatever is happening she can assess the situation and stay logical. She doesn't lose her temper and doesn't fly off the handle and make silly mistakes, like I do.

"Who wants to know?"

The woman smiles with an expression that reminds me of Furukawa Keiko.

"I bet you know who we are, don't you?"

"Yes Yamamoto Miyu, I do."

Her eyes are sparkling through the patches of charred skin and dark makeup, making my stomach tighten again. I try to reach down within me and commune with Lailah once more but nothing happens. I feel so empty and in so much pain from the glass digging into my skin.

"Kyu, I know what you're trying to do, but please stop. I told you, I'm here for you now," Miyu says, turning to the woman, "what were you doing to her?"

The woman shifts slightly, causing plaster to be dislodged from the wall and crumble to the ground.

"You think you have the right to ask? How about I show you instead?"

tsnng

As soon as the last word exits her mouth she's up. The sound of a Fallen teleporting fills my ears and darkness fills my vision. The girl is flying towards me, her black wings blocking out the world as her glinting eyes are matched by the shine of a small dagger she's pulled from a hidden recess. There's a sudden scream inside me but it's drowned out by the depression that fills me up. I can't even muster the energy to close my eyes, instead focussing only on the point of the tiny blade. As it reaches my clothing a small, translucent circle appears to block the attack. It rapidly expands outwards like a supernova, enveloping my body. Within a moment short enough for a thought I'm surrounded and engulfed by a faintly crackling, turquoise bubble which spins gently around me.

The Fallen woman pulls the blade back and swings it hard but it bounces off the edge in front of me and is flung away, along with its carrier, by a small explosion of energy. With the woman shot over the side of the room Miyu gently lower her outstretched hand with fingers splayed. My eyes find hers and a confident smile passes over her face.

tsnng

The Fallen leaps at Miyu, making me reach out instinctively to try and protect her, even though the pain makes it almost impossible to move. My hands touch the edge of the shield, causing a small blast that shocks me like static electricity. I suck on my fingers absentmindedly, trying not to suck any glass shards out of my skin as I stare up at Miyu. She's mouthing an incantation and bounces the Fallen off another wall of energy. Desks and chairs get flung around the room as she crashes onto the floor.

"Kyu, please listen to me. You cannot get out of that spell until I release you. You're in no state to fight, and I will not have you risk yourself again. It's a double-sided protection, for your own good. If you try to leave you will be hurt, but if you stay within, I promise you will not come to harm."

My hands fall back to my lap as I consider this, although I don't really have much of a choice in the matter. Miyu is right, I cannot attempt anything in this condition, even if I could get through her spell. I bring Tenshi over my shoulder and cradle him on my knees, my fingers idly tracing the engravings.

"Do you understand? Do not try to escape or there will be nothing I can do to stop the consequences."

"Yes Miyu," I say as I idly pluck bits of glass from myself painfully.

The Fallen woman climbs up from the floor, pushing a chair violently away from her. It careens into the barrier around me but is thrown away with a crash.

"Who are you, Fallen woman?"

"You don't know who I am? But I know who you are and what you are Yamamoto."

"Whatever you think you know, I doubt it's enough. Now tell me your name."

"Knowledge is power Yamamoto, but for now you can call me...Rama. By the time this night is through I will release that girl from your clutches and I will have her."

The bright smile returns to Rama's face as she flicks her hand from her side and two razor thin needles come firing towards me at eye level, but they don't even penetrate the surface of the shield. She flaps her wings, teleporting before spinning her body around in a corkscrew to hurl a desk towards Miyu with tremendous force. Miyu flexes her hands and pulls it out of the air from between them, holding it before tossing it back at her, although she easily avoids it with another flap of her wings.

"Your magic is strong," Rama says, "but just how strong is it?"

"You will never get through to her. I won't allow that to happen as long as I'm alive."

"Is that so? Let's see if your actions can back up your words."

Rama flaps her wings hard towards the floor, bouncing large fragments of broken window into the air before sending them hurtling towards me with an almighty push. By the time they reach the dome they're burning red with the friction but each one is deflected with ease by Miyu's protective spell. Miyu dodges and weaves as the shards fly off in random directions, burying themselves in the walls.

"I told you, you cannot hurt her," Miyu says to the hovering form of Rama, whose eyes are still fixed on me.

Slowly her head turns to Miyu, an evil grin spreading across her face like a Cheshire Cat.

"Well then, if I can't get to her, I'll destroy you and force you to drop that spell!"

Rama launches herself towards Miyu at an alarming pace with claws at the ready. My grip on Tenshi strengthens as dread rises inside me. Being locked in here, unable to help is agonising. But Miyu holds her own, pushing Rama past her towards the glass spiked wall. She looks so calm and confident using her enemy's momentum against her. Each time Rama jumps towards her she evades as if she can predict these moves in advance. Miyu's sparkling, purple robe looks astonishing as she moves with such elegance and grace in the rapidly darkening evening. Rama launches herself through the air again, faking to jab before swinging her whole body to land a roundhouse kick that sends Miyu flying backwards. She pushes an energy barrier out to clear the glass shards from the wall just before she gets impaled.

tsnng

But now Rama is firing towards her like a bullet, her dark wings flat against the air and her outstretched hand holding another small blade aimed directly at Miyu's midriff. I push against the barrier, only the be thrown backwards. I curl up, wailing in agony as my chest convulses powerfully.

"MIYU!!!"

I scream as loudly as my lungs will let me as Rama plunges the razor thin knife deep into Miyu's stomach. I expected Miyu to shout or scream when the attack landed but there's nothing but a faint gurgling sound of blood in her throat.

"No! Miyu!!!"

Through my distorting tears Rama is laughing maniacally, her eyes bright and wide as she removes and reapplies the knife to Miyu's abdomen over and over again.

"No! No! Stop it! You fucking murderer! I will fucking kill you and everyone you care about you bitch!"

Spittle flecked hatred erupts from me as my control ebbs away again. I shift my weight, driving spikes of glass further into my knees but I can't even feel the pain anymore. Nothing matters except killing her. The feeling of a need for vengeance fills me as I stab the shield with Tenshi's edge repeatedly, sending shocks through my body. I hit it again, and again, and again, grinding my teeth and closing my eyes in an attempt to block out the pain in my chest. Tenshi whines at me as the current vibrates the metal within him. I don't need an Angel protecting me, I don't need Miyu's spell, I just need one shot to take that bitch out.

With jab after jab, I try to break the shield preventing me from taking my revenge. Each attempt makes my body twinge harder until I feel like I'm going to go over the edge and my heart is going to burst. I clutch at my chest, dropping Tenshi to the floor before following him with a clatter. My head hits the tile hard as I curl up into a tight ball to try and pull my body back from the brink. I move gently and brush against the container of magic pills that I've been taking for days. I flick the top off the bottle with great difficulty and crunch four more between my teeth. A sudden wave of calmness crashes over me as my heartbeat begins to slow down. I uncurl slightly and look across the room to Rama and Miyu. She's still there, still ploughing away at Miyu's body, or at least what's left of it, with the blade. The sight of Miyu's blood and shredded organs pooling around her is disgusting, horrifying me to my very core. Rama pauses from her task, breathing heavily. Looking back to me, her face contorts into a despicable, rictus grin.

"That's your little friend done with, you're next."

Chapter 13

She stands up with her bright, gleaming, evil eyes fixed on me. Something prods at my subconscious as I look at her through the barrier.

"Wait," I say.

She starts walking towards me with a gait like a supermodel, taking slow, methodical steps.

"She was so beautiful wasn't she Sasaki?" She asks, taking another step, picking her fingernails with the blade. "Do you want to end up like her?"

A thought suddenly pokes into my head as I catch her eyes through the turquoise defence that Miyu put up.

"I don't think you can, can you?" I answer back.

"Pfft, stupid girl, why do you think that?" She asks as she gets to within inches of my face.

"You can't touch me, because you're not real, are you?"

"Your friend is dead, and you just sit there talking? That's her blood on the floor. That's her liver, her stomach, oh and look there's what I think is her spleen by her feet. You see all of that and you just look on?"

"No, she isn't. And no, that's not her blood."

"You couldn't be more wrong, or more dead Sasaki."

I look directly into her eyes, staring her down with newfound confidence.

"I trust Miyu with my life. She promised me she'd protect me, and she still will. If you think you can, come and get me."

With her hand gripping the dagger hard, she raises it up as if to strike me but then hesitates.

"I thought so. That wasn't the first time you tried to trick me either. What about the bodies when I came in? How could Miyu be dead there and then suddenly be here? You affected my vision somehow didn't you. This isn't real."

A brief pause of complete silence passes between us, with neither of us moving or blinking. We just stare at each other over the broken glass and dried blood on the floor. Eventually Rama leans in and slowly starts applauding, clapping the blade against her hand.

"Yeh, sure, well done Sasaki. I nearly had you."

She starts walking away from me, fading with each step until she completely disappears. As the real world flows back in, I realise I'm still on my knees in the blue bubble with blood congealing around my cuts. Miyu's eyes widen as I awaken, dropping the defensive spell before hugging me close.

"What happened?" I mutter.

"You're back! Oh Kyu! I heard you come crashing through that window and saw her coming at you with a knife. You were unconscious, so I put up a barrier to protect you. You've been wailing and thrashing yourself nearly to death. I kept telling you to stop but you didn't listen!"

Miyu smiles warmly at me. She seems completely unharmed, standing a few feet away with her hands covered by her long sleeves. Rama is sitting in an upright position against the wall in one corner. She looks different, more haggard and frail than what I had seen in the illusion. The brightness she had shining through her skin is now completely obscured by dirt. Her hands are stuck in her lap, encircled by a large pair of glowing restraints. There're no dead bodies, no guts on the floor, no dried blood on the ceiling. Everything felt so real, so tangible. I could touch the blood on the floor and smell the death in the room. But it was all fake. Some kind of illusion.

"Your suspicions are right Kyu. Why don't you tell her what you just told me Rama?"

The Fallen woman groans loudly, shifting slightly before fixing me with a stare. Miyu helps me up to my feet before perching me on a desk. I clutch at my legs as they groan painfully at me.

"Tell her!"

There's an air of command in her voice as it echoes through the room. I stare up at her in surprise at the power she can project, but then down there on the floor is a shackled, defeated Fallen. A powerful supernatural being, captured by this wonderful, brilliant girl.

"Ugh, fine. My name is Ramiel, and I am the Angel of Divine Visions."

"Wait, you're an Angel?" I ask. "You're with Hashimoto and the others? I thought you were a Fallen?"

"You talk and act as if there's some huge difference between us. That dictator gave us that name, and no I'm not with him," Ramiel says, spitting blood onto the floor.

"What do you mean?"

"I don't think you're quite ready to learn that just yet Sasaki. Maybe someday soon you can see for yourself who you really are."

"Can you force her to make more sense Miyu?"

"I could, potentially, but it would effectively be torture and I don't think I can do that, even for you."

"She's tortured me though! She's wrecking my mind and I need to know how. I need it to stop!"

"I'm sorry Kyu, I won't."

"Fine, fine, ok," I say with a snarl, "we'll let you off for now Ramiel. At least tell us what you did. How did I see those bodies and smell that blood?"

I point to the very definitely empty desk at the front of the room. It had felt so real just moments ago, but like a nightmare.

"I am the Angel of Divine Visions; I can overpower the consciousness of those around me and manipulate them."

"How can you make it so perfect, so real?"

"Because I am damn good at what I do, and you are not much of a challenge to overpower. I don't even need a run up to change the way you see things."

Suddenly the walls change colour and the quickly darkening night is replaced with a brilliant morning sun. I hold a bloodied arm up to cover my eyes as my retinas strain in the light. From darkness to daylight in a fraction of a second.

"Cancel," says Miyu with a flick of her wrist.

Miyu makes a hand motion as her magic counters Ramiel's efforts, the light flicking out like a candle being extinguished, immediately returning to the darkness of the evening.

"But I felt that! I felt the warmth on my skin."

"I can control everything you see and everything you feel Sasaki. Everything."

"Don't get clever Ramiel. As soon as I get wind of you even attempting to screw around with her I will stop you."

Ignoring Miyu, Ramiel continues talking to me.

"I can show you what you want to see."

Feeling a presence behind me I turn to see the back of a tall, golden-haired girl standing at the front of the class, writing something on the chalkboard. My eyes widen in shock and my mouth drops open.

"Cancel."

And she's gone again, the chalk kanji fading away, leaving a faint outline in my head.

"I warned you Ramiel," Miyu says.

"I could show you what you don't want to see if you'd like instead?"

A liquid sound fills my ears as a sword pierces Miyu's torso. I know it's an illusion, but it still makes me gasp in agony. I take a deep breath and suppress the vomit rising in my throat. It's not real. It's just an illusion, it's just an illusion, I keep repeating.

"Cancel!"

"How about what you want most of all instead Sasaki?"

And there, wrapping around me from behind, are my wings of beautiful white feathers. The sense of lightness starts to flow through my body. It fills my soul with a glorious feeling of completeness and just as I move to flap myself into the air they disappear into the ether.

"Cancel! That's it Ramiel!"

A pang of resentment spikes in me as Miyu takes away the positive feelings, even if they were an illusion. The fact that it's so easy for Ramiel to read my innermost thoughts disgusts me. Only a few days ago no one even knew I existed, not even my own parents, and yet now everyone I meet seems to know everything about me. I clench my teeth together a little harder.

"Is that really it Yamamoto?" Ramiel says, her Cheshire Cat grin returning, crawling along her face.

She stands up against the window, her hands still bound in front of her.

"Yes," Miyu says matter-of-factly.

Her right hand is up again quick as a flash, a bolt of energy flowing out of it and smashing into Ramiel's chest. I shut my eyes to protect against the glare of the impact but when I open them again, panic starts to rise in me. Ramiel isn't there. Miyu isn't there. Tenshi is no longer in my hands. Everyone has gone. I'm standing alone in the classroom with the desks back the to normal. There's nothing but the sunset pouring through the windows, lighting up the room like a furnace. I turn and look out of the window as the breeze blows through the trees outside.

"Cancel."

Miyu is breathing heavily as she returns to her place in front of me. She stumbles and goes down to one knee.

"Kyu, I can withstand her illusions but she can get to you," she pants.

"Can you beat her?"

"We can bea..."

Miyu's voice gets cut off as the skin melts from her face and off her bones. Her eyes drop from their sockets and she collapses to the floor. I shut my eyes again in disgust.

"Cancel!" and she's back again, the same as she always has been.

"I have a plan but it's not going to be pleasant. Can you trust me Kyu? We can beat her together, but you have to trust me. This is the only way."

I close my eyes again and try to gain the courage to say 'yes', but a mass of swirling emotions has suddenly built up inside me. My previous confidence and trust is being battered down by the sudden surge of doubt and fear, mixing with love and hatred and vengefulness. I want to tell the truth but I can't bring myself to so I nod ever so slightly.

"Ok. We need to do this quickly."

She runs over to me and plants her hand on my head while speaking an incantation of some kind. My legs still hurt from the glass being pressed into me as I shift my weight. At least Miyu will make me feel better. I grit my teeth in preparing for the unpleasantness that Miyu mentioned. I guess removing this many shards from my skin would be horrendously painful, but hopefully her magic will keep the worst at bay. I can get through this, for her.

"Blind!"

She finishes her spell with a sudden snap. I clench my eyes shut tight, but instead of the pain I was expecting I'm only greeted with a strange noise, like a spring unwinding in a metal sink. I open my eyes and see nothing but blackness. I try opening them again. Nothing. Darkness. My breathing immediately increases as I start hyperventilating with the panic.

"M...Miyu?! Miyu what the fuck has happened?!" I shout but the words are soundless to me. I can't even feel my mouth moving.

Since I got wrapped up in all this I've dabbled with fear but I'm not sure I ever really understood it. But this inside me, this is real, cold, hard, dread. The darkness and the silence around me might as well be made of fear. All my senses have gone. I can't smell anything, I can't even feel where my body is, like I'm a ghost. I'm completely alone with my thoughts. Why is this so scary when being alone is all I've wanted for so much of my life?

I clutch at my chest hard, my hand trying to feel the bike chain that holds my arrows on my back. I follow it round to my back and count how many I have left but even that feels off. I feel the wood, the metal, the leather but all the sensations are the same. Even my sense of touch has gone. My whole body is shaking hard as the reality dawns on me. I reach down in front of me to find my bow. For a few seconds, the panic rises further as all my hand finds is the broken glass. It enters my skin smoothly but there's not even any pain. I have literally nothing left.

"*Kyu...I had to do it,*" Miyu's voice reverberates and echoes within my head.

"What did you do to me?!" I yell silently.

"*I can't stop her from using her power on you, and soon she's going to break out of her cuffs and come for me. I can't protect you from her while constantly fighting her off from inside your head. There's no direct attack for me to stop, it's like she's already inside you. She even got to you inside my bubble.*"

"Wha," I murmur.

"*I think Ramiel's power works by affecting your sensory system, so I have detached your senses from your brain. Your optical nerves, auditory system, touch, pain, everything, and that means she can't get to you anymore. I will protect you while you're in this state Kyu, I promise.*"

"She'll get me Miyu!"

"*No. I will not let that happen. You have to trust me Kyu!*"

"I....I c..." I try to yell out but I can't. How can I trust someone who could do this to me?

"**You think you can protect her?**" The second voice scythes through my head like a metal saw.

"Who are you?" I ask.

"**Do you not recognise me? What about when I have come to you before?**"

Yes. It does sound familiar.

"You're the monster aren't you? The Angel monster. I've seen you before in my soul, and in the hospital."

"That's right, I'm the monster in your mind."

"I thought you were in my imagination? In my dreams? You're not real!"

"Oh, I'm afraid I am all of those things and much more. I am in your imagination, but I am also real. I run through your dreams. I run through your mind. Maybe I can make you understand."

I wait as the seconds tick by, nothing but blackness in my vision and the echo of the voice fading away in my brain.

"Hmm, your friend is certainly intelligent. She has found a way to keep me out, but it will be temporary. When my human form kills her I shall take you back and devour you from the inside out Sasaki."

"Kyu do not listen to that voice. She shouldn't have any way in, but her power is in there somehow. I will not let her defeat me. I promise. Please trust in me."

"You're her aren't you, you're Ramiel herself?" I opine. "But I've never met you before today, how come I saw you before?"

"We may not have met in person but I have been with you Sasaki. Ever since you took Lailah I have been inside you. I was inside you in the hospital, inside you when you fought the Angels, and I'm here now."

The first night in the hospital was the first time I saw the monster inside of me. She must have got to me somehow. But with Miyu by my side how could that have happened?

"You were in Lailah's mind already weren't you?"

"Yes, I was in her soul when you took her within yourself. I have been writhing in your subconscious ever since that day and I will take you over. I will completely overpower you. You will join us. If you do you can find out what really happened to your sister."

"Stop talking to it Kyu! She's trying to trick you! If I defeat her then you'll be free. I won't let her take you but you can't go on your own. If you want to survive this then you need to do what I say."

Why am I having to go through this? My mind has been invaded so many times that I don't feel like I'm my own person anymore. I feel dirty and disgusting, like I've been defiled by these monsters.

"Kyu, I know you can do this. I will tell you where I need you to put your arrows. Stand up, do not move, and fire where and when I say."

I stay silent. I can't hear anything. Will I ever be able to see again? How can Miyu do this to me? My only friend. My thoughts flit back to Satoshi and my heart flutters a little. No, the rest of the Angels might not care about me but Satoshi does. No one can be that genuine and still lie.

I flex my fingers slightly, feeling the shallow grooves of design on Tenshi's frame. Even if I can't feel the materials under my hands I know how to fire an arrow. I've done the movements so many tens of thousands of times there's a muscle memory in there even deeper than a physical one. I slowly and shakily get to my feet.

"35 degrees."

I fire as instructed. Even totally blind I nock an arrow and fire it in an instant.

"270 degrees! 50! 240!" Miyu shouts into my head.

My body twists and turns of its own accord as I follow the orders.

"Two shots, straight in front, now!"

Not being able to hear the flight of my shots leave the bow or know if they've hit their target is one of the most distressing things about this. I'm so cut off from the world my knees start to shake and buckle.

"Kyu!"

Six arrows down, four left. Just try and remember what Sis taught you and you'll get through this.

"Kyu, above your head, then 55 and 45!"

"I only have one left, please make it worth it," I yell silently into the aether.

Miyu's voice comes back with an affirmation, but even the voice she projects into my mind is breathy and tired. A few seconds pass with nothing but silence. Eerie silence. Scary silence.

"Now...now Kyu..."

Miyu's voice struggles into my head directly, every word seemingly more difficult than the last.

"Straight...in front. Put everything into it."

I push new strength into my legs and stand again, pulling Tenshi's string back as far back as I can, and after a brief hesitation my hand lets go of the string.

"M...Miyu?" I ask to the world, with nothing in return.

There's a sense of pressure against my leg as I collapse down to the floor, crashing painlessly into the desks and chairs behind me.

"Miyu?! Please God let it be you."

"It's...over...Kyu."

"What does that mean? Where's Ramiel?"

I scrabble around on the floor looking for something, an arrow to fire, or Miyu's body. I resort to holding out Tenshi like a stick, swinging it back and forth as I await something to happen. Something grabs me from behind and I yell, viciously swinging my bow. I panic as Miyu's voice sears into my brain. It might be the last time I ever hear it.

"Kyu..." she says before the voice cuts out.

"Miyu!" I shout as loud as I can muster.

Chapter 14

There's grass around me again. The memory of the chomping sound of teeth on bone and sinew still haunts me. I can hear it ringing through the air from all around, surrounding me. I walk forward but nothing changes. A fog settles in the air, bringing the sound along on the wisps that roll through the field which stretches out to eternity in every direction. I walk, and I walk, and I walk until time ceases to have any meaning and lethargy overtakes me. There's nothing here. Nothing at all. I can't tell if nothing is better or worse than a monster.

***

A heart monitor cuts into my consciousness as I start to stir back to reality. My mind is hazy but the sound piercing through my ears is welcoming. Relief floods through my body. I put a hand to my forehead and feel bandages. I open my eyes, blinking in the harsh white light and try to focus on what's in front of me. For now, that is the long plastic tube going into my hand via a large needle. Nausea overcomes me and I lean over to vomit painfully down the side of my bed. My head is swimming as I look down fuzzily at the scars reaching up my legs until they disappear under my hospital gown.

I turn over to avoid the stench and the beautifully framed features of Miyu come into view in the bed next to me. She's sleeping, face like an angel, a thought that makes me exhale loudly. She's far more beautiful, honest, and true than any of the Angels I've met. Keiko's brutal violence, Hashimoto's intrusiveness, Hiroshi's deep-set depression, even Michihara's short shrift and uncaring attitude. Satoshi is the only one who seems to have even a shred of normality and decency about him. But Miyu is a true angel. She saved me from Lailah, she helped me beat the Denier brothers and now if she's here and alive she must have beaten Ramiel. All this for me, someone who has caused her so much pain. Why would she do it? I need to find out what happened to my sister, but Miyu? She doesn't have any reason to come along with me. Every time she comes to save me she gets hurt.

Suddenly the image of her and Satoshi kissing floods into my mind. Seeing her luscious lips on his and her body enveloped in his arms brings tears to my eyes. She just needs me to get to Satoshi. That's it. What was it, something about creating a powerful child together? Once they're together they can carry on their amazing genetic lines and protect the human race better than I can. Once she has him I'll be discarded.

I turn back, disgusted at both my own thoughts and the horrible smell that accompanies the other side of my bed. The door slams open and the sound of multiple pairs of footsteps scares the sadness back to its hidey-hole my mind. Michihara yanks at my eyes to check them while Hashimoto and Tachibana stand at the foot of my bed, muttering to each other. Michihara checks down my body before whispering something to Tachibana. Hashimoto then glances to his grey haired, one-eyed assistant who nods to him.

"Welcome back Sasaki," Hashimoto says, "it's good to see you back up and more like your old self."

"What happened?" I ask, groggily.

"We were hoping you could tell us that. We found your friend Yamamoto chained to Ramiel with an arrow piercing through both their chests. You were the only other one there."

What? No...

"I must say Sasaki, I would never have put you down as someone who would go through their own friend to get the enemy."

"No! I would never," I shout hoarsely.

"Well, I think we can safely assume it was you. I'm impressed with your single mindedness. I knew it was right to bring you on board with us."

I clutch at my chest with words of anger stuck in my throat. How could Miyu do this to me?! She made me blind and then used me to hurt her. Inside my head there's a horrendous scream of earth-shattering proportions, but nothing comes out of my open mouth.

I fall out of bed, ripping the needle out of my hand and spraying blood on the floor before jumping onto Miyu's prone body. Straddling her hips, I grasp her shoulders and start shaking her. Then the words come flowing like vomit from my throat, covered in bile and viciousness.

"How could you?! How could you sacrifice yourself again?! I told you not to do that. I told you. I fucking told you! You have so much to live for and now you've made me take that away from you!"

The tears roll from my eyes onto her unconscious face as I'm overcome with emotion. The shaking dislodges her sheets, revealing the arrow wound through her upper chest. The sight overwhelms my mind, causing me to freeze. I can't even keep myself up anymore as I bury my head in her neck and wrap my arms around her. Even in a hospital she smells so wonderful.

"Please, please Miyu, please..."

A flash of light in the room accompanies my body being jerked upwards as I'm torn away from her by Tachibana. Miyu remains unconscious despite the disturbance but disappears as I'm spun around and placed on my feet directly in front of Hashimoto. Blood drips from the gash on my hand as he towers over me. Looking back to where Tachibana was is now the single tallest and greyest thing I've ever seen, full of intensity but looking like a statue. Her long, flowing grey curls reach down her full-length dress of the same colour. A bandage across both her eyes surrounds her gaunt face and pallid skin. She must be at least eight feet tall, her head reaching the light fixtures. Her wings are grey too, but barely poking over her shoulders. Even with the bandage over her eyes I get the feeling she's staring right at me. I focus on the floor, concentrating on the small pool of blood on the tiles.

"This is Puriel, the Examiner of Souls. She's someone who could almost match me on her day."

Her eyeless gaze looks to his face and even I can sense the strong bond between the two. Now that I think about it I've never seen Hashimoto without Tachibana beside him. I turn to go back to Miyu's side as the guilt courses through me, but as soon as I do Puriel reaches an extremely long arm out and lifts me into the air with one hand. She's nothing but skin on bone but seems to have a massive amount of strength. She drops me right back down in the exact spot I was, without ever saying a word.

"She can see me?"

"Yes. She is justice, she judges everyone and can see everyone, nothing is off limits to her. Now listen Sasaki, your friend isn't dead. We have healed her while we were reconnecting your entire nervous system back up to your brain. She'll be alright, I promise, but we cannot have you losing yourself like that. You are an Angel; you are a member of our team. You must do what the others do and work together to achieve our goals without your petty, selfish ideals getting in the way."

"P...petty?" I stammer in shock.

"Yes. However much you feel for this person she is just a human being, admittedly one who is particularly skilled in arts we thought were dead, but a human being, nonetheless. She's an insignificant speck in the grand scheme of the Universe. She will die when her time comes and the world will move on, but her time is not now.

"But you, you are an Angel, Sasaki. We are everlasting! We are eternal! And we are here to fulfil our purpose to protect the human race. Right now, that is under threat from the Fallen.

I'm delighted at your progress and the fact you've helped us take out a number of them already, but their ranks will grow unless we destroy them completely."

How can someone who wants to protect humans think that the lives of them are insignificant?

"We must deal with the remaining Fallen Sasaki, before they deal with all of us, including Yamamoto. They are weakened from your assault, and we must land the finishing blow. Do you understand that?"

I pause, leaving the silence filling the room as thoughts race through my mind.

"And what about my sister, Hashimoto? Was she just an insignificant speck on the world too?"

"Except for the Angels and for the Lord himself, all things are low beings. Our job is to protect them as a whole because they need protecting. The fact that they are weak and cannot do it themselves reminds me every day of their inferiority."

His words make my blood boil in an instant. In the split second, before my body can react to strike him, Puriel's arms reach out and wrap around me. Her grip is ironclad, restraining me with the strength of a thousand chains.

"The Fallen killed your sister because they hate humans. They want to see them gone Sasaki."

"But why her?"

Seething with anger I hear the dusty voice of Puriel drift from over my head. It sounds like a library whispering at me.

"We can still find out why they did it. The leader of the Fallen is a meticulous person who plans every move."

"It wasn't an accident?"

"Everything they do is part of their plan, and if he had anything to do with it, which I suspect he did, then he will have a reason. I will face him eventually and judge his actions when his time comes, but for now if we capture him you will have your answer Sasaki."

The whole thing leaves me feeling confused. A plan? They killed her, murdered her! They decimated my family and my home. They destroyed my mother, father, and me. What could they have done it for? Something is going on and I will find out what it is. It doesn't matter what the Angels are doing, or what Satoshi and Miyu will do, I will go after the remaining Fallen and get them to explain what they did. I must have my answer.

"How many are left?"

"Unless they have recruited anyone else then it will only be their leader," Puriel says quietly, "there was a lieutenant but we believe he's already dead."

"What do mean recruit? What are they doing?"

"Sasaki, why do you think that we have such a massive supply of udomite under this hospital?" Hashimoto enquires.

I think back and remember the cavern where I fought with Ariel and Barachiel. It was filled floor to ceiling with the crystalline material. After a few more seconds of silence, he answers his own question.

"Udomite is powerful, as you can tell from the medication. It can heal, it can help suppress negative emotions, and it can also mutate a human's body on a sub-cellular level. We found that by exposing enough udomite to the right conditions we were able to make a stone that allowed us to connect with our ethereal beings. We call it a genesis shard, and when people are exposed to them under certain circumstances they can become angelic beings, or under lesser circumstances they can become mutated into the things you have encountered. We're all linked to it on a deep, deep level Sasaki. It connects us all.

"But if the Fallen had enough udomite and enough power they could make multiple genesis shards, distribute them through the world and transmute innocent people into beasts. We must protect the supply of the mineral so that they cannot get their hands on it. Once they have been vanquished, we can release it upon the world and solve so many of the problems in society. We can turn the human beings into an enlightened race with knowledge and purpose."

Thoughts run through my head one after another. Humanity would probably be fine regardless. If you take all the pain and sorrow I've experienced in the past few years and multiply it by all the billions of people in the world then its...scary, but despite all of that humanity continues on. People go to work and love their families. They learn and experience and grow. They hurt and hate and succeed and fail on their own.

"How long will it be before Miyu can come with me?"

"I don't think she will be conscious again for another day or two Sasaki," Hashimoto says with his hand on his chin.

"Let me go after the leader then."

"You will not be able to do anything alone Sasaki. Your power doesn't seem to be fully under control yet and that's dangerous. We can't risk losing you to them."

"Well, what about you and Puriel? Or Ariel and Barachiel?"

I say the last pair of names through gritted teeth. I don't want to team up with them but if it lets me go after this guy then they're better than nothing. Hashimoto looks up at Puriel who shakes her head gently, her grey curls and wings moving ever so slightly.

"We haven't heard from them for 24 hours now, we don't know where they are. And Puriel is needed here with me. Just go home and wait for our clarion call Sasaki. When we are ready, we will go get him. You can have your answers and we'll destroy him, along with their remaining threat."

No. I must go. I must go tonight. I must find the leader and make him talk. I make a move towards the door when Hashimoto grasps my shoulder with an iron grip.

"Do not go after him on your own Sasaki. That is an order, do I make myself clear?"

I challenge him by forcing myself to look into his powerful eyes. Flames lick around the edge of my vision as his gaze bores into me, but there is one overriding thought in my mind. I do not take orders from you.

"Yes."

With a flash of light Puriel is gone and Tachibana is back again in her stead. The two of them walk out of the room and close the door in complete silence. I decide against going home and instead go and sit on the bed next to Miyu. I raise my hand to touch her arm through the covers, but something makes me pause. After a few seconds the nerves relent and I squeeze her shoulder. Her soft breathing causes her body to shift almost imperceptibly under my touch.

"I'm sorry Miyu, I need to do this now. I must find out what happened. I know you can't be there to protect me but I have to do this anyway."

I let the silence roll in as I sling Tenshi painfully over my shoulder. I stand up and look at Miyu again. She's so beautiful, I just want to kiss her and to make her safe, but not a single muscle moves in my body. A sense of worthlessness rolls into my consciousness. How could I even think that I'm worthy of touching such an amazing person. I try to conjure up the Angel within me to protect me from the terrible feelings but nothing comes. I defeated Ramiel so at least that monster should be gone from my head. Maybe I'm truly alone now. Maybe now it's just me, no Angel, no monster.

I look down at Miyu again to try and steel myself but instead horrible thoughts pass through my mind. What if she hates me for going off on my own? What if her and Satoshi leave me? What if the Angels forbid me from seeing either of them because I'm going against Hashimoto's orders? My brain lingers on the last one as I take five more pills so I can get over the pain in my head as well as from the cuts and bruises all over me. I take a deep breath at the door before sliding it open and striding out of the room.

The hospital almost feels like a second home to me now. I've spent so much time here recently that I've come to be able to find my way through the corridors without thinking. As I reach the front entrance a large set of electric doors slide open, blasting my face with a cold breeze that whips my clothes around.

I start walking through the streets, feeling the wind blow about me. I know I told Hashimoto that I wouldn't go after the Fallen leader, but I feel an urge within me to chase. I'm getting closer to the truth, I swear. With the monster gone from within me I can see more clearly now. When I confront the leader of the Fallen I will get what I want, answers.

Above me the sky is swiftly turning a shade of bright pink as the sun descends to the horizon. The thoughts of finality come back to me. Yes. I will go tonight because otherwise I won't get another chance. But where? Where could this Fallen leader possibly be? I linger on the thought for a few seconds in the middle of the pavement as people stream past me.

Distracted, I reach round to my arrows and count them. Eight. That's not enough, I'm certain I'll need more. I need to be less conspicuous too, and warmer. I better go home and stock up before heading out.

As the distance between the hospital and home passes under my feet I find myself idly thinking about everything that has happened recently. The people I've met, the things I've done, the people I've...killed. My life has been turned completely upside down and I hate it. I don't want to be a killer, or a monster. Sadness fills my heart as I think of the people that came to harm at the end of my bow. Ramiel, Munkir, Nakir, Miyu, Lailah, all of them met the point of my arrows whether I wanted it to happen or not. I pierced each one of their skins and each memory pierces my heart commensurately, but Miyu more so than any of them.

I grimace as pain floods my chest. Miyu, why did you have to make me hurt you? Why couldn't I have been stronger and better? Why couldn't I have avoided it? I can't bear the feeling of self-hatred that courses through me. Hatred at myself for being so weak. Miyu, Sis, I could have saved you without any of this if only I was just that little bit better. The negative emotions feel like roiling clouds within my soul as they take hold of me. It feels like they're filling me up and draining the energy out of my body.

By the time I make it home I'm stumbling on shaky legs. I walk through the door and slip my shoes off, expecting to be greeted by someone but the silence shouts loudly into the evening. No one is even in? I've been gone days! I'm injured! I nearly died and yet no one even cares? Where the hell are my parents? And just like that something snaps in me, like a black hole has formed in my brain and is sucking everything in. Thoughts, emotions, hatred, anger, depression, sadness, it all disappears into the abyss. I begin to move as if in a trance. Staring into the distance unblinkingly, I enter the house. No. One. Cares. The stairs drop away as I move upwards. No one here. I feel like things aren't real. I've been deserted by everyone.

In my room I go to my closet and pick up a black cloak, wrapping it around my shoulders awkwardly. It's not fashionable but it keeps me warm and allows me to still fire arrows. I fill my quiver to bursting point from the stash in my closet before swinging it back into position. I can't even feel the weight on my back as I reattach the chain.

I move back downstairs to the door slowly, the rattle of arrows filling my blank mind. A crunching replaces it when I chew on another handful of pills. Everything I do is unthinking as I find myself at the front door. The darkness has rolled over the world, bringing with it a deep yellow hidden behind dark clouds.

I pull up the hood of the cloak and dash out into the night, letting my body go where it wants to. Something is driving me forward, something in the back of my mind making me twist and turn through the city. I let it take me, until I turn down a side street and realise that there's nothing but tall buildings, broken windows and unkept roads. This is the industrial area of the city, the place where my sister was taken.

Once I realise where my soul has been driving me I push it harder, my feet clacking against the road and the arrows knocking against each other underneath the cloak. There are no cars passing, no people on the streets, just the wind whistling through old, abandoned buildings. Another corner passes behind me and I arrive at the spot. This is it. This is where she was taken from us. I kneel down to catch my breath and stroke the rough tarmac as memories and feelings coming flooding back to me. Imagining the clouds as they were that night, the echoes of my mother's tears sound in my brain.

The wind picks up again, the cloak billowing around me as I stand up and look around. A building site, a car park with two burned out cars in it, and what looks like an old factory that's falling apart. A thought at the edge of my brain finally filters into my mind: what was my sister doing here? I circle the whole area but there's nothing of interest here. Why have I never thought of this before? There isn't anything that would give her a reason to be here. Why did my mother never think about what the hell happened? A hit and run, here of all places?

As the thoughts flow, I suddenly realise that grief must have overtaken both of us at the time, but this place has been deserted for years at this point. Was she bought here after something happened elsewhere? Or was she here doing something, or meeting someone? My sister was never the kind to hide things, she didn't go out and get in to trouble and she never snuck out or missed school.

The hairs stand up on my neck and my stomach curl up; something isn't right here, and no one has ever even questioned it. Maybe if I can find out what she was doing here then it may lead me to who did this and why. The wind is getting stronger now, like there's a storm on the way.

I decide to start my search indoors, but the giant entrance doors to the abandoned factory are locked with a massive chain and thick padlock. I think about getting Tenshi out, but I don't think I'd be able to break a chain like that without an Angels help. I walk around the building but don't see any other doors that I might be able to use. The clouds are starting to swirl above me as if they're angrily fighting with each other. As the first drops of rain start to fall on me I spot the tunnel in the building site opposite me. There are two lights still lit above its entrance and it look likes it descends downwards into the earth underneath the scaffolding, so I dash for it as the rain starts to come down hard. Shelter will do for now. I'd rather be in here than caught in this storm.

The rain echoes through the cave as I reach the inside, pulling my hood down and catching my breath. I stick my head out and a massive drop of rain that had been saving itself especially for me flops down from the interlocking iron girders above straight onto my forehead. It looks like they were halfway through building something here and then just stopped. The ground outside looks like it was the start of the foundations but there's just sand, uneven concrete blocks and broken beams littering the place now.

Turning back to the tunnel it's dark but dimly lit by a few small lanterns, which is odd in and of itself. Around my feet there's a large amount of sand, as if it's been dragged in from outside.

"Hello?"

I call down the tunnel gently, my voice echoing around me. No answer, nothing but myself. I straighten up and realise the roof is lower than I thought. The walls are really close too, not more than the width of a couple of people. The stone should be rough but it feels smooth like marble, so smooth as to almost feel wet. I shift my arm slightly and silently unsling Tenshi from underneath my cloak. Using the end of his frame I can follow the floor like a blind person with a cane.

With one hand on the smooth marble-like wall and Tenshi in my other, I start to take a few tentative steps into the darkness. The clacking of Tenshi's frame against the floor echoes with my slow, methodical footsteps as the light begins to disappear behind me. A flash of lightning illuminates the cave mouth and a roll of thunder crashes over my shoulders. The thunder is so strong I swear I can feel the earth moving under my feet.

I pause until the shaking feeling stops before moving with more confidence, following the path as it trends downwards, doubling back on itself. The walls close in, bringing the darkness closer somehow, like a cloying heat on my shoulders. The beginnings of claustrophobia kick in as my breathing rate increases and my heart beats faster. I come to a narrow turning and realise that it isn't dark anymore. After a total absence of light, it seems almost alien to see the dim, purple light shining against the wall. I adjust my grip on my weapon to bring it up to my side, not that I could fire it in this enclosed space. I reach back slowly and pull an arrow from my quiver, holding it in my hand like a knife. It'll do in an emergency; the tips are razor sharp.

The purple light is upon me now. There's a shadow flickering within it and my chest starts to tense up. I pause for as long as I can, taking breaths as deep and quiet as my lungs allow. The anxiety is in full flight now. I need to get out. I need to go right now. I can't breathe. I turn on my heel to run out but before my foot even hits the floor a voice rings out, causing me to freeze entirely.

Chapter 15

"You, eh, you killed her, didn't you?"

The voice wheezes at me, sounding old and dusty. I manage to unfreeze my body enough to take one step backwards before the voice returns.

"Don't leave Sasaki. Please, come and sit with me for a bit."

The panic in my brain sets my thoughts racing. If he is the leader of the Fallen then there's no point in coming all this way not to stay and face him. I need my answers, and above all he has to hear my questions. He might attack me and kill me right here. If he's the leader of this group he must be pretty damn powerful, and I'm definitely not in my element trapped so far down here in such a small space. But if he wanted me dead he could have already killed me by now, so he must want me alive. He wants me to talk.

I slowly move towards the purple glow spilling around the corner. Before I face him, I pause and consider the weapons I have to hand: a bow I can't fire and arrows I can't hide. One arrow I can use as a stabbing implement but that's really not enough to go against the most powerful Fallen. It'll have to do though. I emerge around the corner and come face to face with the voice for the first time. It belongs to a wiry and tired looking old man sitting in a low chair. He's balding, with white hair around his temples as if his head was rising through a cloud. The purple light that I saw is shining from the object in his hands. He's twirling it slowly between his arthritic fingers, causing the light to dance and float about in the small space. It lights up the coat and long, flared sleeves that cover most of his body. He turns his thin and wrinkled face up to me through the purple light.

"Sit with me" he says, gesturing to the empty chair next to my leg.

I attempt to sit down but only end up knocking the chair with my quiver. A chuckle escapes his lips.

"Please put your weapons down Sasaki. I promise you that you won't need them where we are now. You could probably outrun me on your hands and knees if I did try and attack you. Put them down against that wall, I think we should just sit and talk for a bit."

I hesitate, but he really does look old and decrepit. I put the quiver down gently against the wall with a few clinks and put Tenshi next to it, making sure they're all within an arm's reach at least.

"Thank you for joining me Sasaki. I know this place will probably make you feel a bit uncomfortable but I'm, eh, afraid cafés and restaurants are few and far between in our part of the world," he says, letting out another small chuckle. "You must feel like a caged bird in here, but at least we are safe from the storm outside. I would not want you to attempt to escape through the bars and end up having your wings shredded. It's quiet down here don't you think Sasaki? Considering we are only twenty feet down you cannot hear a thing of the world outside."

"Yes, it's very quiet."

"And lonely," he says, continuing the sentence I thought I'd finished, "yes, eh, this is a very quiet and lonely place now Sasaki. Only a few weeks ago it was bustling with my friends. We were full of life and variety, but now you have shown up, gotten yourself involved in our business, and within that short space of time I find myself here on my own."

He sounds hurt but there is a wry smile on his face. His hands are still for a moment as he trails off into silence. The purple glow illuminates his face from underneath in a creepy way, leaving the shadows floating across his brow.

"Do you know what this is Sasaki?"

I think a bit before I answer.

"Can I see it please?"

He pauses for a good few seconds longer than I expect before leaning across and handing the object to me. A creak of the chair, or possibly his spine, echoes in the room as he sits back and I start turning the thing over in my hands. As I flip it slowly the gem embedded in it reflects the meagre light in here but concentrates it to the point that it blinds me. It's a choker.

"This is Ramiel's isn't it? She had one very similar on her the last time I saw her."

"Yes, it is. In fact, it's the one she wore right up until you killed her."

I startle slightly at the direct accusation, but I can't do anything but look down at the floor. I know that I can't deny it, however much Miyu was ordering me around at the time. I have to tilt the light away from my face so that this man won't be able to see the sadness in my eyes.

"I didn't want to," I say as I hand the choker back to him.

An uncomfortable silence fills the cave as I wipe the moisture from my eyes.

"Oh, don't worry, eh, I know you didn't."

The surprise of this admission stops my emotions in their tracks. Looking into his highlighted face I can't tell what kind of emotion he's feeling.

"I know that you didn't want to kill my friends. It is obvious from your actions that you could not kill unless you were in a desperate position. Unfortunately, *they* keep putting you into those positions, don't they?"

"Who?"

"The Angels."

He seems so calm and knowledgeable, despite talking about the death of his friends at the hands of his enemies. I shouldn't have expected any less from the leader of the Fallen.

"It is them isn't it Sasaki?"

I nod carefully which elicits a sigh from my host.

"I knew it was going to happen as soon as you were taken in by them that night at the hospital."

"How do you know I was at the hospital with them?"

"I have been using my powers to, eh, let's say, keep tabs on you. I was in the hospital that day when you were brought in." His fingers clasp around the choker and grip it tightly as he sighs again. "I guess I should introduce myself properly. My name is Miyake Fumio. I hope that the name stays in your mind for a long, long time."

"And you seem to know me already?"

"Oh, I know you better than you would expect Sasaki. I was in your room when you woke up in the hospital with Yamamoto at your side."

I riffle through my memory to what feels like so long ago. I remember the white lights and seeing Miyu's face lit up by the sunset from the big window. I remember the night terrors and the Angel monster attacking me as I struggled through the grass of my dreams. But most of all I remember the pain, the scything, wretched, mind shattering pain that ran through my body back then.

"Some form of disguise? Were you one of the doctors?"

"Mm, a good, eh, a good first guess. Try again."

I sit and think for a moment. I've just got to get rid of what is impossible and concentrate on what's left, however unlikely.

"Some kind of camouflage ability? Hiding against a wall or a window?"

This draws a raspy chuckle from his throat, the sagging skin under his chin wobbling slightly.

"Close, I'll give you one more guess."

Ok, I've got to think this through. How else could he have gotten in? Was he in the ceiling somewhere? Or have some kind of device that allowed him to spy on the room? No, he implied he was actually there which would rule out using a video camera or a tracker.

"If you were there, but your power stops us from seeing you, then you must be able to absorb light and stop it being reflected."

He laughs loudly and claps his hands a few times.

"Excellent! You're wrong but you are so close that I will give it to you anyway. Your intelligence is as good as we were led to believe. I can bend light around me, so in fact I was standing in that room right next to Yamamoto as you spoke to her."

I knew there was something wrong with the light in that room. Just for a second I swear I saw something, some kind of distortion!

"Why were you there?"

"I told you; I was keeping tabs on you. We knew that they wanted you for themselves to further their power. We needed to know what was happening."

"You were spying on me so you could try and kill me, weren't you?"

"What?"

"You have been trying to wipe out the Angels so you can enslave the human race and destroy everyone else."

Another long sigh escapes his lips as he sits back in the chair and puts his hand to his eyes, rubbing the bridge of his nose.

"Is that, eh, that what they told you?" He asks in a quiet voice. "Was it Hashimoto Shinsei that fed you that story?"

Before I can think it over he continues to fill the silence between us with his low, aged voice.

"I would expect nothing less from that despot."

"How do you know Professor Hashimoto?"

Another long pause passes between us before Miyake looks up at me from underneath his brow. Even I can tell that the seriousness in his look almost verges on shock.

"Didn't he tell you that we all know him? We were all together at one point, in the beginning. I wonder what else he is not telling you?"

He may well be lying. I need to know. Why would Hashimoto keep such an important piece of information from me?

"Will you trust my words if I tell you more? I know that you have are a naturally cynical soul and you think I am your 'enemy'."

He moves his hands to put the inverted commas around the word enemy, making his joints crack painfully. Everything he has done up to now has been peaceful, but he's right.

"I will tell you whether I trust you after I've heard what you have to say."

Silence fills the cave, interrupted only by the occasional whistling of the storm echoing down the halls.

"Who do you think we are?" Miyake asks eventually.

"Hashimoto said you were a group trying to destroy the Angels and the human race."

"That is partially correct I guess. But those people that you killed and those you are working for were all together on the same project when we were created."

The word 'killed' spikes through my chest like a dart again. I try and excuse myself by repeating that I was forced into all of those situations, but ultimately I know I'm a murderer. I grip my chest hard to try and make the pain go away.

"There was an accident at the hospital, in the lab that I'm sure you've been in, caused by the udomite. Even with the, eh, the tiny amount we had back then it was enough to be powerful, enormously powerful. We found out that it had its fantastical properties, and we were all so excited! It seemed too good to be true. We found more of it under the hospital, so we dug down and captured and stored more of it. The advances we made in those initial months were more than anything we had managed to do in years up to that point."

"And you were there were you?" Maybe I can catch him out if he is lying.

"Yes I was Sasaki. I was there with the whole team."

"Who?" I ask quickly.

"What?"

"Who was there with you?" I ask, keeping up the assault to try and get him to slip.

"Hashimoto, Tachibana, the Kagawas, the Furukawas, the Tsumura brothers, myself, my partner, and a couple of others."

I realise it's a stupid question because I have no idea who half these people are. But he does know the names of the Angels and if he was lying he probably wouldn't have encountered them in human form.

"You wouldn't know the Tsumura brothers by name Sasaki, you would have only encountered them as Munkir and Nakir, but they were actually Tsumura Mitsuharu and Tsumura Matsuharu. Twin brothers born to a Swiss father and a Japanese mother. They grew up in London with some of the best schooling around. They were brilliant minds and yet now you have taken their knowledge and power away from us."

"And your partner?"

"Oh, you know her for sure. Mazaki Tami was one of the, eh, the greatest young scientists of her generation. She was a genuine wonder in this world. She graduated university at the age of fifteen and when she joined us I was assigned to her but within a year she was the one teaching me."

"I don't know her."

"Yes, you do," he says with his head bowed before raising the choker at me, "that was hers."

"Ramiel? *She* was your partner?"

"Mazaki and I worked together for a long time. We were awfully close, but now..."

I tense up, fear bubbling away in my stomach at the thought of what he might do if he blames me for her death. Slowly Miyake rises off his chair, his head reaching all the way up into the dark shadows above my head. He's looming over me like the grim reaper come for his subject. Get my arrows and run, yes, that has to be the way. All I have to do is make an opening for myself.

"Come with me Sasaki, let me show you something."

The attack I fear doesn't materialise; Miyake just stands there with one hand outstretched. I take it as he helps me to my feet, but as I reach for Tenshi his arm shoots across to block me.

"That won't be necessary Sasaki. You can pick those up on the way out."

"I...I must have them Miyake," I whisper.

Inside I can see an image of a younger me with tears in her eyes.

"Oh no, I must insist that you leave them here," he says forcefully.

His left hand is gripping the choker harder now, the strain on his skin obvious even in the pale light.

"Can I bring my bow but leave the arrows here please? It's the only link I have left to my sister...surely you can understand?"

He seems to consider this for a moment, probably trying to imagine what harm I could do without anything to fire. Without saying anything, the hand blocking my way drops to his side. I quickly grab Tenshi and breathe a huge sigh of relief. I'm not sure what I can do if Miyake unleashes himself at me but at least I have a chance now.

He turns out of the niche and I follow closely behind him. The tunnel has some very dim light bulbs hung off the walls at distressingly long intervals. Luckily, Miyake Fumio is an old man and only manages a slow gait as our path starts to head downwards again. The walk leads us to a spiral staircase that has been roughly hewn in the stone. The uneven stairs are a horrid trip hazard as I struggle my way down them, while Miyake easily navigates himself around. My own clothing is making the journey a sweaty and muggy experience in the underground. It was cold and windy outside but now there is nothing but heat and pressure. I finally catch up to him at the bottom of the spiral and take a moment to catch my breath in the oppressive air.

Chapter 16

"What is this place?" I pant at the stationary figure.

He turns to me with arms outstretched and a big, genuine smile on his face.

"This is my home Sasaki! Welcome to the, eh, the world's first udomite mine!"

Behind Miyake spans an enormous cavern, far bigger even than the room under the hospital. Udomite crystals spike out from every surface. The whole place is lit with the same shade of eerie purple light which illuminated our little chat in the alcove. In the middle of the floor is the source of the light. It's a giant, rough-hewn lump of opaque udomite, just like the one that was in the Sanctum. The surface shimmers and glows into a million shades that range through violet, blue and black. Its light is just enough to discern a sense of scale about the place, but it's unfathomably large. There're metal struts embedded in the ground everywhere, coiled with crystalline udomite growing up them, but the walls and ceiling they're connected to disappear off into the blackness around us.

Despite being so big, the shards of crystal poking out of every surface make the place seem packed. The purple light bounces through and off them in every direction, making it hard to discern what is and isn't real, like a hall of mirrors. In one corner there are small, symbolic gestures towards life continuing here such as chairs, tables, and papers strewn around.

"Do you like it?"

He walks over to the bright stone in the middle of the floor. When he puts his hand on it the colours react to his touch, chasing and swirling around in a chaotic maelstrom. The shading flickers under his wrinkled chin, making his face light up in a disturbing way.

"Do you like it? This was our base, but as you can see now it is just me. Me on my own. Just me. How can I continue without the others?"

His head drops and his shoulders shake as silence fills the space between us. He looks like he's crying but it could just be a trick of the light. I really don't know how to deal with this. I don't have any support without Miyu, without my Angel, without my arrows, without my sister. How can I be expected to deal with all this stuff that has been dropped upon me?

I take a few steps towards him and a sound that is definitely sobbing filters through to me. Gently I reach up behind him and go to put my arm on his shoulder, and after a moment's hesitation I pat him gently. I circle around the glowing stone so that I can get a better look. When my hand approaches the surface the colours erupt like a tsunami towards me and my arm is flung backwards. The shock travels up my arm and makes me grimace in pain.

"Don't try to touch it!" Miyake yells.

In a brief second he grabs me by the shoulder, forcefully pushing me away from the stone. The sheer surprise that an old man can have such speed and strength makes the tingling sensation in my arm drift away for a bit, but it soon comes back.

"How dare you try to touch our genesis shard! It is ours and ours alone!"

"The Angels have one that looks similar, what is it?" I ask.

Miyake's voice is already louder and more strained than it was before. I really can't risk him getting angry.

"What? You don't even know? What the hell has Hashimoto told you?"

Not much now that I think about it.

"He mentioned a genesis shard but didn't tell me what it was."

"Why are you even fighting with them? Why are you siding with a group you know almost nothing about?"

I drop my head to my chest as I think about it, but the reason I fight has always been the same. It is for my sister and for my friend. Because it's right to protect them. I look into his eyes and remember my purpose.

"I don't fight with them. I have a reason to fight and we happen to have a common enemy in you."

"I am not your enemy. You are mistaken in your beliefs. You have been led here to do their work for them. Hashimoto has manipulated you."

If I tell him that I'm here on my own then it will weaken my position. He will know no one will come looking for me. Time to deflect. I lever Tenshi into my hand and point it towards the stone, making sure to keep a fair distance away from Miyake.

"What exactly is a genesis shard? Why does yours look different to theirs?"

"You really don't know anything do you Sasaki?"

He stands up straight and breathes deeply. The colours in the stone slowly settle back down. I return Tenshi to my shoulder and cross my arms.

"How do you think we were created?"

"An accident involving udomite."

"We were conducting an experiment in the lab…eh, the Sanctum as we called it. All of us. That includes all your so-called allies and all of my friends. Our goal was to take the temporary effects of the mineral and manufacture it into something that could affect people permanently. Something that would transform humanity and lead us to a new age of enlightenment and happiness."

"And the accident?"

"Yes, something went wrong. I was leading the team that was monitoring the experiment alongside Mazaki and the rest of my friends, while the others were working with the material itself."

He pauses and closes his eyes at the mention of her name. Her choker has been in his hands this whole time. He twiddles it between his fingers before gripping it hard again.

"The experiment involved focussing sunlight with mirrors down from the roof and into a sample of udomite, trying to amplify it's capabilities. Something went wrong with our calculations and the light ended up reflecting off every surface in the lab and off every sample of udomite we had until it fed into the experimental core. There was an explosion, a massive one. It ripped through everyone, leaving twisted metal and glass everywhere. So much of our equipment got destroyed, but there sitting in the middle of the floor was the genesis shard."

"Was anyone hurt?"

"Yes, there were injuries, bad ones, especially to Kagawa. There was so much blood on the floor...but I was responsible for setting up those mirrors Sasaki. I was, eh, I was the one that made the mistake. The injuries were my fault. People were on the floor dying because of my error. I still think of it every time I close my eyes."

He puts his hands up to cover his face as he tails off.

"But no one was killed?" I push.

Then he raises his head to the ceiling, hands clasped in a position of prayer.

"No, no one was killed that day thank God. By the time help had made it down to our lab the injuries had already started to heal. Cuts were closing up, blood was drying and bones were knitting back together. We had no idea, eh, what was happening. It was miraculous, but it didn't make the guilt go away. You already know that guilt can be a powerful force."

I nod softly in appreciation.

"No one died that day in the lab but it did set us on the course we are now. That accident created the Angels. They began to come out from their hosts, starting with Meta from within Hashimoto. He spoke to us with a voice of magic and presence. He spoke of ultimate power, and of the responsibilities that came with it. He gestured to the remnant of the experiment and declared that it was what had allowed them to come into being. He called it the genesis shard and said it had called him through to this world and that we could use it to call others.

"Soon him, Puriel and Lailah began using the shard to begin to draw the Angels out of the rest of the members who had been seriously injured that day. But he didn't do it to any of us."

"Wait, Lailah was there? What was her Angel called?"

He gazes at me with a look of puzzlement.

"I think you, eh, are mistaken Sasaki. Lailah was the Angel. She was the Angel that resided in Komoda Yusuke, an immensely bright girl. She was a wonderful scientist."

Her face wanders through my mind and I scrunch my eyes shut to try and force it out again. The memory of her breath in my ear and her honey like voice seducing me make electricity flow through my body. My toes curl up in my shoes and my hands grip my cloak hard at my sides.

"What happened to you on that day?"

There's another pause, longer than before this time. I'm just about to repeat myself but he breaks the awkward moment.

"Nothing."

"What?"

"Nothing happened to me, nothing happened to Mazaki, nothing happened to any of us who were working outside of the main chamber."

I pause, staring at genesis shard underneath his ashen face.

"Why did you repeat the experiment Miyake?"

He looks up at me, the darkness flickering around him like candlelight.

"You are a shock aren't you? Considering how little you've been told I'm surprised you worked that out."

"I just, yeh, er, worked it out I guess."

He looks at me carefully and for long enough to make me start feeling really uncomfortable. My hands twitch and pull at my cloak nervously.

"I see," Miyake eventually says very slowly, "well, eh, why do you think we repeated it?"

I continue to look at the floor. I can't bring myself to answer.

"When the Angels were coming out, those of us on the secondary team were angry and jealous. In the days and weeks that followed Hashimoto and the people following him became progressively more introverted and distant from us. They held secret meetings; they made plans without us. Some of us had been there from the start and we were getting shut out because of those elitists. They didn't want us. They saw themselves as above us as they learned more of their newfound powers. The teleportation, the flight, the strength, the regeneration.

"They started sending us out on missions to try and find more udomite. They were insistent that we needed more, that we needed to try and collect as much as possible so we could continue the various experiments. When out on one of these useless trips I remember the protestations that were thrown out by our group. We were people of science being wasted on a wild goose chase! You have to understand that we felt completely useless. We were being betrayed by those who we had considered our closest friends and colleagues up to only a few weeks before. Our work, to help humanity, was being taken away from us.

"Slowly the team's goals were pushed aside for finding more of this stuff. Our good intentions were being overrun by them and we had no idea what was going on! We were angry."

His voice has been getting louder. He seems like he's getting more out of control just remembering it.

"When we were done that night, another night of fruitless search, we had an argument about what we needed to do. We had reached our limits with the situation and ended up agreeing that we would confront Hashimoto and the rest of them. As the leader of our part of the group I was tasked with leading the charge back at them when we returned to the lab."

"How did it go?"

The reply comes slowly again, even slower than before.

"The argument was titanic. We demanded to be allowed to be brought into the experiments, to be turned in to Angels like they were. We just wanted to be their equals again! They paid some lip service to us, but it was obvious from the reactions that it wasn't going to happen."

"It sounds like it would be dangerous, maybe he just didn't want to put you through it?"

His look makes me realise that was probably the wrong thing to say.

"Really Sasaki? You really think so? We knew it was dangerous! But we were prepared to accept that! We wanted to have the experiences they had and be seen as their equals again. They didn't refuse because they wanted to protect us though, they said no because they were threatened by us. Hashimoto only ever used the genesis shard on those he saw as loyal to him. They saw us as an enemy and a risk to their power and we knew it. That was when things really got heated. Everyone was shouting at each other and nearly coming to blows, but we knew we couldn't win a fight, not a physical one at least," he pants, out of breath from his long recap.

"So, you repeated the experiment on your own?"

"We got together and decided that the plan was to repeat the process on our own, yes. We couldn't let them find out about us, so we did it in secret together. We gathered equipment, planned a place, but needed to get the udomite out. Hashimoto had that gigantic basement dug under the Sanctum to store all the stuff found. He did it soon after Meta had appeared for the first time, almost as if he knew that controlling the source of the stuff was important."

"Did you manage to get everything?"

Another fierce look.

"After many, many months we did. We had some of the smartest minds on the team so we had everything planned out within a few days. We knew we'd be able to pull it off as soon as we found a source of udomite. We continued the search at the behest of Hashimoto week after week, month after month. Until, eventually, we discovered this place!"

He throws his arms out, the light in the genesis shard rushing away from him.

"This is, eh, this is the largest deposit of udomite ever discovered. There was enough here to make hundreds of genesis shards and use them to allow millions join our cause! It was our ticket to freedom! We could finally see a way out! It was so wonderful seeing everyone smiling for the first time in months. We kept the udomite here while we returned to the lab 'empty handed' again. That night we snuck back down here and took our destiny into our own hands."

"How did you do it at night? Where did the light come from?"

"Because we couldn't do it during the day while we worked at the lab, we decided to use moonlight. The moon reflects sunlight does it not? With all of the equipment we had we could make it work. Everyone gathered around the udomite as we activated the machine that would rotate the mirrors into place and waited. Then it happened. The moment arrived. The clouds dissipated and we watched as the light funnelled through our systems. There was an explosion just like before. We were hurt badly but we had planned for it and had enough first aid materials to patch ourselves up enough to see what our efforts had created."

"Another genesis shard?" I ask, even though I know the answer.

"That's right. This! This, eh, beautiful piece of wonder! It spoke to us all that we had done something extraordinary. We all felt a connection to each other and to the shard. We knew we could use it to bring more people to us and give them the security that came with the strength we had unleashed."

"What? You wanted to create more Fallen? Did you want to make an army of monsters underneath you? There's enough here to cover everyone on the planet! You wanted to enslave the human race?"

"No girl! Not enslave. We wanted to bestow humans with the same strength we had. The Angels were dangerous and we needed to stop them. We wanted everyone to have the power to protect themselves, to experience the sublime connection to the world of the divine and to each other."

"Of course they were dangerous. To you! They weren't the ones going after humans and trying to forcibly convert them."

"I said we didn't want to force ourselves on them! We were finally Angels! We could be equals again!"

Silence fills the vacant cavern for a few seconds.

"But, you aren't Angels, are you?"

"We were so happy," he says wistfully, ignoring me.

"You aren't an Angel though, are you Miyake?"

His eyes snap on to me with a look of rage on his face.

"How dare you question us Sasaki," he shouts with a rasping voice, "how DARE you! What makes you so sure of that? We are connected to the divine world just like they are! What makes us any less pure than your precious masters? Our shard looks different and our forms are different but our methods are the same!"

"You're monsters."

I can't stop the words slipping out.

"Monsters?! We came about not by accident but our own efforts! We are as pure as any of that bunch of terrorists! All we wanted to do was our jobs!"

"What, your job of enslaving mankind? Of taking over the world and having it for yourself? Of forcing people to become like you? You're evil!"

Miyake pauses for a brief second, dropping Mazaki's choker to the floor. Before it even hits the ground he circles the genesis shard and leaps towards me with a terrifying speed. I raise Tenshi to try and deflect him but he bats him away with an arm. His hands clench around my throat, lifting me off the ground and slamming me against a wall with such force as to knock the wind out of me and sending jolts up and down my spine.

"Who do you think you are to talk to me like that? You killed my friends, you destroyed our plans and now you want to destroy our legacy, and you want to call me evil!"

His shouts are visceral as the words reverberate around us, vibrating their way through thousands of tonnes of udomite and into my ears. His hands squeeze harder and a gasp tries to escape through my closed throat. I kick and struggle, but I can't make him move an inch.

"Oh, don't bother trying to say anything. No more of your playing dumb! You're a damn liar Sasaki! You speak as if you don't know who I am, or what we are. You were sent on those missions by Hashimoto. He told you everything and you went out there with the intention of murdering them. You went out and you killed my friends! You killed them all by choice! You took them and now you're here for me! You killed Mazaki!"

My eyes are wide with pain and panic as my blood begins to deoxygenate, so I'm forced to see the tears roll from his eyes.

"You took my love from me!"

Even as he tries to strangle the life out of me I can't help but hate myself for what I've done. He's accusing me of doing exactly what I blame him for, so how am I any better? I deserve to die. I stop struggling against him and accept my fate. As soon as unconsciousness starts to drift over me his hands retract, dropping me to the ground. I gasp loudly, pulling as much air as I can through my damaged throat.

"I'm so sorry," I whisper hoarsely into the darkness.

Miyake crawls through the dirt to the choker on the floor, purple light reflecting brightly from the shard. His head bows to touch it as the tears continue to flow down the old man's face. If only I could show him how much I understand how he feels.

"You can't trust him Sasaki. You cannot trust Hashimoto, or any of them."

"I don't want to fight with them. I don't want to fight anyone. I just want to find out why my sister had to be taken from me. Why did you have to take her?" I say with all the ferocity of a mewling cat.

The words echo gently around us, mixing with the sound of our sobs as both of us attempt to come to terms with our losses. Miyake turns his head to look at me over his shoulder, but I can't face him.

"What?" He eventually asks.

"You heard me. I lost the person nearest to me, the only person who could make sense of this world for me. My sister died because of you. You had her killed. I don't want to trust the Angels, but if it means defeating sick monsters like you then so be it. If it means getting justice for my sister, then good. You may have lost Mazaki but you took the most precious thing in the world to me you bastard! Mazaki didn't deserve to die but you sure as hell deserve to lose her because of what you did to me."

We both remain on the floor, silence passing between us for many minutes before Miyake stands up slowly. I use Tenshi to lever myself up to keep up with him. There's anger in his face. Pure spite, malice and bloodlust in his expression.

"That's, eh, that's why you took her from me?!" He says through gritted teeth. Both of his hands are holding the choker now with skin so thin and pale that I can almost see his skeleton through it. "That's your reason? You side with monsters and destroy us because of that?!"

"Yes, and I will defeat you if it means getting the truth about why you killed my sister."

A growl escapes from Miyake's lips.

"I said you couldn't trust him Sasaki. I didn't do it! No one in this group was responsible for your sister's death."

"Oh stop lying," I shout angrily.

"Hashimoto ordered her killing. He wanted you, and he did whatever he needed to get you. He needs you to do his bidding. You're a tool of his, and so was she! You're nothing but pawns in their plans, how can you not see that?!"

All the sorrow and self-hatred in my body morphs to anger in an instant. How dare he talk about her like that. It feels like the air around me is hot from the energy within me. This fucker. How dare he. How dare he! HOW DARE HE!

"If I can't have my sister then you can't have Mazaki. But what's worse is that you don't deserve her for what you've done to me. You don't deserve her and you never did!"

I let out a blood curdling scream so loud that it makes the crystals around us vibrate and split.

- 171 -

Chapter 17

With a swift move that belies his age, Miyake flicks his arm up, tossing Ramiel's choker at me. Circling through the air the light of the genesis shard erupts off it and causes an explosion of purple through the glittering cavern. With my eyes shut momentarily I sense a brilliant flash of white attack my retinas through my eyelids.

When I open them a fraction of a second later Miyake is gone. The only sound in the cavern is the choker rattling to a standstill at my feet. I kick it away and take a couple of steps back, hitting a wall of udomite which pushes little rough spikes into me. My tightly strung nerves cause me to flinch at a sudden noise to the right, but when I look there's nothing there. I try and keep myself calm but my whole body is on fire with anticipation. I hold Tenshi out in front of me to give me some kind of protection, swinging him from side to side. Ok, just...just think. Put the anger to one side, if I attack wildly I'll be dead and the truth will never come out. This lying bastard will be able to live on despite his crimes. I've got to try and think my way out so I can get the truth.

I instinctively reach back to pull an arrow and my hand grasps nothing. Without my arrows and without my Angel how am I going to fight? The man can turn invisible, meaning he has the upper hand so I need to run. Just one opening and I can escape this place. Run. Find help. Miyu. Satoshi. Anyone. My heartbeat is off the charts and my breathing is fractured. Why is my Angel not coming to me? I thought with Ramiel gone I'd be able to unlock my power. I try once again to summon it from inside me, imagining pulling it out of the tree in my soul, but once more nothing happens.

A sound of scraping metal on stone comes out of the blue, sawing through my consciousness and causing my reflexes take over. I roll and feel the wind brush my ear as I collapse to the floor. The wall of udomite behind me smashes into millions of pieces as an invisible attack crashes into it.

"Just what are you Miyake?" I shout.

Another tiny scrape of metal and I'm jumping forward, rolling on to one knee. The ground splinters where I was standing, bits of rock and stone erupting into the air around me. I've barely had enough time to catch my breath before another scrape alerts me to a fresh attack. The metal beam behind me buckles and warps as the invisible force rips through it. Come on! Where are you? Please I need you! I beg to my internal self, as if the power of the thoughts would bring the Angel to me. I grab a piece of broken metal as I get to my feet and look at my reflection in it. I grimace as the seconds tick away but nothing changes. Just my blue eyes staring back with anger and frustration reflected in them.

"Fuck!" I shout as I throw the makeshift mirror into the ground angrily.

The metal bounces away and then abruptly comes to a stop as if hitting something invisible. I swing my bow towards the direction where I think he is, but don't make contact with anything.

"You're still here then Miyake? Hiding somewhere. You won't be able to hide from me forever, and then I'll get my justice!"

Then with a blink he's standing in front of me. To say his form is horrifying would be an understatement. He looks so little like the other Fallen I've seen, but manages to make bile rise in my throat nonetheless. For the most part he looks a lot like he did before he transformed; no bulging biceps, no tree trunk legs, just a very old and very frail looking man with his cloak tied around his waist showing bare torso and shoulders. His ribs stick out from under his pallid, almost grey skin, being wrapped in a tiny pair of wings framing his bony, thin-nosed face. His hair is grey, practically matching his skin. But where his eyes should have been, the ones that were crying so recently, there's nothing. Just a blank patch of skin. I stare in horror at him as he turns slightly, his weapon shifting against the floor. The sword he's moving is the largest I've ever seen. As he drags it around it kicks sparks off the ground. It must be at least eight feet long and a foot wide and looks like it should be ripping his arm right out of the socket.

"How can you possibly swing that?" I ask.

His eyeless head turns to the sword and then back to me. He reminds me a little of Puriel, her blindfolded face seemingly being able to look directly into my soul. When he speaks his voice seems more distant than it was.

"Our results were...unexpected, but not as different as you think. You call us monsters, you call us 'Fallen', but we are merely two sides of the same coin. We are made in the same way as the Angels. We can regenerate just like you. We can fly at incredible speeds, transform, have wonderous abilities. What makes us different? You stand there judging us, but whether you like it or not you are the same Sasaki."

"I have nothing in common with you."

"Really? You house an Angel, you murder those who run against you, you abuse your power. In what way are you different to what you think I am, or to the rest of them?"

His questions pierce through my mind, sending shivers of pain down my spine. I am different. I must be because I protect those who rely on me. I try to speak but nothing comes.

"That's what I thought," he says, slowly turning the sword to reflect the purple light around the room, "why don't you join us?"

I stare at him in disbelief.

"I see all Sasaki. Join us and we can take on the fiends that sent your sister to her death. I can see that is what you want."

"How? How do you see without eyes?"

He waves his free hand in an arc, revealing dozens of dismembered, free-floating eyes around his body. They move up and down slightly as if independent bodies, blinking in strange rhythms.

"I am Dumah, the Thousand Eyed. I see all, I know all, and with this weapon I can kill anything with a single cut."

The sight of all those eyes blinking individually is disgusting.

"A single stab is enough to kill you. It's what will wait for you if you refuse my invitation. Join us. I'll give you one more chance to come and get the revenge you want so badly, as well as the knowledge that you want. Join us and destroy the Angels."

"Stop lying! You killed her! Admit it!"

"I'm afraid I can't admit to something that isn't true. Maybe I can make you see that."

He starts walking towards me, dragging the heavy sword behind him. My gaze flicks back and forth from him to the eyes while I try and keep my distance. I swipe towards him with Tenshi who is long enough to be good for keeping some distance between us as he ducks backwards to avoid the blow. I swing again and again but he easily dodges each one. I try a vertical swing, but as Tenshi's frame comes within an inch of Dumah's head he catches it with a force that nearly knocks me off my feet. He twists his hand to try and wrench the bow from me, but with my reactions taking over I follow the movement by twisting my body into a roll. He may be strong, but I can still outsmart him.

I spring up in the direction of the door. I can get my arrows and get out of here! Yes! Time feels like it slows down as my feet cover the distance between me and freedom. My confidence starts to rise as the glow of the lamps above the doorway come closer and no attack materialises from behind me. Looking back over my shoulder I see him standing, unmoved, just watching me with his disembodied vision. But that's when my world goes tumbling. The scenery spins around as my legs flail out from underneath me. The clanking of the piece of stray udomite I tripped on plinks into the space above me as I hit the ground. I scream out in pain as something pierces my side. My arms and knees are scratched into oblivion and blood is oozing out of me. How could I be so careless? I was so close!

The scrape of Dumah's sword forces me to try and roll as it comes down hard. Despite his Fallen strength the blow is sluggish. Even for a superbeing the sword looks heavy and moves slowly as the blade arcs towards me. I instinctively raise Tenshi up to deflect the blow, just in time to stop it hitting me. The blade pierces my cloak, ripping it from my shoulders and pinning it to the ground. Turning my bow around the visible damage done to him makes anger and bile rise up within me.

"You hurt him! How fucking dare you hurt something so precious to me!"

My ranting is interrupted as black flame erupts from my cloak, causing it to burn away in a matter of seconds and leave nothing behind but a wisp of smoke.

"I wasn't lying Sasaki. If you get pierced by my sword, then you will die. I can make it obliterate everything it slices, even right down to the atomic level. It will burn every molecule in your body and eradicate you from the face of the world."

I try to ignore his warnings as my hand finds the source of the pain in my side. There's a large piece of metal from the destroyed pillar jutting out from me with blood flowing out through my shirt. It's difficult to breathe properly, and my head wound is making blood flow into my eyes and block my vision. When I look back up panic strikes me, as there's nothing but a large empty space where Dumah was.

I try to stand up to retreat but the pain in my side is so bad I can't move properly. I slump against the wall and try to keep myself upright, anticipating another attack. The one thing I have on my side is that the weight of his sword makes him slow. Even in my state I should be able to react quickly enough to avoid him. I just need to keep my guard up and listen.

"Where have you gone Dumah?"

"You know that I can bend light Sasaki. I can lens the light around me making me invisible. I could be anywhere."

Ok. Concentrate. You can track him by sound. During that sentence he moved a few degrees to the left.

"You may be able to become invisible, but your voice betrays you. I know where you are."

I lift up Tenshi and point him directly at where I think he is.

"Yes very good Sasaki," he says to my left side. I shift my bow to point towards the sound. "I am fully aware of the weaknesses of my power. But you will not be able to keep up your strength forever. Your head is bleeding a lot and if you don't get that hole in your side fixed soon you will bleed to death. You will die here and I will go and continue with the job I have to do to avenge Mazaki. Unless you stop this and join me, then I can help you."

I open my left eye and keep it trained at the end of my bow. With each word I shift the point slightly, trying to keep it pointed at my invisible foe.

"You know I won't do that."

scrr

I try to jump away from the attack but the wound in my side makes me cry out and fall to my knees instead. The invisible sword slams into the wall where my neck would have been, shattering the stone and showering my head with tiny bits of udomite and rock dust.

I lash out with Tenshi as far as I can but hit nothing but air. Dumah's sword is so long I can't counterattack him. My wounds are making adrenaline flow and making panic run through my body. One hit and I'm done for. Please come to me my Angel! I need you more than I've ever needed you. I have to keep going right to the end. Miyu would do it for me. No, Miyu has already done it for me. Satoshi has already done it for me.

Both of them have got hurt to protect me and I can't let their efforts be in vain. I owe them.

I force myself to my feet, struggling against the wall. My vision is starting to become hazy. Dumah was right, again, I'm going to die before long.

"You're tougher than Mazaki it seems," I say. Come on you bastard, speak. I wait in silence for a few seconds before continuing. "You speak as if she was some kind of deity but...she wasn't," I wheeze. Every time I take a breath it feels like my diaphragm is catching somewhere. "She couldn't even...beat...two schoolgirls. She couldn't outsmart me Dumah. How does it make you feel to know that she couldn't get past me?"

The seconds tick by again, with pure silence between us. Just as it looks like he's not going to fall for my plan, his voice calls out through the cavern.

"You may have gotten the best of her once but you won't get past me!" Yes! There he is, directly in front of me, about six feet away!

"That once...was all...that I needed."

I put all the effort I can into swinging my leg through the debris that litters the floor by my feet. The kick sends dirt and shards of udomite flying through the air, smothering the previously invisible Dumah in a layer of dust. My plan worked! I can see the dust on him and track him that way. Plus, that should put him on the back foot. A piece of dust in the eye may hurt like hell, multiply by 20 or 30 and you have a recipe for distraction.

"Now I can see you, you've lost your advantage," I crow as he tries to brush the detritus off his skin.

I start to lurch towards the door, dragging my broken body over the ground as Dumah struggles with his eyes. My hand clasps on the frame of the doorway and a sense of triumph bursts through the pain. I've got past another Fallen, and with no weapons except what I can make out of the environment. Not bad right Sis?

I look back up towards Dumah, my mouth turned up in delight, but an empty cavern greets me. The smile falls from my face as I search around desperately for him.

"You thought that something as simple as that would defeat me? Do you not consider that I might just be smarter than you? What makes you think that getting one over on Mazaki will allow you to get past me?"

"H...how?" I force out.

"Do you think that I can only throw light around myself? I can only hide myself? I control the light, and by changing the shape of the lensing I can hide just about anything," he explains.

I hadn't even considered he could be that powerful. To be able to control light on such a fine level is astounding. One hand is clutching my side and the other is holding my bow out as far as I can but I can see my arm shaking with the effort. I'm still close enough to the door to be able to just run for it. His sword might be long but I have a head start, and once I'm in the tunnel he won't have room to swing it.

I try to bound for the exit when the rattling of the chain fills my ears. The hope within me is swiftly replaced with dread as I feel metal wrap around my wrist like a coiling viper. With a yank my arm is ripped backwards and pinned against the wall. Another chain shackles itself around my ankle, pulling me back again. I try to hold on to the edge of the door but within seconds all of my limbs have been constrained, leaving me suspended against the wall a few feet in the air with my arms and legs spread. Spikes of udomite push into my back and arms as the bounds tighten on my wrists and ankles. The pain makes me choke on the blood that has risen from my stomach. Looking down hazily at my blood drying on the floor, I cough again and more pours out. Eventually the vomiting stops and I can only hang my head as the strength drains from me.

"A trap? How did you possibly set this up?" I ask through my strained vocal cords.

Dumah doesn't answer, but as I raise my head and steady my eyesight he appears in front of me. His grey skin and disgusting eyes appear in a blink again. His brow is furrowed as his eyes float towards me, staring at me from all angles. Even I can tell that he looks puzzled, like he can't work out what's happening. I try to avoid eye contact with him but everywhere I turn there's dozens of orbs floating around me. I snap my neck away and another pupil comes homing into view. No. No! No! I can't take this!

"Come on then!" I yell. "You've got me huh?! You set up your little trap and you got me! You're the smartest, the best, and I couldn't beat you! Now kill me!"

He just stands there, not moving an inch. Suddenly something flips inside of me, something visceral. Maybe it's the blood loss and the proximity to death, but something comes up from inside my soul. I splutter out as a maniacal, blood laden giggle escapes from my lips. The laugh gets louder and more forceful as my head drops again. My eyes are wide and dry as I stare at the blood pooling around my feet and down my side.

"Who cares anymore right?! Huh?! No one is coming to save poor, poor Sasaki!" I shout.

I don't know where the words are coming from but the laughter comes back, interrupting my meagre thoughts.

"I mean, I mean...I mean...ahaha, eye mean! You eye monster haha! I'm going to die at the hands of the eyeball monster here haha!"

There's something dark swirling inside me. I raise my head with the laughter still spluttering out of me like a bubbling geyser.

"Come on then! Take me now! Take my life to replace the one you loved. Eye for an eye right?! HAHAHAHA!"

The scraping of the sword along the ground floats through the air as he takes a few slow steps towards me. Yes. Come on! Another ten feet and you can have your sweet, sticky revenge! I wonder what he does if he needs glasses? Or maybe he puts in dozens of contact lenses? The laughter from my throat rings out across the room, echoing around us both and drifting off into the infinite. Then the pain comes. It comes hot like a fire poker through butter, then through the plate the butter was on, then the table, until it feels like it's piercing my very being. I feel like my mind is being ripped in half as the laughter morphs to a scream. It goes on and on as the pain continues to plough through me. It's like something is trying to carve up my brain from the inside. The surge that flows through my nerves make my limbs twitch against the tight, cold metal restraints. Even through everything I've experienced this agony is a thousand times worse than I've ever known.

My eyes force themselves to open through the intense, burning destruction of my mind. My eyesight flickers into black and white as I focus on the floor. I can hear electricity pulsing through my ears and my throat feels like it's filling with water. The screams turn to gurgles as my airways block and my lungs fill. Unconsciousness pulls itself through me within a brief moment, sending my body limp against my shackles.

Chapter 18

For a brief second I look upwards, calmness filling my being instead of anguish, until the flickering above me makes me realise that I'm underwater. The sensation of my lungs filling up forces me to the surface in coughing, spluttering desperation. Every time I come here it looks different, but it's my soul, my mind, I know it. This time, in the middle of my vision behind the giant cherry tree there's a gigantic, swirling vortex of deep, dark green and chromatic, heavy purple energy. The clouds are roiling around each other and piercing through one another in a mass of sheer brutality. Lightning and thunder erupt from the formations, grounding itself through the world. Each strike causes me to wince as a jolt goes through my head.

Thunder rolls back and forth over the world so loud that I cover my ears. It doesn't make any difference to the volume though, if anything it seems to make everything louder. It feels like my head is going to split down the middle from the noise. I cower down to my knees in an attempt to shy away from it but there's no getting away as it keeps on reverberating around me. After a few seconds I'm screaming at the agony. I force my eyes open and in the reflection of the pool the green cloud bursts overhead, splitting the purple cloud like cracks on an ice floe.

The noise suddenly stops, leaving deafening silence rolling around me as I gasp for breath on the water's edge. The pure, still pool only moves when I brush the surface with my hand, causing ripples to flow off through the placid water in a hypnotic way. I find myself almost forgetting about the chaos going on above me as my eyes follow the waves.

I jump as another hand breaks the surface. The pale white arm scrabbles in front of me as if trying to get out. Just as I move to grab them and pull them out, a dozen bolts of purple lightning crash down around me, piercing the ground and locking me in an electrical cage. I touch one of the bolts, but agony jolts through me and pushes me backwards. Kneeling down as close I can without receiving another shock, I try to reach out to the stricken arm. I beat Mazaki before, but something is still here, affecting me. Something wants to stop me helping whoever this is. I can't let it win.

Grimacing hard, I put my hand on the cage in front of me and push. The electricity pierces through me but I keep pushing, forcing myself part way through the barrier. The drowning person's hand falls to the surface as if dead and starts to sink slowly below it. I wail loudly and push with all my might, forcing myself through the gap slightly as the pain takes me over. My voice reaches an ear-splitting pitch as I summon an extra few percent from somewhere deep within and break through. Steam and the sound of sizzling fills the air as my burning body connects with the cold, shallow water. As soon as my hand comes into contact with theirs there is an almighty crash from above as a bolt of green lightning envelops me. A terrifying, blood curdling scream comes from my mouth as the colossal flash fills my world.

***

The faint remnants of the scream die on my lips as I return to consciousness. My breath is loud and rasping as the sight of my rapidly drying blood and vomit on the floor comes back to me, but something feels different. There's a feeling of fire crackling through my veins, making me twitch uncontrollably. With another scream my whole body shudders and briefly I feel like death again. Something is fighting inside me, fighting for me. I'm not alone. I won't die. I can barely think consciously as something animalistic takes over. It pulls at the chains hard, reaching and grasping for freedom. The groaning of the metal creaking under the pressure punctuates the roars of pain. My vision sparks and flames as I pull myself up into the cavern towards Dumah and his disgusting body.

I let out an almighty, indecipherable shriek of power and anger, with the force breaking the chain around my wrist. I watch it shatter into a million tiny fragments as the scream continues to flow from me. Anger and triumph start to mix as the restraints on my feet disintegrate. Thrusting my hands into the sky, I destroy the last thing holding me in place, sending cracks shooting through every wall and piece of udomite in the mine. Dumah's eyes dart around as the crackling of crystals goes on for what feels like forever. Finally, silence fills the air for a few seconds before the walls around us begin to explode in a cacophony of destruction. I grasp my hair as the pain shoots through me intermittently. I have to move before this strength disappears. I reach down and pick up Tenshi from the floor, holding him straight in front of me.

"It's over Dumah."

It seems like we're moving in slow motion as his eyes start to focus on me again, but I know he won't have time to react. Reaching my hand back to where my quiver would be I grasp a huge spike of udomite from the cracked wall. With barely a grunt I rip the stone out, drag it over my shoulder like an arrow and nock it against the string, pulling it back until my bow is groaning under the tension. By the time Dumah has fully caught on I unleash the makeshift missile. The udomite spins through the air like a corkscrew, ploughing through his stomach with barely a touch of resistance before ripping the columns behind him to shreds.

Dumah's eyeless face stares at me with his mouth aghast as the signals from his wound reach his brain. A few of the eyes roll back as he collapses to the floor. He lets out a gurgle of pain as he slowly reaches forward towards Mazaki's choker between us, but he eventually relents, his arm flopping down. His eyeballs drop to the floor like hailstones, hitting the ground and rolling to a halt.

The pain roars through my head again as whatever is going on inside me snaps in and out of my consciousness. I drop to my knees and scream in agony until my body settles again. I look at the metal jutting out of my side and grit my teeth. One more thing I have to deal with before I can get out of here. If I don't do this while the power is still in me the pain will be too unbearable.

I grip the metal with blood-soaked hands and brace myself. I try to pull gently but it doesn't budge. Increasingly desperate I yank at the shard, crying out as it starts to move. Even with the extra strength I have the pain is horrible. I grip harder and brace myself, counting myself down with increasingly desperate breaths. With a huge pull the fragment comes free from my stomach, spraying blood over the floor as the pain overwhelms me. Tears flow into my gaping mouth as I bellow in agony before collapsing to the ground and grasping at my side. Checking my reflection in the dull metal that I removed, I see a remnant of those green Angel eyes staring back at me before they sputter and die like a candle, the pale blue flooding back in.

I can barely move but I have to do something about the bleeding before I can leave. My hand finds a pile of udomite fragments left over from when I burst out of my chains. It's a complete gamble, but the pills heal me, right? So maybe this will? With exhaustion taking over me, I grip as many as I can, take a deep breath, and force the udomite into the wound. I bite my lip hard and stifle another scream before flopping to a complete stop, buried in debris. The bleeding begins to slow down as the udomite cauterises the wound, leaving me panting with relief.

Breathing hard I survey the room. The walls are covered in deep cracks and the metal support pillars around the genesis shard are warped and broken. Almost all the udomite in the place has shattered. Dumah's dead hand rests on the ground next to Ramiel's choker, his fingers clasping for the memory of her. I can feel the adrenaline starting to flow through my veins again, pushing me forward. Groaning, I pull myself upwards causing bits of rock to dig into my hand, before supporting myself against the wall.

The memory of those words that Dumah said about the Angels courses into me. 'Hashimoto ordered her killing', 'she was a tool'. I have to get back. I have to know if it's true. I struggle sideways to the door for the third time, and after a lingering look back at the corpse trudge up the dark staircase and back towards the real world. As I get nearer the top I can hear the wind howling down the cave as I struggle my way back towards the surface.

After a few minutes of using the wall to stop myself falling over I come to the small niche where I pick up my quiver and arrows. My hands hold on to the bike chain clasp as I slouch to the floor. Sis, what did they do to you? How did you get tangled up in all this? My head sinks into my chest and I run my hands through my hair before digging my nails into my scalp as another bolt of pain fires through me. I don't feel in control. In fact, I haven't felt in control since my Angel came to me in the hospital. I need it back. I need control over my own body. However little I can trust Dumah, there is something niggling about his accusations. I have to get back to Hashimoto.

I groan as I slowly force myself up against the wall and limp off towards the outside world again. As I turn a corner I get hit by a blast of icy water from outside. The storm is raging fully with wind that feels like it's going to blow me off my feet and rain that hits so hard it hurts. I huddle under a large iron girder from the carcass of the building works but it gives me no real protection against the elements. With the warm air of the cave still clinging to my clothes I take a deep breath and steel myself before walking slowly and unsteadily out into the rain.

I've only gone a few metres before I'm wheezing and gasping for breath. I can't keep myself going anymore. I can't even breathe without it catching in my diaphragm. I try to keep myself up, but it's just too much and I collapse to the pavement.

scrreee

The familiar screech of metal scraping along the dirt fills my very soul with dread. I roll over onto my back and see the massive blade slicing through the rain drops at the exact height of where my neck was before I collapsed. Dumah stumbles to the side under the weight of the sword strike as fear causes my body to go into overdrive. I scramble to my knees and stagger backwards to get some distance between us. My chest is heaving as I shakily nock an arrow and try to keep the point facing Dumah's back.

"What are you...doing here?" I ask.

My pained voice is barely audible over the torrential downpour, but Dumah still seems to be able to hear me, even though I can barely hear myself. He points to the hole in his stomach, or at least where the hole was. Now all that remains is a large, bloody scar with large chunks of glowing udomite sticking out of it. His voice carries over the distance to me easily but I can hear his suffering too.

"I...saw you. You used the...shards. I thought if it could...do the job for you it could work for me."

"So, you've come to finish me then have you?"

"I want to talk to you. You were acting strangely down there but it's not too late Sasaki, you can still join us. We will have right on our side forever; whatever the Angels have made you believe."

No. He can't be telling the truth.

"Your group killed my sister. You put my best friend in hospital. You wounded others. You want to enslave humanity. I could never join you."

"But we...we just want to protect humanity by giving them this strength. It is our job."

"You're doing a bad job of it aren't you?"

"We need you to take on the Angels, to stop them imposing their will and keeping this power for themselves. But if you won't reconsider then I won't let them have you. I can't let them have you."

"Why me?!" I shout. "What have I done to deserve this? I don't have any power! Not anymore."

For a few seconds there's nothing but the sound of the rain and the feeling of a warm tear drop running down my cheek, mingling in with the freezing rain drops.

"Your powers run deeper than you think Sasaki. Why do you think Hashimoto would lie to keep you on his side? You have a power that they want."

"No! You're the liars!" I screech.

I unleash the nocked arrow but it practically floats through the wall of water. As soon as it's within reach of Dumah his free hand snaps around the shaft, stopping it dead. He holds it for a few seconds before throwing it to the floor.

"You're dangerous Sasaki. Please, one last time, please use the power you have to avenge your sister and to protect everyone else. Don't give it to them and let them use you as a tool for war."

He's using you Sis, he's using you to get to me. The despicable bastard!

"Never!"

Conjuring something from deep within me I start firing a barrage of arrows at him. Even with his sword weighing him down Dumah still manages to dodge my shots by shifting from side to side. I speed up my attacks and feel them getting closer until the point where I force him to deflect an arrow away from his face with his arm, cutting him deeply. His sword swings are getting wider and less focussed now, bringing building materials and girders down around.

I pull one more arrow and put enough power into it to make Dumah stumble to the floor, but the effort leaves both of us struggling to move. He stands up slowly and faces me, visibly in pain, but the wounds around my head, my stomach and my legs are all taking their toll too. I stare with exhaustion into his gaunt face as he gasps for breath.

"I don't want to kill you Sasaki."

"Why not, I'm your enemy?" I stutter.

"You remind me of her. You have the same look in your eyes."

Memories of the vicious and cunning Ramiel flood into the forefront of my mind. I don't want to be like that, an evil, violent, crazy being of malice.

"What look?"

"You know things, and I can sense the power within you. I noticed it as soon as you first sat down with me. Mazaki would always look at me with those big eyes as if she knew everything that was going to happen at every point in time. She made her choices during combat and they were always the right ones. I can see the same thing in your eyes Sasaki."

I can't do anything but stare at him. I don't know how he could see that in me. I've got through the past few weeks on nothing but luck and instinct, and now here I am at the end of the road.

"One time she tracked, attacked, and escaped a pair of dangerous enemies on sheer force of will and reflexes Sasaki. Even when living purely on the edge she knew the decision she had to make to get the outcome she wanted. I've seen you do the same. My friends have suffered at your hand because of that skill you have. My colleagues are dead, and all because of that instinct you share with her. That's why I don't want to have to do this to you, but you leave me no choice."

He stands up and stretches his arms out.

"No!" I scream.

I drop to me knees and instinctively reach out a hand towards him before falling backwards on to the road as he disappears from sight. I scrunch my eyes shut and cuddle Tenshi close to my body like a frightened child holding a teddy bear. Without the time to upkeep him he's beginning to show wear on the metal and scratches in the wood. I'm so sorry I've let him come to harm Sis. My hair is plastered to my face and dried blood is caked all over my fragile body, which is sitting on the edge of death.

"Goodbye Sasaki."

I'm done. I can't muster another arrow, and now I can't track him. My brain is foaming with agony, pushing images of Satoshi and my beloved Miyu across my eyelids. I failed all of them. My grip on Tenshi loosens, my hands finding the clasp on my chest instead. Tenshi and the chain are the only solid things I have left to hold on to in this world.

I open my eyes to look up at the sky and see nothing but the rain which tortures my lungs and throat. Then, slowly, a distortion floats into the edge of my vision where the rain moves in a weird direction. The glitch moves gently through the air before positioning itself a few feet above me. My gaze naturally averts from the large eyes that I know are staring at me from behind their curtain.

Thoughts fall slowly into place as more eyes hover over to me. He can bend light around himself, and he can shape that light around any static object. But it took him a few seconds for him to reassert himself back then. Now he's being hit by hundreds, thousands of rain drops every second and he can't cloak himself properly. A slow arc slices through the rain as he hefts his sword up to his head painfully. I steel myself, and try to conjure up something, anything to help me through. As it reaches the top and begins to drop slowly towards me, something sparks inside me. I don't care if my Angel has deserted me, I can do this without them. I am not an Angel, I'm not a Fallen. I'm only me, but I can do this on my own.

In a snap movement my hands wrap around Tenshi's shaft and jerk him into the midriff of the barely visible Dumah. There's a sickening sound as the hard tip pierces the Fallen's old, pallid skin behind that curtain of water. He gasps and splutters as I roll to my left to avoid the point of his sword. I manage to stumble upright as the sword clatters into the ground, splashing water around us. The storm is unrelenting, and as I reach over my shoulder with my right hand a flash of lightning illuminates the world directly above us.

Silence rings through the air as if to make room for the almighty burst of thunder that will accompany it. I pull a soggy arrow around and load it into the bow. Pulling the string back slightly more than normal to compensate for the friction of the rain and the condition of the arrows, I take my aim. Electricity runs through my soul as my sight fixes on my target.

The arrow flies out straight and true before making a sound like a spoon dipping into a particularly thick trifle, as the point impales itself into a barely visible eyeball. Looking like an olive on a cocktail stick, the arrow appears to be falling so slowly as to be floating in place as I instinctively nock another shot. I fire again and again until the sky seems to be completely filled with strange, bulbous snowflakes. When the last arrow hits home I raise my head to the sky and shut my eyes as thunder crashes through the world, filling the air around me with a raucousness that makes my teeth rumble in my mouth. The sound fills my ears before rolling outwards only to be punctuated with the pattering of dozens of arrows falling on to the tarmac, and then the squelching sound of a body dropping into the water as Dumah joins them.

I open my eyes and see the rain beginning to let up above us. I gaze upon the war zone in front of me, looking upon the sight with a mixture of pride, horror, disgust and most of all, a sense of disbelief. Dumah is lying there, fully visible now, gasping for breath as the last drops of rain fall on to his bleeding, skeletal body. The sparks within me flicker out and the pain comes back again. Using Tenshi as a crutch, I hobble over towards the Fallen monster. No, not a monster. Without the eyes floating around he just looks like a terribly sad and lonely old man. I collapse down by his side as my legs give way. With a slow juddering motion, a single eye floats over my shoulder, looking across at me as Dumah's face turns to mine.

"I guess...I...missed one," I struggle out.

Dumah splutters in my face, attempting a laugh.

"I...told you...you had power Sasa...ki," he wheezes.

"I got lucky."

"No, there is no luck. You have to...to make it yourself," he continues slowly. The rasps between his words are getting louder and more pained. "You are...like her...I promise."

"I do not have the power that she had."

"Sas...Sask...you fired 30 shots in the time it took a bolt of lightning to turn to thunder. What kind of power do you think you don't have?"

A grey hand reaches out and touches mine gently, causing me to look back to Dumah.

"Kill me...please..."

"What? No, I...I can't."

"I'm tired of this world without her in it. I can't carry on anymore."

"No! I literally can't! I can't kill you! I can't do it!"

The hand that was resting on mine moves off slowly towards his sword, half submerged in water. His fingers eventually clasp around the handle. His other hand reaches across to join it with a gasp of pain.

"Help me."

"No, I told you I can't! I can never kill you!"

"Just help me...kill myself then. Please? I lived for our group. I lived to protect humanity, but most of all, I lived for her Sasaki. I lived in the hope of doing the world justice for Mazaki. You must know how that feels?"

Yes. I do. All too well.

"I can't carry on with my quest anymore. But you, you can carry on yours. Make the right decision and live for the woman you came here for. They killed her. We did not. I promise you. Go and find out."

Feeling the tears flow down my sodden face, I look deep inside and know that I have to deal with him somehow. If he escaped he would come for Miyu or Satoshi and would probably be killed horribly by Hashimoto. I have to take this chance to wipe the Fallen out completely, and at least he'll get what he wants.

Shaking, I drop Tenshi to the floor and reach across to embrace his hands with mine. I feel the warmth of his skin and the immense weight of the weapon as I heave it upwards. Between us we manage to lift the blade a few inches above his stomach like the sword of Damocles. A splinter of apprehension pins my heart before gravity sets in and drags the sword into his spongy skin. Black fire erupts from the wound, causing me to flinch. The flames slowly lick down his legs as his Fallen form drops away, revealing his human face to the world. A pale but very much human coloured hand brushes against my check with the warmth of a furnace.

"Thank you. You are special just like she was. You don't believe it, but you are a good person Sasaki. Thank you for allowing me to go back to her. You will always have the power of...those eyes."

There are tears framing a smile on his face as the vaporising flames flow up his limbs and torso. His hand falls away from me as he becomes completely engulfed in fire. As my stubbornness finally disintegrates I begin to wail, the screeching echoing around the empty buildings and roads around us. Tears run from my eyes and drop down onto Dumah's body as if trying to put out the fire, but within a split second there's nothing left. Nothing to leave behind to prove he existed outside of my memories of him. I continue to cry into the void of the world, burying my head in the concrete before eventually letting myself fall asleep.

Chapter 19

My eyes blur into focus on the small bird investigating Tenshi as I wake up slowly. The steaming tarmac is already getting warm in the bright, post-storm sunshine. As I stir to get up the animal flies away leaving me hugging my knees in the middle of the road and trying to take stock of what's happened. I look groggily into the sky and wince as another burst of pain runs through me. My head hurts, I'm exhausted and the pain in my stomach is still agonising. My entire body is covered in cuts and bruises, and my face is stained red with blood. But I discovered the Fallen base and I took out its leader. I did it all. On my own. As Sasaki Kyushiro, not as an Angel.

Looking across to the building site I can see the ruins of what the base had been. The damage Dumah and I did last night caused the building works to collapse and completely cave in the area. The memories of the fight linger behind my eyelids, but at least now Miyu can recover fully without the fear of an attack coming.

Then the words Dumah spoke hit me again. 'Hashimoto ordered her killing'. That can't possibly be true...can it? She was hit by a car while riding her bike. Those feelings of wrongness come back to me again in a flood. Why was she in a place like this anyway? I could barely think about anything for years and yet, now, in the warm afternoon light the strangeness of the situation shines out. Why the hell was a teenager here in the middle of the night? If Dumah was telling the truth then I have no idea what I can do. There's no way I can take on the Angels, and especially not now that I've killed the last of the people who would have at least fought on my side against them.

Another stab in my head and I clutch my hair until the dizziness goes away. I thought I had finished all of this but there's still something going on in my head. I need to sort this out, somehow. I need them to help me get better.

I sling my bow and quiver around my body and stumble off towards the hospital, swaying with a lack of energy. I can't even remember the last time I slept or ate properly. I tip the bottle of udomite pills up and empty the remains into my mouth, trying to satiate my body with medication. Throughout the slow walk my thoughts just keep going around and around about what I'll say and what I'll do when I get back to the Sanctum. If Dumah was lying then why? He didn't gain anything out of it. He clearly knew the pain of losing a loved one and didn't seem like the kind of person who would do that just for vindictiveness' sake. If he wasn't lying and Hashimoto really was behind it all then why?! What would the Angels possibly gain from killing my sister?

The buildings and people begin to get more densely populated as I reach downtown, with more and more people staring at me in my bedraggled state. They're judging me. Please stop looking at me! I want to just disappear! My breathing is fast and my chest is tight as panic sets in. A man stops in front of me and reaches out. I shout and shy away from him, diving down an alleyway between two buildings to escape. I lean against the wall, clutching at my heart until my trembling legs can't keep me up anymore, grasping my knees to my chest as I collapse to the floor, gagging for air. I have to...get to the...hospital. I shut my eyes and try to concentrate on what I need to do. I have to carry on moving forward. I have to find out the truth.

After a few deep breaths and with my bearings stabilised I stand up and set off, slightly unsteadily, down another alley. The city disappears beneath my feet as I flow down the alleyways like blood in a capillary. Keeping off the street makes things so much easier. Every turning I take makes my heartbeat rise that little bit more as I get closer to where I need to be. I can't even keep the thoughts of what's going to happen in my head now.

When the hospital rises into view relief hits my brain, but it's quickly suppressed by the tension within me. I have to go to the Sanctum and speak to the Angels. But...I need to see Miyu. I need to see her and make sure she's ok. I run my hand through my hair as I try to remember where her room was. Using the position of the sun as a guide I set off, circling round the outbuildings until I find a low, open window. I jump into a bush underneath it as a group of people in white coats walk past. I'm trying to keep my breathing as quiet as possible. Why am I doing this? What the hell is wrong with me? No, wait, I can't be seen in this state. Someone will try and take me away and I won't be allowed to see her. That's why I'm acting like this. God, I feel so confused! I place my palms over my face and try to push my feelings down. I've been forced into this. Yes. Definitely!

 Grasping my arrows with one hand and with my heart beating hard against my chest, I flip over the sill and start padding down the corridor as quickly and quietly as possible. As the walls pass by I remember the last time I walked these halls alone. I don't know what happened, but Ramiel must have been behind it because I didn't feel like myself. I felt lost, defeated, like the Fallen were going to come around any corner to destroy me and everything I stood for. The pure heaviness of fear that weighed down on me that day left me crushed. It was such a nightmare. I remember walking the halls for what felt like hours until I was a broken husk, left on the floor paralysed with dread. Then the Angel came from within me and lifted me up, pushed me forward and allowed me to continue. But where are you now and why have you deserted me?

 I round one more corner and come to Miyu's room, hovering outside the door for a second before realising I've been smoothing my shirt out and pulling my skirt down to cover the worst of the scars. I shake my head and take a deep breath in before sliding the door open quietly. I brace myself, but when I open my eyes all that's there is an empty bed. I puff out my cheeks as I let out the breath I'd been holding. Where the hell is she? They said she needed to be kept for a few days and it's only been one night. Oh my god, she can't be...No! Pain pierces my head again, causing me to gasp. Fighting the tears back from my eyes I slam the door shut and speed down to the Sanctum. My legs yell at me as I jump down the stairs three at a time before tripping and falling at the bottom. Adrenaline pushes me to roll and flip back upright straight into a run. I burst through the big double doors with my shoulder and look around frantically. There's no one here at all. Spotting the button to call the lift I rush over and mash it with my thumb.

"Come on!" I yell.

Finally, the doors open and I jump into the small crate before hammering the button for the basement. I can't do anything but jump around on my toes as the shiny box descends slowly. I press the button a few more times in a futile attempt to make the lift go down faster. When it slows to a stop at the bottom the doors just sit there. I wail at them, slamming them with my palm until the vibrations make my arm seize up. Open! Open for God sake! Without a noise the doors slide open so quickly that I fall through them, stumbling to one knee.

"You can't be here Sasaki!" gasps the angelic tones of Hesediel.

I try to squeeze past him into the room but he closes in one me.

"What are you doing?" I yell as he throws his arms and wings around me. He pushes my head down into his chest and I struggle against him.

"Let me through you bastard! What's going on!"

"I can't let you through Sasaki! I'm not allowed to let you through!"

"Is it Miyu?" I shout.

"You can't see! Please!"

I lash out with a strong kick towards his shin which hits with a crunching, leathery sound. The damage causes him to drop to a knee and reveal the reason he was blocking me. Blood seeps into my mouth as I instantly bite straight through my lip. Miyu is in a hospital trolley across the room, propped up at a 45-degree angle and strapped down thoroughly with large leather belts. Her struggles make the whole bed rock even with Naoko and Keiko holding on to the sides. I can hear her muffled screams through the gag placed across her mouth even over the background noise. Hashimoto and Tachibana are standing at the base of the bed, carefully adjusting a set of mirrors on a large experimental bench with the genesis shard sitting in its holder next to it.

I yank an arrow round and pull the string back, aiming directly at Hashimoto. The shock of seeing Miyu in this state pours through my body. Bloodlust and terror fill my veins leaving me without an ounce of doubt that I'm going to kill him.

"No don't!" Hesediel screams at me from behind.

Just as I let go of the string, Hesediel's feathers flap around me and the arrow I had tried to fire is stopped in its tracks. I look up into his purple, sparkling eyes as he grasps me in a firm, unmovable embrace. He pulls the arrow out of the bow with one hand and slams it to the ground. I'm screaming over the noise around me as Hashimoto strokes Miyu's cheek. The cacophonous generator powering the machines shuts off abruptly, leaving my shrill voice bouncing around the place.

"You can't! Get off her!" I bellow in an uncontrolled and vicious way. "Don't you dare touch her!"

"Hesediel, why did you let her in here? I told you to guard the door did I not?"

"I'm sorry Hashimoto, she caught me off guard," he says as Hashimoto shoots him a thunderous look.

"There are no excuses Hesediel! We must stay vigilant at all times lest we let our position slip."

"What are you doing? What the hell is going on?!" I yell at him across the divide. "Let me go! What are you doing with Miyu?! You're trying to make her into one of you aren't you?! How dare you sully her!"

"I had almost forgotten that you seem to be able to pull information out of nowhere. And where did you get that idea from?"

"I spoke to the leader of the Fallen when I was at their hideout. He told me about the experiment that created you. He showed me the genesis shard they had and told me how you used yours to create the Angels. He talked all about how you side-lined those who worked with you when the accident happened. He told me how badly you treated them."

"You did what?"

"You don't, you don't have to fight anymore," I plead with him, "I defeated them. I...I found the Fallen base last night and I killed their leader. Now let Miyu go! You don't need her anymore!"

"Why did you do that Sasaki? I warned you not to do that! I specifically instructed you not to go after him. How dare you disobey my orders."

"The leader of the Fallen also said that you killed my sister as part of some plan, but you told me that they did it so I'm not sure how much I can trust you!"

"Sasaki of course he would tell you that, he was our enemy. What happened to your sister was a tragedy, but I guess that it doesn't really matter anymore."

"Then give back Miyu!"

"Ah, I'm afraid that we do still need her. We never knew that mages were still around, and now that we have one we can't let her power slip through our grasp."

"But you don't need any more power! You don't have any enemies anymore!"

"But what if new enemies appear Sasaki? Udomite is probably everywhere in the world. We can't be sure that there won't be more monsters. So, we'll make her into a truly God-like being to lead the next generation of Angels."

He returns to fiddling with the equipment around Miyu as I turn back to Hesediel. I want to kill him right now, but the mixture of rage and sadness and fear inside me is just too much for my brain to deal with. When I speak there is a pleading tone in my voice.

"You can't let him do this to her. Please save her."

"We need her," he says after some thought, "I'm…I'm so sorry Sasaki."

He looks in so much pain. Part of me wants to just turn and bury myself in his chest and throw my arms around him to try and take the hurt away. But then I look back at Miyu and that part quickly fades into the background underneath the rising bloodlust. I have to get her out. I need to take this chance.

"I'm sorry too Hesediel," I whisper.

I shrug my shoulders upwards and jab the end of one of the arrows into his eye. It doesn't do much, but I know it's coming. As soon as his grip loosens just a tiny bit, I tear myself free, scattering feathers around me as I launch myself towards Miyu. I draw an arrow on the run and pull Tenshi up to murder Hashimoto. Tachibana starts to move towards me as I expected she would. Just as she blocks my view of the leader of the Angels, I duck to my right to work the angle for the shot. But before I can take it the world explodes.

Chapter 20

An earth-shattering roar rips through the cavern, throwing me backwards as large chunks of the ceiling fall down in front of me. In amongst all the destruction I just about make out a silhouette plunge down through a hole in the ceiling, landing on top of Tachibana before a cone of fire erupts upwards through the hole that the assailant came through. The heat flashes over my face and feels like it's frying my skin off. The figure that landed on Tachibana, leaving her still on the ground, rises from its knees until it is standing tall. It must be at least six-foot-tall and has darkness exuding from it which feels almost crippling. Slowly a pair of ragged and damaged black wings unfurl that, when combined with his spiky charcoal hair and floor length black cloak, still billowing from the convection, creates an imposing figure. He turns to look back at me with fiery red eyes glowing through the dust and destruction. I nock an arrow and aim it at him quickly in case of an attack, but instead he looks away towards Hashimoto.

I peer around at the other Angels quickly and see nothing but fear in their faces. Naoko is tending to Keiko who looks to have come off worse from the explosion. Hesediel is still behind me but one of his wings is trapped under a large piece of ceiling and his father is cowering next to the generator. Kagawa Hiroshi looks over towards us but doesn't make any move to help his son. Miyu is still struggling in the bed with tears coming from her eyes. The black clad figure hasn't looked away from Hashimoto since he locked eyes with him.

I take one step towards Miyu and then hesitate as Hesediel's scream of pain cuts through the air behind me. I pause briefly as conflicting feelings swim in my brain before darting to him and heaving the large slab. With a huge, back-breaking effort I manage to lift it an inch off the ground before kicking him out of the way and immediately turning back towards Miyu. Either Hashimoto and his new guest don't care about me or they don't notice as I circle round to her side without alerting them.

As soon as I get near her she looks across at me with eyes wide with terror. I want to stroke her hair and reassure her, but as I can't bring myself to touch her in such a loving way I settle for starting to rip at the restraints holding her in place. As I tear the belts open muffled moans coming from her again. I reach up and pull the gag out of her mouth.

"Kyu watch out!"

My neck flicks upwards at whiplash speed just as the large ceiling block comes down and smashes into Miyu's temple. I scream as her eyes fall shut and her head lolls, blood pouring out of her. I pull the last belt off her and drag her to safety behind a chunk of udomite that avoided the damage, ripping a piece of my shirt off and pressing it on the wound. Putting my head on her chest I can feel her heartbeat and the breath from her nose on my hair and let out a huge sigh of relief. Shooting a look back at Hesediel I see him cradling his broken wing. I knew I should have just left him there. If only I hadn't spent those valuable seconds on him I could have got to her first and protected her! If she dies I will never forgive him for making me make that stupid decision.

"I promise I'll protect you," I whisper to the unconscious body slumped in front of me.

Propping her up against the crystalline pile I poke my head around the rock. Hashimoto is standing a few feet away, staring at the black bedecked stranger who is straddling the decimated and scorched remains of Tachibana. I fight the bile back down my throat after seeing clearly what a gruesome state her body is in. Her chest is entirely gone. Evaporated. The entire bottom half of her face has been burned off, leaving a bloody, charred mess.

Seeing the attackers face for the first time I realise that he looks young, in fact he doesn't look that much older than me. But there is something in his eyes sitting below his crown of black spiky hair. They glow red like the embers of a furnace. Despite looking young I can't help but get the feeling that this boy has seen a lot. The feeling is just radiating off him, like he's seen more than anyone his age should have. Finally, he speaks with a clear voice that rings with power in a way that reminds me of Hashimoto himself.

"Hello Father."

My mouth drops open. Looking back from the son to the father I can start to see the resemblance. Hashimoto looks more wrinkled, more ashen faced, definitely more grey hairs, but they share that powerful presence. The air is practically crackling around them.

"I was hoping that we weren't going to see you, son."

"What a glorious way to greet me! You should be welcoming me like the ancient civilisations welcomed the sun rising every morning."

Looking out towards the pair through a slit in the udomite that is serving as our hiding spot, I realise I have an opportunity here to take one of them out. One shot through the neck should do it. Which one though? I'm sure Hashimoto is lying to me about my sister. After seeing what he was doing to Miyu I can't trust him anymore. Miyake Fumio seemed to have ten times the legitimacy and honesty that the Angels ever had. I need to make him pay for it, but his son just oozes danger. All the hairs on my neck stand on end each time I look at him. He's standing there without a hint of fear, but without arrogance either. He's too confident for someone standing in a room full of supernatural beings that he's just pissed off.

I load an arrow into the gap in the rock like a snooker player using a rest and then raise Tenshi up to connect the string. Pivoting the arrow around I can aim at either of them. I shut my eyes and take a deep breath. My brain is surging with the possibilities of what my shot could lead to. Shoot Hashimoto and all-out war will break loose between his son and the Angels. Shoot the intruder and Hashimoto might go crazy and lash out at me like the Deniers or Dumah did. I take another deep breath to slow my heartbeat. I swivel the arrow, open my eyes, and gently pull back on the string with my calloused fingers. Exhaling slowly, I release the arrow which silently cuts the air towards him. He doesn't notice it, he doesn't move, he doesn't even look. I've got him!

The sound of the flames cuts out my excitement as a wall of fire bursts up from the ground around Hashimoto's son, instantly burning the arrow to nothing but dust.

"Ah, you would be the girl that I have heard so much about. Sasaki, is it? That was an exquisite shot, it really was. You live up to your reputation."

The boy talks to me but he still hasn't moved, one hand on the sword at his side and the other in his pocket. He still hasn't looked away from Hashimoto.

"Sasaki, please can you come out from there. You need to answer to me," orders Hashimoto.

I stand up, take a look at Miyu to make sure she is as safe and comfortable as can be and step into the space beside the pair.

"You told me that you killed this man did you not?"

I'm puzzled by this question.

"I don't know who this person is Hashimoto."

He looks over to me, finally taking his eyes off his son.

"You said you had killed the leader of the Fallen. This, this thing is their leader."

"I, I...I" I stammer.

"Why did you lie to me Sasaki?"

"I didn't lie!" I whine. "I killed Miyake Fumio! He was the leader of the Fallen. I destroyed their base!"

"Oh no, Miyake is dead? Oh dear. He was a truly tremendous servant to me. He was a good friend of yours too wasn't he Father? I remember meeting him at the lab on my visits and you always seemed to enjoy his company. He was very kind to me; how could you kill such a wonderful man Sasaki?"

The words of the Fallen boy pierce my heart like a dagger. How? How could I kill him? He was a brilliant person with nothing but love for Mazaki.

"I don't know how you concluded that Miyake was their leader, but you are sorely mistaken. And your mistake has led to the death of Tachibana. That is on your shoulders. If I had known that this was still alive we could have prepared. Anyway, allow me to introduce my son, Hashimoto Sanzo. He is the true leader of the Fallen, and he's here to destroy our genesis shard and us."

Sanzo bows slightly before me, the flicker of his red eyes burning into my vision. My brain feels like it's overheating. The guilt for Tachibana comes crashing down on top of the guilt about Miyake, pushing me down to my knees. I look back at Sanzo with despair flooding my soul.

"You wish to know a lot, don't you Sasaki?" he asks.

I nod my head.

"Then allow me to show you!"

He unsheathes his sword, the blade immediately becoming surrounded by flames right up to his hand, before leaping towards his father with a flap of his broken wings.

shhnk

Hesediel appears between the two of them, Sanzo's attack bouncing off his shield.

tsnng

The noise that accompanies Sanzo's teleport is one I had hoped to never hear again. That strange vibration of the air that sounds so much like the noise that the other Angels make. He really is a Fallen. Now, ten feet back he stands tall and points his sword at Hesediel.

"You think you can protect him with your power? From me? Let's see if you can handle the heat!"

A laser beam of white-hot fire erupts from the tip of the blade and heads towards them. I go to cry out but the words stick in my throat as I shield my face from the heat. Satoshi said that Hesediel was a defence expert and it shows. He smashes his arms into the ground and pushes energy into his protection, causing it to grow before my eyes. By the time the flames hit him he now has Hashimoto completely hidden, deflecting the heat towards the ceiling and around them.

Sanzo smiles and raises his spare hand to the sword, putting more energy into the beam. The roar of the fire drowns out any noise, but I can see the pain on Hesediel's face as he pushes back against it, until the attack abruptly dissipates, leaving a ringing silence in my ears. The scorch marks in the rock behind the Angels remind me of when Hesediel protected me from Munkir. That atomic blast ripped through the air but we were protected without a scratch, just as Hashimoto is now, standing in front of the genesis shard in a cone of serenity, completely unharmed. I had almost forgotten just how much I owe him for protecting Miyu.

"What is your name?" Hesediel asks as he retracts his shields.

"Did you not hear my father introduce me? I am Hashimoto Sanzo."

"No, what is your Fallen name? What name does your monstrous visage take on?"

"What, this old thing?" he asks, waving his hand down his form. "Why I..."

shhnk

The flap of the wings is followed by a baying roar as a tunnel of wind crashes towards Sanzo's back. Ariel is hovering in the air, arms out, hands splayed. But in an instant Sanzo is gone, reappearing on top of a large outcrop of udomite behind her. He raises his fist and throws his arm into her side, sending her crashing down, landing beside her husband again. She screams in agony as the attack leaves her flesh burning black like a brand.

"I do believe that I told you. I am called Hashimoto Sanzo!" he shouts into the chamber.

Hashimoto Shinsei takes his glasses off and speaks slowly and calmly to us while he cleans them calmly on a handkerchief.

"This is Azrael, the Archangel of Death."

"Oh that! Oh well I guess once upon a time this form would have gone by the name of Azrael, yes. You're right, I had basically forgotten. I knew that Miyake was up to something behind your back, and when I confronted him I forced him to let me in on his plan. Once they had their genesis shard I made sure to be first in line to be changed.

"That night Azrael came to me with his hellfire and wings of black and took me down to Hell where he reigns. He showed me the most horrific images of slaughters, torture, viciousness, and avarice. But do you know what? None of that fazed me at all, I just stared him down. He almost seemed shocked! So, do you want to know what I did? I took him down. I faced the devil and I won. I took his sword from him and slashed his wings apart to make sure he'd forever know what had happened. I, me, Hashimoto Sanzo left him writhing in agony on the floor! I made him bow to me! The devil himself bowed before my strength. He gave me his kingdom, and his eternal service. But that wasn't enough for me, how could it be? So I took his soul and I burned it into mine!

"I, Hashimoto Sanzo am now the most powerful being in this Universe! Doesn't that make you proud Father? I bring mercy to the souls of millions. I give them their justice and reward for their lives of sin and debauchery. All those souls suffering endless punishment that they know they deserve is just delicious, and I rule over it all!"

He cackles, raising his hands above is head and spewing fire all around him, melting the udomite around the room into gigantic blocks. A large chunk falls from the ceiling towards him before he uses the fire to throw it towards his father.

"Hesediel," Shinsei says.

shhnk *shhnk*

Hesediel grabs him, teleporting him a few feet to the side and back again as the large ball of compressed, glassy udomite sails harmlessly over, crashing into the wall behind them. Sanzo lets out another passionate laugh.

"You see, I am Hashimoto Sanzo, the new Archangel of Death, with dominion over all the circles of Hell. The dead souls look upon me from the darkness, and unlike your pathetic band of miscreants they are loyal, because they know that I am their true ruler. They know I am here on a mission to bring mercy to this world and that I am right to do so, and that starts with you father!"

He laughs again, like someone being told a hilarious joke.

"And what of your mother? Did you bring mercy to her?"

Suddenly Sanzo falls silent. Even with the crackling udomite spewing stored heat into the room it feels like the temperature drops a few degrees. The pause goes on for an uncomfortably long time.

"I...gave her an end to her suffering. Is that not what you wanted? She was desperate in the end. Begging for someone to free her of the agony that reaped her heart every day. I just did the merciful thing. Do you even know what mercy is father?"

"And what were you doing to her before she got into that state?"

"Oh, you know, I was trying to turn her into one of us, to come with us into a brave new world and to rid this one of the disgusting monsters like you."

He goes back to laughing again, filling our ears with a piercing, hacking glee. My instincts were exactly right, this person is nothing but evil.

"You have brought nothing but shame to our family. You disobeyed me. You took your group of destructive demons and what did you do? You killed your own mother, my beloved wife. You broke her like a twig because of your demonic lust."

"I gave her mercy! I helped her! If I hadn't you would have gotten her and I know you wouldn't have been that kind father. I helped her and now I'm here to help you."

"Then you shall have to go through everyone here. Everyone, you are now under strict orders to kill Hashimoto Sanzo and protect the shard. Do not let him destroy our stone, remember how important it is to our futures. Take him out anyway you can. You must not fail me."

Chapter 21

Hashimoto Shinsei, the older Hashimoto, does not appear to be willing to join the fight, leaving just Hesediel and the Furukawas against this demon. And yet, there is something about them that feels as if they are doing it out of choice, even though certain death awaits them. Shinsei speaks and his followers do. He seems to inspire some kind of ridiculous trust in these people. Well, he can't have me because I'm not leaving Miyu's side.

"Go. Attack." Shinsei barks.

Barachiel and Ariel spring from one end of the cavern up to Sanzo's position, both flashing through the air with wings splayed. Their understanding means they attack in perfect harmony, teleporting around each other as they converge on the Fallen king. In a pincer movement Ariel slashes her arms across one another throwing out blades of air, as Barachiel swings his staff crackling with electricity towards the cornered Sanzo. He doesn't move or even flinch as they close in, the bright smile remaining resolute on his face. Just inches before the attacks hit home flames erupt up around him, eradicating them from existence. Barachiel flips his staff and stabs it towards Sanzo, causing another rush of fire to erect briefly, the staff bouncing off it.

"Sasaki. Did you not hear me? You are under a direct order to attack."

I catch Shinsei's angry stare, daring me to defy him.

"I am not yours to order around. I'm here to protect Miyu and find out what really happened to my sister. I don't trust you one bit."

"Sasaki, defeat him and we'll give you all the answers you need. I told you at the beginning you'd get what you wanted if you followed us. Now here's your chance, you must take it."

"Even if I did what you want, what would be the point? Can't you see how easy he fights you off? Why order something that won't work?"

Ariel and Barachiel pause their attack and look down at the three of us, breathing heavily, as my words tail off into the cavern.

"How dare you Sasaki! How dare you question my authority! My troops will follow my orders because they know that I will lead them to victory," he rages at me. He puts a hand on Hesediel's shoulder and turns back to his 'troops'. "You will attack again. You will keep going because you know that my orders are absolute. If you want to succeed you will do the right thing, no matter how impossible it might seem. You will attack with all your might!"

After looking into each other's eyes and wordlessly communicating a whole conversation, Ariel and Barachiel swing back into action. Teleporting back, they undertake combination after combination, attack after attack. But every time the wall of fire appears from nowhere, holding firm against their barrage. A flash of light from the corner of my eye catches my attention as tiny slivers of magic fly through the air. Hesediel has pulled splinters of energy away from his shield and shaped them into thin needles that he's flinging with an almost dance like quality. I follow them with my eyes as he sends them over Sanzo before turning them in mid-air to attack from a blind spot. It's a clever move but it still doesn't work as the fire around Sanzo continuously blocks everything that comes near him.

"Sasaki. If you do not attack my son then I will deem you an enemy and I will exterminate you. I will deem Yamamoto as your ally, and I will slaughter her too. You will join in if you value this world, this country, these people, your friend and your life."

I bow my head to the floor for a second as a painful realisation passes through my head; I won't be allowed to avoid this battle even if I want to. I begin slowly taking shots, knowing that each one will be repelled. I can't go too quickly or I'll run out of arrows as each one that gets anywhere near Sanzo gets evaporated. Despite all of our attacks he hasn't even had to move.

"Cease! Fall back," Shinsei shouts.

I lever the arrow I have nocked back into a resting position and pause for breath as Barachiel and Ariel teleport back to Hashimoto's side.

"You will not be able to beat me father. You and your little pack cannot get past my firewall. I am the ultimate leader of the underworld and the billions of souls that live under my reign will throw themselves on to the fires of hell to burn anyone or anything that gets close to their king. They will gladly sacrifice their souls to keep me safe, and you will never, ever have enough attacks to defeat them all. Tens of thousands of people join my army every second that ticks by in a never-ending flow. Do you understand that I WILL deliver mercy to you, and that there is nothing that you can do about it?"

He turns his attention to the rest of us.

"Do not follow this man any longer my children. I can see in your eyes that you have finally begun to doubt his words. His iron clad grasp on you is finally beginning to relent. You will all have mercy as well, but it will be the mercy of being on the winning side. I'm sure you would all make fine compatriots in my court."

The three Angels in front of Hashimoto exchange looks as they consider swapping one bullying, power hungry emperor for another. I take a step back and reach down to touch Miyu's unconscious shoulder.

"He won't get us, don't worry Miyu," I whisper.

Then I notice the wave of black crawling along the floor underneath Sanzo. It looks like a piece of starless night sky, tinged with purple and blue in the darkness, creeping along the floor towards our foe. It reaches his shoes where it begins to wrap around his ankles and crawl up his leg. Then, as if becoming physical, the snake of night suddenly pulls him upwards before hurling him down the thirty or so feet to the floor, smashing him into the rock and sending a wave of dust and debris blasting over us.

I shield my eyes quickly and follow the attacker back down to where a pale, black-haired figure is hiding in the shadows, hands clasped into fists in front of him.

shhnk

The Angel appears twenty feet above the crater left by the attack, supported by a pair of amazingly complex looking black and white wings. As he flexes them the pattern shifts under my eyes. His form is a pale white, so pale as to be almost see through, with a face that even in this form is unmistakably Kagawa Hiroshi. The haunted look on the face and long black hair are still present, accentuated by a steady flow of blackness streaming from his eyes like tears. His eyes are even more deep set and black rimmed, but now they are concentrated on Sanzo as he pulls his hands back to create a ball of the same dark material that he attacked with before. He releases a contracting beam of darkness that blasts into the crater before teleporting back down to his hiding place. As soon as he hits the shadows he vanishes completely.

"That's your father?" I ask towards Hesediel.

"That's Cassiel, the Watcher, my Father's Angel. He's watches over the Universe from the shadows," Hesediel says, keeping his eyes on Sanzo. "Cassiel can control and manipulate an invisible force in the Universe called dark energy, making it solid and bending it to his will."

"But how did his attacks make it past that firewall?"

He looks over to me with a grim expression upon his face.

"Father always said 'even the brightest of flames can be extinguished by true darkness'."

Looking around the room to try and locate Cassiel again, I draw a blank. When Hesediel notices me trying to find him he pipes up.

"You won't be able to find him Sasaki, he can become invisible within the shadows and move his physical form through them instantaneously."

There is something in Hesediel's voice, something that has taken away from his usual upbeat and positive tones. I think it's fear, fear of his father. He's already fought with that being before, he must know exactly how strong he is.

tsnng

Sanzo appears in the air, weaving about on his broken wings, blood dripping off one of his arms.

"You may be able to disappear Cassiel, but let's see if you can avoid this!" Sanzo shouts forcefully.

The floor starts to shake under his power before suddenly breaking apart to show red hot magma beneath us. It forms a tidal wave that begins to flow through the cavern at unerring speed. As the lava passes underneath Sanzo he raises his hands up, causing the wave to rise before ploughing forward again.

The Angels teleport towards outcrops in the wall and ceiling to protect themselves as I grab Miyu and start tugging at her body. I can't escape with her, there's no high ground for me! As I try to drag her away from the forefront of the wave, she falls limply to the concrete. My skin starts to tingle at the heat radiating towards us from a few feet away. I dive behind the large stack of udomite that Miyu was propped up against and reach round for her shoulders.

Just as the wave is diverted around us by the gemstone I manage to pull Miyu's body around to me in a panic, cradling her in my arms and shielding her from the heat as the lava creeps past. Using a nearby boulder I plant my feet and push my body upwards off the ground, yanking Miyu up with me. My foot slips slightly, causing my shoe to break the surface and become engulfed in flame. I suppress the scream and with one last pull I get Miyu off the floor and manage to get my leg back into position. The skin on my ankle is turning black as I look back into Miyu's emotionless, unconscious face. I have to do this for her. I have to protect her!

My legs wobble and my back starts to slip down the rock face as I desperately try to hold on. Then suddenly my foot slides into a crack in the boulder in front of me and my body comes to a complete stop above the ground. Gasping for breath, I scrunch my eyes shut and pray that we won't be swallowed whole. As the heat starts pressing into my back like a solid force I can't help but cry out at the pain.

The plinking of the lava cooling to solid rock permeates through the air just inches from my ears. I snap my eyes open just as my foot slips out of the crack, throwing my body and Miyu down to the rapidly cooling surface. Miyu crashes into my stomach, knocking the wind out of me as the burning on my skin begins to subside. The top layer of lava is hot, but not so bad as to burn. I puff my cheeks out and a let out a big sigh of relief. Levering Miyu off me I go to set her down but realise that I don't want to let go of her. I never want to let her go. The feelings confuse me to my core. I've never felt this way about anyone before. When I finally relent and unwrap myself from her I make sure she's carefully laid down so she won't go anywhere.

There's a loud noise as Hesediel dissipates the magical shield from around him making the thickened lava that had pooled up against him flop to the floor. I take as many deep breaths as I can as I wipe away the ash from Miyu's face. If he's going to put her in danger then I have to do something.

"How dare you try and hurt her," I say through gritted teeth as I stand up, trying to keep my voice steady. I pull Tenshi out and put an arrow against the string, pointing directly at Sanzo. "You have hurt my friends and family too much Sanzo. I will not allow you to go any further."

shhnk

The sound of Ariel and Barachiel teleporting behind Hashimoto and Hesediel punctuates the end of my sentence. Cassiel appears as if from nowhere to stand next to us as well.

"We will not allow you to go any further!" I shout as I release the shot.

The demonic fire springs up around Sanzo as I expected, but I already have another one ready to go.

"Angels, attack!" Shinsei orders us.

For now, I'll be one of 'us' even if I'm just a human, even if these guys aren't trustworthy. We need to stop him from putting anyone else in danger. I unleash a barrage of shots one after the other, aiming at different points of Sanzo's body. Maybe he has a weak spot. Maybe he can only keep up his fire for so long. What the shots mainly are though, is a distraction.

Out of the corner of my eye I see Hesediel launch another package of needles which split and fly apart in mid-air. The co-ordinated attack continues as Ariel, Barachiel and Cassiel all teleport to Sanzo's position in a pincer, trapping him from the sides while Cassiel attacks from above. The coordinated movement and numbers mean Sanzo finally has to make a move to defend himself, swinging his arms around and directing fire from his palms to keep them away. Cassiel smashes dark energy towards Sanzo's defences, so I let off on the tautness of my string just a tiny amount to reduce the speed of my next shot. It arrives just as Cassiel's darkness hits the shields, allowing my arrow to plough a furrow through the flames. I track the arrow as it flies to within touching distance of Sanzo's chest and clench my fist in celebration as the point touches his skin.

tsnng

My head follows the noise as it flows into my left ear where Sanzo appears a foot behind his father, drawing his sword to land the final blow. I don't have time to react as his sword bursts into flames during its upwards swing, landing with an explosion that obscures our side of the cavern.

As the smoke clears my shock transmutes into hope as the glowing form of Hesediel appears, blocking with a semi-spherical barrier doesn't even bend under the explosive fire that is coming from the edge of Sanzo's blade. He drops to one knee, obviously struggling under the weight of the power being placed on his shoulders. Sanzo's wings open up to teleport away, so I snap an arrow into Tenshi and pull the string back to breaking point. My eyes follow the probabilities of where he'll turn up, letting the shot rip through the air as soon as Sanzo reappears. But even with my reactions turned up to eleven Sanzo is too quick. His sword arm flicks in an awkward direction, coming back around to intercept my attack in a ball of flame before circling back around towards Hesediel.

shhnk

Cassiel's white and black form appears between his son and Sanzo. He raises his hands, causing dark energy to form into a solid sheet around them. Bending backwards he connects with his son's shields to form a complete dome over Shinsei and the genesis shard. Sanzo's attack disappears into it as if falling into a black hole. Where the darkness touches Hesediel's shield there is a crackle of energy and sparks flowing between the two. Light and dark, energy and nothingness meeting with the single aim.

Sanzo's shredded wings flap again, leading him back up to his outcrop as the remaining Angels catch up with the action. Cassiel makes a pushing motion with his hands causing tendrils of dark energy fly out from his shield. The coils of negative space fly at amazing speed towards Sanzo, and even through the flame shield rockets up to protect him, one of them manages to break through. Sanzo makes a move to avoid it, but it catches him square on the cheek and tears through his flesh.

"No! How dare you all protect this lowlife!" Sanzo shouts as he teleports back up into the air, hovering in place. One of his hands touches the side of his face and comes back with blood running down it. The expression on the other half of his face can only be described as pure, hellish, rage.

"I will be your rightful king and you will bow to me! All of you! You will pay for what you've done Angels! The world doesn't want you and your monstrous kind here anymore."

As the battle resumes Hesediel and Cassiel drop their protection to join us. We continue to push at him, nicking through his defences every now and then but never getting close to landing a fatal blow. With Cassiel's help and the others as distractions I finally get one of my arrows to graze his skin, taking a layer of blood with it that evaporates from the heat.

"You!"

Sanzo's voice rings through the cavern towards me. His red eyes are glowing with rage, reflecting the fire around his blade which is pointed directly at me.

"You have just jumped to the head of the queue Sasaki! You shall have your mercy before anyone else."

Sanzo tilts the sword away from me slightly before unleashing another laser beam of concentrated fire which pierces the air. Shit, he's not aiming at me, he's aiming at Miyu! I jump towards her and force my body into the line of fire.

shhnk

My world goes dark as Hesediel appears in front of me. His wings brush my face as the attack slams into him, propelling him backwards over us and into the wall with a massive blast of force. I scream as his skin chars, his defences thoroughly penetrated.

"Finally, father, your time has come" Sanzo says as he teleports behind him.

Shinsei falls to his left but it's not enough to avoid the stab. The sword pierces his skin like a hot knife through butter spilling his blood to the floor. Cassiel teleports in above Sanzo and hits him with his dark energy. The attack tears through Sanzo's body but the bastard just rips the sword out of his father's stomach before flitting away to safety. Ariel and Barachiel join Cassiel around Shinsei as he falls to one knee.

"You may or may not live from that wound father. You deserve more of my time, but I finally managed to get your shields down. Oh, thank you for that opportunity by the way Sasaki!"

Through the tears flowing down my cheeks, I shoot him a look filled with anguish and anger. I rush to Hesediel's side where his shouts of pain are fuelling the anger within me. The blackness from the injury is spreading over his side and up his rib cage already.

"Why the fuck did you do that?! Why did you sacrifice yourself for me?!"

"Because...I...I...you..."

shhnk

Cassiel looms over the pair of us, a menacing scowl on his face.

"What did you just do you little bastard? You nearly cost Hashimoto his life! How dare you deviate from the plan. You're a failure of a son."

"Hey!" I shout.

"Shut up little girl," he snaps at me pushing me away as he picks his son up by the throat, raising him to his feet with brute force. "After all you've done to our family you now endanger the entire mission for a stupid girl like this?"

Hesediel's strangled choking noises stab at me.

"Let him go!" I yell.

I reach out and grab his arm to try and free Hesediel, but I can't move it at all. Cassiel puts his other hand on my forehead and pushes me down to the earth with an almighty crash, causing lights to flash before my eyes. Pain surges through my head as I curl up into a ball, arrows clattering out of my quiver and across the floor. I reach up and feel the warmth of my blood from another wound. Cassiel teleports away, dragging his son to his boss.

"Look at what you've done to him! Just look at what your recklessness has caused!"

Holding Hesediel's head up by his hair, he forces him to take in the damage done to Shinsei. Hesediel is isolated, injured, and on his knees in front of the Angels.

"You have failed, Hesediel," Shinsei says, "your mission was to protect me, and we do not tolerate failure."

Chapter 22

"It looks like they're going to kill him doesn't it?"

The familiar female voice whispering just inches from my ear sends tremors through my body and terror flowing through my veins. Suddenly my arms are wrenched behind my back and I feel chains wrap around my wrists, handcuffing me like a prisoner, just like back in the Fallen cavern. A stiletto dagger drops past my eye-line before the cold steel is rubbed against my cheek by a gloved hand. The blade drops from sight as the velvet glove grips my chin hard. She presses herself into my back and puts her arm on my chest, constricting my body, which is wracking with terror.

"Wouldn't it just be horrible if you had to sit here and watch that beautiful young man perish before your eyes? I know you're quite fond of him aren't you, maybe even more than you think?"

I try and struggle against her but her grip is like iron.

"It looks like they're going to tear him apart, all for failing to protect your weak little leader. Oh, how terrible!"

Her mocking tone makes my skin burn with anger as a laugh seeps from her lips.

"Did you miss me, little Sasaki?"

"I...killed you...Ramiel."

She laughs under her breath again and wrenches my head around to stare at me with her gleaming turquoise eyes over an evil, pointed smile.

"Do I look like someone you killed? Huh? Do I?"

I stay silent, fighting against her grip on my face.

"No, I didn't think so," she continues before turning me back to the Angels again.

The large pile of udomite and the crater obscure us from view, but no one is paying any attention to us anyway. I want to scream out, but Ramiel is holding on to my face so hard that I can't.

"He's not such a pretty sight, is he?"

I scrunch my eyes shut but Ramiel's free hand yanks one of my eyes open forcefully. Cassiel raises his hand and lands a massive slap across his son's face. As Hesediel crumples to the ground from the force I put everything into breaking the hold I'm under, but she bats off my weak attempts and comfortably holds me tight.

"Oh no, you can't possibly alert them to my presence little Sasaki. I won't have that now; I wouldn't be able to have my fun!"

"What do you want from me?" I squeak.

"I want you to suffer!" She hisses. "You're going to sit there and watch as Sanzo eradicates your friends, including that little boy you seem to like so much. He's going to burn your friends down to their bones just like he did that old woman, and then I'm going to kill you."

"Why are you here?" I murmur quietly.

"Ooh that's a fun one, but don't you really mean 'how am I here'? How am I standing here, your life in my hands," the dagger reappears, dangling by her thumb and forefinger, "when you saw me die? Well, I did tell you that I was very powerful Sasaki. I told you I could change the way you, and others, see the world. Do you think I couldn't get into the head of that little mage friend of yours, hmm? She thought that she was sacrificing herself to take me out, but do you think I would really put myself in harm's way so easily?"

Miyu made me push an arrow through her stomach when blind and deaf to get rid of this monster. All that pain. All that suffering. How can all of that have been for nothing? How could we be no closer to the end of all this?

"You...weren't there?" I ask.

"Oh, well I was there, but I was well concealed. Fumio taught me a lot about how to hide well."

If she had gotten into both of us she could have been anywhere. She could have been in the same room and we would never have known.

A movement out of the corner of my eye catches my vision. It's Miyu, crawling towards us slowly. I can't let Ramiel know or she'll kill her in an instant. She looks out at me from under her shelter through the dried blood on her face.

"No!" I yell instinctively.

Shit! Oh god no Miyu don't come out here, you'll get killed! Please, I beg you to stay in there. Hide!

"No what?" Ramiel demands of me.

I have to distract her and allow Miyu to escape.

"But Miyake is dead now. He died yesterday."

"What?!"

She grasps a fistful of my hair and pulls my head back until it feels like my scalp is going to tear off.

"I'm...sorry Ramiel. He died at my hand."

I bite my lip and look away from her, back to the side where Miyu has begun crawling out from her hidey-hole.

"You're lying! He could never fall to someone as worthless as you!"

There's a rattle of wood and steel from my left as Miyu disturbs my bow and arrows which are all over the floor. If she can't be quiet then I need to make more noise.

"It's true. I'm sorry, but he made me do it. He thought you were gone, and he couldn't continue. He obviously cared about you very deeply."

"No, just shut up! Shut up with your lies!"

"Accept it Ramiel! He's gone. You can see inside my mind right? You know I'm telling the truth! He made me use his own sword! He was so desperately unhappy at the idea he had lost you that he couldn't face it anymore."

"No! No! He hadn't lost me! Why would he ever do that?!"

"He thought you were dead. Were you not in contact with him?"

"I had to pretend I was dead! I couldn't risk being discovered by these bastards." Flecks of spittle land on my face and shoulder as she spits out the words with venom. "Oh, you thought you were going to suffer before. You stupid, deceitful, murderous bitch! I'm going to cut your skin off inch by inch and make you eat it!"

The poisonous threats continue to pour into my ear as the tiniest of sounds floats into my left. Miyu is whispering something under her breath, but I can't make out what it is.

"I'm going to kill everyone you love and grind them up Sasaki! I'm going to pour the ashes over your skinless body!"

A full-on laugh pours out of Ramiel's mouth. A laugh laced with the kind of murderous bloodlust that is usually reserved for monsters in fairy stories. She's completely lost it. And then I hear it, Miyu's pure and beautiful voice piercing through the madness.

"Give me thine weapon...take up...the...fight."

The soft, squelching noise that follows interrupts Ramiel's laughter. We both look down to see the tip of the arrow protruding from her stomach and into my chest. I try to move but I can feel the shaft running right the way through Ramiel, locking us together. We both sink down to the floor, our blood mingling together and dripping off the tip of the arrowhead. I look back at Miyu as her voice comes again through the ever-closing darkness and the glow in her eyes begins to fade away.

"I'm sorry Kyu. I couldn't stop her before...but you have the chance now. This was the only way."

***

"Oh Miyu, what did you do?" I whisper as I awaken underneath the dark, menacing sky tinted with green.

A groan from the other side of the clearing snaps me back to action. I hop up on to my haunches and reach for Tenshi but grab at nothing but thin air. Surveying the scene there's now a small copse puncturing the landscape behind me in addition to the large cherry tree in front, but other than that there's just the expanse of deep grass pocked with lakes and pools. I take a crab step towards the water by my side as the groan attaches itself to Ramiel who brings herself up to a standing position while holding her head groggily.

"Urgh, this place looks even worse than I remember."

I stare at her as she sighs and rubs her head.

"Can't you put the pieces together by now? I thought you were supposed to be clever Sasaki?"

A small roll of thunder comes from the clouds above me.

"So, you don't just control people's senses but you literally get inside their soul? That's how you control what they see? That's how your power works."

"For the first time in your life you're a winner Sasaki, yes. But not just see. I can manipulate all the external senses from the mind. So many people think that their eyes and ears and mouths control their brains but the reality is that it's almost entirely the other way around. Your brain can trick you into seeing or feeling anything that it wants to. I can pull on those strings in the outside world, feeding information back to your senses however I want."

"How many times have you been here?"

She fingers the handles of her daggers in her belt and looks at me.

"I guess the first time I was here was the night that you defeated Abaddon. Do you remember Abaddon? No, I guess not because you killed him before he could even speak. You didn't even acknowledge his existence. You just executed him in cold blood, like the murderer that you are."

So that monster that attacked Lailah really was a Fallen.

"How could you have been here since then? All this time? I've been here loads of times and I never saw you."

"Ah well, by the time I got here you'd already made her your little bitch by stringing her up against that tree hadn't you?" She says, pointing a thumb towards the tree where Lailah is imprisoned.

In the sky the clouds are roiling and billowing again. Above Ramiel the green lining in the clouds turn to purple, rolling and bashing against one another like they're at war.

"Are these your doing too?" I say, pointing upwards. "You've been inside my head, screwing up my brain?"

"I haven't been able to be here all the time, but when I have I may have helped the process along somewhat. Frankly, it didn't need much help, your mind was completely fucked Sasaki. It was a complete mess before I even got here."

"Sski..."

That voice! It's Lailah, but distant and in pain.

"Saski...save...me."

"What do you mean?"

"Oh, you've definitely encountered it before. In a way I've always been with you even if it was him doing the work while I was away! Don't you remember seeing your little friends bleeding to death in the school? Or losing your wittle way in the hopital?" She says in a mocking, childish tone.

"That was you? All of it?"

She looks smugly at me with a grin that I want to smash right off her face.

"It was both of us. Me and him," she says, pointing behind me.

I turn slowly and come face to face with the featureless, tooth-filled Angel monster towering above me. It sniffs me from just inches away before opening its craw to reveal those shark teeth. Row after row of interlocking spikes fill its elongated mouth. As it roars at me my hair flows back and the stench hits my face, but I remain resolute. The scream dies down to silence and I can hear the ringing in my ears from the brute force of the sound wave.

"We even let you have a taste of Lailah's power at times. It was so glorious to give you those positive feelings and then steal them away from you! You were so distraught! I thought you were going to kill yourself with all the trauma we put you through. Isn't that funny?! It was amazing to feel from the inside Sasaki hahaha!"

"You...must defeat her."

The voice echoes in my mind again. How? I don't even have a weapon!

"This is your soul...you're in more control...than you think. Make yourself a weapon."

Yes, it wasn't me. The self-doubt, the feeling that everyone was going to leave me, it was her! I'm sane, I'm wanted, I'm needed by people. I can't let her control my thoughts anymore.

"You nearly got me Ramiel, you really did. So you left him, a part of you, in here to play with my mind? All the nightmares, all the visions, the bloodlust. It's all been you? You had me believing I was insane, and that I was useless!"

"You are useless! You already feel it, I just brought it to the front!"

Everything makes more sense now. This is me, and if I'm in control I can make this place mine again. I hold up my hand, causing a large bolt of lightning to ground itself through me, covering my whole body in light. When it subsides, there in my hand is a perfect copy of Tenshi, exactly as real as the one back in the Sanctum. I reach back to a full quiver, nock and fire a shot at the Angel monster in a split second, causing it to duck and slither away. A small smatter of blood hits the grass where I nicked it on the side of its snout. When it reaches Ramiel's side it stands up and she rubs it slightly, like an equestrian caring for a prize mare. Blood drips down Ramiel's cheek from a wound that's appeared on her face at the same place. The lightning strikes pick up. Green and purple bolts crash into the ground around us as if attacking each other.

"You have a pathetic little mind Sasaki. You can't even see that you're being manipulated, being controlled by those very beings you try to defend."

"Tell me, when I was fighting Miyake Fumio it felt like my mind was wrenching apart. That was your little creature wasn't it?" I ask.

A low growl comes from the monster. No wonder Miyake looked so confused back there. The chains, the trap, the madness, it all came from that thing hiding away in the recesses of my head. None of it was real. Ramiel trapped me with my own mind while to him I was just yelling about nothing! He could have killed me easily but had no idea what was happening. I thought I'd really got control back of my mind once I defeated Lailah, and then again when Miyu and I defeated Ramiel, but none of that was true. I'll only be free of them if I can take both of them out here and expunge every last bit of their influence from my soul.

Chapter 23

I raise Tenshi to a firing position and pull an arrow out of my quiver. I need to get back to the real world, I need to know Miyu is ok. I have to save Satoshi, and if I don't stop Sanzo then none of that will matter.

I fire at the monster, but they both dive out of the way before bouncing up in perfect unison. They rush towards me, circling in an eerily similar way to how Barachiel and Ariel work in tandem. The monster comes in at my midriff, but I use Tenshi to block his biting attack.

tsnng

In anticipation of her attack, I've already grasped an arrow behind my head, blocking the dagger that Ramiel slashes down with. It's just like when I was fighting with Lailah. I can tell exactly where my enemies are, and I can feel where they're going to go. Even as Ramiel teleports around me I can sense the air move and react quickly enough to block her. We twirl around like a trio of dancers, trading blows.

With her physical attacks not working Ramiel suddenly teleports away from me, disappearing into the ether and leaving her familiar and me one on one. It jumps back strangely and runs at me before dodging my shots. When it gets closer it lunges hard at me, but my reactions are better than ever here.

After minutes of the song and dance, I force it around before catching it with a surprise shot, but just before another shot pierces through the monster's throat its tail hits the ground, propelling it into the air, kicking up soil and turf with each rotation. Something feels different. It's moving around but I can't feel it in the same way.

Suddenly the air behind me moves in the tiniest of ways and I spin only to see nothing there, but reflexively roll sideways anyway. Ramiel's monster appears at my side shrieking and firing teeth at me like missiles from its maw. I cry out in pain as they bury themselves into my shin.

"Sasaki!" Lailah's voice cries out above the pain and into my mind.

I clutch at my leg to try and staunch the blood flow, the monster lifting its head before disappearing completely. Subtle air movement triggers me again as another barrage of sharp, triangular projectiles come at me from nowhere. With the tiniest bit of foresight after the last attack I have just enough in me to push off with my good leg and roll away from them. On the ground, I take advantage of the momentary break to clamp my eyes shut, grip the shrapnel, and yank it out of my leg, turning the beautiful green grass a horrible shade of maroon.

"You're affecting how I feel aren't you? Even here? Just how powerful are you?!"

Ramiel's laugh echoes invisibly over the growing storm. I have to get to safety and calm myself for a bit. My eyes dart to the forest and I make a calculated risk to go for it. I jump up to my feet but my injured leg struggles to hold me up as I push myself towards the cover of the trees. The bark is almost close enough to touch as the Angel's mouth clamps on to my trailing leg, sending me flying to the ground. The pain is so intense as the teeth shred my calf muscles, making me scream at the top of my voice as thunder and lightning break overhead.

I spin round and jab the monster in the eyeless face with the end of my bow, piercing the skin and forcing it to release its grasp. Scrambling up to the nearest tree I start to shimmy up the trunk on my one good leg, using Tenshi as a hook to pull myself into the security of the canopy. The dying bark is flaking, but despite my chunky frame the solid wood seems strong enough to hold me as I escape upwards. I try to control my breathing as I struggle to get from branch to branch without making too much noise.

"*Sasaki,*" Lailah whispers.

"I can't talk to you now. I need to stay hidden," I whisper.

Staring down intently from my vantage point I can hear the padding as the monster enters the forest. Its face is leaking fluid from the attack that let me get out from underneath it. Good, and that means that if they're linked Ramiel will be hurting as well, unless this is all a mirage...No! I try and concentrate, feeling the movement of the trees, the air, the grass. I can work this out if I focus hard enough. I try to stay on the blind side of the monster as it circles around the trees, sniffing at the trunks, attempting to track me down. When it stops at the base of the tree next to me I hold my breath.

"*Sasaki!*"

It jumps into the trunk, attempting to dig its claws into the bark but it's far too heavy to climb up.

"*Sasaki, listen to me!*"

"What?!" I hiss angrily, "can't you see I'm busy here?"

"*You have to release me. That monster has me trapped. If I try to get out it attacks me. It's so dark in here! Please help me! She was here before, and they let me out to talk to you, when you were at the hospital. They made me give you part of my power, but as soon as I tried to escape properly they beat me and shoved me back in here.*"

There's another thump as the monster falls off another tree. Holding on to the trunk I rotate around to the other side.

"Can't you come out now and help me? I could really use another bow around here."

"*I don't have any energy to fight her, and she destroyed the bow I came here with.*"

"Ok, but I can't help you until I've got rid of that thing and Ramiel. If I try and get to you now I'll get slaughtered."

"I can distract it, but if I do you have to kill it. You have to do it in that moment. If you kill the monster it'll take her down too."

"How are you going to distract them?"

"If I attempt to come out they'll come after me. They know if they kill me it'll all be over."

"What?! You can't risk yourself like that."

There's an uncomfortable pause filled only with the padding of the monster below.

"If you don't screw it up then it'll work out. I've been here for what feels like eternity and I need to get out one way or the other. Do not mess this up Sasaki! I'm counting on you."

As the monster gets closer to my position I skip over to the next branch, which creaks before breaking and dropping to the floor. I catch myself on the remaining bough but as the debris hits its head the Angel roars at me.

"Stay out of its way Sasaki!"

As if I needed to be told that. I rush across the canopy as fast as my damaged legs will take me, using Tenshi to swing from tree to tree as the monster follows my trail. Across the field is Ramiel; the thing must have driven me in a god damn circle! And now it's right beneath me. It raises its head and opens its mouth, but before it can fire at me the screeching sound of Lailah's voice pierces the air. Her head pushes its way through the giant tree trunk that was acting as her prison. White light glares out like she's emerging from the centre of a supernova. Her hair is ripped, and her face is covered in scars. As her shoulders make it out she stops and collapses down, half escaped. The monster sniffs before bounding towards her, it's tongue lolling out of its mouth. Ramiel reappears from her hiding spot with a dagger lunging towards Lailah.

"Now!" Lailah yells.

I drop down from my hiding place, making sure to put most of my weight on to my good leg and roll forward as I land. Before I can take the shot a second Angel monster jumps towards me, causing me to panic and fire off target before it disappears. Out of pure good luck it cannons off one of the arrows sticking out of the ground from earlier, piercing the real monster's leg. Both it and Ramiel collapse, Ramiel's dagger falling just short of connecting with Lailah's throat as she lunges out.

"You stupid bitch Sasaki!" Lailah yells. "What are you doing?"

"I'm sorry!"

"You had to take out the monster! Do it now!"

Ramiel, unable to move from her wounded leg, raises her hand and beckons towards me, causing the monster to spin around and leap on top of me, knocking Tenshi out of my hands and all the arrows out of my reach.

"Kill it!"

It snaps down at me but all I can do is grip on to the thing's jaws. The stench of its breath on my face is horrific as it moves to within inches of me. I struggle and squirm against it as hard as I can but I can't stop it getting closer. Ideas speed through my panicked mind, but I can't come up with any way of getting out of this situation that doesn't leave me at its mercy. I look down at the exposed muscle of my bitten leg and a realisation finally dawns on me.

I shut my eyes and take a deep breath before removing my hand from its jaw muscles and stuffing my forearm into the things mouth. As it clamps down on me I can feel the hundreds of pointy teeth sinking into my bones. Lightning begins to erupt from the clouds above as I scream with the breath-taking agony, causing my lungs to falter and tears to stream from my eyes. Blood flows out of the things mouth as my arteries and veins get decimated. It opens its mouth again and I can see the white of bone through the gaps in my flesh.

I hold my good arm aloft and with another flash of lightning materialise an arrow into it. I push it as hard as I can through the thing's jaw, the point plunging into the roof of its mouth, making it bellow alongside my breathless, anguished shrieking. I push the monster over on to its back, straddling it like a love scene from a grotesque horror movie. I raise my hand and make another arrow appear, framing it with the roiling clouds which continue to pound at each other above us. Lightning flashes between them and the thunder is a constant cacophony. I sink the arrow into the Angel's stomach hard. It screams out at me around the arrow in its mouth as I rip the point out of its grey flesh and push once more. Over the noise of the storm, Ramiel's wails mix with the monster's as I thrash the point into its stomach over and over again, spraying blood on to my chest and face. I can taste the warm, ferrous flavour as the blood sprays into my mouth, but I just keep on screaming and stabbing. Eventually the adrenaline that is allowing me to continue fades away and I drop the arrow before falling forwards on to the carcass below me.

"Lai...lah..." I gasp.

"Finish her Sasaki! Kill her!"

Ramiel is clutching her stomach, trying to keep her guts from escaping the deep wound. I get to my feet as quickly as I can but with my devastated leg and shattered arm I can only move slowly towards her. After a few steps I collapse to the ground again.

"I...can't"

"Yes you can! You fucked up by not doing what I said! Kill her before she gets me, or we're both finished!"

One leg, one arm, blood loss. I can't do it. I can't kill her from here. My vision is blacking out already.

"Don't you fucking dare give up Sasaki! I'm here because of you, now do something about it!"

Her words drive through my brain, reaching down into me and pulling out the last drop of energy I have. I roll over on to my back, materialise Tenshi into my hand again and raise my knee up to my chest. I manoeuvre the bow around and pull the string back with my good arm. With my body contorted on the floor, I move around until I'm aiming at Ramiel's head. The green and purple light flashing above me in the boiling sky is blinding, so I shut my eyes and materialise an arrow in the string.

"Do it! Don't be the failure that people think you are. Don't be the person who I thought you were when I first met you."

I groan loudly as I transfer the string from my arm to my teeth and pull it back that little bit more. My groan turns in to a muffled scream as my body threatens to give in.

"Fire!"

As the twanging string slices my lips open, a flash of green lightning smashes down into me. The arrow flies out of the bow sheathed in energy at a speed I can't even comprehend, the force of it ripping up the ground as it passes. It's so quick I barely hear the noise of it hitting Ramiel in the chest. With blood all over me I lay there, breath rasping in my lungs and my heartbeat slowing until it threatens to stop completely. In the haziness of my vision, I notice a bright light flowing in from beside me. It moves up to my head until it's filling my vision.

"Lai...lah..."

"Thank you, Sasaki. I'm finally free."

Her hand touches my head and a soothing calm flows through my body. I hold my arm up and see the muscles knitting themselves together, the skin covering back over miraculously. The pain drops out of my body like a weight falling from my feet. The world rotates around me and I realise I actually am floating in the air on a pair of great white wings.

"Wh...what's happening?"

"With that thing gone we can finally be free to commune together properly. We can finally use our power together. Look."

I follow her eyes and see the banks of grey clouds begin to dissipate, with columns of sunlight falling to the ground. The forest I hid in has already started to bud with new leaves, and the dead bark is renewing and coming alive again. I hold my head up to the sky and drink in the sun, destroying the heavy grey darkness that has been encompassing this place. Now that the battle is over I can finally look into Lailah's graceful face, still beautiful underneath the scars and cuts. A million questions tumble through my head but only one presents itself to my tongue.

"I thought you were dead."

"I was, for a bit, but I'm stronger than you think I am."

I can't look at her anymore, my eyes sink to the floor.

"I saw you get taken, by me."

"It takes more than that to kill me. I had to sacrifice almost every shred of energy to stay alive once that beast was here. It ravaged me for what felt like years within that prison. I have the scars to prove it."

Her clothes are shredded, revealing an emaciated form with ribs sticking out from under the rags. One of her legs looks to be broken at the shin and the long, beautiful hair has been ripped to pieces, leaving it jutting out at random places. Her wings are broken and in tatters. She looks like she's been through a war.

"I fought and fought and fought to get rid of them, but every time I managed to gain the energy to escape my prison, they beat me and put me back in there. It drove me back to the darkness."

"You did all that to help me?"

"Oh don't flatter yourself, do you know what would have happened if you'd died while I was in here? I would have been a goner too. If an Angel's host body dies then the Angel dies as well, so I had to take the beatings and the lashings so that I could force enough of myself out and give you access to my power. Do you think you would have beaten Dumah without my help? I couldn't let you perish at his hand. I need you alive. The plan is still in play."

"What plan?"

"Hashimoto Shinsei's plan. We needed you, and we still do."

She takes her hands away from mine, gently brushing her pocked fingertips against mine. I clench my palms to try and capture the feeling of her skin within them to stop it floating away, but before I can even finish savouring the sensation her hands have snapped around my throat. She thrusts my body down to the floor and crashes on top of me, knocking the wind out of me. Through wide, tear-filled eyes I can see the madness in her face.

"Now I'm out I can finally defeat you Sasaki. I will take your mind and then I will take your body and get back to my rightful place by Hashimoto's side!"

Her anger turns to a manic laugh as her hands grip my throat harder. Her face is contorted with rage, but looking into it I realise that I can still breathe. Oxygen flows through my throat inside a neck that feels like it's made of steel, pushing back against her. I raise myself up from the ground and force Lailah back. Her arms peel off me with the ease of taking a wet t-shirt off after a rainstorm as I grab a hold of them. She's powerless to resist me as I push her hands behind her back, locking her in a close embrace, her arms and wings entirely encapsulated. Our faces are just inches away. I feel strength and light flowing through my heart.

"You think that you have the power to just come out and take over my soul Lailah? You come out in that state and just expect to take over the place? Even after all this time you still think so lowly of me."

I hold her closer to me, so she can feel my breath in her ear as I whisper.

"What is it the Angels want from me?"

"You have...power," she says breathlessly.

"That's right. But now I am free of the burden of that monster, all the guilt of thinking I'd killed you and all the things I've had to do. I can see now they were necessary. They were hard, and violent, but when I was in control I think I always made the right choice to protect those around me. And I'll keep doing those hard things until they're all safe."

She gasps as I clench her closer.

"What would happen if I crushed you, right here and now?"

"I would..." she says before drifting off. I wait a few seconds but she clearly can't say it.

"You would die, wouldn't you?"

As she nods her hair rubs softly against my cheek.

"You don't want to do that Sasaki."

"Then I will give you a choice. Fight with me. Be my power, help me protect my friends and defeat Sanzo and I will return you to the world when we are complete."

"And if I don't?"

"You will never see the light of day again. Don't make me do it. But I will, and you know I will."

I release Lailah slightly so that we can stand face to face again. She finally looks like she realises the gravity of her situation.

"Ok," she murmurs.

Suddenly she pushes her mouth on to mine, our lips entwining. My heart jumps in my chest as the passion flows through my body, setting it on fire. I shut my eyes and my hands drop to my sides as she holds my face. When I open them I see her body melting away into energy in front of me. I put my hands up to her and she flows through them like sand through an hourglass.

Chapter 24

I wake up in a startle, gasping and clutching at my chest, the pain radiating from the arrow still stuck in there. I grab it and pull hard, forcing it to inch slowly out from within my body. The fact I can still breathe properly means it missed all my vital organs, Miyu must have done an excellent job with her aim. Finally, the feathered flight erupts from my chest cavity, spraying blood on to my ragged clothes.

My hands instinctively go to my pockets to find more udomite pills to staunch the bleeding, but the memory of the empty bottle flitters into my mind, and then the wound on my chest starts healing over on its own. Of course, no need for those now that Lailah is free. The angelic power flows through me, healing me as I reach for Tenshi, reassured by the real wood and steel in my hand. I look past the reflection of my eyes, green and fiery in the dull metal, and spy the unconscious Ramiel on the ground next to Miyu.

"Kill her Sasaki."

Ignoring Lailah's voice, I run to Miyu and lift her up from the debris.

"Miyu, are you alright?"

"Kyu! Oh, I'm so happy you're ok!"

I shake my head in disbelief at her. Her cloak is strewn with blood and she can barely move, but her first instinct is to check on me and see how I am. I don't need to be an empath to see that she is not in a good way.

"I'll be ok Kyu, I promise. I'm so glad you managed to get out. I knew you'd be able to do it if I gave you the opportunity."

"What did you even do?"

"You needed to defeat her, and after fighting her before I knew you wouldn't be able to do it here, it'd be too difficult. So, I simply copied the incantation that Lailah used when she originally attacked you."

"And that was simple was it?"

"Well, ok, no it wasn't. I've been working on it ever since Lailah first showed up."

"But it's Angel magic! How could you possibly do it?"

"It's actually not that different to the magic that my family has used for thousands of years. 'Angel magic' isn't really a thing. They might have supernatural abilities, but what Lailah used is actually blood magic. I doubt I could do what Lailah does with it, but I researched in our library at home and practiced on myself. See."

She lifts one of the long arms of her cloak, revealing hundreds of small scars all up her arm. She smiles at me and the dams burst within my mind.

"How could you hurt yourself like that?!" I say, choking back the tears with anger and dismay.

She retracts her arm and puts her sleeve back down before wrapping herself around me.

"I knew you would need it. You saved my life when we fought Ramiel before and I can never repay you for that, but I hope that I did help."

I grasp her as hard as I can. There are so many things I want to say to her.

"Kill Ramiel now!" Lailah shouts inside me.

That damn Angel continues to insist on trying to ruin the moment.

"I...I..." I murmur, before trailing off. I can't tell her that I love her. I desperately want to, but I can't say the words.

"I know Kyu. I've missed you so much all these years. You think so little of yourself, but to me you're everything. It's so sad that it took all this to get you to realise it. My life has always been better with you in it, even if you never knew."

As she pulls back there's tears in her eyes, but there's a smile on her face which warms my heart. Nothing more needs to be said. I can feel my cheeks flushing in embarrassment.

"We need to keep you safe Miyu. We need to get you out of here."

"I won't be able to get out until this is over Kyu. You go and finish this.

"OK, do you promise you'll stay here and stay hidden while I go and deal with Sanzo?"

She nods her response to me silently.

"Do not, under any circumstances come out, even to help me."

She nods again. I help her up and move her across to the wall behind the biggest remaining crop of udomite a few feet away. I collect my arrows up and slot them back into my quiver, shaking as much of the blood off them as I can before stepping over Ramiel's prone body. The wound in her chest is still oozing blood, but it doesn't look like it's going to be life threatening to my untrained eyes.

Suddenly my body goes stiff. It feels like quick setting cement is flowing through my veins, locking my limbs where they are. Lailah's voice crashes through my head like a tidal wave, destroying the control I have on my body.

"How dare you ignore me! Put her away now, make sure that she's dead and she won't come back."

"No! I can't kill an unconscious person! We defeated her, she won't be an issue," I say through a jaw clenched so hard that talking is difficult.

"I may be fighting on your side, but I will not let you act in a way that is so stupid. You'll put us both in danger. Now...kill...her. Put an arrow...through her...head."

As her demands come through, my leaden arms start to move of their own accord. I fight against them, but I can't stop my left arm raising Tenshi and my right arm swinging around to pull an arrow out.

"No! Stop it!"

The arrow comes over my shoulder and into sight. Slowly but unstoppably Lailah uses my body to put the flight into the string. One eye snaps closed and the other looks right down the length of the arrow, the gleaming point staring directly at Ramiel's temple. I fight and fight with everything I've got as the string inches back towards me.

"No…No! I won't…let you…kill her!"

I tense myself as hard as I can and push against Lailah's effort. I flick my aiming eye temporarily away and see Miyu's distressed face looking back at me. She must know what is going on, but I did tell her not to come out under any circumstances.

"We…have…to…"

Lailah tries to make my fingers let go of the string, but I pull every shred of energy I have to keep them curled up. I grit my teeth until it feels like the enamel is going to chip off and let out a guttural, primal bellow, forcing my left hand up as the arrow finally releases. It flies off, burying itself in the ground just inches from Ramiel's head. I hear Lailah's scream inside me and feel her hold on me release, letting me fall to my knees. I quickly grab an arrow and put the point against my own neck.

"No! This is my body. You cannot, and you will not ever do that again. Do you hear me?!"

Silence.

"If you ever, EVER try to do something like that again I will push an arrow through my throat, and you will perish. Do you hear me?"

More silence, broken by a loud slap that rings through the cavern. I turn to see Hesediel falling to the floor, Cassiel's hand still high in the air after the blow he landed upon his own son. From across the cavern, I see that poor boy's face smash into the concrete at the feet of his leader.

Hashimoto finally moves, leaning down and grabbing Hesediel's head. White fire flickers over his hand and down onto him, covering his body in flames and burning at his skin.

Pushing his head back down to the ground, golden light suddenly erupts from his pores. The energy forms into a ball, spinning and undulating until it explodes like a snowstorm. Slowly it comes back together until it forms into a spectral version of Hesediel, floating above Satoshi's body. The Angel glows beautifully with white and gold light, bowing his head to Hashimoto.

"I'm sorry, I've failed you." Hesediel says, his voice echoing strangely.

"You will be missed Hesediel, but you know that we cannot let you continue."

"Yes sir."

Suddenly the spirit dissipates, the golden light scattering until nothing is left to even indicate that it was there. They...they forcefully turned him back? How could they? After a few seconds it's clear that only Satoshi remains.

"Lailah, come to me, now!"

I push my hands back, my chest out and my head up, and feel the purity erupt inside of me, coating me in a film of light. The feathers brush against my hands as I extend them fully.

shhnk

I flap my wings and spring forward to where Satoshi's body is still lying and knock Shinsei's hand away. I cradle his head protectively and look up at the leader of the Angels. Suddenly it dawns on me that he's not breathing. I shake him and start to try to perform rudimentary CPR as the tears flow over my cheeks until Hashimoto picks me up and slams me against a rock.

"Let me go! What did you do to him?!" I shout through the tears and the pain.

"Hesediel failed the mission he was given," he says back through gritted teeth, "and for that he had to be punished. Hesediel is dead as the fitting punishment for his insolence."

"But...Satoshi?" I ask in a pleading tone.

"When an Angel dies the host has to die as well, that's just how it is. The human body cannot take the removal of such energy from within it. Satoshi knew this from the beginning. He knew the mission I gave him was worth giving his life for from the start."

"He can't be...dead," I wail.

"You have to accept it. He's gone."

I grab Satoshi's body before flapping my wings to take him to Miyu. I drop him off and shake my head at her with tears flowing down my cheeks. She puts her arms around me again, trying to take the pain away.

"How dare you focus on your petty, internal squabbles while I'm still here," Sanzo says, rising to his feet after Cassiel's attack.

I heft Tenshi to fire a shot but am forced to stop as Hashimoto strides forward in front of me, blood leaking into his clothes. As he walks, his shirt flows up to show the gaping wounds in his side. He pushes through the Angels in front of him, reaching his arms behind his back and up his long coat before dragging out two wide bladed scimitars.

"I guess I will need to deal with this after all," he says.

He whispers under his breath and slaps the blades of his swords together twice. A blinding flash engulfs us all before it fades to reveal the true leader of the Angels. He's a spectacular vision, bedecked all in white and ensconced in flame. His clothes have morphed into pure white, backed by a long cloak which burns as if doused in petrol. Over that are a gigantic pair of wings, by far bigger than anyone else's that I've seen. The wings burn with the same bright, white fire as the cloak, as does the halo that floats above his head and the blades in his hands. Unlike the fire around Sanzo's being which is a deep, dark combination of reds and oranges, Shinsei's fire seems to contain a light within it. He truly is everything I would have imagined he would be.

"I am worth your effort in the end aren't I?!" Sanzo shouts viscerally. "You thought you could get away without releasing yourself, didn't you? Well now that you're finally here I can get really serious!"

He twirls his arms, raising up a cone of flame from the floor around his body. The tornado rises, whipping the wind around the room, smattering us with shards of rock and stone. Just as the vortex reaches the ceiling it suddenly collapses from the centre, leaving Sanzo crouched on the floor with an aura of flame around him. As he stands up slowly the flames crawl up and down his bare skin, blackening it as if charred. It extends around his wings, down his cloak and up his head where it flickers over the spikes of his hair and around the fangs that frame his mouth. His voice warbles like the harmony of a million individual voices reciting the same lines.

"Hell's fire will give you mercy. We have existed since the beginning of time and our numbers grow by the second. Join the millions of souls that will pass our way and your death will not be violent. This is your last chance to repent your sins and retain your dignity."

"Your numbers do not cause me fear. Come, bring your fire to me."

Sanzo teleports in and his sword clashes into Shinsei's with an almighty impact that sends a shockwave across the room. The force overwhelms me and the rest of the Angels, pushing us downwards.

"Your presence here in this form speaks volumes of your fear Meta," says Sanzo's Fallen form.

"I can say the same to you. This is your true form isn't it Azrael?" Shinsei's Angel replies stoutly.

The clash finally ends, pushing both combatants away before they clash blades again, sending out another shockwave of power.

"No, I told you, Azrael does not exist anymore. I am only Hashimoto Sanzo. Tell me father, how long has it been since you last took that form? You think you can beat me, me who rules the underworld like this every day?"

The Angel, Meta, pushes back, throwing Sanzo off him before pirouetting into an attack. During a twist he clashes his blades against one another, bringing the flames roaring on their edges stronger than before. Sanzo deflects the hits but it's clear he's rattled, even in this form. His supreme confidence has slipped at the sight of seeing his father finally go all out. Sanzo tries to go in for an attack, but Meta blocks it easily with one sword. His second one scythes round at waist height, crashing into the fire barrier that jumps to his son's defence. After a brief struggle, the blade flares and slices through the firewall, the tip grazing Sanzo's stomach.

"Whatever you do, however hard you work, you will never be able to defeat me. It would take you one hundred thousand years just to put a scratch on me," Shinsei says to his son.

The fighting resumes in a whirlwind punctured by clashing blades, erupting fire, and shockwaves blowing apart the environment. I teleport to the remaining Angels and face up to them. They look awestruck as the fighting continues behind us.

"What will you do now?" I ask.

"What can we do Sasaki?" Cassiel responds, still staring at the scene behind me as the ringing of the blades continues. "If Meta has come out then there is already no possible way that we can affect the outcome."

"Why not? He is just your leader. You should fight with him, beside him." Satoshi's face pops into my mind and I'm revulsed at the idea of deifying this being. The one who would rip someone's life from him for saving an innocent person. Cassiel turns to look directly at me through his black rimmed eyes.

"Oh no, he is different. Meta is the Archangel of Heavenly Fire. He carries the fire of God and can wield it in earthly form. His blades, his wings, his halo, they all contain the holy fire. The fact that Sanzo can even keep up with him in this state is a miracle. These are the two ultimate rulers of their domains. They are beings on an entirely different plane to us."

A laser of fire erupts over my shoulder, just a foot or so from decapitating me, which forces all of us to the floor. Looking up from our low vantage point we see them trade blows at lightning speed, constantly teleporting around each other in an attempt to land a devastating hit. Sanzo is keeping up, and the power that radiates from them is practically touchable even from here. We watch as Meta's swords meet resistance of the souls of hell as they burn themselves to protect Sanzo, but it does not take much effort for him to cut through. Cassiel's wings cover his body like he's trying to hide away.

"Sasaki, we must fight where we can. We cannot rely on Shinsei winning this on his own. You must do something," Lailah says to me.

I pull Tenshi round and run my fingers over the damaged ornate workings on his shaft, caressing the rapidly tarnishing filigree. They may be on another level, but we cannot just stand by and let this happen.

Chapter 25

"Stand Angels. This is a fight we all need to be part of. Will you leave your leader to fight on his own or will you give your effort, your energy, and your lives to help us win, together?"

I expected them to jump to action with me but none of them have moved an inch, there's just three scared faces looking up at me.

"Stand! You will fight! Now!"

I spin and fire an arrow, catching Sanzo off guard. Although his firewall eradicates it, it's enough to distract him for a brief moment. Meta ploughs through and slices into Sanzo's shoulder, blood spewing out from the deep wound. He glares at me as he grips his injured arm.

tsnng

Suddenly he's in front of me, his blade piercing the air, aimed directly at my chest. I flip Tenshi round to block and catch the string on the edge of my wing. As the tip of Sanzo's flaming sword moves towards me, Cassiel's darkness rises up to absorb the attack. Sanzo teleports away, pulling his sword out with him but it's straight into Meta's path who grabs his shoulder and slams him to the floor. Sanzo's sword clatters away out of his grasp, the tip shaved off as if cut by a laser.

"You got lucky there Sasaki, Sanzo nearly had you. This is not some stupid back yard archery tournament now. A mistake won't get you a bad score, it'll get you and everyone here killed."

Sanzo escapes up into the air and puts his clawed hands out, spouting two jets of deep red flame towards Meta who swoops around the room to avoid them. They chase each other all around the cavern, leaving scorch marks around the walls and melted rock and gem on the floor. Suddenly one of the jets veers off towards us. I zoom up into the rafters expecting to be joined by the others, but instead they're prostrate on the floor as the attack rushes towards them. Meta appears in front of them just as the laser reaches the tip of the giant, glowing genesis shard in its holder. He blocks the death beam with the flat of his scimitars, diverting it off to the ceiling.

"You must protect the genesis shard from Azrael! That is your order, Angels!" Meta bellows.

Sanzo picks up his sword, struggling to lift it with his injured shoulder. He puts his hand to the wound and a horrid smell washes over us accompanied by smoke and flame as he cauterizes his own wound.

Meta turns to me and I can't help but marvel at his imposing figure. Imbued with flame he stands tall over me with wings outstretched and light illuminating my world. "You must protect the shard Sasaki. You cannot let Sanzo destroy..."

Suddenly his face falters as a beam of fire rips through his side and up his wing. The sound of the attack echoes away into complete silence as he slowly folds to his knees and eventually to the floor. Charred feathers start to fall like snowflakes on a winter's night. As he collapses he reveals Barachiel and Ariel on their knees behind him, having done their best to divert the attack. Silence rolls across us all as we're shocked into inaction. Sanzo gently drifts towards us with a deep, evil smile spreading across his face. The gaping hole in his chest and shoulder has been replaced with a horrific, charred piece of scar tissue. He loses his footing as he touches down, grimacing as he plants his sword into the ground for support.

"I told you that he could not triumph over me and my subjects."

"You think this fight is over?" Ariel shouts. Her voice sounds off though, like she's purposefully using rage to hide how afraid she is.

"My father could not defeat me; do you think you can even come close?"

"You think you can beat us so easily? Well, we're about to prove you wrong!" She looks towards her husband and a confident smirk flows over her face. "Come on dear."

They leap towards Sanzo in unison, combining their powers just like they did against me. However even their best efforts are not enough to break through the damn flames which rise up around him. All I can do to help is shoot at him over and over again, hoping that a shot gets through, but the arrows just can't do enough damage on their own. I drop to my knees in frustration and start banging my fist on the floor as he repels all of us. A rattle punctuates the sound of battle as arrows roll out of my quiver.

"Why do you follow him?!" I bellow, aiming my rage at the souls who are willing to sacrifice themselves for this monster. "Why do you revere him so much that you'll give your lives for him?!"

Just as I go to punch the floor again, a white hand flicks out and grabs my arm. I look down, shocked to see the soft umbra of flame around Meta's skin wrapping itself around my arm.

"Sasaki..." he murmurs, still looking up at the ceiling. Seeing the half-destroyed Angel in front of me forces the rage to turn to grief within my veins.

"I can't do anything to stop him," I whisper.

"It's true he has power, but it is not true to say you can't do anything," Meta says in a breaking voice.

"But why would those poor souls do this to protect him?"

"He has absolute power over them Sasaki. He holds their entire reason for being in his fist. People...respect that kind of power, but it's almost impossible to hold on to that without succumbing to it. To be able to influence people's lives, their deaths, their present and their futures. It warps you."

He holds out his other hand and opens his fist to reveal a single white flame burning on his palm.

"That kind of raw, emotional power burns hot inside a soul. If you do not set up defences then the fire will consume it. It will burn everything to a crisp until the only thing that is left is ashes. Sasaki, I have always tried my best to stop this power corrupting me. But I have not always won the fight. I lied to you about our intentions with your friend. I hid our plan from you."

The silence between us is broken as Ariel and Barachiel's attacks fade away in an explosion of smoke.

"You have the power within you. To lead. To inspire. To win. You have strength you haven't even realised yet. Take this and use it to end this fight. Then take your own power into the world and use it to do what's right."

He picks an arrow up off the ground and clenches his fist around the shaft. As he does, my eyes widen as the fire crawls away up towards the arrowhead. Soon the whole thing is entirely sheathed in the white flames.

"You must not...let the power...destroy you."

I reach out gingerly towards the flaming arrow being proffered to me. When I grasp it I expect it to burn but instead it feels warm and comforting. I stand and draw the arrow, pulling Tenshi's string back until the gentle heat is tickling my ear. As the smoke clears I hold my breath and release the shot. The shroud around the arrow follows behind it like a comet trail as it rushes towards Sanzo. The burning point bursts through the Fallen leader's defences, eating through the hellfire like a rock smashing through glass, shattering it. The shock in Sanzo's eyes is clear as he sees the arrow carrying the message of his father. It punches through his chest, ripping a massive hole in his torso.

As the arrow exits out the other side and buries itself in the wall behind him I notice that the fire has gone from the projectile. Instead, it flickers around the gaping wound, delivering itself to within Sanzo's body. His gargles and groans are the only thing breaking the silence as he collapses to the floor, clutching at his chest.

Ariel and Barachiel appear before me, standing over Meta. Cassiel emerges from the shadows and joins us, kneeling down at his head, placing his pale hand on the Angel's shoulder in silence. I flap my wings and teleport to within inches of a now unconscious Miyu in the corner, feeling her breath on me. I wrap my wings around her and shut my eyes. I've put her through so much.

"Sasaki, you must not get distracted."

Ignoring Lailah, I instead placing my hands on Miyu's cheeks and holding her. When Sanzo's voice growls across the cavern I practically leap out of my skin in shock.

"You think...that you can...beat me so easily?" He asks.

His voice is strained from the massive injuries he's suffered but there is an unmistakable sound of evil flowing out of him. I feel like I should be afraid, but what actually flows through me is anger. I'm angry that he has interrupted such a moment between Miyu and me. A moment of calm in this storm, the same bastard storm that has destroyed everything since it came into my life. I flap my wings and appear, standing over his fallen body. He's on his knees now, one hand clutching his chest.

"Kill this filth," Lailah spits out.

"Gladly," I think back.

I draw an arrow and pull the string back slowly. We can't possibly leave Sanzo alive.

"I'm sorry," I whisper at him, "you hurt Miyu, you hurt all my friends, and you took my sister from me. I can't let you live."

I grit my teeth and hoist Tenshi into a different position.

"Do it!"

"Your sister?"

"You killed her four years ago and my family has never been the same since. You deserve to die."

The rage is starting to build up inside me again, bubbling up through my soul. Sanzo shifts his body slightly. He's going to try and attack me while I'm close up.

"Wait! Please!" He shifts again.

I tense myself, holding my breath. Now's the time to do it Sasaki. But the seconds drift past and nothing comes.

"Why would we kill her?"

The question raises my level of anger one more notch.

"You hate us, don't you? You either want to see us all with you or dead. You tried to turn her into one of you. I'm right, aren't I?" I say through gritted teeth.

"You think we...hate you? You think we ever forced this on anyone."

A noise comes from his mouth that sounds like a giggle combined with gagging on the blood in his windpipe. My breathing is more rapid and uncontrolled as I feel the string sliding back on my fingers. Words float through my brain and out of my mouth before they trigger in my consciousness.

"This was her bow. This was her quiver, held on with her chain. You took her life and now she will take yours."

Sanzo clicks his fingers at me, a sound like a gas fire lighting filtering into my brain from all around as I go to produce the lethal blow. Ignoring the distraction, I release my grasp on the string, or at least I try to. My fingers don't move. Fire is all around me, gripping my arms, around my neck, down my legs. I struggle and just about get enough room to teleport upwards to safety. Back with the other Angels I drop to one knee and gather my breath back.

"Bruv, you let 'er slip through your grasp again."

"She seems a bit faster than last time, don't she?"

I gasp at the voices. There they are, the Deniers, Munkir and Nakir, standing between me and Sanzo, protecting their leader. Their voices sound identical and they look the same right down even to the chain that connects them at the wrist, except for the fact that they appear to be covered in orange flames that lick around their extremities. My chest tightens as I look past them and see Dumah standing at the back of the formation. His blank, eyeless face is pointed directly at me, his eyeballs floating freely around, each covered in fire. On the other side are two women I've never seen before flanked by Tachibana Kameko.

Her huge form towers over everyone as the six of them form a defensive formation around Sanzo.

"My lost souls," Sanzo chuckles, "my subjects, my former team, and even some of yours. I have summoned you to protect me and protect our life's work. You know these people, you know how they've hurt you, betrayed you and in some cases even put you to the sword. Your souls burn with the lust for revenge, now satiate yourselves for eternity!"

The lost souls teleport towards us, fighting against the remains of our group. They seem to have all of the powers they had when they were alive, teleporting around as if they'd never gone. The Deniers and Dumah all appear in front of me, swinging their weapons towards me in a joint attack. I dodge around them, dashing between outcrops in the damaged wall and ceiling to avoid them, but they track me all the way. I teleport back and forth trying to vary my angles, but the resurrected Fallen continue to stay on my tail.

I weave around the rest of the Angels who are facing their own foes while trying to distract my chasers. I swoop over one of the unknown women standing over Meta's prone body before slaloming around Ariel and Barachiel who are deep in combat with Tachibana. I peer backwards but still the chase continues, the Fallen keeping up with my movements despite Lailah pushing power through my veins.

Flapping my wings, I dash forward and nearly collide with the other woman I didn't recognise, who is now standing in front of Cassiel. She flicks her hand upwards and a ball of blue energy encircles them which I clatter into, rolling up and over the top of it until I hit the floor on the other side.

"What have you done with my son?" the woman says.

The Deniers hit the barrier with a loud crash, bouncing them off in different directions, but the two inside don't even flinch.

"I'm sorry, I couldn't stop them," Cassiel blabbers, "he failed Hashimoto and so he had his connection with Hesediel severed. I tried to protect him; I did!"

He points towards Hesediel in the corner as he lies through his teeth. The woman immediately drops her shield and teleports in a flash of flame to be with her son. She cradles his body in her arms in a picture so haunting that makes my heart break.

The moment is broken as the Deniers attack again, making me escape upwards to the safety of the ceiling and leaving them tangled in their own shackles on the ground. But instead of coming to a graceful stop I'm suddenly winded as I smash into the uneven rock. As Dumah drops his light bending the air ripples in front of me, revealing him on an outcrop ten feet lower than I thought it was. His eyes encircle me as he dives towards me, his face a picture of emotionless violence.

"Why Dumah, why are you doing this to me?"

He doesn't answer, instead lunging at me, his ethereal, flame laden sword kicking up sparks on the rock as it slices towards me. Suddenly it feels like there's a flood in my mind as my body begins to move of its own accord. It's like I'm watching myself from behind a window as the ground pivots around me and I spin like a top to avoid the attack. My arms reach out and grab hold of Dumah from behind, pointing him towards Mazaki. When my mouth opens the voice that comes out is not mine.

"She's not dead. You can still see her. There."

Lailah uses my finger to point Dumah towards her, still lying on the floor.

tsnng

Before a second can pass he's gone, disappeared in the blink of his eyes to be by the side of the woman he loves. Lailah returns control of my body to me.

"Thanks," is all I can say to Lailah.

"We're still two against one, don't let your guard down."

She's right, the Deniers are looking up at me with manic grins on their faces, showing their glowing orange fangs. But now that the odds are a bit more in my favour it's time to get my hands dirty. I can feel a sense of control, even a tiny iota of calm within the raging in my mind. The pent-up frustrations of everything that has happened are still there, along with the grief of losing Satoshi and seeing Miyu hurt, but the difference within me from the first time I fought them is night and day. The violence that gripped me that night, the one that destroyed Nakir's limbs and pushed Munkir to breaking point is no longer a part of me.

The realisation helps fuel that sense of control as I flap my wings and drop down before firing two shots, one into the chest of each of them. They reach across and rip the arrows out of each other's mid sections before coming crashing towards me in unison. Something just isn't the same though, they're slower, or maybe I'm faster. I dodge and put a couple in arrows in their backs. With my newfound strength they pierce deep into their muscles, causing each of them to roar with pain.

I reach back for another two arrows but when I run my fingers across the flights I realise I only have a few left. In the corner of my vision, I see bundles with blood rapidly drying on them scattered around the corner where Miyu and the others are. I make it a run for it, teleporting over to the bystanders, holstering Tenshi over my shoulder and fully restocking my quiver. I stop briefly and allow my hand to caress Miyu's face as I pass by her and Satoshi's mother, still cradling her son's dead body. And there next to her is Dumah, kneeling next to the still breathing body of Mazaki. He looks so strange, sitting cross legged on the floor with one hand on her chest, like some kind of priest, with the other hand resting on her head. He seems to be having one side of a two-sided conversation, his eyes shut. I don't even know if he realises he's talking out loud.

"I'm sorry that I couldn't be good enough for you. You do know that was all I wanted, didn't you?" He smiles at the unheard response before continuing. "I thought so. I could never hide anything from you, even with my powers." Another pause before a wider smile crawls over his face. "I'm glad. That gives me so much happiness to hear. I have made the journey, Mazaki, I think we both know it's time for you to do the same."

The life within her fades away as she utters her last breath and I can see the sadness creeping through Dumah's soul. Black fire bursts out of her body before amalgamating itself into an image of Ramiel. She glances at me before leaning in to Dumah and whispering something in his ear before fading from the world.

After a good ten seconds Dumah turns to face me.

"Thank you Sasaki."

"For what?" I ask, taken aback.

"You gave me a chance to see her one last time. She told me about everything that happened. She also told me how you could have killed her while she was suffering, but you stopped that from happening. You may have helped me pass from this life before, but without everything happening the way it has I would never have been able to be by her side when it was her time to leave. She was scared and helpless, her soul was terrified of letting go. But thanks to what happened between you and me I got to make the journey first. I calmed her, told her about it and helped her through it. Ultimately it was time for her to let go but without my advice I don't know how long she might have held on like that for, with all the fear and the pain wracking her soul."

"You're not angry with me, even though I killed her?" I ask as he smiles ruefully.

"I know it might sound strange, but no. You didn't have a choice in the circumstances and now she can take her journey with peace, knowing that she had me by her side."

I don't even know what to say as the sounds of the battle fade and silence rolls over us.

"I can't ever thank you enough Sasaki."

The moment is punctured by a roar from behind me as the Deniers lunge towards us. But before I can move Dumah teleports over me, swinging his sword and cutting both attackers in half. Their returned souls evaporate as the fire burns their atoms to dust.

"I hope that begins to pay back even a tiny fraction of the life debt I owe to you," he says as I look into his pale, wrinkled face, "thank you. For everything you've done for me. Things would have been...very different without you."

He holds out his hand, which I tentatively grasp and shake. The flames around his soul cover my hand but don't even feel warm.

"What are you going to do now?"

He takes a step forward towards his trusty weapon and rests a hand on the top.

"My time here is done now. Mazaki is at peace, and that is all that matters. There really is so much of her in you. I'm certain you'll reach your goal. People like you always do."

In a swift movement Dumah hefts the sword out of the ground, before turning it and plunging it into his chest, slicing his soul in half. I shout and make a start towards him as he begins to burn up.

"I go happily this time, with no regrets, no worries," he says faintly, stopping me in my tracks.

I wonder how many times I have to watch him die as he burns away to nothingness.

"Bye," is all I can manage to say.

Chapter 26

I put my head in my hand to hold back the tears.

"You've grown into such a beautiful boy," says Satoshi's mother, sobbing into her son's chest in a fiery embrace. After a moment the tears stop, resolve passing over her face. She carefully puts him down and stalks back towards Cassiel, anger flowing off her almost as much as the flames that surround her.

"You couldn't stop them huh? There was nothing you could do right? You fought for our son all the way did you?!" She yells at him as he cowers backwards.

To see Cassiel, a heavenly being, so scared is mystifying. This is an Angel who only minutes ago was tangling directly with the king of the underworld and now he looks like a scared child being scolded by a teacher. There's even a distinct warble as his voice shakes and stutters.

"Of c-course dear. I-I-I couldn't stop Meta from p-punishing him."

By now she's right in his face, towering over him. The flames lick around her curves as she jabs a finger into his chest.

"I don't believe you, you slimy little worm. You always despised our son didn't you? You did this to him didn't you?!"

"N-n-n...n"

"Admit it!" She screams at him. "You hated him because you think he caused my death didn't you? Do you know who caused my death? It was you. You were the one who tried to turn me in to an Angel while I was pregnant. It was you who caused our unborn child to become an Angel inside me!"

"No! I didn't know you were pregnant! I never would have tried if I had known."

"You're a liar! You knew!"

"Honey how could I have known?!"

"Don't you dare call me 'Honey'! If you'd paid any attention to me then you would have heard me tell you! But you never fucking listened."

"But I didn't know the experiment was going to fail! If it had worked, then you would have been fine! I didn't know he was going to kill you."

She grabs him by the collar and lifts him up off the floor entirely.

"Let me repeat myself. Our son did not kill me, you did. And you have to live with that guilt forever. I've watched over him as he grew to maturity in just 18 months and became such a beautiful young man. He always loved you because he never found out, and he loved Hesediel despite what happened. Hesediel was my connection to him, and you tore that out of him, didn't you?!"

"No, I didn't do anything, it was Hashimoto! I tried to stop them and save him."

A sudden burst of genuine hatred towards Cassiel punctures my soul. That lying, evil bastard let his pregnant wife undergo a ridiculous experiment and now he blames his son for her death? The rage burns through my heart like acid. Something primal pushes at my brain as the waves of horror and disgust go through my soul. As that deep, dark hatred pierces into my inner being I flex my wings out and teleport behind Cassiel, throwing him to the ground with more force than I intended, causing the ground to crater around us. I swing around and straddle his chest, aiming an arrow directly at his forehead.

"How dare you pretend you had nothing to do with it."

It feels like I'm starting to lose control again. Suddenly the confidence about my newfound stability isn't as strong as it was.

"I always hated that scumbag. He did some truly awful things but never took responsibility," Lailah whispers into my ears.

"Give me one reason why I shouldn't shoot you right here and now!" I shout, attempting to control the anger.

"You can't murder me Sasaki," he pleads.

I push the dark feelings down again and weigh up my options. Tendrils of darkness wrap around my arm like a snake, suddenly pulling on the string to prevent me from shooting. The tentacles lift me up and placing me on my feet in between Cassiel's wife and himself.

"Anyway, you need me to defeat Azrael," he says.

He's probably right, but the revulsion at him still fills me to the brim as he stands up in front of me. As he dusts himself down the fingers of darkness around me begin to wave like long grass in an invisible wind.

"I will kill you scum! You let them destroy my son when you promised me you would take care of him!"

The soul of the woman burns bright as she tries to leap around me and towards Cassiel. I stick my arm out, using the angelic strength to stop her following through with her murderous threat, however much she struggles against me.

"She was a good woman when she was alive, so passionate and raw. Full of that kind of vigour."

I pause a second and shut out Lailah's words.

"You can't kill him, even he doesn't deserve it."

I stare deep into Cassiel's eyes as he stands in front of me, hiding behind his wings again. He looks pained, like he's fighting off his internal demons. Suddenly a muffled scream comes from behind me and I spin to see the errant fingers of dark energy encircling the soul of the woman. In a flash she's entirely cocooned within darkness.

"What are you doing?!" I yell.

I try to grip the dark energy and rip it off but my hand passes directly into it, I might as well be trying to grasp smoke. I can't do anything as her voice gets completely cut off.

"Stop it!"

But he doesn't listen. I swing round to see him close his fist as the soul behind me is crushed under his power, the darkness collapsing into a point. I instinctively fire a shot at him but he's quick enough to teleport back to the shadows of the rocks, where he immediately disappears, causing me to scream with frustration.

"I had to," he says, his voice floats through the air from wherever he's hiding, "if I hadn't then she would have killed me. It was self-defence!"

"You know she wasn't going to really hurt you! You're an Angel!"

"You cannot be certain of that Sasaki, I had to protect myself."

That unknown feeling is suddenly back, sparking again. The one I thought I'd beaten, a feeling of disgust and hatred at the world and those within it. Before I can think about it more though, Azrael's scream rips through the air, interrupting my thoughts.

"What are you doing?!" He yells. "I am your king, and you are supposed to be obeying me! I brought you hear to kill these monsters and you are failures!"

Looking around it appears that Tachibana has been dealt with by Ariel and Barachiel, but both have suffered at the hands of their former teammate. With her gone there's just one remaining of Sanzo's entourage, a beautiful, thin woman with flowing blonde hair. She resembles a fairy queen wrapped in the gentle glow of the fire. She whispers something to Meta. I don't know if Sanzo actually heard it, or if he just doesn't like her talking to his father but it makes him erupt with rage again.

"Mother! Kill him now! You will obey me!"

She stands up from where Meta is still lying on the floor, turning to her son.

"No, Sanzo. How dare you bring me back here to do your dirty work. You speak with the authority of a king and you may have subjects that live in fear, but that is not the same as having followers like he did."

His mother, the one he himself tried to turn into a Fallen before murdering her? I can't believe he would have the guts to bring her back, let alone to set her upon his father. She speaks like Hashimoto did, with authority and power despite being calm on the outside. She doesn't appear to have an ounce of fear in her.

"How dare you lecture me Mother! You lecture me as if you have any form of strength yourself, but you couldn't even survive to follow me. Your own son completely outshone you and now you stand here with absolutely nothing, watching my father die."

"How dare you talk to your mother like that."

Meta struggles to his feet, with copious amounts of blood dropping from his white clothing. He coughs up blood which runs down his chin and neck.

"And what the hell do you want? You couldn't even protect her. You have failed at everything you've ever done and now you will watch as I rip you both to shreds."

Meta pushes past his wife to stand facing his own son.

"You speak as if you have the power of the world underneath you, but in reality, you have nothing. What good did bringing your friends back do for you?"

"They may have been my friends in the real world but in the underworld they are my subjects!"

"No, Sanzo," his mother says, putting her hand on Meta's shoulder, "you think you own them, but you never will. They subjugate themselves to you because they know what you might do to them if they don't. That isn't true power. You trusted them to do your bidding but you saw what happened. That fear was overridden by the experiences that those souls had while alive. The bonds that they made showed them that fear could be beaten. And if you thought that bringing me back here would lead me to doing what you want then you are clearly far stupider than you look. You don't have any power over me, or your father."

Azrael clenches his clawed hands into fists, turning his black skin white with pressure. The breath coming from his lungs becomes rapid and broken as the rage takes over him. His eyes glow bright red as he throws his head back and roars before launching himself at his father. He wrenches his sword up, the blade cutting the air so forcefully that fire erupts from his whole being, destroying the ground as he passes. I nock an arrow just as the sonic boom pushes over us, leaving everyone on the ground except Meta and his wife. Her face contorts into a frown as she pushes past her husband to stand in front of him, but that just causes Azrael to scream over the noise.

At the very last second Meta wrenches his wife out of the way of the attack, the fiery blade piercing straight through his stomach. Hellfire rips through Meta's being as Azrael screams again, filling the air with fury. He snaps his black wings and pushes himself ninety degrees, ripping the blade straight out of Meta's body and through the torso of his mother. It seems as if all the blood that is left within Meta explodes out across the cavern. The floor around him is completely covered as both of them collapse to the ground. He reaches out his hand to touch her face as the flames slowly evaporate from around her. As the last remnants of her being float away Azrael teleports back to his stricken father.

"That is the power I had over her," he shouts, "and now I will show you the power I have over you."

He raises his sword and gently pulls Meta's white clothes apart, revealing his chest. Azrael laughs maniacally, pulling his sword above his head before sinking it directly into his father's heart. Golden light bursts out of his skin, the same way it had with Hesediel. The light soon takes on the form of Meta, the wings evaporating from the back of Hashimoto, leaving the old man's body withered and destroyed on the ground. The spirit of the Angel slowly rotates around to face Azrael.

"Unlike you, I will always be able to trust my friends to do the right thing," it says before disappearing.

The spirit bursts into tiny fragments leaving nothing but a faint shimmer in the air from where he'd been. Ariel and Barachiel are both collapsed on the ground with a look of loss on their faces. Cassiel re-appears from the shadows behind a rock, trembling on his hands and knees. He was a fierce leader, but these Angels went through a lot together. He didn't lead them without the ability to make them trust him.

Azrael takes a few steps forward towards the genesis shard, which is covered in blood from the conflict around it. Even through the red stain the patterns of light can be seen reacting to him as he moves his hand towards it.

"Finally, I can put an end to you all," he says.

Sanzo puts his hand on top of the colossal stone. It reacts painfully to him, the light fizzing and screaming inside.

"Angels! Hashimoto and Meta are gone but you must carry on the mission," I yell out.

The three remaining Angels look up towards me from their various states of stupor. I see tears and loss in their eyes. I bark my order out, feeling Lailah's voice edge into mine.

"Defend the shard now!"

A barrage of attacks rains down upon Azrael, including multiple arrows from my own bow, but he flaps his wings, dispersing everything as he picks up his prize. I can see all the pointed teeth stretching right back into his mouth as he stares at what he came for. He's so engrossed he doesn't notice the shadow crawling up his lower body. Cassiel stealthily wrenches the shard away as the rest of the darkness coils around the demon's form, tossing him heavily across the room. He smashes into the far wall, raining rocks down upon him and burying him from sight.

shhnk

All four of us teleport to the shard as Cassiel places it back on its stand.

"Listen everyone, we need to defend this. We have our orders from Hashimoto and we must honour him," I say with as much authority as I can.

"But how can we?" Ariel wails. "We don't possibly have the ability to beat that thing do we you stupid little girl. We needed Hashimoto!"

Chapter 27

After a moments silence a scream begins to rise inside me. I close my eyes and find myself in front of Lailah roaring at the clear blue sky.

"What the hell is wrong with you?" I yell over the noise. Perhaps it's the shock of me communicating with her or just the bluntness of my tone, but she immediately fades into a strangled gargle.

"You're going to get me killed! You're going to get yourself killed and you're going to get all of my friends killed before I can even see them properly again. I can't believe I'm stuck with you and your stupid decisions."

We stare at each other for a few seconds with nothing but the sound of the slight breeze blowing through the grass disturbing us. Looking directly into those fierce eyes of hers I can see that she really means it.

"You don't trust me?"

"Of course not! You're a bloody kid. You have absolutely no experience of battle."

"No experience? Really?" I say with derision, "you've been here in my head, in my soul, throughout the last few weeks, haven't you? You've seen me fight. You've seen me win with my own skill."

"You got lucky. Half of them practically killed themselves!"

I start counting, trying to calm myself, but the longer I wait the more the anger rises.

"Do you honestly believe that?" I ask through gritted teeth.

In the pregnant pause, the world transitions to darkness as deep, grey clouds have formed over us. Returning my gaze to them I form Tenshi into my hand and materialise an arrow in him.

"If you think I'm so weak then what about this? I could shoot you right now couldn't I?"

She slowly raises herself to her feet, with my arrow following her all the way. What am I doing? This isn't me, is it? I slacken the string and lower the arrow back to my side. Looking at the filigree on my bow I stare at the reflection of my pale blue eyes before sighing and taking a step forward.

"I'm sorry Lailah. To tell you the truth I've been feeling the same way."

"What?" she asks, surprised.

"I'm a fraud, a failure. You know what I've been through and you're right. I got lucky, and even then I've still relied on my friends to sacrifice themselves for me. I've been unable to stop them from being hurt."

"Why are you saying all of this?" She asks as I sigh deeply and rub the bridge of my nose.

"I don't know, I'm just sick of it. Honestly, I don't even want to carry on. I just want to take an arrow and plunge it into my heart. I've done horrible things to people, even if they were terrible. What I did to Mazaki and to Miyake were just...awful. They ended up dead and all they were trying to do was make each other happy."

Lailah stays quiet, looking at me with her chin resting on her hand.

"Lailah, I don't think I'm going to be able to do this without you. If there's one thing I've learned through all this is that is that force is not going to work. I either need you to be on board willingly and truly, or I won't even be able to attempt to take on Azrael. I am not going to try and use threats or force; I need you to come willingly."

I sigh again and drop the bow to the floor, taking another step closer to her.

"Without you we don't have a chance. Without a leader the other Angels won't even be able to try to take him down, and without you it's impossible for me to get close to him. You heard what Hashimoto said about me, that I can lead them like he did. But I can't, I just can't. Not without the kind of power you can give me. I forced you to bend to my will before, but now I am asking you to follow me, to believe in me, to trust me. I have nothing to offer other than my word, but together I think we can do it. Put your life in my hands and let's lead the Angels, together."

I'm now so close that I can feel her breath on me as we stand face to face. She seems to be battling with internal thoughts.

"Look, I know that Hashimoto said that, and it's true that he's an exceptional judge of character," she says, looking directly into my eyes, drinking in my inner being. "I'm scared I won't make it. I don't want to die here Sasaki."

"I know, I'm scared too. But you've seen what has happened before, we have to do what we need to do to get through this to the other side."

I feel myself infatuated with her as we're practically touching.

"Do what's right Lailah, please?"

"Maybe I did underestimate you."

Something flickers deep in her eyes. She slowly puts her arms around me, and we embrace each other. The skin of our cheeks touch and electricity flows through my soul.

"Thank you, Yusuke" I murmur through tight vocal cords.

From underneath us white light spirals upwards, engulfing us in dazzling brightness. From behind me the energy is seeping out from the jewel embedded in the front of my bow, flowing up towards us. The world begins to disappear as the light spins like a tornado around us.

"Let's do this, together, Kyushiro" Lailah whispers back.

And then the light lances upwards into the sky, breaking the deep, dark, clouds. As it reaches the top of its journey another beam of pale blue light crashes down towards us. The blue energy around us pulses and flickers away as the fingers of light connect, writhing amongst each other. I continue to hold on to Lailah's shoulders as we both stare up at the fireworks show going on above our heads. It's so bright now that I can't see a single patch of sky, just light engulfing the entire world.

With a sudden clap of thunder, the light collapses into a ball which swells to absorb the entire world until it begins to dissipate. As the last shred of energy from around us gets absorbed my hands sway down from Lailah's shoulders.

"I believe in you."

Lailah's voice drifts into my ear, sounding like it's coming from a thousand miles away. Her smiling face flitters away like leaves on the breeze as she begins to evaporate into energy again. My inner world collapses down in a colossal explosion that bathes the world in brightness so fierce that I fall to the floor, curling up on myself to try and protect myself from it.

After what feels like years the prickling sensation on my skin begins to relax. The nerves in my ethereal body finally stop screaming at me, instead merely whimpering at the onslaught. I gently open one scrunched up eye and roll over, slowly stretching against muscles that fight me all the way, before gasping at the scale of what's in front of me. Sitting in the sky and completely blotting out the sun is the largest Angel I've ever seen. It must be hundreds of feet tall and glows with an immense shimmer. Its face is hidden by a hood on a white tunic that surrounds its body, but I can feel it staring at me. The wings of the thing span miles across, with flecks of blue diamond punctuating the white feathers, all glowing with a blue and yellow energy. Occasionally its wings flap to keep it airborne, pushing me deeper into the soil. From beneath its cowl, the faceless Angel speaks with a voice that booms around me.

"So, thou hath brought me to the world?"

The sound of the ancient voice fills my ears and stuns me into wordless silence. The Angel cranes its head, looking at itself.

"What hath thou done to me? I am not as I should be."

"I...I don't know" I whisper.

"Did thou summons me or not?"

"I don't think so; I don't even know who you are."

The head tilts up to the sky and then appears to look around to take in where it is.

"I am Rafael, the Archangel of Life, he who controls the flow of life energy through the aether. I was...locked away somewhere."

"Locked away? Where? By who?"

He bends down, pressing his gigantic, faceless form close to me. Even then I can't see anything but darkness underneath the cowl.

"I don't know, it was a woman, but not one I had encountered before. She had a level of power that even I had never seen," he says, straightening up back to his full height, "where is this place?"

I struggle to my feet in the presence of such a being. The light emanating from him feels like it's almost a physical force trying to push me away.

"This is my soul. I came here to commune with Lailah, the Angel that was trapped here. Where has she gone?"

Another giant flap of the wings makes me stumble and cover my eyes from the breeze. As I drop to the ground my hand falls on Tenshi and I grasp my hand lovingly around him. I stand up and hold him close to my chest protectively.

"What is that?"

"This is my bow, it was given to me by my sister," I say carefully. The light glimmers in Tenshi's jewel, reflecting in strange ways around me, ways I've not noticed before.

In a very slow, methodical way Rafael swings his arm over his shoulder. When it returns he pushes what is, unmistakably, a gigantic version of Tenshi into my face. I gasp loudly and put my hands over my mouth, raising my bow to compare. Rafael's version must be 20 times the size and is glowing with energy, but it still sports the same carvings as my own.

"This is mine," Rafael says with a flourish, "look familiar?"

"Why are you here? What is going on?"

"I was trapped and now thou hast freed me. If thou had the power to break the seal that my captor placed upon me then I am impressed. I am bound to thou for my freedom."

"But where is Lailah?"

"I believe her power helped break the chains that bound me. But all things are connected through the aether. Energy cannot be destroyed. She will still exist somewhere."

I can't help but just stand there with my mouth opening and closing.

"How...how can Lailah be gone?" I snivel.

"I told thou, life is eternal, her energy is here within me. She will still be with thou in her spirit."

"So, what does this mean? I needed her power to lead my comrades against the evil we face. Without a leader they will all die, as will my friend. The King of the Underworld threatens everything that we stand for."

Rafael seems to bow his head as if in thought, holding his massive bow in his hand like an ancient colossus guarding a tomb, waiting for someone to cross his boundary.

"So, Azrael has come back has he?"

"Yes, he has already killed Meta, he has killed Puriel. He even brought back the souls of his loved ones to fight with him, against those they so cherished when they were alive. He has caused harm to come to so many, and I will not let that continue."

"Meta is dead?" The sound of surprise edging upon the booming voice sends a shiver through my core. "The situation is graver than I thought."

"So, I needed someone to fight with me. I need an Angel to give me their power. Could you fight with me? As a partner?"

"I cannot dodge the fight against death. Azrael has always stood for everything that I do not, and that I have lived forever to protect. Life is sacred. It should not be abused by anyone. Even in death the soul should be allowed to rest. Tell me thy name."

"Does it matter?" I ask. After a few seconds of silence, it's clear that it does. "I am Sasaki Kyushiro."

Rafael drops down to the ground before moving his bow towards me.

"I am in debt to you and Lailah. I owe my freedom to you, so take this, Sasaki Kyushiro. Let us raze evil from the world as one."

I clasp my hand around the giant, ethereal version of my bow which makes electricity stream through my body and overflow from my pores. I shut my eyes as I try to contain it within me, attempting to stop my body from exploding outwards. There's a flickering of yellow and blue behind my eyelids as I'm overcome by the power. Just as I'm on the brink of letting go the sensations suddenly stop, collapsing down into my chest.

***

Back in the real world, with the new energy burning inside me I raise Ariel up until we're face to face.

"How can we win? Frankly, I don't care. Our mission was to defend the shard. If we can only delay him then we will delay him until our dying breath. Do you understand me?" I ask through gritted teeth.

Rafael's voice is edging out through mine as a glow seeps out of my skin. Something inside Ariel's eyes flickers at the sudden surge of strength from within me.

"We might not have Meta at the helm anymore, but we are still here. Meta believed in us, and he believed in me."

Pulling Rafael's newfound energy from within me, I fill the room with light as my wings emerge from my back. But these aren't the wings I had before, they're massive, with blue shards glowing within the white feathers.

"I am Sasaki Kyushiro, and I am also Rafael, the Archangel of Life. I promise each and every one of you, right here and now, that I will put every ounce of strength that I and he have in our collective souls to protect the shard, my friends, and all of you. Your leader trusted me to guide you in his absence, but if you are not ready to take this fight up with me then leave here and never come back."

I point at the hole in the ceiling to indicate their exit. My heart is pounding in my chest and the neurones are firing in my brain. I drop Ariel back down to the remaining Angels where she immediately shrivels towards her husband while Cassiel just stares at the floor. After a few seconds of silence, Ariel and Barachiel walk to the genesis shard. Cassiel finally follows with his head hanging. Then a hand belonging to Miyu squeezes my shoulder from behind, her face filling with awe as I turn around. I instinctively want to push her away, to remove her from danger and protect her in a fight she cannot possibly be a part of. But in her face I can clearly see resolve, a fiery determination to stand with everyone else. We have our mission; we have our enemy and now we have a leader.

An explosion from across the room clears the rocks which Azrael had been imprisoned under. The monster roars at the top of his lungs, which turns into a strangled laugh halfway through.

"You still think you can defeat me? You cannot stand in the way of our mission."

"'Our mission'? I don't know if you noticed but there is only you left Azrael. We defeated your friends, and we'll do the same to you, because we have right on our side!" I yell.

Hefting Tenshi and loading an arrow into the string, I fire the shot just to see it incinerated as the fire leaps up to protect its master.

"Right is no good without power Sasaki. You may have swayed those pathetic souls that I used to call my friends, but there are billions out there that will fight for me. You and your puny weapon cannot do anything to me."

"He is right, use my weapon instead. Wield the energy of life," I hear Rafael say inside my head.

Concentrating on the feelings inside me, I shut my eyes and channel Rafael's power down my arms and into my bow. When I open them again Tenshi is now covered in an aura that extends his size to more than double what it was before. The glow around him shimmers in hues of turquoise and yellow as it meets the carvings and the gemstone in his centre. When I lift him he's practically weightless, and the string takes almost no effort to pull back. When it reaches my cheek, I concentrate and an arrow of light and energy forms into it, ready to fire. A wide smile crawls across my face as I stare directly at Azrael, unleashing the bolt of light across the cavern. It rips through the air at a blinding speed, far faster than anything I've ever seen before, leaving a rumble of thunder in its wake.

Azrael's fire jumps to meet it but the arrow ploughs into it, distorting it like a weight on a rubber sheet. He pushes his hand forward, reinforcing the defences in front of him and eventually deflects the arrow away where it lands and fizzles into nothingness. The flames fade from between us, revealing Sanzo, but he looks different. No longer the scary, demonic Archangel of Death, but hints of the young boy underneath. Suddenly he is no more a leader of the undead than he is a teenage boy thrust into a position of power, now left alone to face his enemies.

"Wh...what are you?"

I raise the new Tenshi above my head with a fist clenched around it. Flapping my wings, I float up in the air behind my friend and teammates.

"I am sick of people not listening to me! I've told you over and over again, I am Sasaki Kyushiro, and we are the Angels!" I bellow into the chamber.

My eyes, flickering with the blue light sparking all round me, pass across the faces of the four below me. I will another arrow of energy into my palm, gripping it and holding it up as a triumphant signal of my newfound power.

"Let us finish this, Angels! Attack!"

A roar goes up from my companions as I nock and fire the arrow above the advancing crowd. The sound of the Angels teleporting towards Azrael fills the air. He knows he's not strong enough to defend against my newfound power so instead he simply runs, zipping around the room as our attacks rain upon him. Ariel and Barachiel alternate, throwing their elemental powers towards him from all angles while the other teleports to attack his blind spots. Cassiel seems to have disappeared, but fingers of dark energy snake through the air from the floor, the walls, even from my shadow behind me.

I take my time and fire off arrows at the most opportune times, but whatever we do he manages to just escape, moving as someone who has thousands of years of fighting. His movements show a confidence in his own abilities that could not possibly come from such a short time in this world.

The lengthy battle starts to take its toll though, as Ariel and Barachiel's attacks become more ragged. It seems that Sanzo can see it too. He swings away from another blow and spins his damaged body upwards to hit them with a counterattack. With the power of Rafael flowing through me I can predict his moves from the smallest of tells. My eyes flick across to the space above them as Azrael appears above Ariel's head in slow motion. I just about manage to launch an arrow in his direction in time, forcing him to back away again from his target.

"You have to keep going Angels!" I shout in support.

But it's no use, suddenly Azrael is on the attack now. The flow of the battle has transformed in a single moment without anything obvious changing. I fire another warning shot to keep him off Barachiel, but he's already over to me. I teleport away and feel my wings brush against the rock wall behind me.

"Get him here," a voice says from my shadow on the wall.

"What will you do?" I whisper over my shoulder, but there isn't time for an answer as Azrael launches a jet of flame at me.

I push off the wall, soaring down towards the floor. The fire follows me, billowing through the air but not quick enough to catch me as my newfound wings let me swing around at breakneck speed. I keep moving around until I finally see him get angry enough to generate an opening. I pull up quickly and fire an arrow directly towards his attack, splitting the jet in half. He shifts his body away from the arrow as it passes over his shoulder, bringing his other hand round for a more powerful attempt.

"Now Angels!"

Ariel and Barachiel appear behind him, sending a cyclone of electricity and gale force wind towards him. The memory of that attack hitting me just a few short weeks ago makes me wince in recollection. He teleports upwards to avoid it just as my arrow impacts into the ceiling next to his head. The rocks interrupt his vision just enough for him to stay on the back foot as I repeat the trick, each time pushing him back towards Cassiel.

"Ariel, now!" I yell.

She throws another bolt of wind towards him from the side which he jinks around, but he only moves into the path of one of my shots. He flicks his wings and suddenly he's right up against the edge of the room. I fire a shot that ploughs through his thigh, locking him against the wall. Out of his shadow Cassiel flows back into the world with the speed of darkness filling a room after the lights are turned off. His dark energy surrounds Azrael, quickly constricting him before throwing him downwards. A loud roar erupts from Barachiel as he throws his long staff down towards the cloud of dust. A scream also escapes his wife's lips as she entraps his hands and ankles with restraints made from her power, locking him into the ground just before the electricity hits him.

The air clears to show Azrael on his back, his body convulsing against the cuffs of air that Ariel has covering his limbs. With each second that passes Barachiel throws more and more lightning strikes down upon Azrael's prone form, causing his skin to start to char away and for blood to escape from him.

Chapter 28

Flapping my wings, I cross the entire distance between us in the blink of an eye. I throw my bow round in an arc that smashes through Barachiel's column, dissipating the energy and causing the unconscious Azrael to flop back to the ground. Silence fills the room as the final echoes of the static fall away, accompanied by a look of shock on the Angels.

"No! Don't kill him! He must answer to me."

Ariel tries to protest, temporarily forgetting the respect she had for me and my power only a few minutes ago. I fire her a glare tinted in white and blue that stops her immediately.

I drop down and stand over Azrael's body, grabbing his hair and raising his head up as gently as I can. There are patches where his black skin has sloughed off to reveal the muscle underneath it. I'm not angry at him anymore, I just want him to accept the crimes he committed and explain why he did it.

"You nearly destroyed my family Azrael. Why did you do it?"

No answer. I let out a snort of derision and drop his head back to the floor. I magic an arrow into my hand and hold the gleaming, pointed tip against his cheek. As it touches his exposed skin a spark of white arcs from the tip, sending a jolt through his body.

"Did you do that Rafael?" I ask internally.

"I merely pushed a sliver of life into him, to restore his vitality so that he can speak to us. Thou need answers to sooth thy soul."

I quickly put a cautionary hand around Azrael's throat and hold the arrow in front of his eye as he begins to stir.

"I could kill you right now, and the effect on your billions of followers would not even reach a fraction of what you did to me."

"I didn't...I didn't do anything to you," he chokes.

"You took my sister from my family four years ago. If you admit it and tell me why I will grant you a merciful death without pain."

He seems to be looking around, as if trying to work out where he is. I press the point of the arrow closer to him just in case he tries something.

"You think I will accept your mercy without a fight?!"

One second feels like forever as Rafael's instincts take over my senses. My wings carry me upwards and away from the jets of fire that erupt from Azrael's arms and legs. He melts his shackles, using the sudden freedom to flip his attack towards me. With fire coming at me from all angles all I can do is concentrate on dodging through the chaos. I do my best to teleport around the bolts of flame, but as I twirl around the air they catch my shins and thighs.

tsnng

My head snaps around, just catching the moment Azrael reappears. He thrusts his chest out and flames burst from every inch of his skin. The dried blood burns away from his wounds as the fire fully covers his body. He opens his hands and throws two concentrated beams towards me, which I try to arch my back to avoid, but I'm not quick enough. The flames singe the blue feathers at my extremities. The feathers falling off me are barely translucent in the light, but as they burn away I shriek in agony.

tsnng

He appears in front of me, pushing his hand towards my throat.

shhnk

I attempt to teleport behind him but the damage to my wings throws me wildly off course. He catches my eye with a horrific grin of a hunter who has spotted a weakness in its prey.

tsnng

Suddenly he's gone as I fall towards the ground, drunkenly stumbling around the air on burnt wings. I blink the tears from my eyes just in time to see him appear behind Miyu and the genesis shard. I try and teleport towards them but end up crashing into the floor instead. I yell out as his grinning form rises up, murderous intent clearly visible in his eyes and aimed squarely at my friend. Azrael looms over her with the fire surrounding him burning bright as his hands reach out. In slow motion, his fists unclench and the fingers start to splay out, showing a tiny ball of light in his palm. Staring at it as he readies his attack feels like looking at the pilot light in a dragon's throat.
        "Lock!"
        Miyu defiantly shouts her spell into the roaring flames with her hands held out, palms upward. Magical chains erupt outwards, wrapping themselves around Azrael's hands, clamping them shut. What passes across his face looks like pure shock. Miyu must have barely featured on his radar, a slight, waif like girl with charred clothing and covered in blood in the same room as a bunch of extra-terrestrial power mongers.
        "Lock!"
        Another set of chains wraps his arms behind him, intertwining his wings into his constraints as even his honed instincts desert him from shock.
        "Bolt!"

A green cylinder of magic thrusts itself into Azrael's chest, which he looks down on like a mosquito bite. He snaps back to reality, exploding flame and smoke around them.

"I've got you now!" he yells.

The burst from his attack covers the room in smoke and dust, hiding Miyu from view. I can't help but scream her name as I struggle to my knees and try to get to her through the heat and destruction. I stumble forward before a sudden gust of wind through the hole in the ceiling blows the smoke away, revealing the burning, returned soul of Satoshi holding Miyu up, protecting her from Azrael's fireball. His ethereal body has been razed by the flames, leaving him in almost as bad as a state as when he left this world. Struggling to his feet, he turns to face his king.

"How dare you go against me!" Azrael yells at him. "You are MY subject! You will do what I say!"

Satoshi's smile has gone, replaced with a grimace.

"I won't let you kill my friends. This girl has done nothing to deserve to be one of your targets. Leave her alone."

Azrael grasps the spirit form of Satoshi and lifts him up from the floor.

"You are a pathetic ant! You dare believe that you could challenge me!"

"Help me Rafael," I shout in my head, *"I need to save them!"*

"I need to repair our body first, I need time," Rafael intones.

New feathers are replacing their burnt counterparts as his energy converts itself to matter around me, but it's too slow.

"You haven't got time!"

"Thou should trust those people that are protecting what thou care about, even at great risk to themselves."

"You are despicable to rise up against the Archangel of Death. I will make sure you never, ever see another sunrise little girl, and you Kagawa Satoshi, I will make you suffer in hell for all eternity."

"It's worth it to save these people from you," Satoshi says as he spits at Azrael.

His bravery and selflessness make my heart leap in my chest, pushing through the conflicting feelings of seeing Miyu in his arms again.

Azrael has clearly had enough; overcome with anger, he raises his palms, pulling dark fire around him into huge spheres before collapsing them down in to dense, dark-hot projectiles.

"Hurry up!" I yell at Rafael, my heart beating at an incredible pace, *"I can't just leave them to die!"*

Pushing his hands together, Azrael combines the two globes into a neutron star of fire.

"Scum."

He swings his arms, pushing the burning heat towards them.

I flap my wings to try and teleport over to them but they're not fully repaired and I career off course and collapse to the floor as the fireball move towards Satoshi and Miyu. I scream with everything I have, but it gets eaten up by the noise of the air burning. Satoshi turns to look at me and gives me one of his adorable, energetic, passionate smiles as he picks Miyu up by the shoulders and throws her out of the path of the attack. It's the last thing I see of him as he vanishes away, burned back to where he came from.

With the last of my feathers repaired I teleport over to Miyu and pick her up as tears stream down my cheeks. My teeth are clamped together hard as I teleport her away to safety, leaving her on her knees.

"I'm so sorry Kyu, I had to try."

"He's going to suffer so much you know," Azrael says to us, "I'm going to torture him personally for all eternity. But first I'm going to kill you Sasaki, and then I'm going to take you back to hell with me so I can torture you in front of him."

He waves his hands and pulls another fireball in to existence.

"I can't wait to reunite you with that complete and utter idiot," Azrael says as he launches his attack at me.

"How dare you talk about my son that way," Cassiel says, silently rising out of the shadow cast behind Azrael by the attack.

He swirls masses of dark energy around the floor, pulling it up like a sheet, shaping it and moulding it into a rectangle containing a churning vortex between us. It absorbs every single last joule of Azrael's fireball, leaving the room filled with silence. Azrael turns to attack Cassiel with a snarl, but before he can lash out a burst of energy comes spewing out of the darkness. It rips through Azrael's shoulder, causing his arm and wing to fall to the ground and blood to spray out on the already stained rocks. He looks down in shock at the wound as the world seems to stop all around us. When the seconds pass, Cassiel speaks in his reedy, whiny tone.

"Look behind you. That is a black hole waiting to swallow you up if you make a single move."

Azrael's face is a picture of fear as he turns around.

"You're the King of the Underworld, are you? All you do is rule a very small corner of the Universe, my Universe! In all that space, in between all those stars going on for eternity, there is dark energy flowing in the aether. You cannot fathom the realm that I rule. I have formed the energy to my will, collapsing it in on itself until it makes a singularity from which nothing can escape. If you make a move I will envelop you within its boundaries, crushing every piece of matter in your being to a single atom with a gravitational force higher than in the centre of a million stars. Your body will be turned into energy and spewed out back into our Universe."

The anger swells up inside me again, causing me to flap my wings and teleport to Cassiel, drawing an arrow mid-flight aimed at what remains of Azrael. His mouth is hanging open and his body is wrecked. There's blood running down his chin as well as pouring to the ground from his open wound.

"The time has come for you Azrael, accept my offer of mercy and tell me what you know about my sister. If you don't explain why you killed her, why you had your lackeys come after me, why you hurt Miyu, everything, then I will put this arrow through your brain. At this distance, with this much force, with your body in that state there is no way you will survive. And even if I fail to kill you, Cassiel will."

Every word that comes from me feels like it's pushing me further towards the edge. Each sentence is smothered with rage and grief as spittle flicks out of my mouth. I can't take any more. Azrael has to give me what I want or he's going to die. He changes his focus from the point of the arrow to my eyes and for once I can see nothing but the scared eyes of a teenager looking back at me. The boy that is my own age looks up at me instead of the beast that nearly killed us all. When he opens his mouth, I can hear Sanzo's voice and not Azrael's.

"You would kill me for not being able to tell you something I don't know? I can tell you the rest but I do not know what became of your sister."

"Stop lying!" I yell uncontrollably. "You're evil! You're a murderer! You kill innocent humans!"

He coughs blood on to the floor and looks back up at me. He looks like he's starting to fade from the damage done to him.

"You truly are one of them aren't you? You really are an Angel and not a human. You have bought into their lies."

"One more line like that from you and I will fire! Tell me why you've done all this!"

He waves his hand around at the udomite surrounds us, although most of it is now shattered from the crossfire, littering the floor.

"The shard is the link to these beings, it draws out the connection with the person's soul, shaping their power. They've been using it to make more Angels. Every Angel made with their genesis shard is linked back to theirs, and every Fallen made is linked to ours. Or was at least. Before you killed them all."

A pregnant pause cuts through the thick air.

"The stones are the key. The evil and the beauty that exists within everyone has been there forever and will continue on forever. By putting people through these experiments, they've used their stone to bring out people's inner beings. With more Angels they can do anything, unchecked. They want to control this world."

"And you can make more Fallen can't you?"

A brief second passes as he seems to consider this, as another slip of blood flows through his hands.

"Yes, we wanted to stop them gaining their power. But we never did because we wouldn't force anyone into it, and we'd already converted or attempted to convert all the volunteers we had. But my father and this bunch, they didn't have those morals. You saw them try to force themselves on Yamamoto, didn't you? That's what they do. They use force to achieve their goals. The process is...not pleasant Sasaki. I have seen up close the horrors that can be caused by it. I bet my father never told you about the slew of failed experiments, did he?"

I stay silent, the arrow shaking slightly in my hand.

"He forced dozens of people to undergo the transformation just as he was going to do with your friend. Most of them died within seconds, but he just kept going, trying again and again no matter what the results were. He killed so many people Sasaki...we couldn't let him carry on. Every life that was destroyed to get to where we are today was another person wrenched from their family. We wanted it to end. I needed to destroy their stone, to prevent the Angels from doing this to more and more people."

"You mean to prevent us from stopping you taking over the world for yourselves and leaving humanity cowering before you," Cassiel says, "you're a filthy lying demon with evil running through your veins. Whatever you do Sasaki do not listen to him, he's the Archangel of Death for God's sake."

"Stop filling this girl's head with lies about us. I may be the ruler of the underworld, but I don't bring people there myself you capricious fool! You have corrupted her beyond anything that a piece of udomite could have done, you monster," Azrael says angrily.

"You are the monsters! Despicable beings that have killed so many people!" I shout.

"Sasaki, we do not kill humans! We are just trying to protect them. The Fallen have never attacked anyone who isn't either an Angel or someone who works with them. It is your group that have forcibly taken people from their homes and family to be experimented on and put to work. We have never subjected anyone to the transformation that didn't want it, unlike my father. I promise you that."

"Don't lie to my face! You killed your own Mother after forcing her to be a part of your sick experiments. You said it yourself!"

The darkness boils away inside me as I try to work out the truth. Another cough and more blood erupts from his wounds. His head is drooping and lolling as if he's about to lose consciousness.

"Don't you dare leave me yet. You have more questions to answer," I say as I grab hold of him, pushing my arrow against his throat.

His breath is slow and rasping already, but he looks up at me through the fog of his wounds and speaks clearly.

"She wanted to join us. She loved my father but hated Meta. She saw how corrupted he'd become and chose to undertake the process to stop him. And yes, I did kill her. The experiment went wrong, and she was injured...badly. I saw it all so closely. She was completely paralysed but in permanent agony. All she could do was scream out to me in pain and I still hear the sound of her screams echoing in my ears. I took the only decision I could to give her the way out she needed. I gave her relief! It was an act of mercy, and I'd do it again in a heartbeat! Do you think that they haven't made hundreds of people go through that?!"

Suddenly a spike of doubt pierces my brain. Everything about him makes it seems like he's telling the truth, but he can't be. Could Hashimoto lie about the woman he clearly loved so much?

Azrael speaks my name and reaches out to push my arrow away from him gently. He leans ever so slightly closer to me, inching away from the black hole behind him, and speaks in a hushed tone through his torn body.

"You cannot trust them."

"Do not move!" shouts Cassiel.

"They won't help you. They put that girl through the same experiment that could have destroyed her. They don't care for you. They'll use your power for themselves."

"I said stop, now!"

"They knew you had the potential Sasaki. To grow into what you are now. They saw it. They knew."

I can't find any words to say. He inches his way towards me, the smell of blood on his breath.

"She lined you up for them."

"Who?" I ask.

His eyes droop as his hand drops from my shoulder.

"WHO?!" I shriek at an ear-splitting level.

"Mit..."

His lips start to form a word as Cassiel's darkness springs outwards, circling around him and pulling him back. I scream in defiance as he's ripped away from me into the singularity. For a brief second, I stare deeply into the black hole, seeing nothing but the slowly turning mass of dark energy. I cover my face and drop to my knees before I'm abruptly deafened by a roar of energy escaping from the darkness. Azrael's physical manifestation is returned to the world via a laser beam of energy that erupts out of the portal. I turn my head in stunned silence and see the exploded remains of the wall.

Cassiel took my chance. He yanked the whole reason for doing all this away with him into the shadows. I can feel pure hatred and anger filling up the void within as the rest of my emotions are overcome. My entire body feels like it's on fire. Purple light is leaking out from my arms, covering me in a pulsating aura. I make a feeble attempt to keep the rage down but finally feel myself go over the edge. I snap my eyes on to Cassiel and my body goes into auto pilot. My ultraviolet wings curl back and catapult me violently at him, smashing him into the wall. My face is pressed right up against his as the roar escapes my lips, covering him in saliva. My voice comes out with a deep echo that I realise, in a disembodied kind of way, sounds completely different from mine, or Lailah's, or Rafael's.

"YOU WILL PAY"

"What? Why!" Cassiel babbles.

He struggles against me, but even in his Angel form he can't escape my grip.

"YOUR LIFE. FOR HIS."

I bellow again as I reach round and grab an arrow from behind me. I pull it over my shoulder to show him the thing that's going to kill him, an arrow of wood and steel, but where my hand has been touching it the same flickering violet that surrounds my entire body has begun to wind its way around it. In the reflective point I can see a single yellow eye looking out from the girl's chubby face, before turning it towards the Watcher. I swing my arm up in a wide circle, bringing the arrow tip towards his stomach. Just as it begins to push into his skin he vanishes from in front of me. Behind me, Ariel and Barachiel have pulled him away to safety.

"YOU WILL DIE TOO," comes the voice from within me.

Yes, they have to die. Preferably painfully. There's nothing but malice and bloodlust lining my insides as the light continues to roar around me. The three remaining Angels stare at me with fear in their eyes as I hold my hand out, drawing forth the darkness from within me in the form of a massive bow of purple light. I connect my hand to the ethereal string and pull back, materialising an arrow made of that same energy, but there's something trying to fight back inside me. I can feel Rafael's energy within my arms and see slivers of light fighting in the shadows.

"NO. TIME IS NOW," I yell.

Forcing Rafael back down below the seething mass of cruelty, I fire the shot. As the arrow leaves my bow it splits into three parts, each one heading straight for one of the traitors. I throw my head back and roar as they hit, exploding in a massive ball of energy and billowing smoke.

shhnk

The noise accompanies a huge crash from the centre of the room. I look up through the darkness flicking and glowing around my vision and see sunlight cascading through the hole in the ceiling. An arm pushes its way through the smoke, blowing it all away.

"No..."

I drop to my knees, the cruelty evaporating from me like a fire running out of oxygen. The feeling of rage completely drops out of my soul.

"Can't..."

I fall to the floor, my face hitting the stone hard as the energy that had kept me going dissipates. I start dragging myself along the ground towards the figure, standing, glittering golden in the rays of the dawn's light.

Chapter 29

"Sis..."

"Hello Kyu."

There, standing right in front of me is a face that I never thought I'd see again. Bedecked in a white dress and under the mass of her waist length blonde hair, is my sister.

"Sis!" I cry through the blood, exhaustion, and shock.

But this is not my sister, it can't be. She never had a colossal pair of wings sparking with electricity. Her eyes were blue, not shining and glistering gold.

shhnk

She lifts me off the ground, holding me effortlessly as the lightning sparks around us. Staring into her eyes I see my own angelic, emerald greens flickering with Rafael's energy reflected back in her golden irises. I can't help but be overtaken, burying my head in her ample chest and gripping her shoulders. Her wings wrap around me, holding me tight, and mine instinctively do the same to her.

"Is it really you?" I babble at her through the tears.

"It's really me Kyu."

"But...you...you're..."

"Master Seriel! Thank you so much for coming to save us!" Ariel shouts, interrupting us.

"I'm glad I managed to get here in time Ariel, what happened here?" Sis asks as she gently drops me to the floor.

"The fight against the Fallen came about as you prophesied. Unfortunately, neither Meta, Puriel or Hesediel made it through. But we survived. We defeated him."

My sister bows her head and puts her hand to her eyes as if wiping away a tear, but when she looks up there is steel in her voice.

"I'm incredibly sad to hear that our brethren have fallen in the heat of battle. We must make sure their deaths are not in vain."

"What's going on Sis? Why are they calling you that?" I ask as I reach out towards her.

Before I can touch her two pillars of wind crash into me, sending me flying across the room. Instantly, Sis is behind me again, catching me easily and balancing us both in her grasp a few feet above the floor.

"What do you think you're doing?" She says to Ariel.

Peeking through the feathers and electricity Barachiel and Cassiel are having a competition as to who can hide behind Ariel the most.

"Master Seriel, she attacked us! She was going after you!" Ariel shouts.

Sis drops me to my feet and flits over to the Angels, hovering over them. Behind me there's a movement as Miyu puts her hands on my shoulders. Everything that's happened in the last few weeks, all the effort that I've had to expend, all the feelings that are running through my mind. I don't even know what I'm experiencing anymore. Miyu squeezes my shoulder as my feelings flow through her and she gives me a knowing smile.

"I wasn't going after Sis!"

"And another thing, why the hell do you keep calling her that?"

"Oh, yes, I guess you have never heard my true name spoken before have you?" my sister says to Ariel, "I did make sure that Meta never told anyone of it."

"Your true name?"

"And I guess you, Kyu, have never known me by this name have you?"

I stare at her as she pierces me with those glowing, golden eyes.

"I am Seriel, the Archangel of God's Voice. But the body I inhabit is that of Kyu's older sister. I am also Sasaki Mitsuro, pleased to meet you all."

There isn't a sound made after the announcement. It really is my sister standing there, twinkling in the light cascading from above.

"You're an Angel Sis? But I saw you, dead..."

She sighs at me.

"I'm sorry we had to do that Kyu. That wasn't me, it was a fake, an image made solid."

"What? Why?! Do you know what that did to our family?!"

Anger and hurt start pulsing through me again, overtaking the positive feelings quickly.

"I had to. We had to. If I hadn't left then our parents, and you, would have been in danger. As soon as I joined the Angels we knew the Fallen would be after those who I loved. I had to leave and this was the only way."

"The only way?! Bullshit it was the only way! You're saying you couldn't have made contact?!"

"No Kyu! I could not! If I had done they would have gone after you! Even the rest of the Angels did not know who I was. I kept it a secret from everyone to protect you."

The darkness is rising inside me again, the deep, horrendous presence is calling to me. A voice is echoing in my head, calling out to the darkest places in my mind. I begin to panic as the darkness starts to leak out of my pores again.

"Help me Miyu!"

Miyu spins me round and puts her head on mine.

"I don't know what's happening to her! Something big is inside her!"

I drop to my knees and roar as the dark, evil energy envelops one side of my body. I grip my head as I flail around trying to fight the incursion. Rafael is bellowing within me, mixing in the screams of something monstrous. When I open my eyes all I can see is blackness, dotted with stars twinkling in the distance. Disorientated by the sudden void in front of me I fall to the floor. As I reopen my eyes I can see around the shield set up by Cassiel, the portal to deep space. A window to a black hole. Directly in front of me.

"What are you doing Cassiel?!" Seriel screams.

"She really is Samael isn't she?" he says.

She pauses.

"Yes. She is."

"Then we must destroy her!"

"Destroy her? What do you think we've been doing all this time? Why do you think we planned all of this? We need Samael, and now we have him!"

Sis blurs through the air as she teleports over to me. She puts her hands either side of Cassiel's portal, covering the area in a faint glow before collapsing it down to a pinprick of light. She grabs me by the shoulder and hauls me up to my feet.

"You must fight it Kyu! You must fight Samael and gain control. We need you."

"Who is Samael?" I hear Miyu whisper behind me.

"Samael is an Archangel. A powerful one. A being who combines pure hatred, malice, venom, darkness, and vengeance into a single core. He is one of the most powerful Angels in existence. Kyu, you cannot let Samael take you over."

Looking into her brilliant eyes I can feel the power rushing through me. I must do it for her, so she can be proud of me.

"Rafael, help me!"

And then, unexpectedly, the tide of the fight changes. Driven by the belief my sister has in me and the feeling of her breath on my face again, Rafael begins to take over again. His blue and white energy sparks within my body, swamping the darkness. I raise my arms and push the light out towards my fingertips. It spreads through my wings and down my legs. As it fills me up I slam my hands down to my sides, sending a shockwave of energy cascading outwards and leaving glittering blue diamonds filling the air. When I speak I can hear Rafael's echo in my voice, just like it was before. This is how we defeated evil and we can do it again. I look into my sister's face and pride fills my veins.

"I did it Sis. I beat him for you."

But the look she gives me isn't joy or happiness, but an expression of puzzlement.

"I defeated the Fallen inside me, aren't you happy Sis?" I say, with Rafael's tinge echoing between us.

"I was afraid this was going to happen."

"What? What's wrong?"

Anxiety suddenly rises from the pit of my stomach.

"I don't think you quite understand Kyu, we don't need you to hide Samael, we need you to become him. Samael isn't a Fallen, he's your Angel, and we need his power."

"I thought Rafael was her Angel?" Miyu pipes in from behind me.

"He is! I can feel him inside me. I saw him in my mind. We communed and became one, to vanquish the Fallen!"

"That's not strictly speaking true Kyu. Samael is your Angel and has been since we awakened him within you. Once we discovered the genesis shard we had to draw the most powerful Angels out to protect humanity. After I was recruited by Hashimoto I was tasked with finding more people to turn into Angels. I could sense the power within you Kyu, I knew you could become of the greatest Angels there was.

"We took you in secret to the Sanctum and brought you into our holy family. We channelled the genesis shard's energy and brought out your Angel, that was Samael. But he was too strong. He was overwhelmingly powerful and you did not have the capability of controlling him. Your body and your mind weren't ready for such a challenge. But we knew he was the key, the key to our plan succeeding, and we needed his power. So, we had to do what it took to make sure we could get him, eventually.

"I sealed him away within your body, using the power bestowed upon me by God himself. You needed to grow, and change, and suffer, and fear and experience loss and rage and hatred, until you could channel that power to controlling him. We put him back inside of you, hid him within you, and pushed you through the challenges that you've faced so far to give you the necessary strength to become what you are today.

"To stabilise all that hatred within you I needed to build a powerful counterbalancing force to help you. That force is Rafael. You see that," she says pointing at my bow, her old bow, "the gem in it is a piece of genesis shard which contained a link to Rafael. We needed to protect you from Samael at all costs until you were ready. We even created medication that helped you suppress Samael once he started to leak through, and that bought us enough time to get rid of the Fallen and get you to grow stronger. Now I think you're ready to meet your destiny, you're ready to finally become the Archangel of Hatred and Malice."

I raise Tenshi to eye level and look at my green eyes shining back in the metal.

"Is this true Rafael?!"

After a brief pause his voice finally cuts through the silence.

"Yes, it is. I was once imprisoned. It must have been in the bow, in the piece of the shard. All I know is that I have followed thou for a long time."

"Then...the person that put you there?"

"Yes, it was Master Seriel."

"But you are the Archangel of Life! How could she possibly force you in here?"

"I am not sure thou really understand who Master Seriel is. She is rumoured to be the most powerful Angel of them all. She sits at the right hand of God himself."

My eyes had fallen shut during the few seconds Rafael and I had been conversing, but I snap them open and focus on my sister.

"What do you mean you need Samael?"

"What?" she starts.

"You said you needed Samael, but we have destroyed all of the Fallen. Azrael was the last one and he is gone. There are no more enemies left to conquer. We don't even need the Angels anymore. Surely this is all over and we can go back to our lives? You can come home with us. We can be a family again!"

Miyu's hand grips mine down at my side.

"Oh Kyu, defeating the Fallen was merely the first step in the plan. There is a big wide world out there. We must spread our angelic blessings upon the human race. They must experience the happiness and love that God has bestowed upon us. Do you not feel it? Don't you feel the beauty of the Angels within your soul, singing the word of God for you to hear."

I take in the destruction and death that surrounds us. Hashimoto and Tachibana's bodies still sit in piles of ashes in the chasm. The floor around us is made of billions of shards of udomite glittering like stars in the solar system. Sis's golden eyes are wide and bright but over a smile that makes me uneasy.

"The Angels have brought me nothing but...pain and sorrow," I murmur, slowly, "they have brought suffering upon my friends and those I care about most. What about Satoshi? How can a world be beautiful if someone like him can be taken from it?"

"Kyu, can you not see how much better the world would be with a race of glorious angelic beings on it? We can create heaven here! Without any enemies there will be no pain, no suffering."

"But, what if the human race does not want to be Angels? What if they are happy as they are?"

"But they are not!" she shouts with a hint of anger. "They kill each other and hurt each other and fall in love only to have their hearts broken!"

Her voice is visceral and scary. I recoil backwards slightly into Miyu's grip.

"And...what...if what happened to Sanzo's mother happens to more people?"

"Then they will be put to death. Anyone who is not strong enough to go through the process of awakening their Angel and communing with the Lord through them should not continue to exist. This is God's grand plan Kyu. This is what we are here to achieve, heaven in all realms. The human race will be perfect. They won't feel pain again because we will all sing from God's hymn sheet."

This isn't the Mitsuro that I knew. I don't believe that she could talk like this on her own.

"We will let nothing get in our way Kyu. We will force them into it if they do not obey. Who is going to stop us? Their bullets and weaponry are nothing against our power! They can't control us or constrain us. There is nothing that humans can do to stop us!"

Azrael was right...they were forcing Miyu to become an Angel. They would have turned my best friend into a vessel for another being against her will. They would have killed her if it didn't work. They...they did that to me too?

"But I thought the Angels were...good? Hashimoto said we were looking to protect humanity from the Fallen."

There's a quiver in my voice at the thought of being without Miyu, her being replaced with someone else, or even worse, dead. She could end up being someone awful like Ariel or brutal like Barachiel or a paralysed statue existing in permanent agony.

"Kyu I think it's time you grew up a bit. Not all Angels are what you would consider 'good'. We are beings existing on a spectrum, just like the Fallen were. But they decided to stand in the way of us, and of humanity's happiness. Our ideal world is perfect, a world full of Angels. Surely you can see how bad they were for wanting to stop that? They thought freedom and individualism were worth more than us, even though individualism is an illness in the human race that causes so much pain. That makes us better than them. We're the better people, and you helped eliminate them Kyu. You have helped protect humanity from the horrible fate of continuing as they were. You've been a key part in bringing our ideals forward."

No...no, I didn't...

"Think of all those horrific monsters you have killed. You have helped pave the way to the gates of the future Kyu."

The tears start to leak out from the corner of my eyes, slowly dripping down my battle-scarred cheeks. The darkness begins to boil within me again.

"Calm down!" Rafael shouts inside of me, his voice gurgling as Samael rises up to claim him.

"Azrael was right, you really are the evil ones. You called them monsters, but what does that make you?"

Through gritted teeth and the hatred swirling around me I just about manage to control my urges to lash out.

"Kyu do not move against us. I will not let anyone, ANYONE, not even you get in the way of God's plan. Do you understand that? We need Samael to be the vessel of all of humanity's hatred. He can channel their anger and remove it, leaving them passive and less likely to fight us when our plan comes to fruition. We cannot do this without him."

I look deep down inside myself and see the vision of Samael rising out of a deep, writhing mass of darkness. How could they all do this to me? Forcing all humans to become vessels for these...things. It's barbaric. How could they do it? The people I'd been fighting with all this time. My own sister...

"Don't give into him!" shouts Rafael as his voice tails off to nothing.

My own sister. The only person who ever truly understood me. She put me through this, all the pain and loss and hardship. It was her that got Satoshi killed, her that pushed me to the brink. I hate them, I hate them all! As the sadness and grief flows through my brain I can sense it struggling against the multitude of emotional dams I've always had. It feels like it's changing, morphing. Sorrow turns to hatred, hatred turns to rage, and rage flows forth until it is the only thing left in me, swallowing up everything else in its path. Samael's glowing yellow eyes flare up in the darkness. He has come. He has come to claim them all.

Chapter 30

The hatred of the Angels pours out from my chest, covering every inch of my skin. I flex my wings and flick them out, bringing them round and smirk at the delicious feeling of the power within. They shimmer and shine in an otherworldly kind of way. I spread them to their true glory, massive even against the large, open cavern, before cocking my head back and letting out the laughter that bubbles up inside me.

"**FINALLY.**"

All this time trapped in this girl's body and now, finally, I'm free. A broad smile comes across my face as the breeze passes over my cheeks. Looking up into the eyes of Seriel, standing in front of her three remaining disciples, I snort derisively. They put me through all this. But now we can have our vengeance.

"If you cannot control him Kyu then we will destroy him, and you! We can't risk him moving against us," shouts Seriel.

She talks to the girl as if she is still here, but this is my body now. My soul, my actions.

"**YOU WILL NEVER GET HER BACK.**"

"Then we will kill her."

I raise my hand and materialise a dark shroud of energy around the girl's bow. I giggle at the feeling of power in my hands, the sound echoing in the fresh dawn that flows downwards into the cavern. Negative energy calls to me from every being in the universe and I can harvest it all to turn it to my purposes. Through this girl's body I can feel it manifesting itself. I can give it physical form. I run my gaze across the group of pathetic Angels and my eyes lock on to Ariel. Oh yes, you, the girl holds a special hatred for you. Deep down she longs to rip you to shreds piece by piece. She'll never face up to it, but the want is there. How about we make you suffer first?

I draw the bow and materialise a huge, shining purple arrow into it. With the ethereal string rubbing against my cheek, I smile widely again, my face contorted by these wondrous feelings of impending violence. The shot bolts out with a thunderclap, leaving a trail of darkness running behind it. With a movement speed that befits the Voice of God, Seriel rapidly pulls a shield of golden energy up in front of the group.

"NOT GOOD ENOUGH" my voice intones.

The arrow fizzes through the shield, maybe diminished by ten or fifteen percent, but not deflected off its course. It snaps through the Angel's chest just as I had aimed for, causing blood to erupt over the group and guts to fall to the floor. Ariel screams in a pitch that brings rocks down from the ceiling as she catches Barachiel, immediately seeing her pale skin dyed a deep red from his blood. Taking you out first would be no fun would it girl? How about we make your life misery just as you did to this one?

Then suddenly, something pierces the edge of my hearing, the tiniest of echoes, like a single atom squeaking its way out of existence during a nuclear explosion. I shake my head and turn back to the screaming and crying figure of Ariel. She grabs at the air as the golden form of Barachiel starts to flow outwards from his body. It coalesces into the muscular brute of an Angel that he was, pausing briefly to run his intangible hand over her cheek. Her scream fades as the golden particles shatter above her.

"HATE ME!" I shout.

Her voice has faded, but I can see it in her eyes. Pure, utter, absolute revulsion. The feeling of it entering my soul sends shivers through my whole being, it's delectable. It feels so glorious! She drops her stricken husband on the ground and starts forcing the power out from her hands, taking bits of husband's blood with them. I easily bat the attacks way, pushing her even further. She despises me! Haha! This is so wonderful!

shhnk

Ariel teleports up towards me. Her violent movements are so easy to read as disgust drives her forwards, making her do things without thinking. I grab her by the neck and throw her down to the floor before teleporting on top of her and slamming my fist into her stomach. The rocks around her shatter upwards as I push her down into the bare ground. Blood escapes from the thousands of cuts where the shards have entered her body. Yes! Yes! This feels so good! After all she's done, she deserves this so badly!

As I leave her prone on the floor with her eyes glazing over with the pain, Cassiel looks up at me like a wounded deer, his face full of the kind of fear that I could bathe in.

"DO YOU WANT TO BE NEXT?"

I nock another arrow and point it at him, but Seriel puts her hand across his body.

"You do not want him. You want me."

"OH, I WILL GET TO YOU. BUT FIRST YOUR LITTLE LACKEY LOOKS LIKE HE WANTS TO RUN AWAY."

"It's ok Cassiel," she says, turning to him. He nods briefly, his lip quivering as he slips into her shadow and out of the world. "I am the one that locked you away in there, I am the being who imprisoned you for four years. You know that you're the one that hates me aren't you, not the other way around? I need you; I want you, and I love you as one of God's creatures. Come to me and be by my side instead of attacking me."

"HOW DARE YOU TALK TO ME LIKE THAT. YOU DO NOT KNOW HOW BADLY YOU MUST SUFFER FOR WHAT YOU DID TO ME."

"You don't want to do this Samael."

"OH, BUT I DO, SO MUCH."

"Then come and get this over with!"

I swing the arrow up at her, and just as I'm about to fire I feel something, maybe the tiniest flicker of resistance in my fingers. The arrow whistles away, leaving another thunderclap behind it. I stare in shock at my hand before clenching my fist, pushing the feeling away. The arrow fails to hit home as she disappears, teleporting away before flapping her wings and coming barrelling towards me. Her bow comes over her shoulder as she thrusts it towards me like a spear. I dodge sideways easily, too easily.

"HOW DARE YOU NOT TAKE ME SERIOUSLY!"

My arm swings around, an arc of destructive purple energy coming around with it, but her face is gone again in a flash. She flings herself around the room with a precision and speed that was lacking in the rest of them. I start unleashing a barrage of arrows at her, putting more energy in to each one. I can cover enough of the cavern that I force her to alter her tactics. By keeping my shots unpredictable I'm making her live on the edge of her nerves. One shot and she won't be able to fly, one hit and she'll be at my mercy.

"WHY DO YOU NOT ATTACK ME?"

She says nothing as she continues to back off before firing an arrow from her steel bow. I grasp the arrow out of the air and throw it against the wall where it clatters to the floor.

"PATHETIC. I THOUGHT YOU WERE SUPPOSED TO BE STRONG? HAVE THE INTERVENING YEARS LEFT YOU WITHOUT YOUR POWERS?"

A frown covers her face. I'm definitely getting to her.

"Fine," she says grimly as she flicks her hand up.

Below me a huge glacier-like formation of ice in the shape of a hand bursts from out of the floor, reaching up to grab me. I swing my bow and smash through it easily. Another glower from Seriel and another hand flick brings more ice attacks. I dart away as they continue to come crashing towards me, but they're slow and easy to dodge, slower than an Angel for certain. I flap my wings and move upwards, gently avoiding the grabbing fingers. I even taunt her slightly by dragging a foot and leaving it just inches away from their grasp.

As I pass under the gaping hole in the ceiling the sunlight bursts into my vision, blinding me. A noise from above me makes me snap my head upwards to see a hundred ice hands blast out of the ceiling towards me from all angles. The cold starts to encase my body as the fists grip themselves around me.

shhnk

I smash through the ice and just manage to escape, swinging my bow to clear a path out of the surprise attack.

"YOU THINK ICE CAN STOP ME?"

I materialise another arrow and spin away from her before unleashing it into the cavern. As it leaves my bow I point my finger and connect to the end of the ethereal flight. Using the newfound connection, I arc and bend the arrow at will around the room, making it smash through all of the ice hands and leave nothing but crystals floating in the air. As I spin back to gloat over her powerlessness, she raises two hands towards me, teleporting around me gracefully.

Suddenly my vision goes dark as water swirls around me, pushing against my body. It's all around me as it presses down on my bones like a torture device. I try to flap my wings and escape but I can't move. Panic grips me as the girl's lungs fill with water. I have to get out before her body dies! I shut my eyes and force energy out from my skin painfully against the pressure, making the water boil away in an explosion of steam. On the floor I painfully cough up water from her weak, human lungs before choking down as many deep breaths as possible.

Absentmindedly I run a finger through the pools around me, causing more steam to rise up off my boiling skin. She couldn't do this when she awoke me and locked me away in here. Her power was electricity based, not water, the thought passing through my brain just a second too late. A massive electric shock pulses through the cavern, flowing through the water in the air, the ground, and the remnants on my skin. I manage to escape the ground before it hits but the trail of water provides a clear path for the lightning to course over me. I roar as the pain registers through the dark, mean, angry energy that covers the girl's body. A memory flows from her to me of Barachiel doing this to her before...but it seems to hurt so much more now.

"You have to let her have control Samael. If you don't, you know what will happen."

"ONE HIT AND YOU THINK YOU ARE SO FUCKING POWERFUL DON'T YOU?!"

"I am more powerful than I was when I locked you away inside of Kyu."

With panic starting to grip me, I swing my bow around in an arc, leaving a flow of darkness speeding in his wake. Seriel teleports upwards but my arrow is already in the air, hurtling towards her. She spins her body sideways to evade the attack, the arrow just cutting a sliver of hair from her as it misses. I will destroy her. I'll destroy everything here.

"A good shot, maybe you've learnt some skills from my little sister."

"DON'T YOU DARE MOCK ME!"

"You'll have to keep getting better to stop me doing that," she says as she leaps into the air before tearing towards me.

Her blows reign down, a mixture of fists, arrows being swung, fired, thrown like projectiles. Some are steel and sheathed in electricity, some seem to be made of golden energy solidified. I swear I saw one that looked like it was made of binary code. I have to put all my effort into concentrating and deflecting the attacks. Luckily, the girl I'm in had excellent eyes to start with, but I need to break through her attacks to kill Seriel.

There it is again, a sound ringing in my mind, like a piano key played in the depths of the earth's core, filtering it's way upwards through the various layers. She can't be resisting me, that's not possible, and I sent that blasted Rafael back to the depths so it can't be him. As all this passes through my head it becomes clear it's affecting me, making the situation more dangerous. An arrow whisks past my head and buries itself deeply into the ground as the attacks get closer to me. I have to do something to beat this girl. Then this body will truly become the perfect vessel for me, a reservoir for unlimited hatred.

I hold the girl's right arm out and brace myself. As Seriel fires an arrow that seems to be made of pure light, I toss my giant bow towards her, throwing her off balance for a brief second. I call the hatred of this world into my hand, channelling it and forging it to my will. Reaching out with my other hand I catch the arrow mid-flight, letting the momentum spin me round, screaming at the agonising pain as the energy burns my skin. Like a hammer throw I release the arrow during my rotation, returning it back towards Seriel with interest. She drops to dodge it, but I've finished creating a huge shadow blade with the energy in my other hand, allowing me to swing it upwards through her front.

I growl in pain as I catch my bow again, the returning shaft hitting the stinging, burning scar left there from the arrow. Seriel looks up at me from the floor, her front completely burned and a large char mark on her face. When her eyes meet mine I get that sensation again in my mind, louder now but still not audible. It's like an itch that I can't scratch, but I shake my head and force it to disappear briefly.

"Try again," her voice says through a toothless, broken smile.

In a blink of an eye she's gone, faded from sight. As I look around, her voice enters my brain without having the good manners to pass through my ears first.

"You're wondering what I'm doing. You're wondering how I'm doing it. You're scared. You don't know what my powers are and that worries you because you know you can't beat me."

"GET OUT OF MY HEAD!"

I spin around, staring at the destruction as the voice continues.

"You're scared, and do you know what?"

"WHAT?"

"You're damn right to be scared, because I am going to get her back, I will own you, control you, and I will put you to use."

"I AM NOT SCARED! I AM SAMAEL."

I scream and lash out with my bow, letting out huge waves of force that smash through the air, destroying what piles of udomite and rock are left.

"And now I am going to scare you even more," the disembodied voice says, ignoring my protestations.

Then out of nowhere something smashes into my back, sending my body crashing deep into the ground. I spin around, driving shards of rock deeper into my skin to see Seriel floating there, completely unharmed.

"HOW?"

"You want to know my real power? My real power isn't to control ice or lightning or telepathy. My real power is the control I have over you and your fate."

She's making it a battle of wills, of physique, of talent and determination. She truly is a hateful being. I'm going to kill her and make myself perfect though. I am going to kill her...I...I...huh? My train of thought completely derails as if hitting a solid wall. No, I'm going to kill her! I...I'm going to...to...

I scrabble around in the dust, getting on to one knee and flicking my wings open as she reappears, floating towards me. Her golden eyes begin to fill my world.

"I have every power you could ever imagine," she whispers as she fades into nothingness again. "The only thing scarier than you not knowing what I'm capable of, is knowing that I am capable of anything."

"WHAT?"

As her whisper floats through the air and hits my ears from behind I startle and swing round at her, but my hand passes right through another apparition. Suddenly there are Seriels all around me, all talking in unison.

"I am the voice of God himself. Any Angel that has communed with me has gifted me the knowledge and purity of their abilities. All of their powers belong to me."

I stare blankly at the images as they float closer to me. Anything? Any Angel?

The noise of the fire sputtering through the air breaks through the ghostly holograms and smashes into my chest. I cry out as it starts to burn through my skin, the tinge of white on the edge unmistakably meaning that Meta's Holy Flame is consuming me. I flap my wings and burst upwards to escape, smashing into the ceiling as I fail to control my trajectory. When I inspect the damage I can see flickers of my own ribcage through the holes in my charred skin. Fingers of darkness erupt from the floor and wrap themselves around my wings and arms. Cassiel?

"No, it's not Cassiel. It's me. Do I need to prove myself to you any longer?" she asks inside my head, before appearing above me and speaking with her real voice. "Do you want to know where I've been in the last few years?" she asks out loud. "I've been around the world, creating Angels with our genesis shard and communing with every single one of them. I have an unknowable amount of power. I am the one true voice of God."

"I THOUGHT THESE WERE THE ONLY ANGELS?"

The question surprises even me, and my voice sounded different when I asked it.

"I told you she's still in there, that was her question. And no, there are hundreds of Angels out there if not thousands."

Hundreds?! Thousands?!

"Do you want me to prove it to you?"

She doesn't let me answer. Instead, she starts waving her hands, causing her fingertips to spout a thick translucent liquid. With my wings free I teleport away and see the floor where I was laying begin to melt.

shhnk

She's then above me, liquifying the oxygen out of the air and hurling it towards me. Then it's the feathers in her wings moulting, flying at me at breakneck speed like daggers, followed by a laser erupting from the centre of her chest. I can't predict any of the attacks as they all come out of nowhere.

The sound of rock breaking from above gives me just enough advance warning to evade the steel beams that are pulled from the structure and thrown towards me. The sound of them crashing into the ground fills my ears with a metallic ringing until it suddenly stops, replaced by a low fizzing sound. I look from side to side, but the world seems to be covered in a faint green sheen. Nothing is moving outside of what looks like a large bubble around me, one of the girders hanging in mid-air. The buzzing noise gets louder as Seriel appears in front of me.

"Now you can be truly afraid of me," she says, a slight echo in her voice. "I can even stop time. Do you know how little of a match you are for me?"

The time halting field around us drops suddenly, leading to a final crash as the beam resumes its trip to the ground, mirroring my own movement as I hit the floor.

shhnk

Seriel punctures the sudden silence by appearing over me with a smile under those giant, golden eyes that makes dread run inside me.

"I need you, you know that, but if I have to, I will erase your mind, wipe out your consciousness and leave you as a vegetable. Your power will lay dormant until I can find someone else to take over your soul and body, just like I wanted Lailah to."

She reaches her hands out, her fingers clawed around as the light from her wings fills my world. Golden lightning flows from her grip and ploughs into my head. The agony that runs through my body is beyond anything I could ever comprehend, even beyond anything the girl has already been through. All the hate and evil filling my soul begins to get stripped away like houses in the path of an atomic explosion. Darkness evaporates to be replaced with golden light, sheering layers off my very existence. My consciousness begins to fade, replaced by a golden coloured nothingness bit by bit. I try to reach out and summon my bow to fire, but I can't move, I can barely think.

"Cancel!"

The word pierces what little is left in me, like a missile of tranquillity flowing through the golden light within my mind, bringing with it the image of the verdant garden. I blink and it's gone, replaced with the sight of Seriel looking back over her shoulder at the interrupter. The gold lightning floats back towards her hands slowly as they fall to her sides.

"How dare you interrupt me!"

"I won't let you destroy her! My best friend is still in there, and she was suffering."

"I do not care! You may be a mage but to me you might as well be worthless."

"You would kill your own sister? I can sense her in there. You have to know she's still alive in there."

"I will enact the word of God, whatever that is. Right now, I need Samael, but I do not need Kyu. If I have to do this then I will! No one will stand in our way!"

"I will! I might be the only person left here, but I will fight until my dying breath to protect her. She needs protecting right now and you, her own sister, won't give it to her. After all this time, after everything she's been through, you can't be there for her! Kyu was right, you are the real monsters. I swear I will bring her back."

My hand touches my cheek and feels the coldness of a tear running through the caked-on blood. I try and push the girl's consciousness down back under the depths but I can't stop another one flowing through.

"You will protect her will you? Well let's see if you can when you have been burned to ash!"

Seriel teleports into the air and swings her bow up. In her other hand she pulls forth holy fire into a growing ball of swirling destruction. As it grows it begins to elongate until it she fashions it into a large, burning arrow. She places it in the string and pulls it back until it's level with her ear.

"MIYU!"

I scream, my deep voice echoing through the cavern. It was definitely my voice, but the girl said it. I can't get rid of her. Something inside my soul changes and sharpens as the necessity for action becomes an unstoppable force. I flap my wings and cannon upwards, materialising my bow into my hand and crashing into Seriel. As she hits the ceiling I fly into her with a couple of huge punches to her sternum. I reach around and grab the feathers in her wings, wrenching her entire body down and sending her flying to the ground like a bullet. She smashes into the floor with unbelievable force, which I follow by teleporting down and standing over her.

The darkness flows from my pores like a corona around me, causing my vision to have a slight purple tinge as I tower over her. I stamp on her chest and smile the same smile she gave me just seconds ago. Yes! She will perish! I will dismember her bit by bit until she is nothing, just like I did to that Fallen boy in the park! I start to laugh and splutter, the noise rising until it reaches a maniacal volume. When the laughter begins to fade I look away from Seriel's broken face to Miyu. The girl seems to be muttering to herself as she looks up at me.

"THANK YOU. SERIEL WILL PERISH WITH YOUR HELP."

"No!" She screams back. "Kyu will survive, and she'll stop you!"

"SHE WILL N…"

"Transfer!"

Something in my soul changes suddenly. It can't be! This wizard girl cannot have this kind of power! But, unmistakably, Sasaki is flowing upwards through the darkness, leaving a trail of glittering white and blue through the hatred within me. The girl! She found a way to call her back. Quickly I try to unleash the lethal blow at Seriel but I can't move.

"You will not kill her!" says the voice of Sasaki Kyushiro within me.

I bellow with rage as blue light starts intermingling with the aura around me. The arrow in my bow begins to fade as the girl's power comes back through my mind. My scream reaches the highest, most visceral level as the energy takes over me. The girl fills every inch of me, drawing the hatred to a singularity within.

Chapter 31

When my sight returns to me there's sister lying under me, covered in blood. Sighting down the shaft of the arrow at her bleeding, busted up face makes the scream catch in my throat. Relief floods through me as I realise that I'm really back. I fling Tenshi to the ground and throw my arms around her quickly, followed by my white and blue flecked wings. I cry as uncontrollably and as loud as my damaged throat allows me to.

    "Do not worry we can save her," Rafael says within me. *"I will heal her wounds."*

    White light flows out of me, out of my fingers, hands, arms, legs, even my hair. It undulates through the air, smothering Mitsuro in a cocoon of energy, gently swirling around her. I can see glimpses of her face through the light as the blood begins to evaporate from her skin. I smile and feel my eyes go wide as the shell around her explodes into millions of reflections, revealing her raising herself to a sitting position. One minute she looks like she's at death's door, next she looks like she looks as good as new.

    "Thank you Kyu. You saved my life. I always believed you would be able to overcome Samael. I've always trusted in you."

    Pride flows through my body, intertwining with the glorious feeling of Rafael in my soul and the love that I have for my sister as she holds me. I've missed this so much. I commune with Rafael, sending him my deepest thanks as he fills the sky inside me, glowing like the sun over the beautiful, calm landscape.

The hug breaks as my sister takes a step backwards. I can see my reflection in the beautiful golden eyes of Seriel, staring out at me from Mitsuro's body.

"I'm so glad that this is all over Sis," I say with exhaustion.

Even with Rafael within me I still feel tiredness in my bones. It's been a very, very long few weeks.

"I knew you would come with us Kyu. We really will be unstoppable with you."

"Wh...what?" I struggle to get out, "but...no...I can't."

"You will be one of the biggest assets that the Angels could ever have in this world. You will be the person that takes all of humanities hatred away."

"But...no. How could you think I would join you?"

"After all you've done? Everything you've been through? You have beaten one of the most powerful beings this world has ever seen! How can you not see that we are the best to control that immense strength?"

"I, Sis..."

"How could you possibly refuse us? How could you refuse me, your own sister? What we are doing is for the good of everyone Kyu, please see that."

"But I...it isn't that...people deserve a choice don't they?" I stammer.

My voice is childlike in her presence as I avert my eyes to the ground in shame. A change to the stillness of the air pierces my angelic senses making me look up into Seriel's bow raised and a long, silver arrow nocked in the string.

"H...how could you Sis, even after I saved you? It was you who forced me to go through so much," I whisper through the fear.

"I told you this is for the good of humanity. I am doing what I need to do to protect everyone. I will not let anything, or anyone, stand in the way of that. If you will not come with us, then you are our enemy. I...I can't let you stop us Kyu."

My sense of self-preservation takes over as the shot leaves her bow, my instincts teleporting me out of the way of the arrow, which crashes into the far wall. More arrows come at me from all directions as Seriel teleports around the stage. I let Rafael take me over completely as my mind struggles to comprehend reality. I don't know what to do, I don't know what to say.

"If you are so desperate to escape then you can fight me for the right. If I win, you and Samael follow us. If you win, I'll let you go home."

The next shot splits into four small arrows that curve around me in strange patterns, following me like missiles as I teleport around the room. I hit the wall as I run out of space, the points piercing my arms and legs, pinning me against a gigantic piece of fallen masonry.

"I can't Sis," I whisper as the blood trickles from the puncture wounds.

"You won't fight me?"

"I can't! I can't fight my own sister. All these years I've only ever wanted you back! I just want my family back again."

shhnk

She teleports in front of me, face to face, filling my field of vision.

"For the purposes of my plan I am not your sister. I am Seriel, the Archangel of God's Voice."

She hefts another shot and lines it up at me. As she closes one eye to aim I stare deeply into her remaining golden eye. For the first time I really concentrate, forcing past her barriers and look deep inside her soul.

"I do not need you. I need what's inside you," she says to me.

There! A flicker! I'm sure I saw something. Her fingers went to release but they didn't. Sis would never hurt me like this, she wouldn't be so selfish! She must be a hostage in there like I was with Samael! I need to do something to get her out, whatever it takes.

With a scream I rip my arms out of the arrows pinning me to the wall, leaving blood flowing until Rafael's energy swirls out of me, connecting the ends of my blood vessels, muscles and nerves together. Once I can feel my fingers again I raise my bow, our arrows pointing directly at each other. I need to remember that this is Seriel, not my sister.

"Go for it Kyu, you know that you can't fire that shot."

My hand starts to shake as I think about releasing the string.

"I have seen your deeds Kyu. I've known you all your life and I've heard everything about you. I know that you can't kill me. You don't want to, and you couldn't even if you did. Surrender to me and let us use your power for good. You could be a divine being respected around the world and loved by everyone. You could be the being that ultimately brought happiness and peace to the human race. Isn't that what you want? To be loved? By me, by our parents, by everybody?"

I try to hold my quivering lip steady as the tears roll down my face again. So much has happened over the last few weeks, and I don't think I can take it anymore. Seriel has read me perfectly, she knows that that's exactly all I wanted throughout all this. I've never wanted to fight. I've never done anything but try and protect Miyu, Satoshi, my parents, my sister and to be loved by them for doing it.

Through my addled mind filled with exhaustion, pain, and distress Miyu's thoughts arrive directly to me.

"Kyu you know that you can stop her. She may be powerful, but you can beat her."

"I can't shoot at her Miyu; I can't kill her. She's my sister."

"Within she might be, but on the outside, you know she isn't. You have to defeat her."

"If I kill her Angel she'll die! How can you try and get me to kill her? How could you possibly do that to me?"

"I'm not. If you trust me then I promise you we can save her, I'm sure of it."

"What?! How?"

"I can't tell you about the details in case she's in here, but you must buy me some time. Can you do that without killing her?"

Suddenly, a scything golden blade cuts through my mind, severing the link that Miyu and I had.

"I won't let you communicate with that girl Kyu. This is a fight between you and me," she says as I glance back over at Miyu sitting on the ground, her hands resting within her robes, "in fact, I'm going to kill her."

I yell as Seriel teleports above me and fires at Miyu. Action wells up within me as Seriel's shot flies towards her, making me leap to her defence. I swing my body round and snap the string back as hard as I can. A muscle in my shoulder rips, sending pain scrawling through me as I hyper-extend my arm back. Grimacing through it I lean hard on the life energy within me to support me as I fire, the arrow snapping through the air until it crashes into Seriel's attack, knocking both out of the air. I grip my shoulder as Rafael's energy knits me back together again.

"HOW DARE YOU ATTACK HER!" I yell. My voice resonates strangely around the room as I face up to the reality of the situation. There's only one way I can stand up to Seriel. "Miyu, please can you keep her off me for just for a few moments? I have to talk to them."

Miyu doesn't even open her eyes but raises her hands in a swirling formation which forms a ball of cyan light around me.

"You think this pathetic thing will stop me?" Seriel spits.

She flaps her wings and darts towards me. Through the visual distortion I see her take her bow and swing it down towards my protective cell. I immediately sit down, cross-legged on the floor and put Tenshi on my lap, pushing my hands together and closing my eyes. As the screeching sound of the bow slamming into the barrier pierces my ears I concentrate hard and shut it out.

***

When I open my eyes I scoot forward until I can see my reflection in the pool of water surrounded by long grass. The feeling of the air on my face changes as the blue clouds swirl above me until they form the giant being of Rafael.

"Thank you for showing yourself, Rafael. You know what I need to do, right?"

"Indeed," he intones. "Do thou really think this is something that thou can handle?"

"I have to, it's my only choice. I need to get her back to herself."

A long, low rumbling impinges on the idyllic silence as the sound of Seriel's actions filter through to me. I have to be quick or she'll take my life before I even get back. I sigh deeply as I accept that the only way out is going to be to commune with...him.

Looking into my own reflection I begin to raise the hatred of Seriel until the water begins to bubble. All the hate I have for her putting me through everything. Turning me into an Angel against my will, hiding it from me, lying to me, destroying my family, everything makes me despise her. I continue to pull on the feelings until I can sense Samael leaking up into me. The pool turns to a rolling boil as I pull harder and harder, until he finally erupts and appears in front of me. He stands next to Rafael challenging him in height as well as wingspan. His yellow eyes pierce through me as the shroud of energy around him flows in the air. Between the two Angels sparks fly where their auras touch.

"You really think you have the tenacity to do this, girl?" says Samael.

He may look somewhat like Rafael but he has none of the same mannerisms. He speaks directly to me as if he is speaking down to a servant, rather than speaking around me as if I am some kind of alien.

"Do you know what I have brought you here for?"

"It is obvious to both of us," says Samael, nodding towards his counterpart.

"Then will you help me. You know that I need both of you to be able to get through this. I don't care that you're different beings from different times or even that you hate each other. If you do not help me here then the Angel that has control of my sister is going to take everything she needs. She's going to kill me and forcefully repatriate both of you. She will have both of you under her control and she will enslave humanity to her vision."

"And why should I care about that, girl?"

"It is the right thing to care," Rafael bellows.

"Why should I do what is right by you?"

"Thou are just annoyed that thou couldn't defeat her."

"Well neither could you!"

I pause a minute as they growl at each other, the sound of glass breaking piercing the silence. She's broken through the barrier; I've only got a little more time here.

"Together we can defeat her. Come with me for whatever reason you happen to have. Be it revenge, righteousness, anger, duty, I don't care. Just come with me and we can put an end to this."

They both look at me as I extend my hands out. Rafael reaches down and surrounds my arm in his sparkling blue aura. I look up towards Samael who snorts and looks away, with his arms folded. A feeling of loss begins to fall over me until I notice a flicker of purple flowing through the air towards my other hand. A smile breaks on to my face as it wraps itself around my left side. When they meet in the middle of my body I'm lifted off my feet and up towards them, power overcoming me.

"Thank you."

***

I open my eyes to the tip of Seriel's bow inching its way towards me. I put my hand on Tenshi and see light explode around him. In an instant he's covered in the twin angelic power flowing through my veins, becoming an extension of my body. I swing him at Seriel's bow, deflecting her off and past me with ease. I feel like I'm a foot taller as I stand amongst the shield fragments cascading down around me, a white wing falling over my right shoulder and a purple wing over my left. I raise Tenshi to my eye level and use the metal to look at myself. One deep green eye, flickering in blue and yellow, burning with purpose, and one yellow, pupil-less eye stare back at me. The smile crawls across my face as the energy mixes and crackles around me like flames among kindling.

Turning back to my sister, I resolve myself to look directly into Seriel's eyes and to trust that Miyu has the answer. Even in this state I don't think I'll be able to kill her, but if Miyu needs time that's what I'll give her. The voice of Samael inches into my consciousness, almost pleading with me to murder Seriel, but I quickly push him down. I'm not controlled by either of these beings anymore, we are together as equals, not as beings trying to dominate each other. Strength flows through every cell in my body, not physical strength or emotional strength, but something different altogether. It's something that speaks to me on a primal level. A feeling of being a puzzle piece that has finally found its home.

"This is your last chance Kyu," my sister says, her voice pushing on my psyche, making me want to protect her.

My hand twitches as I reflexively make a move towards her. Steeling myself and pressing those feelings down, knowing that they won't save her, I drop my hand and take a deep breath.

Breathe in.

"You do not stand for what I want of this world," I say to her.

Nock an arrow.

"You stand for unhappiness, war, sorrow and hurt Kyu. We stand for peace, happiness and love."

Look at the target. Raise the bow. Pull the string.

"You wouldn't kill your own sister would you?" She asks.

Aim, hold breath, pause as the energy flows around the arrow.

"Try me."

Fire!

The arrow pierces the air, leaving a current of mixed energy behind it. Even with the speed and power behind it Seriel raises her hand, bringing a column of lightning up with her which incinerates it in mid-air. I magic another energy arrow into my bow and put even more effort in, however this one is blocked by shards of rock flying from all angles, compressing it in the core and leaving an asteroid that falls to the ground.

"You can't beat me with these pathetic attempts," Seriel says, "relent to me so we can be together again."

"You're not her, not anymore. Give her back to me."

The final battle for my sister's soul begins as we leap at each other. Positivity and hatred swirl around me and within me as we begin to duck and weave around the now almost completely destroyed cavern. The sound of our wings flapping fills the air as we zoom past one another, putting shot after shot at each other.

As I teleport around I run my hand through the tails of my shots that hover in the air, feeling the tingling as I connect to them. Using the connection, I pull them round the arena after me, trying to get past her defences. Slowly I raise my power until Seriel begins to show signs of struggling, an arrow getting within inches of her, taking a shred of her dress off. She gives as good as she gets though, pulling out different power after different power. Her arsenal truly is scary as she throws lava, particle attacks, gravitational waves and plasma at me. At one point she fires two arrows and pulls up portals on all sides of me, the arrow passing through them and multiplying until they're raining down upon me in the thousands.

I zip upwards, but not without damage as the surprise attack shreds my skin. With blood dripping from me I push myself further, harder. My brain is racing with numbers and angles, planning all of my moves and trying to counteract hers, but we both keep one-upping each other, both of us finding power and strength we didn't know we had. A small shiver goes through me as the end game moves into sight within my Angel eyes. Another one of her attacks draws blood from my side as I try, and fail, to dodge it.

I launch a couple of attacks at different angles towards Seriel, who dodges them, but they push her to the limits of her reactions. She responds with a blast of fire from one hand and an arrow of water from her bow, combining them in between us causing a massive cloud of steam to rise, blocking our views of each other. I react quickly by throwing a few arrows with my hands, arcing them around the outside of the smoke screen. Keeping still I connect my hands to the energy trails and hold them steady to act as trip wires.

Just before Seriel bursts out of the steam I feel her break through one of the energy trails, alerting me to her presence. I'm already there, firing a shot directly at her, forcing her to roll away from me. She skids to a halt in a crouched position with her eyes darting round the room, analysing exactly what I've done. I flick my hands around, bringing with it the arrows arcing back through the air, raining down upon her from all directions. She snaps her wings to rise above them, but I teleport directly in front of her, bow drawn, arrow pointing at her chest.

Her eyes flicker at me, causing me to hesitate for the briefest nanosecond before unleashing the dual Angel power. It smashes through her chest and leaves a crater in the floor behind her as it drags her down to the earth. The explosion rips through the floor and roughhewn walls, debris slicing open my stomach and arms as it flows through the air. One large piece smashes into my head, knocking me backwards until I hit the ground. I gasp through the fog in my vision as an arm materialises through the rock underneath me, grabbing me around the stomach and holding me down. I struggle to teleport away but with my wings trapped I can't launch myself. The face of Seriel weaves around me out of the ground as if she's immaterial, but the grasp holding me down certainly feels real enough. Blood is pouring from my head as a smirking Seriel leans into whisper into my ear.

"I told you, you can't kill me," she says menacingly. "You can try and try but you won't do it Kyu. You will never be able to do it. I have created and communed with every Angel on this continent and many hundreds elsewhere in the world. We are a force of God, driven by the shard that He gave us which links us all to this world. We will win, I promise you that."

"Kyu! I'm ready. Destroy the shard, that will allow us to end it all!"

Miyu's voice hits my eardrums, throwing the fog of confusion away.

"I will stop you from doing that Kyu, and then I'm going to kill your friend because of her disobedience," says Seriel.

I look backwards and see Miyu's upside-down face staring back. Seriel will stop me.

"Trust me Kyu!" she shouts.

In a snap movement she hefts the genesis shard and throws it high in the air where it arcs through the light pouring through the ceiling. Seriel's eyes are drawn to it which allow me to flick my wings free and teleport upwards, leaving trails of blood flowing beneath me. I draw my bow while spinning my body round, creating another arrow made of the dual energies of Samael and Rafael. It flies out through the air surrounded by a tail of white and purple like a comet, flying towards the stone in the perfect arc.

"Oh no you don't!"

Seriel throws an attack to knock mine out of the air, but I use my control to steer it around and towards the shard. Seriel attempts to block it again but my reactions are faster, allowing me to pull the shot around until I get the opening I need, the arrow hurtling through the gap towards the stone. Seriel screams loudly, her voice distorted by the sonic boom behind my arrow, but just before it hits home, she rotates her hands to bring up a green aurora around her. A pocket of time distortion perfectly encapsulates the shard, where it floats in the slight buzzing of the Universe being put through the wringer. The arrow I fired enters the field where it instantly slows to a crawl.

"I told you; you can't kill me! This attack is one you cannot defend against. You cannot deflect or destroy time," Seriel pants, "so you won't be able to stop me as I rip your wings to shreds before pulling that arrow out of the air. Nothing else you can put in that area will destroy that stone before I take you for our cause."

An arrow filled with golden energy appears in her bow pointing at me.

"Lock!"

Miyu's command echoes into the empty cavern as the chains flow from the floor up towards Seriel's arms. With her arrow loaded, she has no choice but to disengage her shot to flick the chains off. It doesn't stop her, but it does delay her enough to allow me time so that when she returns I can deflect the bow from her hands. I teleport to her, clattering into her and rolling across the cavern floor, both our weapons now out of reach.

"I don't need to kill you! All I have to do is delay us long enough until that arrow hits its target!" I shout, as I wrap my arms and wings around her, lifting us both up to our feet. "Now Miyu!"

Miyu uses another lock spell to engulf both of us in chains, knocking us back to the floor. In the cocoon of feathers, metal and flesh we lay on the ground, face to face, with the genesis shard directly above us. Locked in a sisterly embrace, our breath mingles together as we watch the arrow inch its way towards the shard. Staring into those golden eyes I suddenly see a flicker, and fear comes over her face.

"You have to let me go Kyu," my sister whimpers, "I can't stop her."

The pain pierces through my heart as the real Sasaki Mitsuro suddenly appears in front of me.

"This is the only way!" I cry out.

A whining noise cuts in from above us as cracks appear in the luminescence; the time spell is beginning to fail.

"Please trust me Kyu, don't do this, I want to be back with you. Please!"

Her eyes flicker again, and I see the steely resolve of the Angel staring back at me.

"You've lost Seriel, let my sister go."

"You really don't know what you've done Sasaki. You have one last chance to let me go and stop all of this."

"No."

"Then you shall suffer…the consequences," she says heavily, before giving way to Mitsuro. "No, Kyu…please don't…"

"It's ok Sis, Miyu will save you," I stammer, putting my head against hers.

Chapter 32

The sound of thunder crashes above us as the time spell dissipates, leaving my arrow to pierce through the genesis shard with such force that it begins to vaporise it in mid-air. Relief floods through me as the chains unwind from our bodies and disappear in a flash. I roll off Mitsuro whose powerful golden aura has already begun to fade. My body has barely anything left to give either, but I manage to pull myself across the floor to be by her side. As my bloodied fingernails claw at the ground, energy begins to flow out of her pores, pooling in a vortex above her chest. I limply throw my arm across her, raise myself up to see her face and suddenly panic fills my soul. Her breath is catching, and her eyes begin to roll back in her head as her body starts to spasm.

"Miyu..."

"I'm here Kyu," she says as rushes to kneel beside us. She moves her hands around and begins to recite an incantation, surrounding the golden energy in a blue confinement spell. "Leave it to me Kyu."

Weakness overcomes me as I collapse, using the last of my consciousness to grip Mitsuro's hand.

***

Waking up groggily next to the pool in my soul, I gently bring a handful of refreshing water to my face. It's been a long time since I slept properly, or since I had a moment to myself. Even before this whole thing it feels like I've been fighting through every day, one thing after another, over and over again, going on for as long as I can remember. Every time I clear a hurdle something else gets in my way. I splash more water on myself and rub the tiredness from my eyes.

"You seem awfully calm considering the circumstances, girl," the reedy voice of Samael intones from behind me.

"What do you mean?" I ask, keeping my face turned forward.

"The hate-filled one makes a cogent point," Rafael utters.

I sigh and turn around to face them, the two Angels, polar opposites, that somehow co-exist within me.

"But everything is fine now! I destroyed the genesis shard, breaking the bond between the Angels and their host."

They glance at each other before looking back at me.

"Sasaki, do you not remember what happens when an Angel and human break their bond? The Angel returns to God, and the host..."

"The host dies, right?"

"That is correct," Rafael interjects. He waves his arm and the lake in front of me ripples before showing the broken cavern under the hospital. The light is flooding in over my body and that of my sister and Miyu. "Master Seriel is leaving her soul. Thou will watch thy own kin pass?"

"But that is why I have Miyu! She promised me she could save her, and I trust her with everything I have."

In the reflection of the real world Miyu continues her spell. Sweat and dirt covers her face as she concentrates hard on encompassing all of the energy flowing from Mitsuro. After a few seconds she spreads her palms out and begins spiralling her own spell round until it touches Mitsuro's forehead, the energy re-entering her body.

"See! She said she had a plan! She's going to save Sis and we can go back to normal! You told me to trust those I fight with, and I trust her with everything."

"And what about the rest of them? Breaking the genesis shard will sever the link between every Angel that was created with that stone and their host. Every last one of them. You heard Seriel, there are thousands of them. All of those souls will pass into the eternity where they can be reborn."

"What?"

"Their souls will all return to God, Sasaki. You will be personally responsible for the deaths of literally thousands of people."

"No...I didn't...I can't...I was just thinking about my sister."

I put my head in my hands and the tears don't even come this time. My body convulses, overcome with the enormity of what I've done.

"But I can't save them all!" I cry as I smash my hand into my head painfully and bow to the floor.

The sound of two Angels teleporting right behind me floods my ears as one gloved hand and one clawed hand grip my shoulders as they lift me from the ground.

"And nor should you have to," Samael whispers in my ear.

"Souls live and souls die. They will be reborn through God and they will have their time again," Rafael prophesies.

"You've done this before Sasaki, remember, you had to do it even if people died at your hand. You should know by now that you cannot save everyone all the time. People will get hurt. People will love and they will also hate. They will hurt each other and despise each other. They will go to war and kill each other over anything. We all have to bear the consequences of our choices, but even if you didn't make them there would always be plenty of suffering in the world. There's a right way to deal with that guilt without destroying your life though."

Tears begin to flow in torrents, rippling on the image of Miyu as she slumps to one side, struggling with the effort and all the pain wracking her body. She grimaces as a wail escapes from my body next to her and suddenly loses her grip, the flow of energy around my sister becoming disrupted.

"No Miyu! I'm ok! Just keep going," I shout, trying to get my message across to her.

She redoubles her effort, restoring the loop of energy to save my sister.

"But what about you, Sasaki?"

I turn to look at Samael and see something surprising, a look of worry, or maybe confusion in his eyes.

"What about me?" I sob.

"Our time here is almost up; we will return to God as much as the rest of them."

"What?"

"We are Angels, the same as the rest. We were given form by this genesis shard just like Master Seriel was. Did you not think what was going to happen now?"

I hadn't. The thought had never once crossed my mind. I've been concentrating on how to save Mitsuro and Miyu.

"You're going to leave me?"

"I'm afraid so."

The sudden pang of fear that hits my heart causes something to flare in my brain. I hold my shaking hands up slowly, staring at my splayed fingers. No, I can't die…after all this.

"There must be something you can do!" I shout at Samael. He looks away quickly as I turn to Rafael. "You're the Archangel of Life! You must be able to do something magical!"

He looks down, or at least bows his hooded head.

"I am sorry, Sasaki. Even with my power, I cannot prevent death from taking the souls that are His."

"But I can't die! I can't die! My family needs to be together again," I wail madly at them like a scared child.

I smash my hands into the water, distorting the image of Miyu struggling to save my sister. My mind has gone into overdrive as I madly dash around, desperately trying to think of a way out. In the sky a pillar of light begins to rise from each of the Angels. They're starting to disappear. No! Samael looks up to his own dissipating form, the energy falling apart as it reaches the zenith of its journey.

"When we are gone, you will pass, but there is nothing you can do. We will return to God, and so your soul will face judgement. But that is a thing that everyone has to deal with Sasaki. Everyone in the world will eventually die."

"No!" I bark. "As long as I'm breathing, I will do everything I can!"

As the image in the lake settles, I see Miyu with sweat dripping down her face and her teeth clenched together hard. Something catches my eye as, next to my sister, a faint glow begins to leak out from the heart of my own unconscious body. No! I have to do something, it's starting already! The options race through my head, but only one presents itself to me. Moving my hand slowly through the grass, I wrap my fist around Tenshi lying next to me. I jump to my feet, quickly spinning on the spot, materialising an arrow out of thin air and nocking it against the string.

"And what if I destroy you, right here, right now? What if I kill you and absorb your souls into mine? You won't leave me and so I won't die right?"

A look of shock passes across Samael's face.

"You think you can destroy me? On your own? Have you truly gone mad?"

"You said I had to make hard choices! Well, I'll do whatever it takes!"

"Sasaki this isn't the right way to do things. Our souls have to be judged by God just like yours. If you want to try and destroy me then go for it, but I won't go easy on you."

Without a moment's thought I fire my arrow, only for Samael to dodge around it.

"Accept it. You can't do it. You can't defeat me, let alone both of us."

"Both of you?" I ask as Rafael slowly floats towards his angelic opposite.

"If thou want to kill him, thou will have to kill me too. He is right that our souls must be judged."

I materialise another two arrows and fire them both at the same time, but both Angels easily avoid the attack.

"Why don't you kill yourselves? That would work right?" I ask manically. "I am more important than you! You will die at my hand!" I shout.

I feel like I'm losing myself again as my vision blurs. I have to be with my family again, whatever it takes! And to be with them to see Miyu's and Mitsuro's happiness I need to be alive. So, I *can* kill these beings. I *will* kill these beings.

My opening salvo is easily deflected by both of them. I rain arrows upon them, teleporting to different angles, but nothing works. Nothing I do even gets close to landing a hit on them.

"Stop this now Sasaki, this is not the right way to deal with your fear! You have to control yourself and try to do what's right."

I fly up in the air, staring down at the two of them, pulling the string back and materialising another arrow.

"I. Will. Not. Stop!" I screech, breathlessly.

The sound of energy flows around me as hundreds, thousands of arrows appear in the air. I draw a deep breath and let out another bellowing scream as they burst out towards Samael and Rafael. The two Angels disappear into a cloud of energy and dirt as the blows smash around them. With the energy draining from my soul, I drop to the ground, falling to one knee and breathing heavily. The cloud around them begins to dissipate, slowly revealing them both still there, completely unharmed. No! I put everything I had into that. Both of them are enshrouded in the pool of light that continues to drift upwards as they fade away.

I fall to my side as my legs give way entirely, my head hitting the pool and submersing half my face. Samael and Rafael teleport towards me, standing over me with blank stares.

"Thou must calm thyself. Thou cannot go on like this. Thou cannot ruin thy entire life because of grief," Rafael utters.

"He's right Sasaki, there's a right way of doing this, and this isn't it. Trust me, I know how hatred can ruin people, but you have to be able to control it," Samael whispers.

Trying to keep my mouth above the water, I take a couple of deep breaths and realise they're right. I can't do this. It's not right. I need to accept my fate, that my family will never be whole again. But at least they can be happy without me.

Both the Angels reach out their hands and will a bow into existence, each of them a facsimile of Tenshi. Slowly they place arrows in their hands, nocking them and draw the strings back with ease.

The surface of the water flickers suddenly. With half the image in reverse I can see into the cavern where Rafael's and Samael's energy unmistakably begins to flow out of my chest, gathering above my body. The intermingling of light and dark energy mixes above me in a swirling vortex.

"I'm so sorry Rafael, Samael," I whisper, hoping they'll hear me.

A sudden convulsion in my heart makes me gasp, and I look on in horror as my body begins to spasm at the souls of the Angels leaving my body. I try and speak but water rushes into my mouth, choking me. I yank myself out of the lake and back on to my knees as Miyu looks over at me, panic in her eyes. I try to scream at her but the water in my throat rasps my vocal cords. She looks across, then down at my sister before breaking her spell, darting over to me, and beginning to weave her hands again. The cage that held Seriel's energy dissipates and reappears above my chest. The joint energy of the two Angels seeps into it, circling around like sands in an hourglass before flowing back to my body.

"No! Save her! Not me!" I try to yell, pointlessly. "She's the one my parents need most!"

I can't help but stare wide eyed with horror as my sister starts to shudder as Seriel finally leaves her body. The tears slowly drip down my cheeks, obscuring my view as Miyu abandons my sister to her fate. I raise my hands to my face in a horrifying scream as I watch my sister begin to pass away. Behind them in the reflection I can still see Samael and Rafael aiming arrows at the back of my head. Mitsuro's body suddenly flops down to the ground, the energy taking the form of Seriel above her. The spirit of Seriel mouths something at Miyu, who nods at her grimly before showering my sister's body with rapidly vanishing flakes of golden light.

I throw my head to the sky and wail with all my heart. The sorrow smashes through my chest like an arrow as my scream turns into a cry, before fading into a soundless whisper. My neck finally stops being able to support my head as I fall forwards, breathing heavily and staring at the image of my dead sister. I reach out my hand to try and touch her through the water, but as my hand broaches the surface the world goes white.

It takes a while for my eyes to readjust, flashing dots all over my vision as the blinding light leaves its impact on my retinas. When I turn I gape at the sight silently at the sight filling the sky. Standing above me are the destroyed bodies of Samael and Rafael, each one's heart ripped out by the arrow of the other, which is sitting embedded in their chests.

Staring at the tableau sends shivers down my spine and shocks through my body. I clutch at my head as scything pain rips through me. As the Angels collapse, dead, I join them, crashing to the ground. I scream out in agony as their energy floats up into the air where it lingers in the forms of Samael and Rafael. They hover there, flickering like an image on a screen before me. Digging my fingers deep into my scalp, I grit my teeth to try and control the pain. The Angels float down towards me slowly before I finally give in and have to scrunch my eyes shut. I hear them whisper to me, like cherry blossoms on the breeze. The words are almost inaudible, and through the blinding pain in my soul I can't make them out. I feel the touch of their words in me pause as they both finish their platitudes, leaving nothing but silence amongst the agony.

For a moment nothing happens, until the air is punctuated by the explosion of their forms into nothingness. The energy floats down on to my skin, causing electrical reactions on its surface, and as the pain overtakes me again my hearing fades out. The screaming soundlessly comes back to my throat as I become overwhelmed, and with a final bellow I pass into the darkness.

***

When I open my eyes light flows back in, flooding and burning my optic nerves. Squinting through my pained eyelids I see the ground in front of me, which is dark, rocky and covered in tiny fragments of udomite. I inch my vision upwards, taking in the shards of stone, most of which are covered in blood. Devastation. Blood. Pain. I sniff and the place reeks of blood and death and burnt flesh. Panic streams through my brain, but my body feels lifeless. I try and move my hand, managing only to drag my fingers through sharp fragments which stab into my skin. The electrical signals reach my brain but the whole thing feels sluggish, damaged, broken.

"Kyu..."

The voice.

"Kyu..."

"Mi...yu."

"Kyu!" she shouts. My view of her knees gets blocked as she drops her head to the floor, grovelling and crying and babbling. I can't make out the words as she goes on and on relentlessly sobbing. My eyes focus on what's behind her before snapping open in horror. Mitsuro's hair is draped over her face as she lays there, completely still. No...she can't be... My brain finally shifts into gear as I begin to drag myself towards her. Miyu is still crying but I bypass her completely, falling down at my sister's side as I gasp for breath. I let my head touch hers, which causes her limp, lifeless body to shift. I shut my eyes again.

The world turns upside down and then warmth flows across my face as the sunlight streams across my skin. Miyu's face comes into view casting me into shadow, her tears flowing down her cheeks and onto my face.

"I'm so sorry Kyu," she sniffles, "I tried to save her. I really did."

Her eyes are scrunched shut, forcing even more tears to drop on to me. I want to speak. I want to say something, to reassure her, but I don't have the strength. I try to send her a message through my mind but she doesn't react. In the end I do the only thing left open to me. I summon every bit of energy in me to raise my hand and drop it on to Miyu's head, letting gravity drag her unprotesting face down to mine. Her forehead drops on to my lips, and with every sinew I have left firing, I plant the lightest of kisses on her.

***

I wake up to bright, white, cold lights filtering through the ceiling above me. A voice says something above me, but I can't work out what it is before my chest is suddenly compressed by someone throwing themselves on top of me. Miyu stands over me with tears in her eyes, in fact she looks like she's cried enough for a thousand lifetimes.

"I was so worried about you Kyu. I'm so happy you're awake."

"Where...am..."

"You're in the hospital."

I try to move my hands to pull myself up, but I can't, so I continue to stare into Miyu's face as thought returns to my brain slowly.

"It's good to see you awake again after so long, Kyu."

Cognisance begins to ratchet itself up in my brain as some of the fog fades. Electrical signals blitz their way through dormant pathways and a flicker of hope filters through my mind, causing me to choke on my words.

"Thank God, it wasn't real," I manage to say between the pain.

It was a dream, a coma, a fantasy. None of it happened. The Angels or the Fallen. The destruction, the pain and death. The images of all of my friends and foes flicker through my mind as I start to come to terms with it. It felt so...real. So tangible and physical. Then the quietness hits me. Nothing but silence filling the room and emanating from the corridors.

"Where are the doctors?"

"They all evacuated when Azrael turned up. Everyone is gone except for us."

Panic stabs my chest, gripping all my nerves in a vice like grasp.

"But that wasn't real, right? The Angels never existed; it was all in my brain!" I shout through the dread filling my heart.

"Kyu," Miyu says, gripping my shaking hands, "I'm sorry I couldn't save your sister. I did everything I could, but when I saw that you were suffering I had to save you instead. I thought you were going to die! I had to! But you stopped them Kyu, you stopped them from forcing that upon all of us. You're a hero."

A memory of Miyu's voice stings the back of my eyes.

"You promised you would...save...her," I force out slowly through gritted teeth.,

"I couldn't let you die! How could I let you go?! You mean everything to me," she says as she breaks down at my side. "I've missed you so much and reconnecting to you made me so happy. I had seconds to decide! I had to make that choice. I had to try and save you instead! I'm sorry!"

"How could you save me instead of her? What the fuck am I worth to anyone? She would have made my parents happy again. How could you stop that?! Why did you save me?!"

"I had to try! As much as she means to them, you mean a thousand times more to me. How can you not see that after all we've been through?!"

Silence passes between us.

"Anyway, I tried, but it wasn't me that ended up saving you Kyu. There was too much energy coming out of you for me to be able to contain it. Both of your Angels were leaving, but then...they just vanished. It all just...stopped."

A flash in my mind brings back the destroyed bodies of Samael and Rafael, falling to the ground with gaping holes in their chests and their energy bestowing itself upon my soul.

"The Angels killed each other," I whisper.

"What?"

"They shot each other, killed each other at the same time, and gave themselves to me so I would survive."

I look over her bruised and battered body. Her skin is still charred from the fight, one arm held at her side in pain.

"You're hurt, because of me, again. I've hurt you so much."

"I'd do it all over again Kyu. I'd make that choice to follow you again in a heartbeat."

"But why? Why me?!"

"How can you not see the power you have?"

"But I don't have any power left do I? I'm worthless again," I whimper, trying and failing to flap my non-existent wings. No Angels, no speed, no power.

"How can you say that?! After all that you've been through, please can you just realise how important you are to me and to others? No matter what happened inside you, we followed you because you are who you are, not because of some magical power. Samael and Rafael followed you too, and I'm only here because you saved me from all this."

"Why though, why did you follow me, Miyu? Why couldn't you stop and save my sister instead of me? If you knew anything about me, you'd know my family would be much happier with her back and me gone."

"Shut up! Shut up Kyu! Don't say things like that!" Miyu shouts, bursting into sobs, "you mean everything to me. I love you so much. Please don't let all the hardship they made you go through all be for nothing. Don't let what they made you do break you. You're so close to being through it, please just keep going. I can't bear to think about being apart from you again! I love you; I always have. Just being at your side has always made me happy even if you never realised it. That time we spent apart was torture. You're my soulmate and I know your family loves you too. They need you and I need you! I know it's selfish of me, but I can't live without you anymore. Please keep going for me."

The enormity of her words hit me like a train. Everything's been so hard. There's been so much pain and death around me for so long. But this is the girl, the one person through it all which has made it all worth it. I can't let the negative thoughts win. I drop my hand painfully onto hers and grip it tightly.

"I...love you too..."

Epilogue

fwip...*thud*, *fwip*...*thud*

I let my bow drop to my side and smile as the shots hit the bullseye of each target. The setting sun bathes my little practice range in a golden glow, punctuated by the glinting of the arrows as they vibrate to a standstill. I turn the bow around and stare at the body, running my fingers over the decorated wooden shaft to where the piece of genesis shard sits. As I trace the stone a pang of longing spears my conscience. I wish I could still feel the speed of flying through the air, teleporting around, to feel the cold air blast my face.

Even months after the battles, months after having Rafael and Samael wrenched from me, I still feel emptiness inside. But Miyu was right, something has changed in me. I feel whole, finally, like I fit better in this world and within myself. As I think of my sister's beautiful face fading away in the cavern my head drops to my chest. Sometimes the grief still comes to me, not just for those that fell to my own hand, but those that I never even met; the ones Sis talked about meeting and communing with. There's the feeling that I could have saved Mitsuro, somehow. I could have done better. I should have.

"Are you ok Kyu?" Miyu asks, looking up from the book that she's reading, interrupting me just as I start to feel myself spiralling again.

Her voice invokes a sudden flood of relief in me. Miyu and I have been inseparable since we confirmed that the Angels had gone. I turn around and give her a cheesy smile and a thumbs up. I am ok.

I don't remember much about what happened after I passed out in the deserted hospital. When I woke up I was at home, with my family and Miyu staring at me with looks of anguish and exhausted worry on their faces. My mother broke down and cried on my body as I stirred, closely followed by my father. They cried and cried tears of happiness at me being back. They went on and on about how they couldn't lose me after the pain of losing Mitsuro.

Without the Angels inside me, the healing process was long and painful. I spent months recovering and Miyu never left my side for a second. She was with me as I managed to start eating and when I took my first steps again. She helped me pick my bow up and held my hands as I fired my first arrow. I felt her in my mind as the memories of Mitsuro, of the Angels, and the Fallen all passed through me, trailing pain and sorrow behind them. She gave me the strength to grieve in a healthy way.

My mother calls at the door of the house for me to come inside and I feel myself jerk involuntarily. As Miyu closes her book and puts it into her bag I want to reach out and get her to stop. I don't want her to leave. She says goodbye, picks up her things and heads towards the gate, causing me to shut my eyes as I well up slightly. Don't leave, please?

Suddenly the weight of Miyu's body hits me as she throws herself at me. I gasp, dropping Tenshi to the ground before wrapping my arms around her. The scent of her hair fills me up as I bury my head in her shoulder. She pulls around and I caress the scars on her arms morosely.

"I'll be back tomorrow morning Kyu so we can go to school together."

And then she kisses my cheek, leaving me frozen in the instant with the feeling of her lips upon my face. Joy spreads from my heart and around my body as she stares deeply into my eyes.

"Thank you, Miyu."

"What are you thanking me for?"

"I...I don't know, I just feel like I have to keep saying it, for everything you've done. I think of all the times you were in danger because of me."

"Don't be silly Kyu, I've told you a thousand times that if I had to make every choice again I would do it exactly the same way."

I look away, blushing in a sudden wave of bashfulness. I don't know what I've done to deserve someone so perfect in my life, someone who would put everything on the line for me and cause herself endless pain just to support me through my struggles.

"Your actions may have caused pain, but you helped save the human race. I think that if anyone deserves to be happy, it's you."

"Don't do that!" I shout playfully, bopping her on the head with an arrow, "I told you not to read my mind without explicitly warning me first so I can make sure I'm not thinking anything...embarrassing!"

"It's hard to surprise an empath Kyu! I've been with you through all this and felt your emotions every step of the way. I know the bad in you, and I've felt the good too. I like you for exactly who you are."

Maybe I do deserve her.

"Yes, you do."

"Miyu!" I laugh, knowing that she's provoking me on purpose.

As she leaves the garden via the side gate, I watch her go until my mother calls to me again, impatiently. I pick up Tenshi and swing him round gymnastically in my hand, dashing for the house. By the back door I prop my bow up and take off my quiver, putting them next to the small shrine we have for Mitsuro. Putting it up helped me and my parents grieve for her and move on with our lives. I pause briefly and pray for her, reaching out to touch the picture of her before continuing on inside.

ABOUT THE AUTHOR

Steven was born in Watford but now lives in Wokingham. He has a degree in Physics from Reading University and never had any dreams of becoming a writer, but a lifelong love of anime and manga means he appreciates how powerful and impactful a good story can be. While waiting for a train home from a late-night shift in 2010 he was visited by the main character of his first novel, Angel Eyes, and that night began his writing journey to deliver Sasaki Kyushiro's story to the world.

Printed in Great Britain
by Amazon

39454345R00199